Praise for Dianne's
The Gifted Ones Books

*"The Gifted Ones series is **nothing short of perfection** itself. I can't wait to see where she takes us next!"* —Scandalicious Book Reviews

*"You will smile, swoon and have **a lot of fun** with this."* —Books and Things

*"Full of **danger, intrigue and passion.** Dianne Duvall brought the characters to life and delivered an addicting and exciting new series. I'm hooked!"* —Reading in Pajamas

*"**Addictive, funny and wrapped in swoons,** you won't be able to set these audios down."* — Caffeinated Book Reviewer

*"I loved this book! It had pretty much all of my favorite things — **medieval times,** a **kick-ass heroine,** a **protective hero, magic, and** a dash of **mayhem.**"* —The Romance Reviews

*"Dianne Duvall has delivered a **gripping** storyline with characters that stuck with me throughout the day... **A must read!**"* —Reading Between the Wines Book Club

"A great beginning to a new and different series." —eBookObsessed

Titles by Dianne Duvall

CLIFF'S DESCENT

A VAMPIRE'S TALE

NEW YORK TIMES BESTSELLING AUTHOR

DIANNE DUVALL

For my family

Acknowledgements

As always, I want to thank Crystal. You're amazing and such a pleasure to work with. I don't know what I'd do without you. I also want to send hugs and a great big thank you to my fabulous Street Team. You all rock!! I hope you know how much your continued support means to me and how very much I appreciate it. More love and hugs go to the members of my Dianne Duvall Books Group on Facebook. I have so much fun in there with you and can always count on you to spark smiles and laughter.

Thank you, Kirsten Potter, for giving my characters unique and entertaining voices that continue to delight listeners. More thanks go to my editor, Anne Victory, who is such a joy to work with, as well as the other behind-the-scenes individuals who helped me bring you *Cliff's Descent*.

And, of course, I want to thank the Immortal Guardians fans who requested this story and all of the other wonderful readers who have picked up copies of my books. You've made living my dream possible. I wish you all the best.

Preface

I F YOU CHAT WITH ME on social media and/or join me on my blog tours, then you already know I'm a pantser, not a plotter. By that I mean that instead of carefully plotting out my next novel or novella before I write it, I fly by the seat of my pants. That's right. I just sit down, start typing, and let the story unfold however it will. This does not mean, however, that I have no notion of the plot. I always know the beginning, middle, and ending of a story—as well as a few key scenes that have been dancing through my head—before I get started. I just don't always know the path that will lead me there.

This holds true not just for individual books but also for the Immortal Guardians series as a whole. Though I didn't know exactly how many books the series would entail, how many characters would get their own stories, or in what order those stories would come, I *did* know several key elements of the overall series arc before I began writing Roland and Sarah's story. I knew, for example, that Seth's book would end the first series arc and how the jaw-dropping climax would unfold. I knew the ghost of Bastien's sister, introduced fleetingly in *Darkness Dawns* and *Night Reigns*, would return later in the series and find love with an Immortal Guardian. I knew Ami's brother Taelon would eventually make an appearance. I knew all of the d'Alençon siblings would find love. And I knew how and when Seth's origins would be revealed.

All of the little—and sometimes big—things that surprise me along the way as I write are what make being a pantser so fun. And sometimes those surprises come in the form of characters… like Zach. When I introduced him in *Phantom Shadows*, I initially intended for Zach to remain a mysterious background character who only made brief appearances here and there. I knew who he was and his relation to Seth. But I had no solid plan for him… until he perched on David's roof with Ami and accepted a lollipop. That scene changed everything, fueling me with a determination to help Zach find love and give him his own story.

Cliff is another character who surprised me. I never would've guessed when I launched a series in which vampires were the bad guys that one of them would come to mean so much to me. One might think it impossible since all vampires go insane and become monstrous killers in my books. But there you have it. I also did not foresee how much Cliff would come to mean to readers and audiobook lovers. Yet I have received countless emails, messages, and comments on social media posts asking if the Immortal Guardians and the doctors at the network will be able to save him.

Naturally I didn't answer that question… and not—as some of you jokingly suggested—because I love to torture you. I just wanted very much to tell you Cliff's story before I revealed his fate. This presented me with a bit of a quandary though that no other book has. There have been a few times in the Immortal Guardians series in which stories have overlapped. While Bastien was falling in love with Melanie, Richart fell hard for Jenna. While Lisette was falling in love with Zach, Yuri fell in love with Cat. My Immortal Guardians family is a big one, and sometimes they aren't always content to fall in love one couple at a time.

Cliff's story, on the other hand, didn't overlap one book or even two. It overlapped them all. It began in *Darkness Dawns* and has slowly and steadily progressed until we've reached the point at which it all must come to a head. And thanks to snippets in *Blade of Darkness* and *Death of Darkness*, you've already come to understand that somewhere along the way, he fell in love. I've known for some time now that—whether Cliff's ending would be a happy one or a tragic one—I wanted you to see what has been unfolding behind the scenes, which did indeed pose a unique challenge: how to tell a tale that spans nine novels and almost six years.

That was a challenge I readily accepted because I really *do* want to share with you what has been transpiring in my imagination. Since Cliff's story encompasses the entire series, it won't be told in the same way as previous books. A six-year tale requires one to skip ahead here and there to indicate the passage of time. And you *will* see a few scenes you've encountered before. These were, after all, pivotal moments in Cliff's life that I believe were integral to his story. In *Cliff's Descent*, however, they're either told from a different perspective or expanded to shed new light on those events. And don't worry. There is a lot you *haven't* seen before, too.

Although I know I could've begun Cliff's story *in medias res*, as my literature and creative-writing professors would say (which just means in the middle of things), I chose to start at the very beginning, where we first encountered Cliff in the series.

I hope you enjoy it.

Best,
Dianne Duvall

Prologue

"AWAKEN, VAMPIRES!" BASTIEN BELLOWED. "THE immortals have found us!"

Cliff jerked awake. Bolting upright in bed, he glanced over at Vince and Joe.

Both vampires sat up and regarded him with wide eyes.

Boots pounded through the subterranean tunnels at preternatural speeds.

"How many did you count?" Someone with a... British...? accent asked grimly somewhere outside.

"Fifty-seven vamps below," another man—this one definitely British—replied. "Four humans above."

Cliff rolled off the cot he'd claimed and grabbed his blades while Vince and Joe did the same.

Bodies raced past the doorless entry to their room. Other members of Bastien's vampire army, snarling and growling like animals.

"If you can prevent Roland from killing Sebastien," the first Brit said, "do so."

"Oh shit," Cliff whispered. The Immortal Guardians *had* discovered Bastien's home. Or his *lair* as some of the vampires housed here called it. Had Bastien's quest to kill Roland—the Immortal Guardian who had brutally murdered his sister and her husband—led them here despite the care they'd all taken not to leave a trail?

Cliff loved Bastien like a brother. The elder vampire had found him shortly after Cliff's transformation and had taken him under his wing. The psychotic bastard who had transformed Cliff had disappeared before Cliff even fell ill and had been so deranged when he'd reappeared some weeks later that Cliff had wanted nothing to do with him. Bastien, on the other hand, had given Cliff shelter and guidance and helped him come to terms with his frightening new reality.

And Cliff was not the first. Bastien had done the same with nearly a hundred others, feeding them and sheltering them and doing everything he could think of to help them stave off the insanity the peculiar virus that infected them seemed to spawn. He even provided them with lists of pedophiles they could drain so they wouldn't do what so many other vampires did and kill innocents.

Cliff respected the hell out of Bastien. But since he had launched this war against the Immortal Guardians, intent on killing the man responsible for his sister's death as well as all the other Immortal Guardians who brutally preyed upon vampires...

Well, there had been instances when Cliff had worried that Bastien's thirst for revenge might have outfitted him with blinders.

"Go on," a female with a French accent said upstairs. "I'll see to the humans."

A barrage of gunshots broke out above, followed by the thuds of bodies hitting the floor.

Cliff seriously doubted those were Immortal Guardians falling.

The murmur of the female's voice confirmed his fears as the sounds of battle erupted in the basement, drowning her out. The *shicks* and *tings* of blades meeting blades competed with thuds and cries of pain.

"What do we do?" Joe blurted.

Cliff shook his head. "Protect Bastien." Judging by the fear that filled his friends' faces, they held as little hope as he did that they'd succeed.

Lunging through the doorway, Cliff led the other two through the winding hallways. Every vampire who lived here had helped dig and shape these tunnels. Four of them branched off the original basement the farmhouse above them had boasted. One led to whatever room Bastien rested in. Cliff had never seen it since Bastien forbade them all entry.

Cliff didn't blame him for taking that precaution. Bastien had slain several vampires during Cliff's acquaintance when the insanity those men suffered drove them to defy his orders and attack humans who weren't on the lists provided. It only took a few years for the madness to seize total control of those infected. So the vampires who were well on their way down that path and worried they might be the next to lose their head—literally—at the edge of Bastien's sword sometimes tried to sneak up on him while he rested and behead him first.

They didn't know what Cliff had already divined: that the tunnel that led to Bastien's room branched into numerous others that proved to be as confusing as a maze in a cornfield. Only Bastien knew the layout. So those who went looking for him always ended up getting lost and meeting the same fate they sought to avoid when Bastien tracked them down.

The other three tunnels that branched off the original basement led to small rooms like Cliff, Vince, and Joe's that were outfitted with surprisingly comfortable cots and folding stadium chairs in which they could kick back and relax after a hunt.

The metallic scent of blood—coupled with the acrid odors of gunpowder, sweat, and fear—flooded the hallway as more gunshots joined the din and blades continued to clash.

Cliff's heart slammed against his ribs as adrenaline flooded his veins.

Vampires crowded together at the end of the hallway, forcing him to stop. All pressed forward, eyes glowing, eager to jump into battle and slay the immortals who had invaded their home.

Immortal Guardians had recently slain some of their vampire comrades in a skirmish Bastien himself had limped home from. And everyone here wanted those bastards to pay for it with blood.

Cliff leaned this way and that, rising onto his toes and peering over the vamps in front of him, trying to get a glimpse of what the hell was happening.

When he did, his blood froze.

Three men and one woman—all garbed in the long black coats, shirts, and cargo pants Immortal Guardians favored—fought with preternatural speed that was so much greater than Cliff's that he sometimes had difficulty following their movements. Each male immortal had planted himself in front of the entrance to a tunnel and proceeded to cut down vampire after vampire who emerged and attacked them. The woman stood near the stairs leading up to the ground floor, spraying any vamp who made it past her brethren with bullets. Blood splattered every immortal and painted the walls and ceilings. Bodies littered the floor.

Vampire bodies that shriveled up as the symbiotic virus they housed devoured them from the inside out in a last desperate bid to continue living.

The bitter taste of fear filled Cliff's mouth. Was Bastien one of those bodies?

The long, twisting tunnel that led to his room was the only one left unguarded. Had they already slain him?

Cliff strained to hear anything that might indicate Bastien still lived and nearly sagged with relief when he heard Bastien snarl something at... Roland? He was fighting Roland Warbrook?

Determined to find a way to help him, Cliff tightened his hold on his bowie knives and tensed as Mike and Wes, the last two vampires in front of him, lunged forward to attack an Immortal Guardian who must be at least six foot eight with a long black ponytail that reached his ass.

The Immortal Guardian swung a katana so quickly Cliff couldn't see it. He could only hear the whoosh of its movement.

Mike's head leaped from his body and landed in Wes's hands. Cliff sucked in a breath.

Wes yelped and dropped it a second before the Immortal Guardian decapitated him, too.

Vince gasped.

Joe swore.

Cliff stared in horror. Despair inundated him as he gaped up at the immortal who now stood before him.

All of the other Immortal Guardians' eyes glowed amber. But this one's eyes glowed golden, and he radiated power like no one Cliff had ever encountered. Was this their leader? Had the leader of the Immortal Guardians come to personally bring a halt to Bastien's quest? Had he come to *kill* Bastien?

The immortal gave Cliff, Vince, and Joe a curious look, then glanced over his shoulder.

He wasn't even breathing hard!

"How many more of these bastards are there?" a British warrior growled with aggravation as he cut down another vampire.

The tallest one responded with a casual shrug. "I don't know. I've lost count."

His voice... This was the man Cliff had heard tell the others to keep Roland from killing Bastien. Why? Because he wanted to kill Bastien himself? Make an example of him?

Cliff glanced at Vince and Joe.

Panic painted their features. Like him, neither seemed to know how the hell they could defeat this immortal *and* his companions *and* stop Roland before he killed Bastien.

If he hadn't already killed him.

Had Roland killed him? It was hard for Cliff to hear with his heartbeat pounding so loudly in his ears.

He focused on the golden-eyed leader. Even three against one, he had no hope of defeating him. And he did *not* want his head to end up on the floor beside Mike's and Wes's...

The immortal arched a brow. "Well?"

Joe's throat worked in a hard swallow. "You guys are Immortal Guardians?"

"Yes."

Cliff shifted his weight from one foot to the other and tightened his hold on his weapons. "Did you kill Bastien?"

"No. We have no intention of killing him. Bastien is one of us."

Shock tore through Cliff. His jaw dropped. "Bastien is an immortal?"

"Yes."

No way! He couldn't be! Immortal Guardians didn't help vampires. They *killed* them. That's why Bastien wanted to wage war against them. At least, it was *one* of the reasons. "He said he was a vampire like us!"

"Because he thinks he is," the leader replied matter-of-factly. "Bastien is... confused. He was fed false information by the one who transformed him. We're here to help him, not hurt him."

Before Cliff could call bullshit, Vince motioned belligerently to the carnage around them. "Then why are you killing all of us?"

Joe nodded, his face dark with fury.

"Bastien's vampire followers have not been confining their feeding to those on the lists they were given."

Cliff frowned. Every sunset, Tanner—Bastien's human assistant—gave each vampire a list of men they could drain. Every name on the list was that of a pedophile. And Cliff, Vince, and Joe had steadfastly stuck to those lists. It was a win-win. They got the blood they needed to survive and at the same time protected who knew how many children from the monsters determined to prey upon them.

Had some of the other vampires strayed?

As if to confirm his thoughts, the imposing warrior continued. "They're killing innocents. I'm afraid we cannot allow such to continue."

Joe shook his head. "But Bastien said *immortals* kill innocents."

"As I said, he was misinformed. Immortal Guardians only kill those who prey upon the innocent, those who threaten to reveal our existence to the mortal world, and those who seek to harm us. We *protect* innocents."

The giant sheathed one katana, pulled out a throwing knife, and hurled it into the throat of a vampire who had snuck past another Immortal Guardian and was circling around to attack his back.

Cliff glanced at his friends and jerked his head toward the tunnel behind them.

All three took a couple of steps back and huddled together while they kept an eye on the immortal blocking their path.

"Do you think it's true?" Joe blurted. "Do you think Bastien is an immortal?"

Cliff strained to hear what was taking place at the end of that unguarded hallway and finally managed to glean a little information. "Bastien is injured, but Roland hasn't struck a death blow."

"Yet," Vince added.

Joe nodded.

Cliff's glance strayed to the powerful immortal who left them to their discussion while he tossed daggers and throwing stars at other vampires as casually as one might toss bread crumbs to a flock of pigeons. "Before they struck, I heard this one tell the others to try to keep Roland from killing him."

"What?" Joe asked, eyes widening.

Vince scowled. "Maybe he just wants to kill Bastien himself."

"Or maybe," Cliff forced himself to say as doubt crept in, "he's telling us the truth. Maybe Bastien *is* an immortal and was fed a bunch of bullshit by the vamp who turned him. I've spent more time with Bastien than you have." The two of them had forged a strong friendship. "I know his history. The vamp who turned him was his best friend. Bastien would've had no reason to doubt whatever he told him."

Vince's scowl turned into a pucker of worry. "Bastien *is* the oldest vampire I've ever met."

Cliff nodded. "Most of us go crazy within a few years of transforming. Bastien didn't." It made what the Immortal Guardian leader had told them frighteningly plausible and pretty much annihilated their reasons for fighting.

Straightening his shoulders, Joe cleared his throat and addressed the immortal. "What exactly are our options here?"

"How long has it been since you were turned?" he countered.

"Six months."

"Fourteen for me," Cliff said.

"About two and a half years," Vincent answered.

"How's the bloodlust?"

"Controllable," Joe answered.

Cliff nodded. "Same here."

Vincent hesitated. "It's pretty bad," he admitted, surprising Cliff with his honesty. "I... I've been having... thoughts... lately that scare me."

"Have you acted upon them?"

"No."

Cliff hastened to assure the immortal. "He hasn't killed anyone who wasn't on Bastien's list."

Joe nodded. "We made sure. One of us is always with him." Because both had seen the signs that Vince was beginning to struggle with the madness the damned virus caused.

The immortal regarded them thoughtfully. "You have two options then, gentlemen. We can either fight to the death today — *your* death, I'm afraid." Yep. That was what Cliff had thought. "Or should you prefer it, you can be taken to one of our research facilities. You'll be given individual apartments and anything else you need to be comfortable. You will be supplied with bagged blood and food as well. But you will not be able to leave the building without an immortal escort. We can't risk your killing an innocent."

Cliff's stomach sank.

Joe frowned. "Research facility?"

The leader nodded. "Our scientists are attempting to find both a cure for the vampiric virus and a treatment that will alleviate or prevent entirely the madness that inevitably afflicts your kind. Perhaps you would like to be of some assistance."

A faint glimmer of hope flared. Bastien had enlisted the aid of a scientist to do the same: find a cure for the virus or alternately a treatment for the madness it induced. Unfortunately, he'd had little luck. But these guys looked like they had a lot more resources at their disposal.

Vince snorted. "So you want us to be your guinea pigs? Your lab rats?"

"Look," Cliff said, not as ready to dismiss the idea, "if there's a chance they can keep us from going crazy, it's worth it."

"I agree," Joe said somberly.

"But we'd be like their prisoners," Vince protested.

Yes, they would.

A tense silence ensued.

The big warrior threw another knife.

Joe shook his head. "Killing pedophiles is one thing. I don't want to end up killing women and kids and people who aren't violent criminals. If being locked up is the only way to ensure I don't..."

Cliff nodded. "Yeah, I don't want to end up like the one who turned me. He didn't just *feed* on people, he *tortured* them." At least, the vampire who *claimed* he'd been the one to turn him had. That bastard had been seriously depraved.

"The guy who made me tortured people, too," Vince admitted reluctantly.

"So did mine," Joe added.

The Immortal Guardian lobbed another knife at one of two vampires who fought the female, who had abandoned her guns and now wielded shoto swords. "You won't be treated badly," he assured them. "And should we not be able to help you, when the madness grows too uncomfortable, you can choose your own end. We won't force you to linger in such a state."

The three stared at each other for a long, somber moment.

It really seemed the only way. Dying today wouldn't help Bastien. If this immortal was truly on the up-and-up, then maybe Bastien, Vince, Joe, and Cliff could all make it out of this alive *and* get help staving off the madness as well.

"Fine," Vince said finally. "Let's do it."

The formidable immortal sheathed his other katana. "I don't have any rope with which to restrain you so… sorry about this." Lightning quick, he punched Vince and Joe. Cliff drew in a breath to protest. But the immortal was quicker.

Pain exploded in Cliff's face as a big fist struck. The room around him tilted as all strength left his legs.

I hope this isn't a mistake, Cliff thought just before darkness enveloped him.

Chapter One
Two years later

C LIFF LISTENED TO THE ACTIVITY in the hallway outside his apartment. Male voices murmured. Boots clomped on the floor as additional guards joined the already large contingent that manned sublevel 5 of network headquarters. Weapons clicked and clacked as guards checked magazines. Rustling sounded as tranquilizer guns slid into holsters.

One might not think all that would be necessary to keep two vampires in check. And on an ordinary day it wouldn't. But apparently Bastien was bringing in a new vampire he had managed to recruit.

Cliff, Joe, and Vince had been the first vampires in history to essentially surrender to the Immortal Guardians when the latter defeated Bastien. Cliff loved the two-century-old British immortal like a brother. But damn, he was glad Bastien hadn't won that last horrific battle in the basement of Bastien's home. He knew his friend wasn't happy. Seth, the immensely powerful Immortal Guardians leader who had punched Cliff in the face that fateful day, had pretty much forced Bastien into the fold. And neither Bastien nor his new immortal brethren were the least bit thrilled with the situation.

Cliff still held out hope, however, that Bastien would eventually find happiness among their ranks. Particularly now that Bastien had clearly developed feelings for Melanie Lipton, one of the doctors Cliff worked with on a daily basis.

Seth had delivered on his promises. Or most of them anyway.

Cliff, Vince, and Joe had not been thrust into jail cells. They had been given very nice apartments at the headquarters of the East Coast division of the human network that aided Immortal Guardians.

Cliff glanced around. He wouldn't have been able to afford anything so ritzy before his transformation. His apartment rocked. But he had not been allowed to leave sublevel 5 once since his arrival. And no matter how nice the premises were, they hadn't alleviated the difficulty of going two years without setting foot outside.

True to Seth's words, researchers here at the network toiled pretty much night and day, searching for a cure for the virus or a way to keep humans infected with it from going mad. Alas, they had not yet succeeded. And Vince had not been able to hold on.

Sadness struck at the memory of the friend he'd lost the previous year.

At least Vince had chosen his own end, one far more honorable than embracing the madness and inflicting untold horrors upon random, unsuspecting victims.

Cliff was beginning to fear he and Joe would suffer the same fate.

Joe wasn't doing well. Even though he hadn't been infected with the virus as long as Cliff, Joe had had a number of psychotic breaks in recent months and had begun to rant maniacally in his apartment.

Kinda like he was doing now.

"Don't let them take you! Get out while you can!" he bellowed in the apartment next door.

Cliff winced, his enhanced hearing allowing him to hear every word despite the heavy titanium-and-concrete-reinforced walls that separated them.

"Run! They're lying! If you let them take you, they'll steal your thoughts! They'll steal your memories! Big fucking chunks of them! And they'll plant new ones! They'll brainwash you! They'll brainwash you the way they have me! They'll make you think it's you! That you're fucked up in the head! But it's them! It's always been them!"

Cliff's stomach churned. Joe was getting worse. The madness

that seeped into him bore a heavy dose of paranoia. In his lucid moments, Joe knew Melanie and Linda and the other doctors here at the network were trying to help him. He even felt great affection for the former. Neither woman had ever treated the vampires like monsters. Though they must have been nervous as hell—if not downright terrified—the first time they met Cliff and the others, Melanie and Linda had shown them only kindness... even while combating violent outbursts.

Could network headquarters sometimes feel like a prison? Yes. Cliff missed having the freedom to come and go whenever he liked. He missed fresh air. And moonlight. Feeling a breeze on his face. Hearing the crickets chirp. But he would willfully surrender all of that again and again to keep from harming men, women, and children whose only offense would be crossing his path. He didn't want to brutalize and butcher people the way he'd seen vampires consumed by madness do. *Or* vampires who *weren't* consumed by madness but simply got off on the strength vampirism gave them.

Joe felt the same way Cliff did. In his lucid moments.

But he wasn't lucid now.

Cliff heard Melanie talking to Chris Reordon, the head honcho at the network, out in the hallway. Crossing to the coffee table, Cliff snagged a pen and a piece of paper, then scribbled a quick note.

YOU NEED TO SEDATE JOE. HE'S RANTING AGAIN. AND IF THE NEW VAMPIRE HEARS SOME OF THE THINGS JOE IS SAYING, I GUARANTEE YOU HE'LL BOLT.

As soon as he finished, he folded the paper and moved to stand beside the door to his apartment.

Though the network had done a nice job coating the door with a thin sheet of wood, it didn't change the fact that the damn thing was as thick and heavy as the door on a bank vault. So were the walls. Chris Reordon left nothing to chance, so he'd made damned sure any vampires housed here couldn't break or tunnel their way out.

Cliff listened to the conversations that filled the busy hallway beyond. Carefully timing the delivery of his message so it would miss Chris Reordon and attract the notice of Dr. Melanie and Dr. Linda, he slipped the piece of paper under the door.

A few seconds later, paper rattled.

"What is it?" Linda asked. A moment passed. "I'll take care of it."

"Thanks," Melanie said.

If the two said anything else, they did so with sign language, having learned it shortly after the vampires' arrival so they could converse without the vamps listening in.

Cliff paced his apartment. Joe might rant and have violent breaks on occasion, but even when the voices he heard were at their loudest, he didn't direct his aggression toward the women.

At least he hadn't yet.

A knock sounded on the door to Joe's apartment.

Joe quieted.

Cliff tensed.

A clunk sounded.

"Knock, knock," Linda called cheerfully. "Hi, Joe. Can I come in?" The door clunked shut.

"What's that?" Joe asked, a reserved tone tinged with a hint of suspicion replacing his shouts.

"I think I've finally perfected my praline recipe. But just to be sure... I was hoping you'd taste them again for me and tell me what you think. Your taste buds are so much more sensitive than mine. If *anyone* can tell me what I did or didn't do right, it's you."

Silence fell... and stretched long enough to worry Cliff.

"Did you use less vanilla this time?" Joe asked slowly, haltingly, as he struggled to achieve lucidity and beat back the voices.

"I did," Linda said, a smile in her voice.

"Okay." A rustle sounded, followed by crunching. "Mmm. These are good."

Cliff relaxed.

"You really think so?"

"Mm-hmm."

"Anything else you think I should change?"

"No," Joe responded, sounding a little more like his usual self. "I think you nailed it this time."

"Thank you!"

More rustling ensued that Cliff suspected resulted from Linda giving Joe a hug.

Damn, he loved that woman.

He loved *both* women. Melanie and Linda were the perfect combination of sweet and ballsy.

"You seem a little tense," Linda said, concern entering her voice.

Joe's crunching slowed.

"Do you want me to give you something to take the edge off?"

More silence. Then... "Yeah. I think... I think maybe you should."

And there was just something about the women that touched the vampires so deeply that Melanie and Linda were always able to reach them even when the vamps were at their most unstable, their most violent. When Vince had been in the grips of his last psychotic break, he had attacked pretty much everyone within reach *except* Melanie and Linda.

Cliff sank down on his sofa. He hoped like hell the same would be true when *he* started to have psychotic breaks. Because he would rather die than harm those he cared about.

Linda stayed with Joe until the sedative she administered banished the voices and eradicated for a time the paranoia that plagued him. Then she returned to the infirmary to continue her research, leaving the pralines behind for Joe to enjoy.

Sublevel 5 quieted.

In her office across the hall, Melanie suddenly gasped. "I see why Seth calls ahead to warn Sarah."

"Sorry it took so long," Bastien said.

Richart must have teleported him in. Damn, Cliff envied him that gift.

"Did something happen?"

Richart answered. "There were other vamps at the rendezvous site."

"Pissing on my property," Bastien grumbled.

Cliff frowned, angry on Bastien's behalf. The Immortal Guardians might have demolished Bastien's farmhouse and the tunnels beneath it, but it was still his place. He hoped Bastien kicked their asses.

"I didn't know 'em," a new voice blurted. "They just happened to be there, checking out Bastien's legendary lair." That must be Stuart, the new vampire.

"Ah," Melanie said. "I assume you kicked their asses?"

"The madness had progressed too far in all of them," Bastien told her. "They were beyond our help, so we destroyed them."

A smile entered her voice. "And enjoyed it a little too much, I'm guessing."

"Just with the pisser."

Cliff grinned.

"Dude," Stuart said, fascination entering his voice, "you're dating a human? Y'all can do that?"

Melanie must have made some kind of affectionate gesture.

The quiet that followed made Cliff shake his head in amusement. Bastien still couldn't believe Melanie cared for him and constantly worried about the possible repercussions fraternizing with him might have for her here at the network.

"Yes, we're dating." Melanie sounded as though she was trying not to laugh. "And the jury is still out on whether or not it's acceptable because Bastien has a bit of a checkered past."

Cliff had to laugh at that. *Checkered past* was a hell of an understatement.

"I didn't formally introduce myself the other night," she continued. "I'm Dr. Melanie Lipton. It's nice to meet you, Stuart."

"Yes, ma'am. I'm sorry I cut you."

"Don't worry about it." Cliff knew she didn't mind the skirmish that had resulted in Stuart wounding her because it had led to her first kiss with Bastien. "Welcome to the network."

"Thank you."

"I head the viral research we're doing here and frequently work with the other vampires. There are two currently in residence — Cliff and Joe."

"Welcome, Stuart," Cliff said. He didn't raise his voice. Vampire hearing was so acute Stuart would have no difficulty hearing him despite the thick walls that separated them. "I'm Cliff. It'll be nice to have another vampire to hang around with." Although he hated to admit it, having a vamp around who wasn't yet battling the madness would help him when his own fight began.

"You're one of the vampires?" Stuart asked hesitantly.

"Yes. I know you're probably scared…"

"Is Cliff talking to him?" Melanie murmured.

"Yes," Bastien said softly.

"*I* sure as hell was." Cliff had been terrified he had just handed himself over to people who intended—as Vince had accused—to use him like a lab rat. Particularly after he met Dr. Whetsman. That asshole had refused to work with the vampires unless they were restrained. "But you can relax. Dr. Lipton is great. So are Dr. Machen and some of the others we work with." Hopefully he wouldn't meet Whetsman for a while because the man was still a prick. "And you don't have to constantly be on your guard here, worrying about humans discovering what you are or vampires attacking you or wondering if you'll find a safe place to rest during the day. You made the right decision."

"How do I know you're not an immortal just saying that to get me to drop my guard?" Stuart asked, his tone vacillating between suspicion and hope.

"Well, for one thing, immortals are powerful enough that they don't *need* to coax you into letting down your guard," Cliff responded candidly. "They can overpower you and do whatever it is you think they might do with very little effort. For another, I was one of Bastien's followers. I surrendered the night of the final battle with the immortals at his lair and have been living here ever since. But you'll learn all of this and more eventually."

"What about the other one? Where is he?"

Cliff wasn't sure how to answer that.

"Where's Joe?" Bastien asked.

"I think he's resting," Melanie answered slowly. Apparently she wasn't sure how much to say either.

"I'm here," Joe said, his voice low and emotionless now that the sedative had kicked in. "The virus is fucking with my head today. Listen to Cliff. He isn't as far gone as I am. I think… I think I'm not seeing things clearly right now. Cliff is."

Silence fell.

"Can you help us?" Stuart asked, his tone subdued.

"I hope so, Stuart," Melanie said. "That's why I'm glad you're here. The more I learn and the more insight you and other vampires can provide me with, the closer we'll get to finding a method of preventing the madness."

"What can I do?"

Relief suffused Cliff.

"For now?" Melanie asked. "If you aren't averse to it, I'd like to take a small sample of your blood, then we can get you settled in your new apartment."

"It's… it's really an apartment? It's not a cell?"

Cliff answered swiftly, afraid the query might start Joe ranting again. "This isn't a prison, Stuart. We live well here. We each have our own apartment with whatever furnishings and electronic gadgets we want, though our phone and internet activity is monitored for safety's sake."

"So… I get my own place?"

"Yes," Melanie said, the smile returning to her voice. "We want you to be comfortable and, more important, happy here."

"I've never had my own apartment before," Stuart said with a note of awe. "Or my own room. I always had to share… with my brothers or with a dorm mate. *Man*, I had some sucky dorm mates."

After living in close proximity with nearly a hundred vampires in various stages of insanity, Cliff could relate.

Melanie laughed. "Well, let's hurry and do your blood work so you can get settled."

Bastien and Richart left to continue their night's hunt. A moment later, Cliff heard beeps as someone typed the security code into the electronic keypad outside his apartment. A clunk sounded; then the door swung inward.

Melanie smiled as she pushed the door open. "Hi, Cliff."

He rose and circled the sofa to join her. A lanky guy who looked like he couldn't be more than twenty years old stood behind her. When he peered into Cliff's apartment, his eyes widened and his jaw dropped.

Cliff smiled. Most of the furniture was brand-new. An impromptu (or not so impromptu) sparring session he and Bastien had engaged in when Bastien tested the stimulant Melanie had developed to counter the tranquilizer mercenaries used on Immortal Guardians had reduced most of his old stuff to splinters. Everything he and Melanie had ordered to replace it was top of the line. Very posh, as Bastien would say.

When he reached them, Cliff offered his hand. "Hi, Stuart. I'm Cliff."

"Hey," Stuart murmured distractedly as he shook it. Then he pointed behind Cliff, his finger wagging back and forth. "This is your place?"

"Yeah."

The younger vamp seemed stunned. "It's like something out of a movie."

Cliff laughed. "Like I said, we live well here."

When Stuart stopped gawking at the apartment, he looked at Melanie and Cliff as if he couldn't quite believe it all.

Melanie winked up at him. "Want me to pinch you so you know you're not dreaming?"

That managed to spark a smile. "Maybe."

She grinned. "I thought you might feel more comfortable in the lab if Cliff came with us. Let's get that done, then I'll show you *your* place."

Cliff accompanied them and kept up a running conversation with Stuart when his unease returned in the infirmary. He seemed like a good guy. Once Melanie led Stuart to the apartment that would officially be his, all his nervousness evaporated. He didn't even seem to care that he couldn't leave the apartment without Melanie or one of the others unlocking his door. He was too jazzed about having his own place… and a roomy one at that.

Cliff shook his head with a smile as he sank down on the sofa in his own apartment afterward. It looked like Stuart was going to be a nice addition to sublevel 5.

He heard Melanie call Bastien on the phone and tuned out whatever they said in case their talk turned amorous. Some things he just really didn't need to hear.

"Hey, Joe," he called as he picked up the PlayStation controller. "You up for some gaming?" He felt a little guilty that he hadn't checked on his friend since Stuart's arrival.

The pause that followed lasted so long Cliff wondered if perhaps Linda had given Joe a strong enough dose of the tranquilizer to knock him out.

"Sure," Joe responded finally, sounding exhausted. "Okay."

Sobering, Cliff grabbed the remote and turned on the big-screen television that graced his wall. He'd asked Melanie to test the tranquilizer on him when she'd developed it. He'd been curious to see if it would calm the anxiety that sometimes gripped him and, at the same time, concerned about testing *anything* on Joe while he was unstable.

While it had definitely eased the anxiety, he hadn't liked the sluggish way it left him feeling.

"What do you want to play?" he asked Joe.

"How about—"

A thunderous boom drowned out whatever Joe said. The floor shook so violently the sofa shifted underneath Cliff. Chunks of Sheetrock dropped from the ceiling, exposing the titanium it concealed. Dust and smaller pieces floated down like snow.

"What the hell?"

Another boom followed, seeming to rock the whole building. Framed artwork leaped off Cliff's walls as he clung to the sofa cushions. Books fell off shelves. Shit tumbled out of his kitchen cabinets and littered the countertops and floor. Then the room plunged into darkness.

Seconds later, dimmer reserve lighting he hadn't even realized his room possessed flickered on as an alarm began to blare.

Wonk! Wonk! Wonk!

"Code red! Code red!" Chris Reordon shouted over the hallway intercom.

Oh shit. Cliff had been around long enough to witness the drills the network periodically ran. And this one—a code red—meant the network was under attack.

Chapter Two

"H EY!" Emma jumped, then scowled at the woman who'd poked her head in the doorway. "Don't *do* that! You scared the crap out of me."

Grinning unrepentantly, Cynthia strolled inside and sank down in the comfy chair on the other side of Emma's desk. "Kinda jumpy tonight, aren't you?"

"Not until you shattered the quiet with your near shout."

She laughed. "My mom has complained all my life that I was born lacking an indoor voice."

Emma smiled as she leaned back in her chair, content to take a break. "You leaving early?" Both women worked the night shift at network headquarters, and dawn wasn't far away.

"Thinkin' about it. But that's not why I'm here." Eyes brightening, she leaned forward. "Did you hear the news?"

"What news?"

"Sebastien Newcombe brought in a new vampire."

Emma's eyebrows rose. "Really?"

"Yes. A buttload of guards went down to sublevel 5 earlier to beef up security."

"Todd told you that?"

"No. I had to take some paperwork up to Mr. Reordon's office and rode back down on the elevator with some of them." She shook her head. "Damn, they look good when they're all decked out for war."

Emma had to agree. Both the network guards and the Immortal

Guardians garbed themselves in all black. And there was just something about it—as well as the confidence and general badassness with which they conducted themselves—that made even the least attractive of them freaking hot.

Which was likely what had first attracted Cynthia to Todd.

Emma narrowed her eyes playfully. "You didn't start dating Todd because he works on sublevel 5 and can give you all the juicy gossip, did you?"

"No." Her friend laughed. "Welllllll, maybe in the beginning. I was just so damn curious."

They all had been. No other network headquarters had housed vampires who presumably wished to work *with* the Immortal Guardians instead of *against* them.

Hell, as far as she knew, no network headquarters had ever housed vampires who *didn't* wish to work with the Immortal Guardians. This was new territory.

"And you know I used to have a thing for bad boys," Cynthia went on.

Emma shook her head. "Until Todd charmed your socks off?"

"Yes." She smiled. "He's such a sweetheart."

He really was. And the two of them were adorable together. Emma envied them. "So what do you know about him?"

"About Todd?"

"No!" Emma said on a laugh. "The new vampire."

"Oh right. Well, Todd said he seems really young."

Emma sobered. "He's a kid?" No one knew how the virus would affect a vampire who wasn't fully grown when infected, if he or she would age or remain forever trapped in the body of a child.

"No. Todd just thought he seemed... I don't know... naive, I guess? Like he hadn't seen or experienced much before his transformation. But he's definitely college age. Chloe was charged with digging up everything she could on his background."

Emma sent her a wry smile. "While you peered over her shoulder?"

Cynthia laughed. "Only until she told me to bugger off. Apparently his name is Stuart. He's from a large family that rarely had enough money to keep their bellies full, poor guy, and was going to college on a scholarship when a vampire transformed him.

I tried to pump Todd for more information, but he and the other guards are trying to stay out of sight while Dr. Lipton and Dr. Machen show Stuart around. He said the kid was really nervous. But Cliff is helping out, trying to ease Stuart's fears and make him feel more comfortable."

That didn't surprise Emma. Everything Todd had told Cynthia about Cliff indicated he was a good guy. She hoped like hell the network would be able to cure him or at least prevent him from losing his sanity. Cliff was the only vampire of the three Seth had initially brought in who hadn't yet had a psychotic break.

He was also the only brother in the mix. And incredibly good-looking. Cynthia had badgered Todd into snapping a pic of the vampires a few months after they'd arrived, then shown it to Emma. Cliff had been laughing at something Vincent, the Latino vampire, had said. As had Joe, the blond vamp. The three men had looked so happy and carefree. Now Vince was gone and Joe was struggling.

Emma spent far too much time thinking about that photo. And Cliff.

What must it be like for him to watch his friends succumb to insanity and see firsthand what awaited him? Did he still harbor hope that the network could spare him that fate? Did he still smile and laugh as he had in that photo?

If so, it said much about his character, his strength, and his courage.

"Hello? Earth to Emma."

She blinked. "What?"

"I said I'm going to try to get Todd to snap a pic of Stuart."

Emma rolled her eyes. "You're going to cost that poor man his job one of these days if you aren't careful."

"No I won't. Who's going to know?"

"Everyone in this building who has preternaturally sharp hearing."

"Oh. Damn it! That's right. I keep forgetting." Her voice dropped to a whisper. "Do you think the vampires heard me?"

"You know whispering won't help, right? Even four stories below, they can still hear everything that happens up here."

She grimaced. "Sheesh. I hope they can't hear *everything*. I love

Todd's spicy veggie soup, but he insists on putting both broccoli and cabbage in it."

Amusement filled Emma. "Ka*blammo*."

"Exactly. You know your man truly loves you when he doesn't complain about his cooking making you super farty."

Emma laughed.

A thunderous boom pierced Emma's ears and seemed to vibrate through her at the same time the floor and walls shook.

Starting violently, she grabbed her desk and held on when her chair started to roll away from it. Her pen and pencil holder tumbled over the side and hit the floor. Dust and pieces of Sheetrock fell from the ceiling.

Cynthia yelped and held on to the arms of her chair.

Silence fell as they stared at each other with wide eyes.

"What the hell was that?" Cynthia whispered.

Emma's heart slammed against her ribs. "I think it was an explosion." Her mind raced, seeking a possible explanation. Had the new vampire smuggled in a bomb or something?

"An explosion?" The light color Cynthia's Latina heritage lent her leached away. "What—?"

Another explosion rocked the building, this one so violent—or perhaps so close—that Emma's chair rolled out from under her, landing her on her ass. Her computer crashed to the floor on the other side of the desk. Her lamp, too. Paper rained down amid more Sheetrock.

"Emma!" Cynthia cried.

Grabbing the edge of her desk, Emma pulled herself up onto her knees and peered over it. Cynthia still sat in the chair, expression terrified.

Darkness swallowed them.

Dimmer reserve lighting flared to life.

An alarm began to blare. *Wonk! Wonk! Wonk!*

"Code red! Code red!" Mr. Reordon shouted over the building's intercom system.

"Oh shit." Emma scrambled to her feet. During the drills, Mr. Reordon always said he would only issue that order if the network fell under attack.

Cynthia stared at her, frozen in fear.

Emma hurried around the desk and grabbed her friend's arm. "We have to go. Now!" Yanking Cynthia up, she propelled her out into the hallway.

More explosions rocked the building. Screams and shouts filled the voids between. A crush of bodies flooded the corridor as employees stumbled out of their offices and headed for the elevator and stairwell at the far end.

"Go with the others!" Emma shouted over the noise that now included rapid gunfire as well. She gave Cynthia a push in the right direction, then turned away.

Cynthia grabbed her hand. "What are you doing? You have to come with us!"

Emma shook her head. "I have to get Sadie!" The elderly woman treated everyone under the age of sixty as if they were her grandchildren. She even baked them cookies. And though her mind and wit were sharp, her body was frail.

Understanding dawned in Cynthia's expression. "I'll come with you!"

"No. We'll catch up. You go! Check on Jasmine and Chloe on the way!" Both women were hugely pregnant.

Eyes widening, Cynthia gave a jerky nod. "I'll get them out! Be safe!"

"You, too! And take the stairs, not the elevator!" Though she was sure the elevator must have some kind of emergency brake, Emma thought it best not to take any chances.

Cynthia disappeared from view as the flood of employees carried her away.

Emma squeezed over to the wall, then forced her way against the tide until she reached Sadie's office. Someone bumped into her, sending her stumbling inside.

Debris cluttered the office, which appeared empty.

Good. She must have already evacuated. But just in case... "Sadie!"

A head adorned with a gray chignon dusted with bits of Sheetrock popped up behind the desk. "Emma?"

Swearing, Emma hurried toward her, staggering as the building shook again. "What are you doing? Mr. Reordon issued a code red. You're supposed to evacuate!" She helped the woman to her feet.

"I forgot." Looking frazzled, Sadie shook her head at herself. "In my day, when you heard an alarm like that, you were supposed to duck and cover."

Emma didn't think *duck and cover* was going to help with this. It sounded as if someone was dropping freaking bunker-busting bombs on them. "We have to get down to sublevel 5." Nerves jangling over the slow pace they had to maintain, she ushered Sadie over to the door.

Maybe she should just hoist the woman onto her back and try to piggyback her?

When they reached the hallway, Sadie turned left instead of right.

"No. It's this way!"

Sadie shook her head. "We have to get Wayne and Lloyd!"

Crap. She'd forgotten they had offices down here. Both men were as old and frail as Sadie. "I'll get them!" she shouted over the booms. "You head for the stairs!" Once she found Wayne and Lloyd, Emma would have to haul ass to help Sadie down the stairs, a task that might actually necessitate that piggyback ride.

She glanced around frantically. "Miles!"

The portly blond looked around, squinting his eyes.

Emma pushed her way over to him. "Miles!"

"Emma?"

"What happened to your glasses?"

"I don't know! Somebody knocked them off!"

She had intended to ask him to help Sadie navigate the stairs. But Miles was so nearsighted she worried he might take a tumble himself.

After urging him along with the others, she shouldered her way farther back and sighed with relief when she saw Lloyd and Wayne shuffling along with the rest of the crowd.

"Where's Sadie?" Lloyd called.

"Up there!" Emma stood on her toes and pointed to the dusty chignon bobbing ahead. A blur of motion at the far end of the hallway caught her attention. As she pushed Lloyd and Wayne ahead of her, she caught a glimpse of glowing blue eyes.

Oh shit. Had Vampire Joe escaped?

She lost sight of him.

Then glowing amber eyes appeared.

Was that Bastien, coming after Joe? She couldn't see clearly for all the dust and smoke and bodies ahead of her.

Someone stumbled into Emma.

Dropping her heels to the floor, she turned around.

Light and sound exploded above her. A roar filled the hallway. Screams erupted. Pain struck as something fell on Emma's head and back, so heavy it forced her to the ground. Agony shot through her arm. Dust filled her mouth and nose.

Darkness.

Chapter Three

C LIFF GROUND HIS TEETH IN his apartment. He should be out there. He should be helping. But no way would Reordon allow it with so many civilians in the vampires' paths.

The French immortals fought the mercenaries aboveground. Bastien started summoning reinforcements while Melanie helped the injured.

"Cliff," Bastien said.

"I'm here," he called. "How bad is it, because it sounds fucking cataclysmic."

"It's bad."

"Dr. Lipton's okay?"

"For now. Cliff, you up for a fight?"

"Hell yes, man. Let me out and I'll help you kick some serious ass." From the sounds of it, they were critically outnumbered. There were a hell of a lot of mercenaries topside.

"Me, too," Joe added. "I'm a little out of it from the drug, but I can hold my own against humans."

Cliff's pulse picked up as he paced, dodging the debris that cluttered his formerly pristine apartment, eager to get out there and *do* something. He wished for the thousandth time that his kitchen were outfitted with a nice set of knives, but the network balked at providing the vampires with sharp implements.

Bastien engaged in a quick argument with Melanie that he ultimately lost when she refused to evacuate with the others. Cliff wasn't surprised. Melanie was the kind of person who always placed the needs of others above her own. As a doctor, she wouldn't leave until every wound had been tended. And Linda had already evacuated so she could tend the wounded on the other end of… whatever means they were using to evacuate people. Reordon had always been hush-hush about that during the drills, as if he didn't want the vampires to know.

Speaking of Reordon… Chris joined the crush of people out in the hallway.

"Étienne and Lisette are up on the ground," Bastien shouted to the human. "David will be here any minute. Richart is fetching Roland, Sarah, Marcus, and Ami."

"Why the hell is he bringing Ami here?" Reordon yelled back.

"We have a plan! I'll fill you in later! Right now you need to let the vampires out to play!"

"Now I know you're crazy!"

"They want to help! And we need all the help we can get! It's going to take all of us immortals to handle the human firepower. We need the vamps to keep the damned building from collapsing until the rest of you can evacuate! Let them out! I'll take full responsibility!"

"Which doesn't mean shit! Because once Seth hears you put Ami in danger, he's going to kill you!"

Cliff sure as hell hoped not. But Seth *did* love Ami like a daughter. Even the vampires knew that.

"What other choice do we have?" Bastien countered.

"You'd better be right!" The volume of Chris's threat increased as he neared Cliff's door, passing Stuart's. "You're dead, motherfucker!"

"He didn't know they were tracking him!" Bastien yelled.

"You won't kill me if I help, right?" Stuart asked. "You aren't going to let those guys capture me again, are you? I mean, I can help, right?"

"Yes," Bastien answered while someone swiped a card and entered the security code outside Cliff's door. "Help the humans get their wounded to the tunnel."

Cliff stood just inside his door. After a clunk, it swung open to reveal Bastien and Chris Reordon. Behind them, dozens of men and women adorned with soot, powdery bits of rubble, and bleeding wounds limped toward the far end of the hallway. Cliff stepped out and glanced in that direction.

A hole had been blown into the wall, revealing a long tunnel through which the wounded filed.

He met Bastien's gaze. "I can help up on the ground."

Bastien shook his head. "I don't want to risk your being tranqed."

Reordon moved on to unlock Joe's door.

Joe stepped into the hallway, eyes glowing a vibrant blue.

"Help with the evacuation," Bastien said, face grim. And a feeling of nostalgia rolled over Cliff. It felt so much like old times—when Bastien would issue orders and Cliff and the rest of his vampire army would follow them—that he might've smiled if circumstances weren't so damn dire. "Check the upper floors. See if anyone is trapped. Get everyone out you can."

Nodding, Cliff and Joe took off down the hallway, zipping past humans in a blur. A never-ending river of employees flowed forth from the stairwell. So they forced the doors of the elevator open.

The bodies of four men lay crumpled on the floor, explaining the screams he'd heard earlier. The damn elevator cable had snapped and whatever explosion had caused it must have taken out half the ceiling as well as whatever safety mechanism was supposed to prevent the thing from free-falling to sublevel 5.

"Shit," Joe muttered.

Nodding, Cliff leaped up through the hole. The mercenaries had wrought so much damage to the building that he could see stars twinkling in the sky far above him.

That sky was beginning to lighten with the approach of dawn, so he and Joe would have to work fast to keep from frying.

The two of them catapulted up from floor to floor until they reached sublevel 1.

Cliff stared. It looked like a damned war zone. Huge pieces of concrete and rubble formed jagged hills as employees coated in dust and blood limped toward the stairwell with expressions of panic, pain, and shock. Those in front stopped and stared when they saw Cliff and Joe. Most stumbled backward when Joe approached them, his blue eyes identifying him as a vampire, not an Immortal Guardian.

"It's okay!" Cliff called. "We're here to help."

That appeared to do little in the way of assuaging their fear as

Joe shot forward, tossed a man over his shoulder, and zipped back toward the elevator shaft.

Cliff would've taken another minute to calm their fear, but more crap fell from the ceiling with every blast. Dashing forward, he lifted a woman into his arms. Her shrieks pierced his sensitive ears, sparking a grimace as he raced for the elevator shaft.

"Hold on!" he ordered.

Her arms locked around his neck as he stepped off.

A longer shriek nearly deafened him as they plummeted toward the elevator at the bottom. Shortly after he had transformed, Cliff had delighted in testing his new strength and endurance by jumping off higher and higher buildings, enjoying the rush without suffering injuries. So he had no difficulty landing smoothly on the part of the elevator roof that was still intact while protecting his cargo from the jolt.

"Almost there," he told her as he dropped through the hole in the ceiling.

Joe and Stuart zipped past them, going the opposite direction and disappearing up the shaft. The woman's cries dwindled to whimpers as Cliff swept through the throng to deposit her at the entrance to the escape tunnel.

He returned to the elevator shaft and leapfrogged up the other floors to reach sublevel 1 again.

The other vampires raced by, already on their way down with more injured.

Sublevel 1 had taken a big hit in the short time he'd been gone. Part of the ceiling had buckled. Sheetrock continued fall like rain from the rest of it. At the far end of the corridor, through the chaos and dust and dim lighting, he saw a sister with a crown braid herding several others toward him, no doubt intending for them to use the stairs. But Cliff doubted the elderly woman in the front would be able to navigate them easily. She looked so skinny and frail a breeze could probably tip her over. And she moved with short, stiff steps.

Cliff started toward her.

Light and fire burst into life as the building shook with another explosion.

More of the ceiling collapsed. Furniture and debris from the ground floor fell with a rumble atop the evacuating men and women. Something heavy struck Cliff's back with enough force to make him stagger.

Shaking it off, he lunged forward and began to yank office furniture from the top of the pile, then jagged flooring, insulation, and Sheetrock until he found the old woman tucked beneath a tilted stretch of granite that had probably topped a desk.

Blinking against the dust, she peered up at him.

"It's okay," Cliff told her, hoping she would think him an Immortal Guardian and not be afraid. Unlike Joe and Stuart, Cliff had brown eyes that glowed amber. "I'm here to help. Are you hurt?"

She tried to answer but coughed instead when dust entered her lungs.

He quickly went to work unburying her. "Are you okay?"

She managed a thumbs-up.

As soon as he could, Cliff reached down and gingerly helped her up out of the pile.

"Thank you," she wheezed. "Where's Emma? You have to find her."

"I'm going to carry you down to sublevel 5 first."

"I can walk," she said gamely.

"I can walk faster."

"But—"

"I'll come back for Emma. I promise." Lifting her frail body into his arms, he swept her down to the mouth of the evacuation tunnel.

An Immortal Guardian he recognized as Marcus and a petite redhead stood beside it. Was she Ami?

As soon as he saw Cliff racing toward them, Marcus stepped in front of the woman and raised his weapons.

Shit. He wouldn't attack Cliff, thinking he'd escaped, would he?

Melanie finished tending an injured man nearby and hustled over to place a hand on Marcus's arm. "Wait."

He scowled at her. "Is that—?"

Cliff skidded to a halt.

Melanie addressed the woman. "Ma'am? Are you hurt?"

The woman shook her head. "The ceiling collapsed. I was trapped and couldn't move until this young man freed me. I told him I could walk, but—"

Cliff lowered the woman to her feet. "I said I could walk faster."

The woman nodded, her expression slack with amazement. "He could."

Cliff took a step back and sent Marcus a cautious glance. Then, after nodding to Melanie, he shot back toward the elevators and returned to sublevel 1. Stuart and Joe had already dug two men out from under the wreckage. They had also uncovered the bodies of three who didn't make it.

Cliff looked around for the woman he'd seen helping the others and saw no sign of her. Swearing, he tore through the wreckage in search of her. An explosion took out more of the ceiling. Rubble rained down on the other side of the pile he dug through. "Come on," he whispered. "Where are you?"

A moan reached his ears, followed by a cough.

Leaping toward it, he grabbed slabs of concrete and flooring and tossed them aside, reducing the pile until he found her.

Dust coated her like ash, powdering her braid and turning her smooth brown skin a grayish white. She blinked up at him. Her forehead glistened with blood that oozed from a gash on one side.

"It's okay," he told her. "I'm here to help. Don't be afraid."

Her chin dipped in a brief nod.

Another explosion hit what was left of the ground floor.

Cliff swiftly leaned over to shield her as flaming bits rained down around them.

As soon as it stopped, he knelt beside her.

"Y-Your eyes are glowing."

"It's okay. Don't be afraid. I just want to help. Are you injured?" He swept his hands over her in a quick, impersonal search for injuries, concerned by the splotches of blood that marred her clothing.

"Th-there's a woman," she said. "Sadie. Sh-She's old. She can't make it down the stairs."

"I already got her to safety. Are you Emma?"

Surprise lit her dark brown eyes as she nodded.

"I think your arm is broken, Emma. I need to bind it." Tearing a strip of cloth from his T-shirt, he wrapped it around a deep gash on her arm. Then he tore another and—preternaturally fast—fashioned a sling.

She moaned.

"Sorry," he said, knowing every movement caused her pain.

Nodding, she gritted her teeth. Her lips pressed tightly together as he lifted her into his arms, spawning even more pain.

"I'm sorry," he said again as he dashed over to the elevator shaft.

She looped her free arm around his neck and looked over his shoulder. Her hold tightened.

"It's okay," he said. "Don't be afraid. I'll keep you safe."

"Mercenaries," she whispered in his ear, her warm breath sending a shiver through him.

Mercenaries? Behind him?

Well, *shit.* He couldn't fight them and protect Emma at the same time.

It took mere seconds to jump down to sublevel 5 and ferry her to the tunnel opening.

Melanie hurried over to him.

"Her arm is broken and bleeding." Cliff carefully lowered the woman to her feet. "And she has a gash on her head."

As soon as Melanie nodded to him, Cliff returned to sublevel 1.

A dozen mercenaries crept through the wreckage.

Joe suddenly appeared at Cliff's side.

The mercenaries hadn't noticed them yet. Smoke and dust and fragments that steadily rained down from the ground floor obscured their vision too much.

But Cliff and Joe could see just fine.

"Kill them," Cliff murmured. "Quick and quiet." The immortals battling above sure as hell weren't taking prisoners, so Cliff felt no need to hold back.

He and Joe flew forward.

The first mercenaries to fall didn't even see them coming. The rest saw them too late. The vampires might not have the blades Immortal Guardians wielded or the weaponry of the mercenaries, but a punch backed by preternatural strength could kill a man in seconds, as could a swift twist of his head.

Another explosion rattled the floor beneath his feet as the last man collapsed.

Worried that this level would soon collapse as well, Cliff

nodded to Joe, and the two of them dropped down to sublevel 2 to evacuate more employees. They took out a few more mercenaries and shuttled multiple injured employees down to sublevel 5.

Cliff waited while Joe handed off another wounded man to the guards at the mouth of the tunnel. "We're both pretty banged up," he told his friend. "Let's stop off and get some blood before we go back."

Joe nodded.

Cliff didn't need the blood. He'd only acquired a few scrapes and bruises here and there and felt fine. But Joe was looking a little ragged. He'd suffered some gashes, two of which weren't healing. The scent of blood was every-freaking-where. And Cliff wasn't sure what effect killing the mercenaries might have on Joe, who'd already been struggling before the attack. Cliff worried the strain of everything would send his friend over the edge. If Joe replenished the blood he'd lost though, it might help him maintain control.

Cliff gave Marcus a nod, unsurprised when the large warrior didn't nod back.

The Immortal Guardian radiated fury and looked ready to rip everyone to shreds as he stood sentinel in front of the petite redhead. Ami's eyes were closed, her brow furrowed as if she concentrated very hard on something.

Maybe she was an immortal with one of those cool gifts. All of the male Immortal Guardians he'd encountered had black hair. But maybe there were some redheads among the females.

Joe made his silent way to the lab. Dr. Lipton kept a special refrigerator stocked with blood in there.

Cliff followed. The crowd in the hallway began to thin.

A hell of a lot of explosions continued to rumble overhead. And quite a few humans were still trapped on sublevel two, so this thing was far from over.

A few steps inside the lab, Joe stopped short.

Cliff bumped into his back. "What is it?"

Joe didn't answer.

Cliff stepped around him and felt his heart drop into his stomach.

The new vampire was down on the floor with Dr. Lipton in his lap, his fangs buried deep in her neck.

"What the fuck are you doing?" Cliff bellowed and rushed forward. Stuart raised his head and snarled something.

Dr. Lipton lay still, eyes closed, blood trailing down her neck.

Cliff lifted her with care, then backhanded Stuart, sending him flying across the room to shatter the already cracked Sheetrock on the far wall.

"Dr. Lipton?" Fear filling him, he placed his hand on her neck to try to staunch the flow of blood. "Melanie?"

Joe watched with wild eyes. "I can't hear a heartbeat."

Neither could Cliff. He'd like to think it was because there was so damned much other noise going on, but…

She was pale. And her lips held an alarming bluish tint.

Come on, come on, come on. Don't die. Please don't die.

"What happened?" Stuart asked, slumped across the room.

Joe turned blazing eyes on the vampire. "You killed her! You fucking killed her!"

"Wait!" Cliff shifted his warm, bloody fingers on her neck. "I-I-I think I found a pulse. She's not dead yet." But she was completely unresponsive.

"*Yet*," Joe repeated and backed toward the doorway.

Cliff frowned. "Joe? What are you doing? Get help."

But his friend just kept moving, his head rocking back and forth. "I can't do it."

"What?"

"I can't do this. Not without Dr. Lipton. Not without Melanie. I can't be here."

"She isn't—"

"You know what they'll do to us! They hate us! They'll blame us! They'll kill us!"

Cliff gaped as his friend disappeared through the doorway.

Stuart didn't even seem to notice. His wide-eyed gaze remained fixed on Dr. Lipton. Crimson liquid trailed from the corner of his mouth. "I did that?"

"Yes!"

"I didn't mean to!"

Cliff could believe it, but… *Shit!* Joe was on the run. Dr. Lipton's heartbeat was faltering. He had to do something. Fast. "If you didn't mean it, get your ass over here."

Stuart scrambled forward.

Cliff passed him Dr. Lipton and hoped like hell he was doing the right thing. "Keep pressure on her neck. I'm gonna go for help."

Stuart nodded. He should be flushed from feeding, but his face was pale as death.

Cliff took one last look at Melanie, then bolted from the room. Down the hallway toward the elevator he raced, moving so fast he would probably kill a human if he bumped into one. "*Bastien!*" he shouted.

Up through the roof of the elevator he jumped.

"*What?*" Bastien called back from somewhere outside.

Cliff leaped up two floors, grabbed the edge, and propelled himself up two more. "*Melanie needs you! She's hurt real bad!*"

One more leap and he ran smack into Bastien on the ground floor... or what was left of it.

"What happened?" Bastien demanded.

"Stuart drained her."

Bastien's eyes flared with panic as he turned to the elevator shaft.

Cliff grabbed his arm. "Joe's gone. He saw Dr. Lipton and freaked out. I have to go after him."

"The sun's coming up."

"He can't be alone. He's too close to losing it."

Bastien nodded and pulled him into a rough hug. "Be careful. If you don't make it back by sunrise, I'll find you."

Cliff nodded and watched Bastien drop through the opening and free-fall to the bottom, where he landed smoothly in a crouch.

Cliff eyed the chaos around him. There was fire everywhere. Bullets whipped past. Immortals...

He swallowed. *Holy crap.* No wonder Bastien's vampire army had fallen beneath the immortals' swords. Once again he marveled over their speed, strength, and intensity.

Cliff's heart began to pound. His chest felt tight. He felt exposed up here. Terrified. He hadn't been outside by himself in over two years. Had he become agoraphobic as a result? Because his feet felt frozen to the pitted floor.

Until a freaking missile shot past.

Cliff ducked behind what was left of a desk. The ceiling was gone, the remains of the roof mingling with the other rubble beneath his feet.

Where the hell was Joe?

Smoke stung his eyes as he peered around, trying to locate the blond vampire.

There! Diving into the trees.

Cliff took off after him. Leaping over a pile of mercenary bodies, he dodged as many bullets as he could. The damned things flew every which way like angry bees. A blurred form sailed past, eyes flashing bright amber.

Terror cut through him like a blade.

Would the immortals think he was trying to escape and kill him?

When the dark-as-midnight figure kept going, Cliff allowed himself to breathe again.

Apparently he wasn't their highest priority right now.

Relieved, he headed for the trees, intent on finding Joe.

Something stung his neck.

Reaching up, he slapped at it and came away with a tranquilizer dart. His vision wavered. His knees buckled.

The ground lurched up and hit him hard.

A shadow fell over him.

Cliff squinted up at two soldiers. "Ah shi—"

Chapter Four

C LIFF'S KNEE BOBBED UP AND down, nearly dislodging the elbow he'd propped on it.

Swearing, he rose and began to pace. Agitation crawled through him like ants, making it impossible to sit still.

"Fucking mercenaries," he muttered.

Fury suffused him. Curling his hands into fists, he took a deep breath and fought it back.

A month had passed since the mercenary attack that had resulted in him and Joe being captured and tortured, the trauma of which had driven Joe to succumb to the madness entirely.

Cliff swallowed hard as sorrow rose. He hadn't gotten to say goodbye to his friend. He hadn't been *able* to. That ate at him. But Bastien had said Joe wouldn't have recognized him if he had. Joe had been so far gone that he hadn't even recognized Melanie and Bastien. All he'd done when they'd tried to help him was snarl and rant and fight his restraints.

"We tried so hard to reach him," Melanie had told Cliff, tears coursing down her cheeks as she fought back sobs. "We tried so hard to guide him back to us." But they'd ultimately had to admit defeat.

Abiding by his wishes, she and Bastien had sedated Joe, then drained his blood and… let him go.

Cliff had been oblivious to it all because whatever torture he had endured at the hands of the mercenaries had triggered his first psychotic break. He didn't remember any of it. The torture. Being rescued. Coming back to network headquarters.

He glanced around. Or rather to the *new* network headquarters. The original one hadn't been salvageable.

Even the days that had followed his return were a bit of a blur.

Hell, he barely remembered the mercenary attack itself. Just little flashes here and there. Few specifics.

His inability to recollect his actions that night troubled Cliff deeply. Vince and Joe had suffered the same selective amnesia after their psychotic breaks. Neither had recalled the rage that had gripped them or the injuries they'd inflicted upon others.

Had Cliff injured anyone that night? The night of his break?

He didn't care about hurting the damned mercenaries but felt sick at the notion that he might have harmed one of the employees or guards here at the network.

Or maybe more than one.

Bastien and Melanie had assured him he hadn't. They'd painted him a hero, going on and on about the lives he'd saved. But was that true? Or was it bullshit spouted with good intentions?

They had always downplayed the violence and harm Joe and Vince had spawned during their breaks. Cliff had too, not wanting his friends to have to contend with guilt as well as the madness. So he couldn't help but wonder if Bastien and Melanie were doing the same for him now.

Pacing did little to calm Cliff's mind or banish the anxiety that rode him.

Crossing to the phone, he stared down at it a moment, shook his head, then took another deep breath and dialed the infirmary.

"Dr. Whetsman," a man answered.

Biting back a curse, Cliff advised himself to remain patient. Whetsman was his least favorite doctor at the network. "It's Cliff. I could use some exercise. Would you open my door so I can run some miles on the treadmill?" Melanie and Linda wouldn't hesitate. They even left his door open for hours at a time now so he could roam sublevel 5 and visit Stuart. But it was lunchtime. Melanie and Linda worked the night shift. And Whetsman—

"No. You should be resting."

—was a prick. Cliff ground his teeth and kept his response calm and casual. "I can't sleep. I think I just need to get some exercise. Wear myself out a little." He forced a light laugh. "A run should help."

Silence. "I think it inadvisable. You can exercise tonight." Whetsman ended the call.

Cliff slammed the receiver down. "Pussy." Whetsman was so terrified of the vampires that he made damn sure he was never alone with any of them and was too stupid to realize his fear and his persistence in treating them like escaped serial killers constantly on the prowl for new victims was so fucking annoying that he actually *triggered* some of the vampires' breaks.

Cliff resumed his pacing and again found no relief. Stopping, he perused his apartment. His shoulders slumped. Looked like he'd just have to play some video games to try to—

His doorbell rang.

Cliff spun toward the door as someone typed a code into the pad outside it and swiped a security card. Hope rose. Had Whetsman actually manned up and changed his mind?

A clunk sounded. The door swung inward.

Cliff remained where he was, not wanting to spook the asshole.

Instead of Dr. Whetsman, however, Todd—one of the guards who usually manned this floor—poked his head in. "Hey, Cliff."

"Hey."

"Mr. Reordon would like to see you in his office."

Shit. Had Whetsman called Reordon and complained? *What a dick.* "Okay."

Smiling, Todd backed away to give Cliff room to exit and join him in the hallway.

Todd was a good guy. He had been the first guard to stop reaching for his weapon every time the vampires left their apartments. And his relaxed demeanor had gone a long way toward ending the other guards' tendency to tense up... *and* had helped Cliff and the other vampires feel more comfortable in their new home.

The guards manning the desk in front of the elevators nodded a greeting as Cliff and Todd approached them.

"How's it going?" Cliff asked.

A jumble of the usual "good" or "not bad" responses ensued.

When Cliff and Todd stepped into the elevator, five guards joined them.

Todd swiped his security card and typed in a code.

The doors slid closed.

Normally Cliff would crack a joke to ease the tension, but he was too damn agitated today to come up with anything. "How's Cynthia?"

Todd grinned. "Out of my league."

One of the other guards snorted. "*Way* out of his league."

"Hell yes, she is," another agreed.

Unoffended, Todd shrugged. "But she loves me anyway."

Cliff forced a smile. "Lucky man."

"Damn straight."

As soon as the elevator reached the ground floor, the guards escorted him to a long hallway that he assumed led to Reordon's office. Though Cliff didn't look back to confirm it, his acute hearing told him more guards entered the hallway behind them, hands probably on their weapons.

Cliff didn't know what to think of it all. This was the first time he had been above ground — except for the night of the attack, that was — since he had surrendered to Seth and the Immortal Guardians. Disappointment filled him as he took in the lack of windows. It would've been nice to see some greenery. Some sunlight. Though he supposed it was better for him that there *weren't* windows. If any sunlight touched his skin, it instantly began to burn and blister.

Todd led him through a doorway, then paused.

Cliff looked around. The room reminded him a little of the reception room at a high-end doctor's office. Comfortable seating took up half the space. File cabinets and a large desk decked out with lots of computer paraphernalia occupied the rest.

A pretty brunette woman seated behind the desk looked up at their entrance.

A slew of guards filed past Cliff and fanned out around the edges of the room.

But the woman paid them little heed as her hazel eyes met his.

Cliff waited for her to tense up, pale, or make some other involuntary display of nerves.

Instead she smiled.

Did she not know he was a vampire? Because her heartbeat didn't even increase.

Rising, she rounded the desk and approached him. "Hi, Cliff. I'm Kate." She offered him her hand.

Surprised, he took it and gave it a firm shake. "Nice to meet you."

Her smile broadened into a grin. "I'm so glad you're back and that I have this chance to thank you."

He glanced at Todd, who just watched them with a smile. "Thank me?"

Nodding, she patted their clasped hands. "We've actually met before. I don't blame you for not recognizing me. I looked like I'd been rolling in dirt and ash and didn't even recognize *myself* when I looked in the mirror." She loosed a self-deprecating laugh that drew a smile from him. "I'm one of the employees you saved when the mercenaries attacked."

He stared at her in surprise. "Oh." He had no memory of that. At all.

"Thank you again." After one last pat, she released his hand.

"You're welcome."

She wrinkled her nose. "Oh screw it. I hope you don't mind this." Leaning in, she stunned the hell out of him by giving him a big hug. "I never would've survived if you hadn't gotten me down to that escape tunnel. I was injured and barely made it to sublevel two. And mercenaries were right behind me."

Cliff darted the guards a wary glance and spread his arms slightly, hands open, afraid to make even the slightest move that might inspire them to tranq him.

Though the guards he didn't know narrowed their eyes and tensed, those who had accompanied him from sublevel 5 remained relaxed. Some even appeared amused when he just stood there, afraid to respond.

Kate backed away and scowled at the guards. "Oh, would you guys just relax already? We're trying to have a freaking moment."

Todd snorted when he tried and failed to hold back a laugh.

Cliff didn't expect the men to react. But damned if they didn't immediately snap to attention, release their weapons, and shift their gazes to stare straight ahead.

"Better," she said with a smile, then gave Cliff another hug.

Amusement sifted through him, dispersing some of his anxiety. Smiling, he wrapped his arms around her and returned her hug.

Out of all the things becoming a vampire had deprived him of, Cliff thought he missed human touch the most. He had gone a long damn time without it. So long that he had nearly wept the first time Melanie had hugged him.

Though taller than Melanie, Kate was still a little on the short side and smelled like cucumbers.

It was nice.

"I'm glad you're okay," he said.

She backed away with a smile. "I'm glad you are, too."

Movement drew Cliff's attention to a doorway on the other side of the office.

Chris Reordon stood there, watching them.

Oh crap. First Whetsman tattles and says who-knows-what to lead Reordon to summon Cliff to his office, then Reordon finds Cliff hugging his assistant?

This wasn't going to go well, was it?

Chris strolled toward them, his expression inscrutable. He stared at Cliff a moment, then nodded *not* at the doorway that led to his office but to the one that led *out* of Kate's. "Walk with me."

Cliff couldn't decide if that was a request or an order but opted to follow him. Not that he actually had a choice.

Reordon didn't speak as he led Cliff back to the elevators.

Todd and the other guards followed at a not very discreet distance.

The guards from sublevel 5 squeezed onto the elevator with them. The rest remained topside.

The short ride only took them down one floor to sublevel 1. According to Melanie, this network headquarters building was an exact replica of the old one. Cliff had reportedly been all over sublevel 1 the morning of the mercenary blitz, but—again—he had no memory of it, so he was seeing it with new eyes.

He glanced around curiously as Reordon led him down a wide hallway. Aside from those that accompanied them, no guards were in sight. No doctors or researchers wearing white physician coats or scrubs were either. Instead, men and women in casual business attire slowed their steps and stared as Cliff's group approached, then passed them.

Did they know he was a vampire? Was that why they stared? Or did they simply not see heavily armed guards on this level very often? Sublevel 1 had the lowest security clearance, so he doubted anything or anyone here needed to be guarded.

They passed several offices, some small with only one occupant and some large with multiple desks or cubicles. The largest room they passed housed rows and rows of fitness equipment currently being utilized by dozens of sweating employees. Across the hall from that lay a gym in which more employees trained in hand-to-hand combat.

"Are those guards training in there?" Cliff asked.

Reordon shook his head. "Regular employees. Before the mercenary attack, the training was optional. Now it's mandatory."

"Even for the elderly employees?"

"Yes. We temper the lessons according to each employee's physical capabilities. And physical therapists help those who wish to increase their strength."

That explained the conversation he'd overheard in which an older man had bragged with a laugh that most of his arthritis pain had gone away after his trainer talked him into *pumping iron*.

Chris turned in to the next room they encountered.

Cliff followed. Surprise darted through him as he found himself standing inside a large cafeteria.

"Join me for lunch?" Chris asked, continuing forward without waiting for an answer.

"Sure."

Men and women of all ages and races occupied dozens of rectangular tables.

The armed guards stationed themselves at the edges of the room.

Conversation halted and silence fell, broken only by Cliff and Reordon's footsteps as the two of them crossed to the service counter.

Awkward.

Chris pointed to an electronic menu that hung above the counter. "That's what they're serving today. Anything look good to you?"

Conscious of the dozens of eyes boring holes into his back, Cliff felt his anxiety levels rise. It didn't help that the burly man behind the counter stared at him with wide eyes and a gaping mouth. "The lasagna and a salad?"

"Are you the vampire from sublevel 5?" the man blurted in what sounded like a Brooklyn accent.

After glancing at Chris from the corner of his eye, Cliff nodded. "Yes."

The man's face creased with a huge grin. "I thought so but wasn't sure. You were all covered in dust and shit the last time I saw you." He thrust out a beefy hand. "Nice to meet you. I'm Mason."

This was… weird. Cliff shook his hand. "I'm Cliff. Nice to meet you."

"You really saved my ass when the mercenaries attacked," he declared, still pumping Cliff's hand. "Thank you."

"Um. You're welcome."

Mason finally released him, his grin growing so bright you'd think his favorite professional football player had just given him an autographed jersey. "You say you want the lasagna and a salad?"

"Yes, please."

"You got it. What about you, Mr. Reordon?"

"I'll have the soup and a salad."

"Yes, sir. Coming right up."

As Mason hustled away, Cliff turned to Reordon.

The network head looked as though he wanted to laugh. "Not what you were expecting?"

"No."

Conversation resumed. Cliff heard his name whispered multiple times as employees expressed their surprise that one of the resident vampires would be dining with them this afternoon. But none fled.

Mason reappeared and handed Reordon a tray with a medium-sized bowl of soup and a small salad, then left again. When he returned a moment later, he proudly offered up a second tray.

Cliff stared. It sported a plate heaped with a massive portion of lasagna that smelled incredible, a bowl twice the size of Reordon's overflowing with salad, and two baguettes.

Mason grinned. "I heard you guys need a lot of carbs because of all the extra energy you burn with your superspeed and strength."

A genuine smile curled Cliff's lips as he took the tray. "We do. This looks and smells delicious. Thank you."

"Anytime. You let me know if you want more."

Chuckling, Reordon turned away and led Cliff to a table near the center of the cafeteria.

Reordon returned to the counter for a pitcher of tea and two glasses, then seated himself on the other side of the table.

Cliff's stomach rumbled as he sank into a surprisingly comfortable chair.

Reordon smiled. "Dig in."

The two tucked into their meals.

Damn, it was good. Reordon always insisted on the best for his employees. The best work environment. The best office furniture. The best trainers. The best chefs.

And they really were the best chefs. Cliff had been stunned by the quality of the meals he and the other vampires had been provided. But Reordon insisted on treating everyone—regardless of his or her hierarchical status here at the network—equally.

The delectable meal Cliff consumed distracted him for a time from all the stares directed his way.

"Good?" Reordon asked.

"Very good." Once the worst of his hunger was assuaged, Cliff studied the network head. "Any particular reason we're here?"

Reordon swallowed the mouthful of salad he chewed. "Whetsman's an ass."

Cliff laughed, some of the tension in his shoulders easing. "Glad I'm not the only one who thinks so."

Reordon nodded. "Unfortunately, he's a brilliant ass. So I can't fire him."

That *was* unfortunate.

"A little birdie told me he doesn't work well with vampires."

Melanie, perhaps? "He doesn't," Cliff admitted hesitantly.

Again Reordon nodded. "I wanted to gain a better understanding of the situation, so I'm having someone monitor him—both his actions and the calls he makes and takes—temporarily."

"And?"

"And the employee who's stuck surveilling him today informed me a short while ago that Whetsman was being a dick. After listening to your conversation with him, I agreed."

Cliff would balk at Reordon listening in and violating his privacy. But it wasn't anything new. All of the vampires' phone and internet activity was closely monitored for security reasons. Reordon was responsible for the safety of every man and woman in this building. Cliff didn't blame him for ensuring vampires couldn't blab to all and sundry online that vampires and immortals existed or invite vampires or more mercenaries to attack and rescue them when paranoia struck. "And?" he asked belatedly.

Reordon grimaced. "And I still can't fire his ass."

Cliff resumed eating with a grunt.

"I can, however, do two things for you." Setting his fork down, he reached into a back pocket and withdrew something.

Cliff stared at the flash drive the blond laid on the table. "What's that?"

"Proof."

He arched a brow. "Of Whetsman being a dick?" What good would *that* do? "I already have ample proof of that, thank you."

Reordon laughed. "No. It's proof that Bastien and Melanie aren't bullshitting you about what happened the morning the mercenaries attacked."

Cliff's chewing slowed as he stared at the small drive. He swallowed. "What makes you think I believe they're bullshitting me?"

"Because it's the one question I would keep asking myself if I were in your shoes."

Cliff ate another bite of lasagna. The Immortal Guardians *did* often say Reordon thought of everything. Cliff just hadn't realized the man paid much attention to the vampires beyond providing them with food and lodging and keeping them in check. "What kind of proof?"

"Video." He pointed to the ceiling in each corner of the room. "There are surveillance cameras all over this building. And they're connected to backup generators located on one of the lower basement levels so they won't stop recording if we suffer a power outage… even if that outage is caused by a military bombardment. It would basically take a bunker-busting missile to *possibly* wipe them out." Forking another bunch of salad into his mouth, he chewed thoughtfully. "Actually, even that may not take the generators out. But it *would* destroy most of the cameras."

Seriously?

Reordon shrugged. "Anyway, every camera that wasn't destroyed in the mercenary attack kept rolling. I'm a paranoid bastard," he stated matter-of-factly, "so I've been combing through all the footage to ensure Bastien wasn't full of shit when he told me Stuart hadn't intentionally lured the mercenaries to us."

More like he just didn't like or trust Bastien because he had succeeded in breaching network security at headquarters the previous year. And, on a more personal note, he also harbored a grudge over Bastien punching him in the face and kidnapping Sarah while Chris was supposed to be keeping her safe.

"I also wanted to evaluate our response to the attack and see what—if any—changes I can implement to make my employees safer in the future." He swiftly finished off his salad, then sat back. "While doing so, I saw you hauling ass to get network employees— *many* network employees—to safety." He tapped the flash drive. "It took me a while to piece it all together into one continuous video for you, but there it is: a second-by-second replay of your every action that morning."

Cliff stared at the drive, his heart pounding a little as hope rose.

"Parts of it are blurry because you move so damn fast. But every time you stop or slow, you can see it's clearly you in the video. And it cuts off when you go aboveground because that floor was pretty much leveled, destroying the cameras up there."

Relief poured through Cliff, loosening his limbs and damn near bringing tears to his eyes. He really *had* helped. Bastien *hadn't* been lying to spare his feelings. And Reordon was offering him indisputable proof to quash his doubts.

It was a really nice thing to do.

He glanced at the other man, wanting to ask him why. This had not been a simple skim-through-the-footage-of-a-single-camera task. This had taken time. A hell of a lot of it.

"It's my way of saying thank you," Reordon said somberly, "for getting Kate and so many others to safety." He shook his head. "I shudder every time I think about how many would've died if you,

Joe, and Stuart hadn't helped evacuate the building while the Immortal Guardians defended it."

Cliff picked up the flash drive and curled his fingers around it in a loose fist. "Thank you."

Reordon leaned forward and crossed his arms on the table. "The other thing I can do for you is this." He nodded to the room around them.

Cliff arched a brow. "Take me on a lunch date?"

Laughing, Reordon shook his head. "Give you more leeway, more room to breathe." His expression sobered. "I know you've been... antsy since your return. Those fuckers tortured you and drove you to experience your first break. Who *wouldn't* be antsy? I also know you've been having trouble sleeping."

Cliff hated that Chris knew he was struggling.

Hell, he didn't like *anyone* knowing he was struggling.

"So I thought you might need a distraction." Reordon studied him carefully. "*Do* you need one? A distraction?"

Though it galled him to admit it, Cliff sighed. "Yeah." Reordon had done him a solid. The least he could do was be honest in return.

"Then from now on you can leave your door open at night and roam sublevel 5 freely. Just don't disrupt the researchers' work too much. We don't want to do anything that might slow them down. And anytime you need to stretch your legs during the day, Todd and the other guards who accompanied us can bring you here for lunch. You can even use the exercise facilities on this floor if you need a workout and don't want to deal with Whetsman's dickishness. I can have a treadmill capable of supporting vampire speeds added to the rest of the equipment in there by the end of the week."

Cliff stared at him. "Really?"

"Yeah."

He glanced at the men and women dining around them. Many a glance skittered away from his in a lame attempt to hide the fact they were staring. "Don't you think some of these people would object to that?" Particularly if Reordon didn't intend to accompany him.

Chris shrugged. "It might make some a little nervous." An understatement, to be sure. "But they'll eventually get used to it."

Get used to it... as if he expected Cliff to visit the cafeteria often.

Cliff thought about how nice it would be to move around during the day without having to deal with Whetsman's sorry ass. "Can Stuart come, too?"

"I'm afraid not. He's still new here, and none of us know him well. Plus if both of you left sublevel 5, I'd have to up the number of guards who accompanied you, which likely *would* make the rest of the employees nervous. I like to keep everyone here as happy as I can. A happy employee is a productive employee. And I appreciate everything they do for me."

Damn. This all made Reordon seem like a good guy. Cliff was going to have to reassess his opinion of the man.

"I was also thinking about having Todd interview you," Reordon continued. "He and Sheldon have interviewed a few immortals for the network's classified internal newsletter. According to Kate, a lot of employees—particularly those you saved and those who have heard about it—are very curious about you. So it would be a good way to help them get to know you and see you as a person rather than a vampire."

"Okay." It was worth a try.

"Great. Let's bus our trays, then I'll show you around the gym. Todd will take you back to sublevel 5 once you're finished."

Returning Reordon's smile, Cliff rose, tucked the flash drive in his back pocket, and grabbed his tray.

Chapter Five

"EMMA!"

Yelping, Emma jumped and banged her head on the underside of her desk's keyboard tray. "Ouch! Damn it, don't do that," she grumbled, backpedaling on her hands and knees. Sitting up, she glared over the desk at Cynthia and rubbed the back of her head.

Cynthia rolled her eyes as she entered. "Oh please. Your hair is so thick and pretty it's like wearing a cushioned helmet. You probably barely felt that."

Emma laughed. She'd pulled her hair back from her face in braids today and wore the rest in a fluffy Afro Cynthia had repeatedly said she envied, usually after disparaging her own hair, which Emma thought was lovely but Cynthia wished was thicker and curlier.

"What are you doing under there anyway?"

"Trying to see how many miles I've pedaled. I got one of those under-desk ellipticals Mr. Reordon offered to buy employees, and the display is too dark to read unless I get right up on it."

Surprise lit her friend's face as she sank down in the visitor's chair. "You did? Why?" She motioned to Emma's body when Emma rose and returned to her chair. "As Todd would say, you're smokin' hot."

Unease slithered through Emma, driving her to fiddle with her keyboard's position as she debated answering her friend's innocent query. "You're going to think I'm weird if I tell you. Or paranoid or something."

All humor left Cynthia's countenance, replaced by concern. "Why? What's wrong? Tell me."

Emma considered refusing but reluctantly admitted, "I've kinda been on a big exercise kick lately." She darted her friend a look, then shifted her keyboard again and fiddled with a pen. "Since the mercenary attack."

Cynthia's gaze turned watchful as she leaned forward. "Go on."

Emma sighed. "It's just... I keep thinking about it. And I know it will probably never happen again. But if it *did*..." She shrugged. "What if Mr. Reordon hadn't let the vampires help us that day? What if the ceiling hadn't collapsed on us and Sadie and I had made it down the hallway on our own? The elevator wasn't functional." It had already plummeted to sublevel 5, killing those inside it. "And there's no way Sadie could've made it down four flights of stairs without help. So I thought I might have to piggyback her and..." She shook her head. "I don't know if I would've been able to do it. I don't know if I would've been strong enough."

"I'm sure someone else would've taken up the slack and helped you."

"But what if they didn't? What if they couldn't because they were injured?"

"Oh honey." Cynthia's features softened. "Is *that* why you've been lifting weights? So if the network falls under attack again, you'll be able to sling people over your shoulders in a fireman's carry and get them to safety?"

"Maybe?" Emma responded, thinking it sounded lame and hoping Cynthia wouldn't worry she was suffering from PTSD or something. She wasn't. At least she didn't think so. She just wanted to be prepared.

For anything.

Rising, Cynthia circled the desk and wrapped her in a hug. "Well, now I feel bad."

Emma hugged her back with a smile. "Why?"

"Because while you've been doing the whole heroic *Let me build greater strength so I can save more lives in the future* thing, I've been more like *I'm going to eat all the junk food I want because who knows what tomorrow will bring*."

She laughed.

"It isn't funny," Cynthia protested as she released her and backed away. "I've gained like fifteen pounds since the mercenaries struck."

"Is Todd complaining?" He'd better not be. Emma would kick his ass if he so much as —

Cynthia snorted. "Hell no. That man loves me. *And* my curves."

"He really does." And Cynthia did indeed have lovely curves.

Her eyes lit with excitement. "Which is why I'm here."

Because Todd loved her?

Emma stared. "Oh crap. Did Todd propose?"

Her friend laughed. "No. He just gave me some news that's going to make you *very* happy."

Wariness rose. They weren't going to try to set her up again, were they? Because the last double date Cynthia and Todd had dragged Emma on had been a disaster. The guy had been attractive and polite but had talked incessantly. He'd spent so much time bragging about his job and his bank account, his fancy car and ludicrously expensive watch, that the rest of them had barely gotten in a word or two. "What news?"

So excited she practically jumped up and down, Cynthia blurted, "Vampire Cliff eats lunch in the cafeteria now!" Throwing her hands up in the air, she gave a delighted scream as if she had just found out she was going to have a one-on-one meeting with Dwayne Johnson.

Cynthia *loved* Dwayne Johnson, also known as The Rock. Which made her devotion to Todd all the more adorable. While Dwayne Johnson could easily sweep a woman off her feet, Todd was more likely to trip her.

Emma smiled, not quite sure why Cynthia found the news so exciting. "Good for him. I didn't know they had a cafeteria down on sublevel 5."

"They don't. They only have a break room."

"Oh."

Cynthia stood on the opposite side of the desk, watching her expectantly.

"I don't—"

"He's eating lunch in *our* cafeteria now."

Emma's eyes widened. Her heart gave a little leap. Her pulse quickened. Excitement warred with disbelief, soon joined by nervousness.

Cliff ate lunch in *their* cafeteria?

Cynthia pointed at her with a knowing grin. "And *that's* the reaction I was waiting for. If you were white, you'd totally be blushing right now. You have it so bad for him."

"No I don't," Emma hissed. "And would you keep your damn voice down? They can hear us down there!"

Cynthia's eyes widened. "Oh crap. I forgot. Sorry."

"Anyway, I don't know why you're making such a big deal about it. We work the day shift, and he's a vampire. He probably eats lunch at midnight."

Shaking her head, Cynthia retook her seat and lowered her voice to a whisper. "No, he doesn't. Most days he eats lunch the same time we do." Some of the joy left her pretty face. "Todd said Cliff has been... struggling a little since the attack. Since he had his first... you know."

Psychotic break?

Emma nibbled her lower lip as worry blossomed. Once the smoke had cleared and Mr. Reordon had gotten everyone settled in the new network headquarters building, then briefed them on the injuries and deaths among employee ranks, the first thing Emma had wanted to know was if the vampires had survived the blitz. If *Cliff* had survived.

Mercenaries had already begun to infiltrate the building when Cliff had unburied her, gently tended her broken arm, and whisked her away to safety. And she'd spent much of the ensuing hours wondering if he had returned to sublevel 1 and confronted them. If he'd had help or if he'd fought them alone. If they had wounded him. Or killed him. There had been so many...

It had never occurred to her that they might capture him. She had assumed they were there to nab an immortal. So her heart had gone out to him when she'd learned those bastards had captured him and tortured him to such an extent that he'd experienced his first psychotic break. And he had lost his friend Joe, too.

"It's okay," Cynthia said softly, dragging her from her thoughts. "He's doing okay." Leaning forward, she whispered, "Todd said he's been doing better since Mr. Reordon showed him footage of his actions the day of the mercenary attack. Apparently Cliff worried everyone was bullshitting him when they said he'd helped. He was afraid he'd hurt someone or something."

Poor guy.

"So," Cynthia said louder. "No more eating lunch at the picnic tables outside. You're eating lunch in the cafeteria today."

A little zing of excitement shot through her. Whenever weather permitted, Emma ate lunch outside at the picnic tables around back. She liked the quiet, the fresh air, the wildflowers, and enjoyed getting in a little uninterrupted reading while she ate.

She looked at the comfortable slacks and casual blouse she wore, then raised her hands and patted her hair.

Cynthia grinned. "You look fine. Beautiful as always. Let's go."

Nerves jangling, Emma rose and rounded her desk.

Her friend glanced down, then winced. "Well, maybe wear some sexy pumps tomorrow."

Emma wiggled her toes inside her running shoes. "Nope. It's this or nothing." She'd done the whole attractive but uncomfortable savvy suit, high heels, and perfect makeup thing in the past but would do so no more. Anyone who didn't like her the way she was could kiss her ass.

Grabbing her cell phone, she followed Cynthia out into the hallway and closed her door. She didn't bother locking it. No one would slip in to steal her purse or disturb anything while she was gone. If anyone did, the plethora of surveillance cameras would swiftly identify the culprit. And if any doubt remained, Reordon would simply summon a telepathic Immortal Guardian to ferret out the thief.

So... yeah. No one so much as stole a pen around here.

Her heart beat a little faster as they approached the cafeteria. And she discovered she was actually holding her breath as she passed through the wide doorway. Pausing just inside, she swept the large room with an eager gaze.

Disappointment struck when she didn't spy Cliff.

Beside her, Cynthia made a *hmmm* sound. "Maybe he's running late."

Or not. Cliff didn't show the whole time they dined. Nor did he appear the next day or the day after that.

"Well, now I feel like crap for getting your hopes up," Cynthia said in the privacy of the soundproof women's restroom as she washed her hands. "Sorry."

Emma smiled to hide her disappointment. "I'll take it as a good sign. Maybe he's sleeping better."

"Could be. Todd said Cliff seemed to relax quite a bit after viewing that footage Mr. Reordon showed him."

Emma hoped so. Just in case though, she found herself once more dining in the cafeteria the following week. Cynthia was spending her lunch break running errands, so Emma chose to sit at a small table in the corner where she could lose herself in a sci-fi romance novel while she ate.

She had barely made a dent in the spicy fried rice on her plate when a hush fell over the room.

Pausing with the fork halfway to her mouth, she looked up.

All eyes focused on the doorway.

Several network guards garbed all in black and sporting semiautomatic rifles and tranq guns entered and took up positions around the room like Secret Service agents preceding the president of the United States. Her heart stopped, then began to pound when a familiar figure stepped into the doorway and paused.

Cliff.

Chapter Six

H E WAS EVEN MORE HANDSOME than Emma remembered, with broad shoulders, the beginnings of dreads, and perfect brown skin that even cover models would envy. It looked so smooth and soft where he didn't have a five-o'clock shadow, begging to be touched.

Uncertainty painted Cliff's features as he glanced around. Giving his wide-eyed audience an abrupt nod, he directed his gaze straight ahead and crossed to the counter. Emma couldn't help but stare like the others. The jeans he wore looked faded, comfortably worn, and clung to powerful thighs. A white T-shirt contrasted nicely with his skin and outlined a muscled chest and abs.

"Cliff!" a booming voice greeted him, so loud in the silence that Emma jumped. Behind the counter, Mason grinned at him. "Good to see you again. What can I get you today?"

Some of the tension in Cliff's posture eased as he smiled in return.

Damn, he was handsome.

Whatever Cliff said next was spoken too low for her to hear from her position in the corner.

"Yes, sir. Coming right up." Mason left and returned with a tray heaped with so much food it practically hung over the edges.

Emma stared.

Cliff laughed, the deep rumble drawing a smile from her. "Thank you." *His* smile, however, faltered as he turned to face the room. She thought his hands might've tightened a bit on the tray, too.

As he strode forward, the thud of his boots seemed unnaturally loud in the quiet that had fallen.

A quiet broken by furtive whispers.

Cliff seated himself at an empty table and gave no indication he noticed when two men nearby rose and moved to a table farther away. Three more did the same.

Emma glared at them. *Pussies.*

Keeping his gaze on his tray, Cliff began to eat.

Tension thrummed in the air.

Lowering her fork to her plate, Emma added her phone to her tray, then rose and strode toward him. Her pulse picked up as she stopped a few paces away. "Hi."

Cliff glanced up, his pretty brown eyes reflecting surprise that anyone other than Mason had spoken to him. "Hi."

She motioned to the chair across from his. "Is this seat saved?" Cynthia had mentioned that Mr. Reordon had dined with Cliff the first couple of times he'd ventured up here.

"No. You can take it."

She smiled. "Actually, I was wondering if I might join you."

His eyebrows shot up. "Oh. Sure." Rising, he motioned to the chair, then waited for her to settle in it before he retook his own seat.

How sweet and gallant.

Reaching across the table, she offered her hand. "I'm Emma."

A little frisson of awareness raced up her arm when he clasped it and gave it a firm shake. "Nice to meet you. I'm Cliff."

She even liked *that* about him. Sometimes when men shook her hand, their grip was annoyingly weak—as if they thought she might break if they clasped her hand as tightly as they would a man's.

But Cliff's merely fed her attraction.

Not even a flicker of recognition lit his eyes though.

Picking up her fork, she consumed another mouthful, then motioned to his tray. "You appear to be a fan of the fried rice, too."

He chuckled as he tucked into the mound. "Yeah. The chefs here rock."

"They really do."

As he chewed, he studied her thoughtfully.

Emma willed herself not to feel self-conscious beneath his piercing gaze but couldn't help but wonder what he was thinking.

He paused to drink some tea, his strong throat working with each swallow. And those brown eyes never left hers. "You do know I'm *the* Cliff right?" he asked as he set his glass down.

She smiled, understanding now. "You mean Vampire Cliff?"

He nodded.

"Yes."

Relaxing, he gave her a tentative smile. "Just making sure." He loaded up his fork. "They don't really call me Vampire Cliff, do they?"

"I'm afraid so."

He looked comically pained to hear it.

She fought a laugh. "Maybe they just don't want to confuse you with Cliff in Accounting."

He chuckled. "Maybe so."

"With your exceptional hearing, I'm surprised you haven't heard that."

He shrugged. "I usually sleep during the day, and the night shift tends to be more furtive in their comments about us because they know we're awake and may be listening."

"True." She sipped some tea. "When I worked the night shift, most vampire-related gossip was passed around in the soundproof restrooms."

He laughed, unoffended.

A comfortable silence fell between them as they satisfied their hunger.

Conversation resumed among the other employees as they finally got over the shock of having a vampire in their midst who wasn't accompanied by Mr. Reordon. But most continued to dart looks their way.

Emma glanced at the guards stationed around the room. When Todd grinned big and gave her a thumbs-up, she rolled her eyes.

"I'm curious," Cliff said.

Returning her attention to him, she raised her eyebrows.

"Why did you ask to sit with me?" He surveyed the room. "I think most people here are understandably leery."

Her hackles rose. "Well, they shouldn't be," she snapped, then cursed when her sharp tone drew another look of surprise from him. "Sorry. It's just…" Relinquishing her anger, she smiled. "We've actually met before."

His brow furrowed. "We have?"

She nodded. "The morning the mercenaries attacked. I was on sublevel 1 when they started bombing the place. The ceiling collapsed and buried me before I could evacuate with the others. I think it knocked me out for a minute. And when I came to… there you were, hauling away concrete and whatever else fell on top of me."

His chewing slowed.

"My arm was broken." She waggled the arm that bore not a single scar from the incident thanks to the healing touch of Seth, the powerful Immortal Guardian leader. "You bound it as carefully as you could, picked me up, then spirited me away to sublevel 5, where Dr. Lipton saw to my wound and ensured I made it safely through the tunnel."

He studied her. "That was you?"

He remembered? A little thrill shot through her. "Yes."

"You were going back to help some of the others."

"Yes." Sadly, both Wayne and Lloyd had perished when the ceiling had collapsed. She likely would have, too, if Cliff hadn't responded so quickly. Giving in to impulse, she reached across the table once more and rested a hand on his forearm. "Thank you, Cliff, for saving me."

He glanced down at her hand on his arm. "You're welcome."

Though she wanted to linger, she withdrew her touch.

"I have no memory of that." The words came soft and slow, as though he wasn't sure he should admit it.

"You don't? I thought… You seemed to recognize me once I mentioned it."

His mien turned somber. "Most of what happened that night is a complete blank, so Reordon showed me the surveillance footage. I saw myself dig a woman—dig *you*—out of the wreckage. But I don't remember doing it."

Emma wasn't sure how to respond to that without mentioning the torture that had robbed him of those memories. And she didn't want to bring him down. She wanted to see him smile again. "Well," she said after a moment's consideration, "I can see why Mason heaped your plate with carbohydrates. You must burn a lot of energy, because *damn* you're fast."

He grinned. "Yes, I am."

Success! He looked so young and handsome when he smiled. "What's that like? I mean, you moved so quickly that morning that everything around us was a blur. How do you keep from bumping into stuff when you run that fast?"

His brown eyes sparkled with amusement. "I didn't at first. There was a bit of a learning curve."

"I bet."

The rest of the conversation flowed smoothly as he shared some of his earliest fails as a fledgling vampire and she relayed her astonishment at learning the job she had applied for involved working for immortal beings. Needless to say, they laughed a *lot*. Emma found Cliff to be utterly charming and immensely likable.

It seemed as though only minutes passed before he announced with reluctance, "I'd better go. The guards can't have their lunch break until after they escort me back to sublevel 5, and I can hear their stomachs growling."

She stared. "You can? Over all this?" Dozens of conversations and the clatter of utensils filled the air.

"Yes."

She glanced at the guards. "I have to admit, it was pretty cool the way they entered first and fanned out around the place... as if you were the president and they were your Secret Service detail."

He laughed. "I wish."

When she glanced down at her watch to check the time, her eyes widened. "Has it been an hour?"

He nodded.

No wonder the guards' stomachs were rumbling. "I'd better go, too."

They bused their trays, then strolled over to the entrance together. There they paused as Todd and the other guards approached.

"It was nice to meet you, Emma," Cliff said with a faint smile.

"Nice to meet you, too, Cliff."

Turning, he headed for the elevator as the heavily armed guards closed in around him.

That had sounded a little too final for her liking.

She *would* see him again. Wouldn't she?

Chapter Seven

C LIFF CAREFULLY RESTRAINED HIS PACE to a casual stroll and kept his face impassive as Todd and the other guards escorted him to the cafeteria the following week. Would Emma be there, already sitting at what he had come to think of as their table?

Their table, as if they were a couple with regular reservations at their favorite restaurant.

He shook his head at himself.

She had joined him for lunch every day the previous week. And just that quickly, he had come to crave her company so much that he had felt ridiculously disappointed—considering the brevity of their acquaintance—when he hadn't seen her on Saturday or Sunday.

He didn't think he had ever greeted a Monday with such eager anticipation before.

Todd kept up a rambling conversation as they walked, one that fortunately only required Cliff to nod here or there while he searched the faces they passed. A few smiled and nodded. Most just stared like a toddler seeing a larger-than-life mall Santa for the first time.

"If it helps," Todd said, "they do the same thing when an immortal is on-site."

The other guards nodded.

Cliff arched a brow. "You mean Bastien?"

Several men issued derisive snorts.

Todd laughed. "No. When *he's* on-site, they shake in their boots and lock themselves in their offices."

Cliff scowled, pissed on his friend's behalf.

"He *did* make a pretty bad impression when he breached network security and broke a lot of guards' limbs that time."

He had a point. But Bastien wouldn't have done that if Reordon hadn't been a dick and refused to let him see Vince.

"Bastien scares them," Todd continued. "But Seth, David, and some of the other immortals intimidate the hell out of them. So they look at Immortal Guardians the same way they're gawking at you." He shrugged. "Just thought I'd put that out there."

Knowing that did help a little. "Thanks."

When they reached the cafeteria, most of the guards entered ahead of him and spread out around the room.

That grated a lot less when he recalled Emma's Secret Service comparison.

And there she was, the woman he spent far too much time thinking about, sitting at their table, head down while she read a book on her phone. She wore a yellow dress that looked fantastic against her beautiful brown skin. It hugged her slender torso and flared out into a loose skirt beneath the table, hiding most of her lovely legs.

Her hair was pulled back into a puffball ponytail that managed to look both cute and alluring at the same time, baring a smooth neck he had pressed his lips to in a dream last night. As far as he could tell, she wore no makeup beyond something that made her lips shimmer temptingly.

Silence continued to fall whenever Cliff entered the room.

When it did, Emma glanced up. Amusement twinkled in her eyes as she watched what she now called his entourage take up their usual positions.

Cliff's pulse picked up, but he gave no indication of it. Offering the room in general his standard abrupt nod, he headed over to the lunch counter where Mason grinned and bellowed another boisterous greeting. Damn, he appreciated that. Whetsman was being a dick again, so it was nice to *not* be treated like an ax murderer.

After receiving another tray heaped with scrumptious food, he crossed to Emma.

Her pretty face lit with another smile as she turned her phone off and gave him her full attention. "Hi."

"How's it going?"

"Same old, same old. Care to join me?"

"Yes, thank you."

Whispers erupted as he seated himself across from her.

"What about you? How's your day been so far?"

He shrugged. "About the same. What are you reading?"

"Another sci-fi romance." Her smile turned wry. "I've been needing more of an escape lately."

He could relate. "Can't get more of an escape than by leaving the planet."

"Exactly," she agreed on a laugh.

While she summarized the plot for him, the whispers of the other diners carried to his ears via his exceptionally sharp hearing.

They're sitting together again, a man said furtively. *This is the fifth or sixth time. Do you think they've got a thing going on?*

I don't think so. I mean, that isn't allowed, is it? He's a vampire.

He may be a vampire, but clearly he ain't dead. Look how he looks at her.

Shit. Look how she *looks at* him.

Unease rose.

Why is she sitting with him? a woman on the opposite side of the cafeteria asked softly.

Because he's freaking hot, her female companion responded.

But he's a vampire. Isn't she scared?

I would be. Rumor has it they can be fine one moment and snap the next without any warning.

Maybe we should tell Mr. Reordon. Do you think he knows? I doubt he'd approve of...

One of his employees doing a vampire? Yeah. I'm pretty sure he wouldn't approve of that.

"Oh, for fuck's sake," Todd hissed in a whisper. "They're just eating lunch."

Shit. Todd must have been standing near enough to hear the women.

"Cliff?"

Blinking, he realized Emma had ceased speaking. "Yes?"

"Is something wrong?"

He wanted to say no. To hell with those people. If he wanted to have lunch with Emma, he would have lunch with her. Who were *they* to object? It was none of their damn business.

But he suddenly understood Bastien's reluctance to embark upon a relationship with Dr. Lipton. Bastien feared fraternizing with him would reflect poorly on Melanie and might threaten her position here at the network.

Now Cliff feared the same for Emma.

Granted, all they did was sit at the same table while they ate lunch. They didn't sneak kisses or caresses or do anything even remotely amorous. They just talked and laughed together. But tongues were already wagging, and…

His hands tightened into fists.

Emma glanced down at them. "Cliff?" she repeated softly.

"I don't think we should eat together anymore." The words left a sour taste in his mouth, but he'd rather eat at a separate table and still get to see her than have Reordon restrict him to sublevel 5 again.

"Why?" Nothing in her posture indicated he'd offended her. Rather she leaned forward, her pretty face somber.

He glanced to one side, then the other. "They're talking."

She followed his gaze, undoubtedly noticing the number of occupants who quickly looked away. "About us?"

"Yes."

She seemed to ponder that. "What are they saying?"

He didn't want to scare her by telling her they thought he wanted her, but he dreaded her response when he told her the rest. "They think you're having lunch with me because you're attracted to me."

She studied him. "And?"

He stared. "And?" he parroted, caught off guard by the one syllable reply. He had expected her to laugh or deny it or say that was crazy.

Rolling her eyes, she motioned to the other employees. "Half the women here are probably attracted to you, Cliff. You're freaking hot. What does that have to do with anything?"

His mind blanked. And his treacherous heart began to pound. *Was* she attracted to him? How could that be? "I'm a vampire."

Her lips stretched in a smile. "I'm aware." Her complete lack of concern confounded him.

"They don't think Reordon would approve and are wondering if they should say something."

Her smile vanished as her brows drew down. "Really? Crap. I didn't think of that." She nibbled her lower lip.

And damned if he didn't feel desire slither through him as he watched. He swore silently. This would *not* be a good time for his eyes to start to glow.

"Did Mr. Reordon tell you not to fraternize with the employees?"

"No. But if he thinks there's even a remote chance that—"

"Oh good!" a bright, feminine voice trilled. "You're here."

Cliff's eyebrows shot up when an elderly woman stopped beside their table and beamed at him. She didn't look a day under ninety, had a sweet smile bracketed by wrinkles, skin so pale he could see the veins at her temples, and snow-white hair pulled up into a tidy bun. The biceps left bare by her dress looked thinner than his wrist, and she seemed to weigh little more than the large clear container full of cookies that she carried.

Emma offered the woman a warm smile. "Hi, Sadie."

"Hello, sweetie," Sadie said, then swung her attention back to Cliff. "I'm so glad I caught you today, young man. Here. I baked these for you."

Cliff's jaw dropped when she held out the container. For a moment he could only stare in stunned disbelief. But the muscles in her bony arms began to tremble, so he hastily took the cookies. "I think you must be confusing me with someone else."

She waved a hand and issued a *pshaw* sound. "I may be old, but my memory's as sharp as a tack. You're Vampire Cliff. Now set that down so I can hug your neck."

What... was happening?

He shot Emma a glance.

Her lovely lips stretching in a grin, she looked as though she were struggling not to laugh. "You'd better do as she says."

Cliff set the container down.

Sure enough, Sadie moved closer, wrapped her arms around his neck, and gave him a hug. The scents of lavender and vanilla wafted over him. "It's okay," Sadie told him cheerfully. "You can hug me back. I won't break."

Nonplussed, he closed his arms around her and gently patted her back.

After a moment, Sadie withdrew with a smile. "As soon as I heard you'd been spotted up here in the cafeteria, I knew I had to bake you some cookies. I hope you like them. It's a recipe passed down by my Danish grandmother."

"I'm sure they're delicious," Cliff said. "Thank you."

Maybe she didn't understand what a vampire *was*.

Emma smiled at the woman. "Sadie, would you like to join us?"

"Oh yes, dear, I would. Let me go get my lunch first."

Cliff watched the woman shuffle over to the serving counter, then looked at Emma.

She grinned. "I wish you could see your expression right now. It's absolutely priceless."

"I have no idea what's happening."

She laughed. "I know. She'll explain it when she gets back." Leaning forward, she nodded at the container. "Sadie treats everyone under the age of sixty like they're her grandchildren. She's ninety-three, so to her we're all just kids." Her eyes crinkled with mirth. "I even heard her refer to Sebastien Newcombe as *that handsome boy with the glowing eyes who caused such a fuss.*"

He laughed at the description. "Bastien is more than a century older than Sadie."

"I know. But he *looks* like he's thirty, so to her he's just another kid in need of cookies."

Sadie returned and shocked Cliff again by setting her tray down beside his.

Rising, he pulled her chair out for her.

"Oh my. So gallant," Sadie said with a happy smile. "You remind me of my Henry."

Cliff retook his seat. "Who's Henry?"

"He was my husband for sixty-two years until the cancer took him." She spread a napkin on her lap and sighed. "He was so handsome. Tall and broad-shouldered like you. And he always did little things that made me feel special." She winked. "Like pull my chair out for me."

Cliff smiled as he watched Sadie take a delicate bite of her sandwich. "May I ask why you baked me cookies?"

"Of course! I did it because I wanted to thank you for saving my life." She smiled at Emma. "*And* for saving Emma's. This precious girl means the world to me."

Emma smiled. "Awww. Thank you, Sadie." She patted the woman's hand. "I'm afraid Cliff doesn't remember much about that morning though."

Sadie sent him a commiserating look. "I know how that is." Leaning closer, she whispered, "I lied. My memory isn't what it used to be. I forget stuff all the time. Mr. Reordon only keeps me around because he likes my cookies."

Emma laughed. "I'm pretty sure it's because you're a whiz with the stock market and make the network tons of money."

"That, too," she agreed.

The next hour passed quickly. Cliff enjoyed the women's banter. They seemed to really care about each other. He also enjoyed the Danish cookies. "Mmmm. Sadie, these are delicious."

She grinned big, the wrinkles in her face multiplying. "Oh, I'm so glad! That's really saying something, coming from you. I imagine your taste buds are so sensitive that you could tell me every ingredient."

He nodded as he devoured another. "But not the proportions. These are perfect. Have some, Emma."

Emma took two. "Thank you. The only thing I *don't* like about Sadie's cookies is that they're incredibly addictive."

"I can see why." The cookies were so good they almost made him forget his concerns about Reordon.

He didn't know how many cookies Sadie had baked, but there were still a dozen left when Emma's lunch hour ended. Cliff handed the older woman the container.

She waved a hand. "Take it with you and bring it back when you're finished. If you don't see me, just give it to Emma and she'll pass it along."

Since it would give him a legitimate excuse to approach Emma after they stopped sitting together, he agreed.

Todd and the other guards closed in around him after he bid the women goodbye. Their stomachs growled as they eyed the treats he carried.

Cliff waited until they were all ensconced in the elevator with the doors closed, then took the top off the container. "Anyone want a cookie?"

They were stuffing their faces before he even finished the question.

He laughed. But his amusement couldn't quite take the edge off the sadness that filled him now that his time with Emma had come to an end.

Damn. He really liked her. Hard to believe he had only known her for a week.

But he was a vampire. Vampires didn't get happily-ever-afters with women like Emma.

Vampires didn't get happily-ever-afters at all.

Nothing but darkness lay ahead of him.

⸻◊◊◊⸻

Emma paused when she reached Cynthia's office. Much larger than hers, Cynthia shared it with nine other employees who closely monitored the internet for mentions of Immortal Guardians, *gifted ones*, and vampires.

Cynthia had grumbled that the last was a pain in the ass because there were so many vampire wannabes out there. So weird.

Emma poked her head in. "Hey, Cynthia?"

Her friend looked up with a smile. "Hey, girl."

"Hi, Emma," the others chorused.

Emma tossed them a hello and turned back to Cynthia. "You got a minute?"

"Sure."

Cynthia rounded her desk and stepped into the hallway.

Without saying a word, Emma led her to the nearest restroom and ducked inside. Once there, Emma made sure the stalls were all empty before she spoke. "I need a favor."

"Okay." Cynthia was such a great friend. She didn't even ask what it was before agreeing.

"I need you to see if Todd can have lunch with us."

"By us do you mean you and me? Or—"

"Cliff is worried because he heard some of the other employees gossiping about us, speculating that I'm having lunch with him because I'm attracted to him."

~ 69 ~

"You *are* having lunch with him because you're attracted to him."

"*I* know that. And *you* know that. But *he* doesn't. And apparently the loose-lipped jackasses who are talking about us think they should tell Mr. Reordon so he can... I don't know... step in or something."

"What?" Scowling, Cynthia propped her hands on her hips. "That's total bullshit!"

"I know. But I'm afraid Mr. Reordon might ban Cliff from eating up here. And Cliff needs this, Cynthia. Especially after what happened with the mercenaries."

"I agree. Todd said Cliff has been way more relaxed since he started venturing out of sublevel 5. He's even laughing and joking again."

Happiness filled her. "He is?" Was it because he was exploring other areas of the building or because he was spending time with her?

Emma quickly shut the thought down.

"Yes." Cynthia touched Emma's arm. "But honey, you know this can't go anywhere, right? You and Cliff?"

"We're just friends."

"But you want to be more."

Hell yes she did. "We *can't* be more. The only time we see each other is at lunch."

"And you don't want to lose that?"

Emma hesitated. "No." Cliff made her feel things she never had before. "I mean, no one else will sit with him. So if *I* don't, he'll have to eat alone while everyone else gawks at him."

Cynthia smiled in a way that said she knew Emma was full of crap.

Emma laughed. "Well. It's true."

"Uh-huh. So you want Todd and me to start eating with you?"

"Yes, please."

"You aren't worried that it'll look too much like a double date to the gossipmongers?"

Emma bit her lip. "Oh. Right. I didn't think of that." Throwing up her hands, she exclaimed, "This is so ridiculous! What does it even matter? It's not like we're going to start groping each other right there in the cafeteria!"

Cynthia laughed. "That would rock! Talk about jaws dropping."

Emma eyed her balefully. "So happy I can amuse you."

Still chuckling, Cynthia waved a hand in dismissal. "Don't worry about it. I've got this." She winked as she headed for the door. "See you at lunch."

Cliff glanced at the guards as they crowded into the elevator with him.

There was one more than there had been the day before. Why? Had someone complained?

He frowned. About what? Cliff had been on his best behavior while on sublevel 1 and had done *nothing* to scare *anyone*. All he'd done was chat with Emma.

His frown deepened into a scowl. Wait. Had someone tattled to Reordon? Was the extra man coming along to ensure Cliff would keep his distance from Emma?

He grumbled inwardly. What a crock. He had already decided to keep his distance from her. He wasn't sure how he would do that exactly. If she approached him and asked if she could sit with him, he knew he wouldn't have the heart to say no.

But when Bastien and Melanie made their attraction known, things had gotten a little snippy for a while between Mr. Reordon and Melanie. Cliff didn't want the same to happen with Emma, particularly since he wasn't sure Reordon considered Emma as irreplaceable as Dr. Lipton.

Todd offered no explanation, and Cliff didn't ask.

Dread pooled in his stomach. Irritation rose until he swore inwardly. Couldn't he have one damn thing he could look forward to each day? Just one. Damn. Thing? Was that so much to ask? A nice meal with a beautiful woman who made him smile and laugh? Who made him feel like a man rather than a crazed vampire whose days were numbered?

A ding sounded shortly before the doors slid open.

Their boots clomped on the floor like a drumbeat as they strode forward. Every fascinated, curious, or nervous stare that met his made Cliff's ire rise. Which one of them had run tattling to Reordon? Was it him? Or her? Or them?

"You okay there, Cliff?" Todd asked, sliding him a sidelong glance.

"Sure." When anger continued to rise within him — something it did more often now — Cliff drew in a deep breath and forced his tight muscles to loosen. "What's the extra man for?"

Todd shrugged. "I missed breakfast today." As if on cue, his stomach rumbled. "I'm hungry as hell, so Simmons is going to take my watch while I eat lunch."

Cliff looked at him in surprise. "Oh."

"What's wrong?" Mischief lit Todd's green eyes as he smiled. "Did you think Simmons asked to come along so he could ogle you while you eat? You're not *that* good-looking, you know."

Cliff laughed.

The other guards laughed too as Simmons gave Todd a hard shove.

As they entered the cafeteria, Cliff wondered if the occupants would ever stop going silent and gaping when he entered.

Emma was nowhere to be seen, he noted with disappointment. Had she chosen not to come so the gossip would die down?

"I like this," Todd murmured, nudging him with an elbow.

"What?"

"Everybody going quiet and staring." He puffed out his chest and adopted an exaggerated swagger. "Makes me feel like a celebrity."

Smiling, Cliff shook his head.

Once Mason happily provided them with lunch, they headed for Cliff's usual table.

Cliff arched a brow when Todd pulled out the chair next to his, sat down, and began to inhale his lunch.

"What?" the other man asked around a mouthful of burger.

"Is there a reason you're sitting beside me instead of across from me?

"Yep."

If he thought sitting beside Cliff would make it easier to tranq him in a worst-case scenario, Todd was mistaken. "And that is?"

"Wait for *iiiiiiiit* — "

"Hi, baby!" a cheerful feminine voice called.

Cliff looked toward the entrance.

A pretty Latina woman was grinning and waving. Beside her,

Emma walked quietly, a slight smile curling her lips as her eyes met Cliff's.

"Hi, gorgeous," Todd replied with a grin as they approached.

This must be Cynthia.

"Give us a minute to get our lunch," she said.

"Sure thing."

Cliff forced himself not to turn and watch them as they continued on to the lunch counter. Heart lightening, he instead kept his expression impassive and focused his attention on consuming the gargantuan bowl of salad Mason had prepared for him.

Todd grimaced. "I don't know how you can eat that shit without salad dressing."

Cliff shrugged. "As long as it has lots of walnuts and raisins in it, I don't need the dressing." Although he still wasn't a fan of celery. Mason must've caught on to that though, because he'd left the celery out this time.

Nice guy.

The women returned.

Cynthia paused long enough to give Todd a quick kiss, then set her tray down across from his.

Emma set her tray down beside her friend's.

Cliff rose.

Todd glanced up at him, then hastily rose, too.

Both women smiled and took their seats.

Cynthia smiled at Cliff as he sat down once more. "You're a good influence on him." She extended her hand. "Hi. I'm Cynthia."

He gave it a shake. "Nice to meet you. I'm Cliff." As soon as the words left his mouth, he felt stupid.

"I know." She grinned. "Sadie's been singing your praises."

"She has?"

Cynthia nodded. "Ever since I heard you were eating lunch up here, I've been wanting to join you, but work kept getting in the way." Wrapping an arm around Emma, she drew her tight against her side in a hug. "Thank you for saving my bestie. *And* Sadie. I love them both to pieces."

Smiling, Emma hugged her back.

Cliff didn't know how to respond, so he just nodded. "I'm glad I was there to help."

Cynthia gave him a teasing look. "So modest." She jerked her chin toward Todd. "Unlike *some* people, who think I should be eternally grateful if they load the dishwasher."

Todd laughed, as did the rest of them.

Cliff shifted his gaze to Emma as the couple bantered.

Her brown eyes met and held his, happiness brightening them.

She had done this. She had convinced her friends to eat with them to try to deflect any suspicion that they were interested in pursuing more than friendship.

And hell, if friendship was all he could ever have with Emma, he would take it. And appreciate it. And appreciate *her*.

The next day, Todd, Cynthia, and Emma joined Cliff for lunch again, as did Sadie. The day after that, a man named Miles joined the growing group at their table. Then a couple of brothers who were part of Reordon's weapons development team. And so it went for weeks. Then months. Sometimes the table was full. Sometimes he only had a handful of companions. But Emma was always in the mix. And she always sat directly across from him, her eyes meeting his much more often than that of the others'.

Affection for her grew. And admiration. She had succeeding in finding a way for them to continue seeing each other five days a week without either of them facing negative repercussions. The whispers gradually stopped. The silence and staring that always greeted Cliff's entrance gradually shortened until he hardly noticed it.

While he missed being able to spend time alone with Emma — or as alone as they could be in a room full of other people — he knew this would have to be enough.

His heart still lightened whenever he saw her. His pulse picked up. His lips stretched in a smile whenever hers did. And just the sound of her laughter made him happy.

How he wished he could touch her. Cover her soft hand with his. Cup her lovely face in his palms and brush her lips with a kiss.

Did she want the same? Did she dream of the two of them coming together, bare flesh against bare flesh, the way he did? Did she even think of him as more than a friend or work acquaintance?

Since she never gave any indication, he honestly couldn't tell.

Until one day a few months later.

Chapter Eight

C LIFF HAD TO REALLY FIGHT to keep from quickening his pace. He and his guards were later than usual heading up to the cafeteria. Todd had delayed them while he checked on something. Cliff didn't know what—he hadn't really paid attention to Todd's mutterings because he'd been too distracted eyeing the clock and counting every minute they wasted.

Minutes he could be spending with Emma.

But they were finally on their way.

As usual, Cliff's attention shot straight to Emma when he entered the cafeteria.

She wore a colorful, casual shirt that hugged small breasts he spent far too much time thinking about and a narrow waist. Short sleeves bared slender arms that bore a little more muscle definition now than they had when he'd first met her. Arms he had on many occasions fantasized about stroking, wondering if her skin was as soft as it looked. Her hair was arranged in a half-up, half-down style, the front pulled back into a puff and the rest left down.

Every time he saw her, his heartbeat stuttered an instant before it began to beat harder.

It took a moment for him to realize that the table was packed today. Only one seat remained unoccupied. The one across from her and next to Cynthia.

His heart sank. Would he not be able to have lunch with Emma today?

Beside her, Sadie glanced up, met his gaze, then turned to smile at Emma. "Well, I'd better get back to work. That darn trainer is going to come get me in an hour for another torture session."

His time at the network had vastly improved his ability to pick and choose which conversations—of the many that took place at once—that he wished to use his acute hearing to eavesdrop upon.

Emma smiled and patted the older woman's hand. "Okay."

"Give him hell, Sadie," Cynthia called as the woman rose.

Sadie laughed. "Oh, I plan to."

Apparently nearly every trainer at network headquarters was also a physical therapist. And one had been working with Sadie for some months now to help increase her mobility and strength.

Cliff strolled forward with Todd.

Sadie *did* seem to move more smoothly and with more confidence now as she approached them with a smile. One of those reusable cloth grocery bags dangled from one hand. "There's my hero!" she called.

Several heads turned.

Stopping in front of him, she wrapped her skinny arms around him and gave him a squeeze.

Cliff smiled and hugged her back. Had she chosen that moment to leave on purpose so he could sit beside Emma? Or had it been a coincidence?

When she backed away a step, she held up the bag. "I baked you some more cookies."

He took it when she thrust it toward him. "You don't have to do that, Sadie."

"I don't have to work at my age either. But what the hell else am I going to do with my time now that my Henry's gone?" She sent Todd a squinty-eyed look. "And don't think I don't see you, boy, already drooling over that bag."

Todd assumed an exaggeratedly innocent expression. "Who, me?"

"Don't you go pouncing on him as soon as I leave the room. Those cookies are his." She gave Cliff a sweet smile. "But you can give him one if you want."

"One!" Todd protested.

Laughing, Sadie left the cafeteria.

Todd and Cliff crossed the rest of the distance to the lunch counter.

"You *are* going to give me more than one, right?" Todd asked.

Cliff laughed. "Right."

Todd kept up a rambling conversation as they collected their trays and headed for the table.

Relieved that no one had taken Sadie's seat, Cliff slowed his steps as he waited to see where Todd would sit.

Yes! He sat beside Cynthia.

Cliff set his tray on the table and lowered himself to the last remaining chair—the one beside Emma.

"Hi," she said, her greeting friendly but no more so than the one she offered Todd.

He set Sadie's bag next to his tray. "Hi."

"Hi, Cliff," Cynthia said with a smile before she turned to Todd. "Hi, baby. How's your day going?"

He pressed a quick kiss to her lips. "Better now that I'm with you."

"Awww." She ruffled his hair. "You're such a sweetheart."

Some of the others at the table greeted Cliff and Todd, then resumed what became an animated discussion of the latest Marvel movie.

Cliff barely heard it, too focused on the woman seated to his left. He drew in a subtle breath.

Emma smelled of coconuts and cucumbers.

As she reached for her glass of water, her elbow brushed his and sent a shock of awareness up his arm.

Did her heartbeat pick up? Or was that just his imagination?

He smiled and tossed in his opinion of the film, drawing both agreements and protests.

"You're just saying that because you're strong enough and fast enough to kick his ass," Todd proclaimed with a grin.

Laughing, Cliff shook his head while under the table he slid his boots a little farther apart and splayed his knees comfortably until his thigh touched Emma's. A seemingly innocent contact no one would notice, particularly since his attention remained on Todd.

But Cliff heard her breath catch. And her pulse picked up until it matched his, which now raced.

Time stood still while he bantered with Todd and awaited her response.

Would she pull away?

No. The pressure of her thigh against his increased, the simple reciprocation firing his blood so much it was all Cliff could do to keep his damn eyes from glowing as arousal shot through him. But a lot of employees watched them. A *lot*. And he could — *would* — do nothing to start tongues wagging again. Even though he wanted nothing more than to drag Emma onto his lap, bury his fingers in her soft hair, and devour her tempting lips.

The women left first. The others at the table straggled away shortly thereafter, leaving only Todd. Cliff finished his lunch slowly, needing time to bring his body back under control. Though sad to admit, it had been so long since he'd felt a woman's touch — *any* touch beyond one of Melanie's or Linda's sisterly hugs — that he had a hell of a hard time tamping down the arousal that burned through him.

A brush of her arm. The press of her thigh.

Cliff closed his eyes.

He wanted so much more than that.

Chapter Nine

M ORE MONTHS PASSED. ONCE A week, Emma managed to arrange things so Cliff could sit beside her. Twice some weeks. Those were Cliff's favorites.

Fevered dreams of peeling her clothes off and exploring her beautiful body began to infiltrate his sleep. But in the cafeteria, he always restricted their talk to casual banter none could find fault with and their touches to simple things like his shoe nudging hers, or his thigh, or his elbow.

He really came to dislike weekends. Like this one. Because they kept him from seeing Emma.

Cliff settled himself on a barstool in his small kitchen, picked up the foot-long sandwich he'd just put together, and took a big bite.

Stuart spoke in a room down the hallway. "Hey, Cliff. You want to join us for a poker game later?"

"No, thanks," he said. "I want to put some miles in on the treadmill."

"Okay." Some of the smile left Stuart's voice, hinting that he'd guessed Cliff's reasons.

Cliff had begun to hear voices. Voices that urged violence and anger and filled his mind with images that sickened him.

Those voices were louder today. *Much* louder. Something he'd begun to notice tended to happen on days he didn't see Emma.

Damn, he wished she worked weekends.

As soon as the thought dawned, he swore and called himself a selfish bastard. She deserved some time off and no doubt needed it after the long workweeks.

How do you think she spends that time off? a sly voice sneered. *Alone?*

A gravelly laugh filled his head. *Not hardly. You think she's saving herself for you? A fucking vampire?*

She's probably out with another man right now. Letting him kiss her. Letting him touch her.

If it weren't for the network, you could be that man. You could be with her right now.

You should kill them.

Kill them all.

Cliff clenched his fists, squishing the hell out of his sandwich as gruesome images filled his mind. Every muscle tensed as he closed his eyes and struggled to quiet the voices. To shut them out. To forget the things they showed him.

This is not who I am, he told himself mentally. *This is* not *who I am.*

He wasn't a monster. He didn't slaughter men and women who tried to help him.

He *saved* them. He protected them.

Every time a murderous vision leaped to the forefront of his mind, he superimposed one over it of him helping network employees the day the mercenaries attacked. Of him digging Sadie out of the rubble. Of Sadie hugging him and calling him her hero. Of rescuing Emma.

Emma.

So beautiful and so kind.

Emma smiling.

Emma laughing.

Emma touching his arm.

Her thigh pressing against his.

The violent images faded. The voices quieted.

Relief left him a little light-headed as Cliff opened his eyes. When he saw his mangled sandwich, he shook his head and tried to piece it together enough to eat without having to grab a spoon.

Yeah. He definitely needed to put in some time on the treadmill. Running himself ragged often helped ease some of the agitation that had begun to afflict him with more frequency and greater intensity. But he would have to wait for that. Bastien and Melanie were in the lab with the treadmills, and it sounded like things were turning amorous.

"The vampires will hear us," Melanie protested softly in the other room.

Yep. Things had definitely turned amorous in there. He glanced around for his earbuds.

"What happens at the network," Bastien murmured persuasively, "stays at the network."

Melanie's breath caught as fabric rustled.

"Um," Cliff said with a grimace. He really wasn't in the mood to listen to them engage in a quickie and wasn't seeing his earbuds anywhere. "That doesn't mean we *want* to hear it. It'd be too much like listening to our brother and sister do it." Not quite, but close enough.

"Dude, speak for yourself," Stuart said. "They won't let me subscribe to the porn channels here."

Laughing, Cliff shook his head.

Though several more vampires now resided on sublevel 5, Stuart was Cliff's favorite.

Bastien sighed. "And I believe that's Chris and Seth striding up the hallway, so…"

A hasty rustle of clothing ensued, making Cliff wonder just how far Bastien had managed to coax Melanie into going. He grinned, imagining how red her face must be a moment later when Chris Reordon and Seth entered.

"You need to add a quiet room down here," Bastien drawled.

Yes, they did.

"Why?" Chris asked. "For interrogation purposes?"

"Okay," Bastien replied, voice bland.

A moment passed. Then… "Oh hell no," Reordon blurted. "I am *not* spending tens of thousands of dollars to soundproof a room down here so you two can have sex without the vampires hearing you."

"You *want* the vampires to hear us?"

Cliff and the other vampires laughed.

"No," Chris sputtered. "I mean, I don't want you having sex! Not while you're both on the clock. Melanie is supposed to be working—"

"She is." Bastien defended her, an edge entering his voice. "*Long* hours."

"And *you* are supposed to be serving as guard. Seven vampires live across the hallway. What are you going to do if a couple of them have psychotic breaks and try to escape while you two are having a quickie?"

"Chase them down bare-ass naked and give the human guards an eyeful."

That was one hell of an incentive not to escape.

"I don't know about you," one of the new vamps said in his apartment down the hallway, "but I'm pretty sure even total mind-fuck madness wouldn't make me risk that guy chasing me down and tackling me while he's naked and has a hard-on."

Every vampire and immortal laughed.

"What?" Chris asked, unable to hear the vamps.

"Nothing," Bastien said. "Forget I mentioned it."

Cliff doubted that. Reordon never forgot *anything*, especially if it pertained to Bastien.

"Ready?" Bastien asked, then his voice softened with affection the way it often did when he spoke to Melanie. "I'll see you later."

"Be careful," she said.

Good. Maybe now Cliff could hit the treadmill and —

A perfunctory knock sounded on his door.

He stuffed the last bite of sandwich into his mouth, leaving only a few crumbs behind.

A clunk sounded. Then his heavy door swung open, revealing Bastien.

Swallowing, Cliff slid off the barstool and smiled as his friend entered. "Melanie is so going to kick your ass when you get home tonight."

He chuckled. "Not if I'm busy *kissing* hers."

"Damn it, Bastien!" she said from across the hallway.

Cliff laughed. All amusement died away, however, when Seth entered the apartment behind Bastien. Shit. Cliff immediately banished all thoughts of Emma.

The moment he did, the damned voices inundated him, calling for violence.

He ground his teeth.

Seth was a good man. Or immortal. A good immortal. He was the reason Cliff was still alive today. He had even healed Cliff on multiple occasions in an attempt to stave off the madness and repair some of the progressive brain damage the virus caused. Then Joe had begun to accuse Seth of stealing his thoughts. And Cliff had met...

Don't think of her. Just kill them all.

Kill them all.

Nearly growling in frustration, he beat the voices back.

Bastien had ultimately told Seth he simply made the vampires too uneasy and increased their agitation, so Seth had stopped coming.

Cliff wasn't the only vampire housed here who felt uncomfortable around the Immortal Guardian leader. They all did. But Cliff had been infected the longest. He struggled the most with the oncoming madness. And he hated that Seth could see the ugliness that now writhed inside him.

This is not who I am, he told himself again as he forced a smile and greeted Seth. "Hey."

Seth nodded. "Good evening, Cliff. How are you?"

"Fine, I guess." Was the ancient immortal even now scouring his thoughts and seeing the horror he fought so hard to suppress? Why was he even here? Did he know about — ?

Don't think about it. Think about something else.

Yes. Think about killing them. Kill them all! Fuck them up!

No, damn it! Shut the fuck up! Cliff looked at Bastien. "What's up?"

"Feel like taking a trip?" his friend asked.

A trip? As in... leave network headquarters? With Bastien and Seth?

Alarm bells rang. He swallowed. "Now?"

Bastien nodded.

He knows, the damned voices announced with glee. *Seth knows. He's in your head right now. He knows and wants to put you down. He knows everything. Every loathsome thing you've imagined doing. Every grisly act you've envisioned, painting your hands* and *the network with blood. The monstrous impulses. The sickening —*

Shut up! Fuck you! That isn't me! That isn't who I am! This is not *who I am!*

Fighting down a surge of panic, Cliff asked, "Aren't you on guard duty?"

Bastien shook his head. "Sean is on his way over to take my place. He'll be here in a few."

Shit. Bastien was *always* on guard duty this time of night. Were the voices right? Was… was this it? Though he tried to hide it, everyone knew Cliff struggled. Even now he had to fight to remain still and had been counting the minutes until he could hop on the treadmill and run until he was too physically exhausted to act on the violent urges rising within him.

"Oh. Okay."

Had Seth and Bastien come to… put him down?

That's right, the voices hissed. *They're here to put you down like a rabid dog.*

I'm not a rabid dog, he growled.

But isn't that what you're destined to become? A mindless killer?

Yes, damn it. Had he reached the point that they'd begun to fear he might hurt Melanie? Or had they merely decided the kindest thing they could do was kill him now, before his mental state deteriorated further, in order to spare him?

Cliff kept his expression blank as he bent down, retrieved a pair of sneakers from beneath the sofa, and donned them. Straightening, he wiped sweaty palms on his jeans. "Can I say goodbye to Melanie first?" He wanted to hug her one last time and thank her for everything she'd done for him, make sure she wouldn't blame herself for not finding a cure in time.

"Bye, Cliff!" Melanie called merrily from across the hall.

He failed to find a response. Did she even know what they planned? Had Bastien opted not to tell her? Did he intend to watch Seth decapitate Cliff, then say it was some kind of accident after the fact? Maybe let her believe Cliff had tried to escape?

Though it rankled, he supposed that was the nicest way to deliver the blow.

"Shall we?" Seth asked.

Cliff wanted to say, *No, I'm not ready* but lacked the time.

Without waiting for a response, Seth touched their shoulders.

Everything around Cliff went black as a feeling of weightlessness engulfed him. Seconds later the darkness lessened, broken by the moonlight that fell upon them.

He glanced around as Seth released him and stepped back. The three of them now stood in a field beneath a sky that sparkled with stars. No structures lay in sight. Only lumpy, uneven ground covered by grasses and weeds that swayed and rustled in the breeze. Nevertheless, Cliff recognized the place and was so surprised that the voices retreated momentarily.

Bastien's home had once stood here. Or his lair, depending on who you asked. As Cliff surveyed the area, a feeling of peace suffused him along with nostalgia. "I never thought I'd see this place again." He drew in a deep breath. "Or smell it. Damn, it smells good out here." It had been so long since he'd been outside, inhaled fresh air, and felt the wind on his skin. He supposed if it was his time to go, this was a far better place to do it than strapped to a table in network headquarters like Joe.

He studied the ground around them. Not even a cement slab remained. "The old place is gone, huh?" He couldn't help but be saddened by the sight.

"Yes," Bastien said, "as are the caverns we constructed beneath it."

"Wow. All that work..." Vampires might be stronger and faster, but they'd still had to work their asses off to create the labyrinth that had resided beneath Bastien's home.

"I know." Smiling, Bastien tossed him a duffel bag. "This is for you."

Cliff caught it easily. When the two immortals watched him expectantly, he unzipped it.

Inside lay black fabric.

No, he discovered as he shifted it around. Not fabric. Clothing: black cargo pants, a black shirt, and a black coat identical to Bastien's.

Metal gleamed at the bottom of the bag.

His heart stuttered when he pushed the clothing aside and revealed beautifully crafted weapons.

Cliff looked from the contents of the bag to Bastien. "What's this?"

Bastien clapped him on the back. "You're going hunting with me tonight."

Cliff stared. There was no way in hell Seth would allow Cliff to hunt. Not in his current state. Not with the fucking voices urging him to do things that made him sick to his stomach.

It's a diversion, the voices whispered, rearing their unwelcome heads as if just thinking about them had issued them an invitation. *So you won't see the blow coming.*

His hands tightened on the bag.

Bastien's smile lost some of its brightness. "I thought you'd be pleased."

The chirping of crickets sounded abnormally loud in the void that fell.

"He thinks we've brought him here to execute him," Seth said softly.

Bastien lost his smile. *"What?"* He looked at Cliff. "Why the hell would you think that?"

Cliff glanced at Seth.

The stoic leader looked at Bastien. "Because the violent thoughts are growing louder and harder to ignore, and he knows I can hear them."

A stricken expression washed over Bastien's expression before he hastily replaced it with a frown. "Why would I give you a bag full of hunting clothes and weapons if I intended to kill you?"

Cliff tried but couldn't muster a smile, so he shrugged. "I thought maybe it was like people getting their dog all excited about going for a ride in the car so he wouldn't realize they were taking him to the vet to have him put down."

Bastien stared at him with what appeared to be very sincere consternation. "That's fucked up."

"Yeah."

"Cliff," Bastien said earnestly, "when the time comes, I'll either take care of it myself like I did with Vince, or Melanie will sedate you and drain you as she did with Joe. Either way, it will be on *your* terms."

His heart began to pound when Seth nodded.

Had he really misread the situation so badly?

"And," Seth added, "the hope remains that Melanie will discover a treatment before it comes to that."

Damn the voices! *They* had done this! *They* had made him think...

Swallowing hard, Cliff nodded and looked down at the bag of goodies. "So... this is real?" His eyes met Bastien's as dread succumbed to burgeoning excitement. "You're really taking me hunting with you?"

Bastien smiled. "Yes."

Cliff glanced at Seth, still afraid to believe it. "And you're okay with this?"

Seth nodded. "You've proven yourself to be a valuable member of our family. We could use another good hunter."

Elation rose within him. He wasn't a monster. He was a *valuable member* of the Immortal Guardians family.

He grinned big. "This is so cool!"

Seth smiled. "I'll leave you to it then. Enjoy your hunt."

As soon as the Immortal Guardians leader vanished, Cliff stripped down to his skivvies and donned the hunting garb. Black pants. Black shirt. Black coat outfitted with numerous pockets and sheaths. He both looked and felt like an Immortal Guardian and loved it.

"Will the coat be a hindrance to you?" Bastien asked. "You aren't accustomed to fighting in one."

Cliff picked up a couple of daggers and flipped them end over end, catching them with a flourish, then performed several experimental swings, kicks, twirls, and thrusts at preternatural speed. "No. I'm good with it."

He was also very good with weapons. Chris Reordon and the other humans at the network would probably crap their pants if they knew Bastien didn't just sit on his ass and play video games when he visited Cliff. He trained him. And he'd been doing so regularly ever since the night Bastien had injected himself with an untested antidote Melanie had created to see if it would counteract the sedative. Afterward he'd told Cliff to attack him in earnest, and boy had it taken the edge off. So the two had secretly begun sparring on a regular basis.

Cliff was now almost as good a fighter as Bastien.

"Shall we go then?" Bastien asked.

Cliff nodded eagerly. "Where to?"

"I thought we would see what's happening at UNCG tonight."

Sounded good. "Wanna race?"

Bastien shook his head. "Let's save that for the end of the night if you still have the energy. I've got a car parked through there."

Cliff followed him through the trees to a Chevy Volt. Once he tossed the bag into the back, he settled himself in the passenger seat. Cliff smiled. "It smells like Melanie in here."

Bastien nodded. "It's her car."

Cliff raised an eyebrow. "It also smells like sex."

He winced. "Yyyyeah. Melanie and I sometimes…"

"Go at it like teenagers?" he supplied helpfully.

Bastien laughed. "Yes. Just don't tell her I told you that."

She would blush every time she saw him if he did.

Cliff peered through the windshield, eagerly devouring the beautiful countryside he hadn't seen in so long as Bastien started the engine and headed for UNCG. Rolling down the window, he drank in the fresh air and absorbed the night sounds that eluded him at network headquarters, drowned out by six floors full of activity.

How he'd missed this.

He wished the drive would last longer, but they weren't that far from the university. So in no time at all, Bastien parked the car.

"I'm glad you two found each other," Cliff commented, his mind circling back to Melanie.

"Me, too."

It felt almost like old times as the two of them strolled onto the quiet campus. They had spent a lot of time together and become close friends before Bastien's army had grown so much that monitoring it consumed almost every waking hour.

Bastien had tried so hard to help them all. To protect them. To save them.

"Do you still feel like you don't deserve her?" It had been a common complaint when Melanie had made it clear that she was attracted to Bastien.

"All the time."

Cliff had suspected as much. "Well, you do," he said. "Deserve her, I mean. You're a good guy, Bastien. I wish you could see that."

Bastien looked at him askance. "You aren't going to get maudlin on me, are you?"

Cliff laughed. "No, I just wanted to put that out there in case I don't have a chance to say it later." In case his mental state deteriorated to the extent that he *couldn't* say it later. Or in case a future hunting trip should end the way he'd thought this one would — with Seth or Bastien decapitating him. "I really appreciate everything you've done for me. You've been a good friend."

Bastien stopped. "Cliff, if you're thinking of running, I've been ordered to —"

"I'm not," he assured him. "I don't want to hurt anyone. I don't want to torture and kill innocents the way other vampires do." And he trusted Bastien and the others to keep him from doing it.

"Joe didn't either," Bastien said somberly, "when he surrendered and sought the network's help. But he wouldn't have hesitated to run if I'd taken him hunting with me."

Sadly, it was true. "I'm not suffering the paranoia that struck Joe. I just have... violent thoughts." It shamed him to admit it. "Really ugly violent thoughts." But Bastien deserved the truth. "It's getting harder and harder to not act upon them when I'm around Dr. Whetsman."

Bastien snorted. "Hell, *I* have violent thoughts when I'm around Dr. Whetsman. Even *Chris* has violent thoughts around Whetsman. He's a total prick."

Cliff smiled, his mood lightening. "I still laugh when I think about the time you got all up in his grill about talking down to Melanie and giving her a hard time. I thought for sure he was going to wet his pants." As Emma would say, that moment had been priceless.

Bastien grimaced. "I almost wish he would've. Whetsman doesn't wet himself when he gets nervous. He farts."

Cliff laughed. "I know. Melanie has a hell of a time keeping a straight face when he's around us vampires. You know we terrify him."

Now Bastien laughed, too.

A cool breeze toyed with Cliff's dreadlocks. "Wow, you smell that?" Tilting his head back, he drew in a deep breath. "The three B's: bad breath, BO, and blood. Ahhhhh. It's like we're back in your lair again." While Bastien had ensured his vampire followers were well fed, he hadn't succeeded in getting them all to maintain good hygiene.

Bastien shook his head with a smile. "Let's go check it out."

When he started forward, Cliff stopped him with a hand on his arm. "Wait. What's my role here? When you said I could hunt with you…" What did that mean exactly? Tag along and watch?

"I meant you could help me locate and kick some vampire ass."

Releasing him, Cliff grinned. "Seriously? I get to join the fight and everything?"

"Absolutely."

"Awesome! Let's go!"

Just like the old days, the two of them shot forward. Except this time, instead of hunting nefarious humans with revolting intent, they tracked down two vampires feeding on a couple of female students in the shadows between two buildings.

Bastien stopped and nodded for Cliff to take the lead.

This was so cool!

"Hey," Cliff said cheerfully, stopping only a foot or two away from the vamps. "What's up?"

Raising their heads, they turned glowing eyes upon him and bared fangs that dripped with crimson liquid.

The blond vampire hissed like a cat.

Cliff burst into laughter. "Dude! Seriously?"

Frowning, the blond released the woman he clutched.

Cliff couldn't tell if she was a student or a young professor. Eyes unfocused, she staggered a couple of steps backward, then slid down the wall to sit on the ground. Blood trailed from a wound on her neck and dirt marred the front of her shirt, as if the vampire had been groping her while he fed.

The vampire's brunet companion shoved his victim toward the other woman and faced Cliff. That woman definitely looked like a student. Hell, he didn't think she was even out of her teens yet.

"Who the fuck are you?" the second vamp demanded.

"I'm Cliff," he answered, maintaining his genial smile as cold fury built behind it. What if that had been Emma and Cynthia? What if these vampires had cornered Emma and her friend when they were out for a girls' night or something?

The two vampires looked at each other, their blood-streaked faces blank with confusion.

"What did you *think* I would say?" Cliff asked. "That I'm your worst nightmare?" Drawing two long daggers, he displayed them in a series of showy swirls, flips, and tosses as the voices in his head jumped on board his anger and begged for blood. "I probably *am* but thought it would be rude to say so."

The blond drew a bowie knife. "You're an Immortal Guardian?"

"Sadly, no," Cliff said. *It could have been Emma*, the voices taunted. *That could've been Emma he was groping. That could be* her *shirt he left his filthy paw prints on.* "But I *do* still plan to kick your ass." As soon as the words left his lips, Cliff dropped his smile and let the fury consume him.

His fangs descended. Adrenaline flooded his veins. And he attacked.

Swearing, the vampires scrambled to fight him off and avoid his blades.

But Cliff struck with vicious intensity.

It could have been Emma. It could have been Emma. The mantra continued in his head, egging him on.

Thanks to Bastien's training, the vampires proved no match for him. Cliff drew blood with his first swings. Then drew some more. And more, toying with them like a cat with mice. Hoarse screams poured forth from the vampires' lips as they swung their own weapons wildly.

He'd seen what vampires did to female victims. He knew these two wouldn't have stopped at taking blood.

It could have been Emma.

Satisfaction filled him as he hurt those bastards.

One vampire collapsed to the ground, already starting to shrivel up.

Cliff grabbed the other by the hair, yanked his head to one side, and started to sink his fangs into the dying vamp's neck. *Let's see how* you *like it, motherfucker.*

Bastien shot forward and stopped him before he could, inserting his arm between Cliff and the vampire. "Don't."

Cliff glared up at him and tried to shove him away.

But Bastien didn't budge. "Don't," he repeated.

"Why?" he snarled. "They were draining those women. Why not give them a taste of their own medicine?"

"Because Melanie is worried that drinking the blood of another vampire will increase your viral load." He frowned. "Or is it viral count?" Frustration rippled across his features before he shook his head. "I can't remember. I just know she's afraid that it will make the brain damage and madness progress faster."

Cliff blinked. His viral count? Melanie had said that?

Or was it his viral load?

Like Bastien, he'd heard Melanie mention something along those lines before but couldn't remember the specifics.

Dragging in a deep breath, Cliff realized the voices had receded, taking the rage with them. He dropped the vampire. "He'll be dead soon anyway."

Bastien clapped him on the back. "Good. How do you feel?"

Cliff thought about it as the vampire at their feet drew his last breath and began to deteriorate. "Juiced. Relaxed. Relieved that I didn't lose it completely and try to bail on you or something."

"I knew you'd keep it together."

"Yeah, but I *really* wanted to bite that guy. I mean, I wanted to rip his throat out."

"Don't let it disturb you. I feel the same way every night. I'm not exactly what one would call even-tempered."

Cliff laughed. "I think you would bore Melanie if you were."

Bastien knelt before the women.

Cliff sank onto his haunches beside him. "Are they going to be okay?" he asked softly.

Both women had lost consciousness during the battle, but his acute hearing told him each had a strong pulse.

"They'll be fine." Bastien drew his cell phone out and dialed.

Cliff was glad neither woman would remember the attack, let alone be haunted by it.

Glancing around, he grimaced. Or be horrified by the ferocity with which he'd dealt with their attackers.

"Reordon," a male answered faintly.

Oh shit. Did Reordon even know Bastien had taken Cliff hunting? Because if he didn't and Seth hadn't given him a heads-up —

"It's Bastien. Cliff and I found a couple of vampires feeding on two human women. Can you send a cleanup crew out here to see them home?"

"Sure. Where are you?" Evidently he *did* know.

Bastien gave him their location.

"How do you like hunting, Cliff?" Chris asked.

His eyebrows flew up. "It's weird," he responded, loud enough for his voice to carry to the human.

Chris laughed. "I know, right? Jack will be there in ten to take care of the women."

The line went dead.

"That was weird, too," Cliff commented as Bastien tucked away his phone.

"What was?"

"Reordon's asking me what I thought about hunting instead of asking you if I'd lost my shit."

Bastien shrugged. "I can't believe I'm saying this, but I think I'm actually starting to like that asshole."

"Chris?"

"Yes."

"Reordon's a good guy," Cliff said slowly. "He's been really nice to me ever since the mercenaries got their hands on me."

"Good. He should be. You saved a lot of lives that night."

Cliff smiled.

"So," Bastien said, "once the cleanup crew arrives, do you want to call it a night? Or are you up for more hunting?"

"More hunting," he said quickly. This was the best night ever.

Chapter Ten

E MMA SMILED AS SHE WATCHED Cliff banter with Todd.
Something had changed in recent weeks. Cliff had seemed
more relaxed lately, less on edge. She didn't like to think about it,
but for a while there...

Well. The madness that was destined to consume him had
appeared to gain a toehold. He had continued to come to the
cafeteria, but his easygoing nature had struck her as being blunted
somehow. Or maybe more subdued? His handsome smile
sometimes seemed forced, as if he knew he should find whatever
sparked it amusing, so he made the requisite motions. And he
laughed less. His shoulders often looked tight and knotted with
tension... or perhaps poised for action. His languid stroll had
grown stiffer, as though he believed that controlling every
infinitesimal motion of his limbs would enable him to control
whatever was going on inside his head. And his eyes had begun to
flicker with amber light.

She wasn't sure if they did that in reaction to something
unpleasant his amazing hearing carried to his ears or something
transpiring in his head, and she didn't ask. The luminescence
rarely lasted more than a second or two before he brought it under
control, so she didn't want to draw attention to it.

Since no one watched Cliff as closely as she did, most probably
hadn't noticed it. But it had worried her.

Now, however, Cliff's lips turned up in genuine smiles once
more. His deep brown eyes sparkled with mirth as he razzed Todd.
He laughed and talked more.

He seemed happy again. Or as happy as a man in his position could be.

Today his gaze strayed to her more often. And his smile seemed to bear some hidden meaning she couldn't discern, as if he knew a secret and couldn't wait to share it with her.

Sitting across from him, Emma found herself mesmerized. Her own lips lifted in a smile that pretty much remained in place the entire time she, Cliff, Cynthia, Todd, Miles, and a few others ate lunch together.

Cliff's boot nudged her running shoe.

When she reciprocated, his smile broadened into a grin even though he directed his attention at Todd.

"We'd better go," he told the guard. "I can hear the other guys' stomachs growling, and they're starting to get cranky."

Todd shoved the last bite of his sandwich into his mouth, then kissed Cynthia and rose.

After tossing the table a goodbye, the two men bused their trays and left.

"I'm going to head back to my office," Emma told Cynthia.

"Okay." Smiling, her friend tapped her phone to wake it up and opened an e-book. "You want to come over tonight? Todd and I are going to binge-watch *Game of Thrones* for the dozenth time."

Emma laughed. "No, thanks. It's been a long week, so I'm just going to curl up with a good book." After turning in her tray, she headed down the hallway and opted to duck into the restroom to check her hair and wash her hands.

Sadie exited one of the stalls as Emma entered. "Hi, darlin'."

"Hi, Sadie."

The elderly woman crossed to the row of motion-activated sinks and washed her hands. Today she wore a casual dress with a long skirt that ended just above thick-soled sneakers. Emma smiled, pleased to see her moving with more confidence now. She was still reed thin but didn't seem as heartbreakingly frail as she headed for the hand dryer. Those training sessions must be paying off.

Turning back to the mirror, Emma patted her hair.

Sadie shook her head and gave her a wry smile as the dryer shut off. "What I wouldn't give to have hair like yours."

Emma grinned, imagining her with a big snow-white Afro.

"My hair's so thin now I barely have enough to pull back into a bun," she grumbled good-naturedly.

"You have beautiful hair," Emma protested.

The woman harrumphed. "So how's my hero today? I missed lunch because my torture session ran late." Torture session being her term for her physical therapy/weight training session.

Emma glanced at the stalls behind them.

"Don't worry. They're empty."

She smiled. "He's good. He seemed to be in high spirits."

Sadie winked. "Because *you* were there." Sadie had been the one to arrange things so Emma could sit beside Cliff that first time. The sweet woman had baked cookies she knew would lure more people to the table, then plunked herself down next to Emma. And as soon as Cliff had entered the cafeteria, she'd abandoned her spot for him.

Unexpectedly, sadness filled Emma because she knew the other woman's matchmaking efforts would never garner the results she wished. "Sadie…"

Her smile softening, Sadie patted Emma's cheek. "I know. I'm sorry, sweetie. I can't help it. It's just that I see in you two what Henry and I had for so long." She headed for the door but paused before opening it and turned back. "I had a lot of years with him, you know." She shook her head. "His battle with cancer was a long one. A hard one. Every time we thought that damn disease was gone, it came back." Her expression turned earnest. "But I'm telling you, Emma, every minute I had with my Henry made getting through the bad times worth it. That kind of love doesn't seem to come around much nowadays." She smiled. "So I'm going to keep hoping you and Cliff will find a way." She opened the door. "You have yourself a nice weekend."

"You, too," Emma belatedly called after her as she left.

<hr>

Emma couldn't stop thinking about Sadie's words as she drove home at dusk. Nor could she stop thinking about Cliff.

She rolled her eyes at herself. As if that was anything new. She *always* thought about Cliff. Tragic though it might seem, Sadie was right. The connection Emma and Cliff shared was real, not imagined.

What she felt for him wasn't simple infatuation. It wasn't lust, easily assuaged. It wasn't a desperate attempt to escape boredom or alleviate loneliness. It wasn't *any* of the things she had experienced with the few boyfriends and even fewer lovers she'd had in the past.

It was so much more than that. If she was honest with herself, what she felt for Cliff made everything that came before him feel like a teenager's fleeting crushes.

Reducing her speed, she waited for a logging truck driving in the opposite direction to pass, then turned onto the long dirt road that led to her small country home.

She was falling in love with him.

Her hands tightened on the steering wheel. No. She already *had* fallen in love with him. She'd *never* felt like this before... like she would walk through fire just to have one more minute with him. She'd never met a man who so enthralled her that she would rather have a platonic friendship with him than take another man as a lover.

Which was not to say she wasn't physically attracted to Cliff, because... damn, that man was hot. Just the press of his muscled thigh against hers under the table left her all hot and tingly.

Pulling into her driveway, she cut the lights and turned off the engine. Though the house had an attached two-car garage, her car wouldn't fit in it. Ever since she had proudly withdrawn a sizable chunk of her savings account to put a down payment on the house, she'd been using the garage as a workshop for all her fixer-upper projects. Tools and materials occupied half of it while the other half accommodated the old economy car her parents had taught her to drive in and given her when she'd started college. Emma had thought it might be smart to keep it on hand as a backup in case the newer one ever gave her trouble.

A sense of satisfaction filled her as she crossed the grass.

The place hadn't been much to look at when she'd decided to make the leap and purchase it, but it'd had what her dad called good bones. Her parents had always instilled in her the importance of owning property. She glanced around. Now this—and several acres surrounding it—was hers.

She smiled wryly. As long as she kept up the mortgage payments.

Fortunately, the network paid her well enough that she was able to make two mortgage payments a month and was already a couple of years ahead on her payments now. The network also offered employees no-interest home loans for the duration of their work tenure.

Thanks to people like Sadie, the network was seriously loaded and went above and beyond anything she'd seen any other company do to keep its employees happy.

No wonder Sadie and other elderly employees were loath to retire. Free meals—breakfast through dinner if one so desired—prepared by talented chefs. Free healthcare with on-site clinics that required no appointments. Free childcare for employees with little ones. Mr. Reordon even offered grants to college-bound children of employees.

And from what she understood, other branches of the network did the same.

A cool breeze set plants to dancing and swaying as she headed up the pretty stone walkway that led to the porch. She had laid those stones herself. The lawn that had been patchy at best the year she bought the place was now thick and green. She smiled. The shrubs she'd planted along the front of the house on either side of the path were coming along nicely. Hanging baskets overflowed with flowers on the front porch. She wrinkled her nose when her gaze went to the wood siding.

The rest of the exterior, unfortunately, looked pretty shabby. Paint that used to be... peach maybe?... flaked off in sizable strips. Emma had already bought some cheerful yellow to replace it along with bright white for the trim, but that was going to be an exhausting job. She'd have to sand off the flakes and—

Nope. She didn't want to think about that tonight.

Unlocking the front door, she entered and flipped on the lights. Much better.

She'd stripped the shudder-worthy wallpaper off every wall—and it had been on *every* wall—and painted each room with colors that appealed to her. Though the wood floor that ran throughout the house was scuffed and faded, she still loved it. She'd had the warped Formica countertop in the kitchen replaced with gleaming granite. Once she repainted the cabinets and added modern hardware, the kitchen would look fantastic.

Her gaze went to the treadmill parked in the space meant for dining.

When she'd bought the house, she had intended to purchase a nice table and chairs to fill the pretty nook, imagining inviting some special guy over for a candlelit dinner.

Then she'd met Cliff and...

Well. Not much point in buying a table she wouldn't use. She couldn't imagine any other man sitting in that nook with her and didn't really want to. So she'd opted for a treadmill and was content to eat her dinner at the coffee table every night while she watched the news.

She sighed. As much as she loved the place, tonight it seemed too quiet.

Fortunately, her nearest neighbors were far enough away that she could crank up some tunes without disturbing them. Hendrix helped her shake off the restive feelings that tried to creep in while she showered, donned a tank top and some soft pajama pants, then whipped up a quick pasta dish.

Once she ate and did the dishes though, the restlessness returned.

Emma settled on her comfy sofa and tried to dive into a new e-book. But it failed to snare her interest. She tried another one. And another with the same results.

What was wrong with her tonight?

Giving up on reading, she turned the television on and surfed Netflix until she found a horror flick that looked promising.

Half an hour later, just as the action in the movie was picking up, a faint thump outside reached her ears.

Frowning, she muted the volume and glanced toward the front of the house. Blinds shielded the windows, beyond which a lone bulb lit the porch and part of the yard.

No shadow passed by them. Nor did any more thuds break the silence.

Had she imagined it?

When it didn't recur, she chalked it up to the movie making her jumpy. It *was* pretty creepy.

Or perhaps she'd simply heard some nocturnal creature pouncing on unsuspecting prey. Nature surrounded her on all sides, and she'd seen a wide variety of animals pass by on their hunt for food. Maybe something had decided to snag itself one of the little field mice she'd had such a hard time keeping out when she'd first bought the place.

With a mental shrug, she turned the movie back on.

A loud knock shook her door.

Emma damn near jumped off the sofa. Her neck popped as she jerked her head around to stare at the door with wide eyes. Her heart began to slam against her ribs as fear trickled through her.

Who the hell would be knocking on her door this late at night?

Who the hell would be knocking on her door at *any* time of day or night?

No one she knew would do so without calling first. And deliverymen and women didn't drop off packages at freaking midnight.

As quickly and quietly as a mouse, she darted into her bedroom and grabbed the 9mm her father had bought her and trained her to use. Flicking off the safety, she returned to the living room and swung by the coffee table to tuck her phone in her pajama pants pocket in case she needed to call 911. Only then did she cautiously approach the door.

Another knock thundered through the house.

Adrenaline spiking, she peered through the door's peephole.

Shock rippled through her. "Oh shit," she whispered. Setting the gun on the coatrack bench beside her, she hastily unlocked the dead bolt, then the knob, and flung open the door.

Cliff stood before her, his big body blocking her view of the yard.

Emma gaped up at him.

He wore the standard blacks of network guards covered with a long black coat similar to that of an Immortal Guardian. His face, neck, and hands were streaked with blood. His clothing glistened with wet patches. And his eyes shone bright amber.

She had never seen them so bright and knew it meant that whatever emotion roiled inside him was intense.

Panic consumed her. "Cliff," she breathed. Stepping onto the porch, she swiftly glanced around, terrified she might see soldiers in black approaching with weapons raised.

When none materialized, she grabbed his wrist and yanked him inside.

Her hands shook as she closed and bolted the door, her fingers leaving little streaks of blood on the white surface.

Spinning around, she stared up at him. "What happened? Are you hurt?" Her gaze swept over him, noting every wet patch on his clothing, every ruby-red splotch on his skin. Was that *his* blood or someone else's? "How did you get here? Are you hurt?" Closing the distance between them, she began to run her hands over his chest in search of wounds.

Cliff grabbed her wrists to halt her frantic movements. His glowing eyes dropped to the points at which they touched. He drew his thumbs over her skin as if to confirm she was real. Then he met her gaze. "I need your shower," he said, voice gruff.

Heart pounding, she nodded. As soon as he released her, she pointed. "It's through there."

Without another word, he strode toward it. His heavy boots thudded loudly in the quiet as he entered the short hallway, then turned in to the bathroom. The door closed. Water began to pound tile.

Emma didn't move.

Cliff was *here*. In her *home*. What the hell had happened?

Her thoughts raced around and around in her head, scrambling for purchase.

Had he escaped? How the hell could he have escaped? There was so much security at the network! So many guards!

But hadn't Sebastien Newcombe successfully plowed his way through security two or three years ago?

Yes. And rumor claimed Mr. Reordon still had it in for him. Some said Reordon had even gone so far as to call for Bastien's execution after that.

Oh crap. Reordon.

The head of the East Coast division of the network would already be assembling special-ops teams to search for Cliff. He might even have Immortal Guardians out looking for him. And while she knew Bastien wouldn't harm his vampire friend, the others would. They might even kill Cliff on sight.

"Oh shit," she whispered again. When she glanced down at her crimson-stained hands, a little shudder shook her. Racing over to the kitchen sink, she washed off the blood. She didn't take time to dry her hands afterward. She just wiped them on her pants as she ran to her bedroom, her bare feet barely making a sound.

Flipping on the lights, she dove for her closet and yanked out an oversized duffel bag. Tipping it upside down, she shook it hard. Skeins of yarn, long bamboo needles, and round plastic looms tumbled out, leftover supplies from when Cynthia had gone on a crafting kick and tried to teach Emma how to knit.

Emma shoved it all aside and tossed the bag on the bed.

She was darting back and forth from her dresser to the bed, stuffing clothing into the bag, when the bathroom door opened. Emma glanced toward the hallway.

Cliff stepped out, his big body bare save for a white towel wrapped around his hips. Broad shoulders, a muscled chest, and washboard abs gleamed with a hint of moisture left behind from his shower. Little beads of water clung to the ends of some of his dreadlocks.

Though she'd love to take the time to admire every delectable inch of him, Emma only looked long enough to determine he bore no injuries before she went back to packing.

"I have a shirt that will fit you." Sometimes she slept in large men's T-shirts. "But you'll have to wear the pants you came in."

He said nothing for a long moment. "Okay."

Delving back into her closet, she drew out the heavy lockbox. "Keys, keys, keys," she whispered absently as she dropped it beside the bag on the bed. Where the hell had she put them?

Right. The kitchen.

Hurrying past Cliff and into the kitchen, she yanked open the junk drawer and retrieved the little ring of keys. She swung by the coatrack bench to retrieve the 9mm. Best to keep it handy since she had no idea when network soldiers might arrive and she was *not* going to let them shoot him. Then Emma headed back to the bedroom.

Cliff still stood in the hallway outside the bathroom. Her bare arm brushed his as she swept past him. But she was too rattled to relish the brief skin-on-skin contact.

"How long do you think we have?" she asked, setting the gun on the bed.

"A couple of hours?" he said, the words ending on an up note as if he wasn't certain.

A couple of hours. "That's more than I would've thought." Frowning, she glanced over at him as she unlocked and opened the small safe. "Why aren't you putting your pants back on?" Inside lay a stack of important documents; two exterior hard drives with backups of all her don't-want-to-lose computer files, family photos, and videos; some keepsakes; and an envelope full of cash.

She had thought her parents paranoid for recommending she keep the last on hand but was glad now she had done it to pacify them.

"Emma," he said softly.

"What?" she responded absently. Where could they go? Where could they go that would make it harder for the network to find them?

It would have to be someplace remote. Out of the country. With Cliff's speed, he could get them across borders without needing passports. So that was a plus because she doubted he had one, and she didn't want to use hers in case Reordon could track it.

Maybe they could lose themselves in South America.

"What are you doing?"

She looked at him. "Packing." The amber glow in his eyes had diminished a bit. And now that he'd washed off the blood, he looked healthy and perfect and so damned lovable. "Right. Sorry." Yanking open another dresser drawer, she drew out a green shirt in a men's size large and tossed it to him. "Here."

He caught it easily but made no move to don it.

"I don't think we should risk taking the time to wash your pants." She tucked the cash and hard drives into the bag, then added the laptop from her corner desk.

"What exactly do you think has happened?" he asked, his voice cautious and quiet.

Something in it made her pause. Turning, she stared at him. "You escaped," she said. "And I don't think it's going to take the network two hours to send teams out looking for you, Cliff, so we need to hurry. Come on. Get dressed."

Clothing. Money. Laptop. Hard drives. Phone.

Wait. Should she take her phone? Could the network track her that way?

Maybe leave the phone.

What else, what else, what else?

The green shirt clutched in one fist, Cliff moved to stand before her, so close she could smell the soap he'd used when he showered and feel the heat from his body.

Cliff was six feet tall or thereabouts. Emma was five-five, so she had to tilt her head back to look up at him.

"And now you're packing?"

"Yes."

"To come away with me?"

"Yes."

His eyes flashed bright amber. "You would do that? You would leave everything behind and just… run away with me?"

"Of course I would." Reaching up, she cupped his strong jaw in one hand and stroked the stubble it bore. How often had she dreamed of touching him like this? "I don't know how long we'll be able to elude them, but—"

He covered her hand with one of his and shifted it so he could press a kiss to her palm.

The tender gesture made her fall silent, her heart aching. How she loved him. Sadie was right. Whatever ugliness lay ahead was worth every minute she could spend with him.

"The network won't be hunting me," he told her, his deep voice gentle.

If network special-ops teams weren't hunting him, that could only mean one thing.

A lump rose in her throat. Blinking back tears, she withdrew her hand, then slid her arms around his waist. The curly hair on his chest tickled her nose as she pressed her face to it and squeezed him tight… as though by doing so she could shield him and protect him. "The Immortal Guardians are hunting you?" she forced out, the words thick.

With a two-hour head start, she had held at least *some* hope of escaping. Seth might be able to sense the location of other *immortals*, but he couldn't do the same with vampires. Once she and Cliff got in her car—the old one, not the one she drove to work that the network had LoJacked—long miles would eliminate any path Cliff's scent might leave for them. Avoiding main streets with traffic cams would further increase their chances of throwing them off. And the farther they drove, the more their chances of getting away would increase.

But if immortals were already tracking him…

Cliff's strong arms closed around her. He rested his cheek on her hair and cuddled her close.

Tears spilled over her lashes and coursed down her cheeks. This was all she'd wanted. To have Cliff in her arms. To have the freedom to love and be loved by him.

But Immortal Guardians could arrive at any moment and —

Wait. What the hell was she doing? Giving up?

Though it killed her to do it, she gently backed out of his embrace. "Hurry and get dressed." She swiped the tears from her cheeks. "If we leave now, there's still a chance we can—"

"Emma." Cliff's voice was oddly calm as he clasped her hands in his.

"What?"

"No one is hunting me."

She stared up at him, uncomprehending. "They don't know you've escaped?" She shook her head. "How is that possible?" Now that he ate lunch in the cafeteria, *everyone* knew what he looked like. So it wasn't as if he could just knock out a guard, put on his clothes, and slip out without anyone recognizing him.

He squeezed her hands. "I didn't escape."

She blinked. "I don't understand. How else could you be here?"

He smiled, the glow in his eyes dimming to brown. "Bastien has been taking me hunting."

"What?"

"He's been taking me out hunting a few nights a week."

Her chaotic thoughts struggled to catch up. "Hunting what?"

His teeth flashed in a grin. "Hunting vampires." But his grin faltered and fell away as uncertainty rose in his handsome features. "The… voices have gotten louder. It's been harder for me to ignore the violent impulses they inspire." And how she loved him for telling her that, for being honest about his condition. "Bastien hoped that giving me an outlet for the aggression would help, so he's been taking me with him on his nightly hunts."

"*Has* it helped?" Was that why he'd seemed more relaxed lately?

Some of the tension left his form. "Yes. It definitely helps."

Good. She squeezed his hands. "Why didn't you tell me?"

He shifted his weight and—releasing her—took a step backward. "I wasn't sure how you'd feel about it." He offered another helpless shrug. "It's a hard thing to admit—that killing makes me feel better."

Of course it was. Cliff was a good man. "But you're doing the same thing Immortal Guardians do. You're killing men who murder innocents. Men who *torture* their victims before they drain them."

He shook his head. "I could've been one of those men, Emma."

"But you aren't. Because you sought help. Because you're *fighting* the madness instead of embracing it. Are the vampires you and Bastien kill fighting it? Do they want help?"

He sighed. "No."

She shook her head. "I'm not going to fault you for executing serial killers, Cliff. I don't think less of you, if that worries you."

He relaxed even more.

"Where's Bastien?" she asked. "Is he waiting outside?" Bastien had never accompanied Cliff to the cafeteria, so she had assumed he didn't know she and Cliff had feelings for each other.

He smiled. "No. He started letting me roam around unsupervised for a couple of hours each night. He thought I would have an easier time chatting up other vampires and surveilling them if I wasn't accompanied by an Immortal Guardian."

Worry rose. "You're surveilling other vampires? By yourself?" That sounded dangerous.

He nodded. "Some of the other Immortal Guardians don't like it, but they need information and Seth gave us the okay, so Bastien doesn't care."

It still sounded too dangerous for her liking. "Does Bastien know...?" *Does he know about us?* she wanted to ask but was hesitant to say it because it sounded so intimate and their relationship had been strictly limited to friendship thus far.

"Does he know about *us*?" he asked, apparently lacking her hesitation.

"Yes."

"No." His brow furrowed. "I wasn't sure how he would react."

Then Bastien must think Cliff was out spying. "So in addition to hunting with him, you're mingling with other vampires? Vampires you *don't* kill?"

"Yes." His look turned watchful. "Are you worried they'll sway me into joining them?"

"What? No. Of course not. I'm worried they might realize you're a spy and hurt you."

He laughed. "They can't hurt me, Emma. Bastien trained me well. I'm as strong a fighter as he is." The words were not spoken boastfully but matter-of-factly.

At last it all began to sink in. Cliff hadn't escaped. Bastien had taken him hunting to quell the voices, then let Cliff do whatever he wanted to for a couple of hours a night.

Her heart began to pound.

And tonight he had chosen to spend those hours with her.

"Cliff," she whispered.

His look turned watchful. "Do you want me to leave?"

"No."

Closing the distance between them, he cupped her face in his big hands and stared down at her with a tender smile that sent warmth coursing through her. "I can't believe you were going to run away with me," he said softly, his face full of awe and love and so much more.

She swallowed hard. "I still would if you asked me to."

Those eyes of his flashed bright amber a second before he dipped his head.

Her breath caught as he pressed his lips to hers in a tentative first kiss that was both sweet and sensual, as if he were waiting to see if she would pull away. But Emma had been fantasizing about this—about kissing him and touching him—ever since they'd started having lunch together in the cafeteria almost a year ago.

Cliff hummed his approval when she kissed him back and explored his soft lips with growing fervency. Dropping his hands to her hips, he drew her closer and increased the pressure.

Emma's heart began to pound as desire heated her blood. Parting her lips, she invited him inside, then moaned at the first touch of his tongue. Every brush and stroke increased the fire building within her. Sliding her arms around him, she flattened her hands on the muscles of his broad back, his smooth skin warm beneath her fingers, the intimate feel of bare flesh against bare flesh merely heightening her need.

A deep growl of approval rumbled up from his chest as he urged her tighter against him, breasts to chest. Abs to muscled abs. Hips to hips, letting her feel how hard he was beneath the towel.

Excitement skittered through her. He felt so good. And damn, he could kiss. She didn't think she'd ever been so turned on by the press of lips or the stroke of a tongue. But Cliff set her on fire.

She'd wanted him for so long.

The muscles of his back flexed beneath her fingers as she caressed them.

And now, it would seem, she could have him.

Chapter Eleven

C LIFF'S HEART HAMMERED IN HIS chest.

She was going to run away with me. Emma was going to leave everything behind to run away and be with me.

The knowledge staggered him. Humbled him. Moved him deeply. As did her touch.

Drawing back a fraction of an inch, he stared down at her, mesmerized by her beauty, her bravery, and the love that shone in her eyes beneath the reflection of the amber glow in his own.

Emma loved him. She hadn't said it. But he knew it as surely as he knew he loved her.

Groaning, he claimed her lips again, more fervent and aggressive. She tasted so good. Smelled so good. *Felt* so good. And he'd wanted her for so long. He could barely believe she was finally in his arms. He had thought this moment would never come. That they could never be together like this.

And her touch…

He'd been so starved for affection, for physical contact, that just the feel of her hands on the bare skin of his back could practically make him come.

Almost as soon as the thought flitted through his mind, she slid her hands around and rested them on his bare chest.

Please don't push me away, he silently pleaded with sudden panic. *Please don't push me away. Not yet.*

But she didn't. Instead, she curled her fingers in the hair there and gave it a tug that sped his pulse. Then she slid her arms up around his neck and, rising onto her toes, realigned their hips so the erection constrained by his towel could press against her center.

She moaned and fisted his dreadlocks when he rocked against her.

He moaned, too. *Nothing* could compare to this. To the feel of her in his arms.

Her tongue stroked his as he ravaged her lovely mouth.

Cliff slid a hand up to cup her breast. Small and firm, it fit perfectly in his palm. No bra hid the stiff peak, only the thin material of her tank top. She moaned again when he toyed with the sensitive tip, stroked it, pinched it. Her hips arched into his.

He slid his other hand down over the firm ass he'd fantasized about and pressed her harder against his erection. Breaking the kiss, he buried his face in her neck and squeezed her tight, though he was careful not to let his enhanced strength come into play and squeeze her *too* tightly.

"I need you," he told her, his voice hoarse.

She slid one leg up his and draped her knee over his hip, bringing them into even more intimate contact. "I need you, too."

How he wished the towel and her pants didn't separate them so he could plunge his hard cock into her slick warmth right now.

Abandoning her breast, he slipped a hand up her pajama-clad thigh to press her knee against his side and hold it in place. "I don't have condoms." Because he had no money. When Cliff had surrendered to the Immortal Guardians, Reordon had faked his death to explain his absence to the outside world. So his bank accounts had long since been closed.

She drew back just enough to look him in the eye while their quick breaths mingled. "It's okay. It isn't my fertile time."

Hell yes. But his love for her outshone the lust that begged him to instantly ditch the towel and rip off her clothes. "We should talk first." Before their relationship became physical. Or more physical than it was now. It would be much harder to walk away from her once he'd—

"Later." She pressed a kiss to his neck.

A shiver rippled through him when she followed it with a lick. "Emma..."

She touched a finger to his lips. "Please, Cliff. I need you. If Bastien finds out you came here, we may only have tonight."

His hold tightened instinctively in protest at the thought.

She delivered another slow, sensual kiss. "We can talk later."

We may only have tonight.

He nodded.

Releasing his dreadlocks, she slid her hands down over his shoulders to his chest, slipped her knee from his grasp, and stepped back. "Let me clear off the bed."

Cliff shot into motion, clearing the lockbox, duffel bag, and gun off the bed in a blink. "Done."

Her eyes widened. Then she grinned big. "That is so cool."

Smiling, he took her in his arms. "Now where were we?"

"I believe we were right about here," she murmured and tilted her face up for another kiss.

Even that—just the pressure of her lips on his, the teasing stroke of her tongue—ratcheted up his need.

Cliff fingered the hem of her tank top, then drew it up over her head.

Her beautiful brown skin looked as soft as silk beneath the overhead light and *was*, he discovered as he slid one hand up her side to palm a breast and toy with a taut, dark peak.

Her breath shortened as desire flooded her features.

Cliff stroked her other breast as well as his heated gaze roamed her. "You're so beautiful," he murmured reverently. Her shoulders were much narrower than his, lending her an air of fragility the light muscle definition in her arms and abs belied. Those muscles twitched and jumped as he teased the tips of her breasts with strokes and flicks and pinches.

"Cliff," she breathed, swaying toward him.

"Lose the pajama bottoms," he ordered, voice hoarse.

They were down around her ankles within seconds, exposing nicely rounded hips, shapely legs, and a dark thatch of curls at their juncture.

Cliff's control began to fray.

Emma dropped her gaze to his waist. "Lose the towel."

Gladly. As soon as it hit the floor, he lifted Emma into his arms. "Wrap your legs around me," he murmured.

"Hell yes," she breathed, locking her ankles behind his back and trapping his hard length between them.

He groaned when she ground against him. He wanted their first time together... perhaps their *only* time together... to be perfect. He wanted to take his time and worship every inch of her. But he'd been celibate ever since he'd transformed roughly four years ago, and he needed her now with a desperation that made him tremble.

Turning around, he knelt on the bed and leaned down to gently lay her against the pillows.

"Finally," she moaned, urging him to rest more of his weight on her. "Take me."

Cliff shook his head. "Not yet."

When he started to move away, she tightened her legs around him and made a sound of protest.

Amusement sifted through him, just enough to take the edge off. Smiling down at her, he patted one thigh. "Let me go."

"Never," she breathed.

And oh, what that declaration did to him. "If you don't, I can't taste you." He cast a heated look down over her breasts and farther, to the point at which their bodies strained together, then met her gaze once more. "*All* of you."

Her heartbeat picked up as she unwound her legs and dropped her feet to the mattress on either side of him.

Cliff ducked his head and ravaged her lips one more time, then trailed a path of hot kisses down her neck.

She gasped when he closed his lips around the sensitive peak of one breast while he stroked and squeezed and teased the other. He sucked hard. She moaned. He delivered a light love bite, careful to keep his fangs from descending. She jumped, then writhed against him and drove her fingers through his dreads. "Cliff."

Then he trailed his lips down her stomach to the mound below.

She was already wet for him and grew wetter still when he touched his tongue to her clit. "Yes," she moaned. He licked it, flicked it, circled and sucked it. "More."

His cock jumped when she arched up against him and gave his hair a tug. Her breath shortened. Her heartbeat quickened. The muscles in her thighs tightened as she strained against him. He slipped a finger inside. She was so tight and wet. He added another, curling them up and stroking her at the same time he flatted his tongue against her clit and moved it so swiftly it would feel like a vibrator.

Emma stiffened. Fingers clenching in his hair, she cried out as her inner muscles clamped down around his fingers in rhythmic pulses and she came hard.

She was still panting when Cliff withdrew his fingers and rose above her.

His heart pounded wildly in his chest. But when he settled himself between her thighs, he paused and met her gaze, asking a question with his own.

Reaching down between them, she curled her fingers around his erection and guided him to her entrance.

Yes. Cliff thrust deep inside her... and groaned. With his heightened senses, he could feel everything so much more now. And she was wonderfully tight and wet and ready for him, her inner muscles still twitching with residual ripples from her climax.

Withdrawing nearly to the crown, he drove deep again.

Emma slid her arms around him and splayed her hands on his back. "Yes," she moaned, nails biting into his flesh and sparking a flash fire.

Again he withdrew, then thrust deep.

"More," she begged.

And Cliff gave her what she wanted. What they *both* wanted. Pounding into her. Holding nothing back.

Sliding her hands down, she gripped his ass and urged him on as she arched up to meet him, thrust for thrust, breath shortening.

He groaned, drove deeper, harder, altering the angle so he could grind against her clit with every thrust.

"Yes. Cliff." Tilting her head back, she cried out as ecstasy claimed her once more.

Her inner muscles clamped down around his hard cock, squeezing and gripping him, increasing the pleasure until an orgasm seized him and he poured his heat inside her.

Chapter Twelve

E MMA FOUGHT TO CATCH HER breath as Cliff rolled them to their sides, bodies still joined.

His eyes shone bright amber as he rested his head on the pillow beside hers and stared at her as though she were the most precious thing in the world to him. Reaching up, he drew the backs of his fingers down her cheek in a caress that was so tender it brought tears to her eyes. "Are you okay? Was I too rough?"

Catching his hand before he could lower it, Emma pressed a kiss to his knuckles. "You were perfect."

The corners of his lips curled up as he rubbed noses with her. "I haven't been with anyone since I was transformed. I was worried I might…"

She arched a brow. "Squeeze the breath out of me?"

He laughed. "Maybe."

"It was perfect, Cliff." She brushed his dreadlocks back from his face, relishing her ability to hold him and be this close to him after having to assiduously keep their distance for so long. "I can't believe you're really here with me." In her bed. In her arms. She stroked the coarse stubble on his jaw.

"I can't believe you were going to drop everything and run away with me."

"I'd do anything for you, Cliff." Her lips brushed his in a light kiss that was heavy with meaning. "I love you."

His hold tightened. "I love you, too." Sighing with contentment, he pressed his forehead to hers. "I'm so afraid I'm going to wake up and find this has all been a dream."

She smiled. "If this is a dream, I don't *want* to wake up."

"Me either. This is *so* much better than having to share you with a table full of coworkers."

She laughed. "Absolutely."

"Thank you for that, by the way."

"For what?"

"For finding a way we could continue to have lunch together." His forehead rocked against hers as he shook his head. "By the end of that first week, I was already falling hard for you. And when people started whispering about complaining to Reordon, it tore me up to think I'd have to give up that time with you."

"Well, I wasn't willing to give it up, so I got Cynthia to help me out."

"And Todd?"

She chuckled. "Yes. And you can thank Sadie for finally enabling us to sit together."

His straight white teeth flashed in a boyish grin. "How'd she manage that?"

"She baked cookies, set them in the middle of the table, and plunked herself down next to me, knowing they would lure more bodies to the table."

"I can see why. That woman makes damn good cookies. It doesn't surprise me at all that people would brave sitting at a vampire's table to get one."

Emma laughed. "That's exactly what happened. Cynthia set her purse on the chair next to her to save a seat for Todd. And Sadie saved hers for you."

"So it was no coincidence that she left every time I arrived?"

"No."

"That was kind of her."

She shrugged. "Sadie's a real sweetheart." Again she stroked his stubbled cheek. "She's also very perceptive and empathizes with us."

"I wish I could thank her. But I don't think she should know we meet outside network headquarters. I don't think *anyone* should know."

"Even Bastien?" She regretted asking him when the joy left his handsome features.

He sighed. "I love Bastien like a brother. I feel like shit keeping this from him. But I'm not sure how he would react."

"Are you afraid he'll stop taking you hunting?"

"No. He'd still take me hunting to dampen the voices, but..." A look of amazement swept over his face.

She frowned. "Cliff? What is it?"

A huge smiled dawned. "The voices."

"What about them?"

"They're gone."

Her eyebrows flew up. "What?"

"They're gone."

Confusion rose. "I thought hunting quieted the voices."

He shook his head. "Hunting just lowers the volume, which really helps. But *you*..." He stroked her face, the love and happiness that shone in his eyes piercing her heart. "You eradicated them, Emma. They're completely quiet now."

And she'd thought she couldn't love him more.

"Wow." She winked. "I must *really* be good in bed."

He barked out a laugh. "You are. You definitely are."

Grinning, she rolled him onto his back and straddled him. The long length inside her hardened. "Let's just test that out, shall we?" Bracing her hands on his chest, she curled her fingers in the hair there and gave it a tug the same time she circled her hips.

Sucking in a breath, he gripped her thighs and arched up against her. "Yessss."

⊰◈◈◈⊱

An hour and a half later, Cliff pressed a soft kiss to Emma's lips and said with much reluctance, "I have to go."

Regret filled her pretty brown eyes. "Already?"

He nodded and slipped out of bed. "I'm supposed to meet Bastien at his lair in fifteen minutes."

"I thought the Immortal Guardians destroyed that place."

"They did. But it still means something to him. To us both really."

She leaned up on an elbow. "I'm sorry it's gone."

He shrugged. "If Bastien hadn't riled up the Immortal Guardians until they came gunning for him, Seth wouldn't have brought me to the network, and I never would've met you. Which just makes the place all the more meaningful for me. Living there led me to you."

Sitting up, she threw back the covers and rose.

Cliff stared at her alluring skin, so soft and warm, traced a visual path to the lovely breasts he'd teased with fingers, lips, teeth, and tongue, then down to the dark thatch of curls that lay at the juncture of her thighs.

"Cliff?"

He met her gaze. "You're so damn beautiful," he professed, his voice deepening.

She smiled. Stepping closer, she rose onto her toes, wrapped her arms around his neck, and kissed him. Though his body instantly responded to the press of hers, Cliff merely held her and relished the love and affection she granted him.

"This *is* real, isn't it?" he asked softly, almost afraid to believe it. "I mean, I'm not... back at network headquarters hallucinating or something, am I?"

She kissed his chin, then dropped back on her heels. "Come back tomorrow night and I'll show you just how real this is."

Happiness welled within him, nearly bringing a lump to his throat. It had been so long that he'd forgotten what true happiness felt like. "Really? You want to see me tomorrow?"

She smiled up at him. "Tomorrow and every night thereafter."

Cliff drew her into another quick hug, delivered an exuberant kiss, then zipped into the bathroom. Seconds later, he zipped back and stopped before her, once more decked out in his bloody hunting clothes.

Still gloriously naked, she gaped up at him. "Okay. *That's* going to take some getting used to."

He laughed, feeling lighter than he had in...

Well, since before his transformation.

"So I'll see you tomorrow?" he asked.

She smiled. "I'll see you tomorrow."

"Good night, Emma."

"Good night, Cliff. Be safe."

"I will." He had good reason to now.

Giving her one last kiss, he dashed out into the night. A cool breeze buffeted him as he headed for Bastien's place. He would have to run at top speed to get there on time but didn't mind a bit. Energy surged through him, fueled by happiness.

He shook his head at himself as his lips stretched in a grin. One night with Emma and his inner monologue sounded like the corniest of chick flicks. The stars seemed brighter. The air smelled fresher. His feet felt lighter. If he wasn't careful, he might soon find himself bursting into song as he twirled around on a hilltop while cartoon birds fed from his hand.

Laughing at the image, he skidded to a halt.

Bastien lay on his back a couple of feet away, ankles crossed, fingers linked behind his head.

Still grinning, Cliff nodded at him. "What happened? Did some vampire lookie-loo come searching for your legendary lair and knock you on your ass?"

Bastien laughed. "No. I just got bored waiting and thought I'd do something I rarely have time to anymore."

Cliff arched a brow. "Stargaze?"

"Yes."

While Bastien rose, Cliff propped his hands on his hips and studied the sky. "They *are* pretty, aren't they?" No clouds hid their sparkle, and the new moon allowed them to dominate the night.

"Yes, they are." Bastien swept some dirt and grass from his coat tails. "You seem awfully chipper tonight." Had his voice not been so dry, Cliff might've worried he suspected something.

Instead he laughed. "I guess I am. Must be the fresh air."

His friend grunted. "Anything alarming happen I should know about before we head back? You leave any bloodbaths the network might grumble over having to clean up?"

Cliff grinned. "Nope. I was on my best behavior."

Bastien snorted. "Sure you were." Together they started strolling in the direction of network headquarters, having left Melanie's car behind tonight. "How are the voices?"

Cliff couldn't seem to wipe the smile from his face. "They're gone."

Eyebrows rising, Bastien halted. "Completely?"

"Completely. I haven't felt this good... this *normal*... in a long time."

The British immortal's lips stretched in a smile. "Excellent." He clapped Cliff on the back. "I'm glad hunting is helping. You want to go out again tomorrow night?"

"Hell yes."

He laughed. "I bet you do. How would you feel about having more time to yourself while we're out and about?"

"Really?" Excitement filled him at the prospect of having more than two hours with Emma. "You'd do that?"

"Of course. I know you've missed having the freedom to come and go at will. And clearly having at least some of that restored is helping."

"Won't Reordon object?"

He shrugged. "Can't object to something he doesn't know about."

"What about Seth?"

Bastien shook his head. "Seth has so much on his plate right now I doubt he'd even notice. Just don't do anything that would make Reordon complain to him."

"Okay. Thanks."

"No thanks necessary. I wasn't just thinking about you." His lips quirked. "If you're off doing your own thing, I might be able to coax Melanie into indulging in some illicit midnight rendezvous." He waggled his eyebrows.

Cliff grinned. "Maybe so."

"Aside from the voices being gone, how do you feel? Want to race home?"

He let his shoulders sag and injected his voice with fatigue. "I don't know. Honestly, I'm feeling a little—" Cliff took off like a rocket toward network headquarters. "Tired!" he called and laughed when Bastien swore far behind him, then belatedly tried to catch up.

Chapter Thirteen

E MMA WOKE WITH A SMILE the next day. She'd never been much of a morning person. But after Cliff had left, she'd showered, tumbled into bed, and slept like the dead.

She couldn't remember the last time she'd felt so rested. Or so happy.

After tugging on a pair of paint-splattered sweatpants, a stained T-shirt, and some old sneakers held together with duct tape, she ate a quick breakfast, then headed into the garage. The dusty economy car took up almost half of it. A washer and dryer with cabinets above them occupied the space in front of it. Beyond that lay a conglomeration of materials and tools that might seem chaotic upon first inspection but were actually organized into categories.

Emma hit a button just outside the door to the house. Sunlight flowed in as the garage door rolled up with nary a squeak or rumble. Dust motes danced on a light breeze, sparkling like fairy dust.

Grabbing a pair of sturdy work gloves, she tugged them on as she made a mental list of what she'd need today. She'd have to lay down a drop cloth of some sort.

It didn't take long to retrieve one and spread it across the shrubs and ground out front.

Crossing to the aluminum ladder, she hoisted it up and carried it outside. It was heavy. Much more so than the one she remembered her dad using around the house when she was a little girl.

She smiled, thinking of her dad, who lived with her mom in Michigan. He'd been so proud of her when she told him she was buying the house. He'd ordered this ladder online and had it delivered the following week. More tools he deemed essential had followed in a fairly continuous stream until she'd laughingly told him that if he kept sending them, she'd have to buy another house just to store them all.

A few more trips and she was up on the ladder, safety glasses and mask in place, rocking out to one of her dad's favorite groups—Sly and the Family Stone—as she scraped flakes of paint off the house's siding. Memories of the time she and Cliff had spent together kept a smile on her face as she worked. She couldn't wait to see him again.

The knowledge that she *could* see him again—here, away from prying eyes—left her as giddy as a schoolgirl.

Emma had just moved the ladder over and climbed to the top to begin scraping another section when the sound of gravel crunching beneath tires infiltrated the music. Frowning, she glanced over her shoulder.

A Chevy Volt in need of a wash crept its way up her driveway.

Unease rose. She wasn't expecting company and didn't know anyone who drove a car like that.

Descending the ladder, she removed her safety glasses, mask, and gloves, tossed them down, and turned off the music. A surreptitious pat of her pants pocket confirmed her cell phone was still there. Retrieving the narrower metal scraper with the sharper edge, she pretended to scrape something off one of the ladder rungs, then kept it in her hand as the car slowed to a stop.

The vehicle only had one occupant as far as Emma could see.

Thrusting the driver's door open, a petite brunette emerged. She looked to be about thirty years old and was four or five inches shorter than Emma. Blue jeans and a Tar Heels T-shirt accentuated her slender figure without being too tight. A brown ponytail swayed in the breeze.

"Hi there," she called, her smile fraught with uncertainty.

"Hello." Who was she? Something about her seemed familiar, but Emma couldn't quite place her. "Are you lost?"

"No." Her smile faltered, and her pretty face scrunched up a little as though the awkwardness of their brief exchange grated. "I'm Melanie Lipton."

Emma's breath stopped. That's why she looked familiar! She had checked Emma's wounds the night of the mercenary attack before sending her through the evacuation tunnel.

She was also one of the doctors who worked with Cliff and the other vampires down at network headquarters.

Why was she here? Had she found out Emma and Cliff were seeing each other?

Terror filled her. Or had something happened to Cliff?

Damn it. She couldn't ask about the last without revealing the first.

Dr. Lipton closed the car door and held up both hands in a take it easy gesture. "Okay. You're looking a little panicked right now."

Emma swore. She'd tried to keep her expression blank!

"So let me first say that Cliff is fine. He's actually sleeping right now, which is great. He hasn't been doing enough of that lately."

Because of the voices.

Emma's heart broke for him. "Why are you here?"

Dr. Lipton lowered her hands. Glancing around as though searching for an answer, she ultimately gave a helpless shrug. "Because I know you're the reason he's sleeping. I know you're the reason the voices are quiet today."

Emma struggled to find a response that wouldn't confirm her relationship with Cliff if the woman was merely fishing for answers.

With a long sigh, Dr. Lipton took a step forward. "Bastien told me Cliff visited you last night."

"Why would he think that?"

"Because he followed him."

Emma's hackles rose as anger on Cliff's behalf filled her. "If he doesn't trust Cliff, why did he tell him he could hunt alone for a few hours?"

"Bastien *does* trust him." She frowned as she continued forward, her steps more bold, until she reached the edge of the shade provided by the oak trees sprinkled about.

Only a few feet separated them.

"Bullshit," Emma countered. "Bastien wouldn't lie to Cliff and follow him around if he trusted him."

"He didn't lie."

Emma arched a brow.

Melanie grimaced. "Okay. Damn it. I guess he did, but *not* for the reason you think. He trusts Cliff. We both do. Cliff is a good man, Emma. An *exceptional* man. Honorable to his core and *so* strong. The other two vampires who came to live at the network the same time Cliff did succumbed to the insanity in an alarmingly short period of time. One asked Bastien to end it for him. The other…" Her throat worked in a swallow. "The other was too far gone after the mercenaries' torture. We tried to reach him but couldn't. So we had to let him go."

She blinked several times, dispelling the moisture that rose in her brown eyes. "One of those vampires had been infected a year later than Cliff. We don't know why or how Cliff has held on to his sanity this long. Most vampires don't. But he has defied the odds, Emma. Cliff is incredibly strong-willed and determined not to become…" She shook her head helplessly. "Well. He's determined not to become what he's destined to become if my colleagues and I can't find a cure for the virus that won't kill him."

What was left of the afterglow that had remained with Emma all morning vanished.

Resentment flooded her. Why was this woman here? Why couldn't they just leave Cliff alone? Leave *her* alone? She'd been happy. *Cliff* had been happy. Couldn't they have one damned night and day of bliss without someone shoving doom and gloom down their throats? "So while Cliff thinks he's been given two hours of freedom," she said tightly, "Bastien has been following him around and — what — waiting for him to lose it?"

Dr. Lipton's eyes widened. "No! No, of course not!" She bit her lip. "I mean, that *is* a concern. It would be much better for Cliff if any psychotic breaks he experiences take place in the safety of the network. But our primary concern is that Cliff may inadvertently go too far to gain information for the network and end up being attacked by whatever pack of vampires he's pumping for information." She reached out as though to touch Emma's arm but stopped midmotion and lowered her hand. "It meant so much to Cliff when he saw with his own eyes how many people he helped the morning mercenaries blitzed the network. He's so afraid that if we aren't able to halt the brain damage, people will only see him as a monster. That that's how he'll be remembered."

How he'll be remembered after the insanity progressed to the point that he chose to die.

Just the thought of it sent pain streaking through Emma.

"We're just worried he'll try too hard to avoid that fate by being the hero and will seriously endanger himself. That's why Bastien secretly followed him and stayed downwind. He wants to be close so he can jump in and protect Cliff if the vampires realize he's an ally of the Immortal Guardians and attack. Vampires are traveling in larger groups now. Cliff is a superlative fighter, but even Immortal Guardians can find themselves outnumbered."

Emma's anger receded. Everything about the woman shouted sincerity. And the argument seemed both logical and worrisome.

Was Cliff taking unnecessary risks while he was out hunting alone?

She glanced down at her shoes. Dr. Lipton's name had come up at lunch on multiple occasions. Each time Cliff's words and mannerisms had made it clear that he trusted and cared about her. "So Bastien followed Cliff here last night?" she asked, her voice low.

Melanie nodded.

Emma closed her eyes, replaying everything she and Cliff had said. Everything they'd done. Every word they'd spoken. Every touch. Every gasp or moan of ecstasy. "How long did he stay outside and listen?"

Again Melanie bit her lip. "Long enough to ascertain the depth of your relationship."

Swearing, Emma turned and paced away. "And by that you mean…?"

"Long enough to know you slept together."

Fury returned, fast and fierce. Bastien had *listened* to them. He had stood outside and *listened* while they made love!

Spinning around, she pointed at Melanie. "That is an *incredible* invasion of privacy," she came close to shouting. "He had *no* right!" No right to tarnish such a beautiful moment. Just the thought of it made her feel sick inside.

Dr. Lipton threw up a placating hand and spoke quickly. "It isn't what you think. As soon as he heard enough to know you welcomed Cliff's presence —"

"Of course I welcomed his presence! The fact that I yanked Cliff inside as soon as I found him standing on my doorstep made it abundantly clear that I *welcomed his presence!*" The bastard had *listened* to them!

"I know," Dr. Lipton said, her voice annoyingly calm. "And Bastien would've left then, but you started packing, and it sounded as if the two of you were about to go on the run."

Oh. Yeah. That *would* have sounded pretty damning, she grudgingly admitted. "I thought Cliff had escaped."

"I know. Bastien told me. And as soon as Cliff cleared that up with you and things turned... amorous..." Pink crept into her cheeks. "Bastien left you alone. He didn't stay and listen further. He really did leave to give you privacy." She forced a smile. "He was nervous as hell though until Cliff made an appearance at the rendezvous point. It was the first time since he came to the network that Cliff was truly on his own. And Bastien was terrified that the two of you might really try to disappear."

Would that be so bad? a voice inside asked tentatively.

Yes. It would, the logical side of her insisted. Cliff needed whatever this woman and the other network doctors could do for him.

"We're on your side, Emma," Dr. Lipton proclaimed softly. "Even more so now that we know how you feel about him, that you love him so much you would leave this life behind and take off with him at a moment's notice if you thought that would keep him safe."

Sighing, Emma let her anger drain away. Upon realizing she still clutched the scraper, she tossed it to the ground. "Did Bastien tell Mr. Reordon what happened?" If Mr. Reordon knew, he would surely put a halt to Cliff's nighttime excursions. Maybe even their lunches, too.

Despair rose. Was that it then? Would they really only have the one night together? Was that all they would be allowed?

The backs of her eyes burned with tears she hastily blinked back. Emma wasn't usually one who cried easily, but *damn*, the past twenty-four hours had been an emotional roller coaster.

"No," Melanie said decisively. "And Bastien has no intention of telling him. Neither do I. It's none of Chris's business."

At least there was that. "Did you come here to tell me I shouldn't see him again?" Emma still didn't know the reason for this visit.

"Absolutely not. Cliff has not been happy for a long time, Emma. He lost everything when he transformed. His life. His future. His family. Then Vince and Joe. But Bastien said when Cliff left here and met him at Bastien's old place... he was smiling. Even *I* noticed a difference in him when they returned to network headquarters. Cliff was more relaxed and at ease than he's been in two years. And he said the voices were gone." Reaching out, she took one of Emma's hands and gave it a squeeze. "You aren't the only one who loves him, you know. We love him, too. And we desperately want him to be happy."

Emma stared at her for a long moment. "If you aren't going to tell me not to see him, then why are you here?"

"Because I care about you, too, and there are some things we need to discuss."

"You don't even know me."

"I know you make Cliff happy. That's enough," she declared, her voice ringing with sincerity.

Emma squeezed her hand, thankful that Cliff had someone like this on his side. "All right, Dr. Lipton. What do you want to talk about?"

She smiled, a genuine one this time. "Please, call me Melanie."

Emma nodded and shook her hand. "Nice to meet you. I'd tell you I'm Emma, but..."

"I already know that," Melanie finished for her as she withdrew her hand.

Emma motioned to the open garage door. "Would you like to talk inside?"

"Yes, please. I love the view you have here. But my damn skin burns even faster now than it used to." She held up the hand she'd extended to Emma.

Emma stared. "Oh shit." The skin on Melanie's hand and much of her forearm was an angry pink from the little bit of sunlight that had touched it. "I forgot you're an immortal."

Melanie laughed. "I do, too, sometimes."

"Does it hurt?" Emma led her to the garage via the most shaded route.

"A little," she admitted. "Roland Warbrook transformed me, so I can actually tolerate more sunlight than Bastien can. But the ride over here was a long one."

Emma led her into the house. "Do you need a bandage or something to wrap it?" She was pretty sure her first aid supplies consisted solely of rubbing alcohol, antibiotic ointment, and a single box of Band-Aids.

"No, thank you. I'll be okay."

"Would you like something to drink?"

"Yes, please."

"Would you like water? Or maybe tea? I also have some—"

"I'll take water, thank you."

Emma filled two glasses with cold water from the filtered pitcher in her fridge, then sat with Melanie on the sofa. "Does Bastien know you're here?"

"Yes." After downing several swallows, Melanie smiled wryly. "I had a hell of a time convincing him not to accompany me."

"How did you manage it?"

"I told him we were going to talk about…" Widening her eyes, she intoned dramatically, "…woman stuff."

Much to her surprise, Emma found herself laughing. "And that entails?"

Again Melanie widened her eyes and intoned meaningfully, "Female issues."

Emma laughed. "I guess immortal men aren't so different from mortal men then."

Melanie grinned. "Not when it comes to stuff that might drive one to seek the aid of what Bastien would call a vagina doctor."

Emma damned near spat her water across the room at that. "A what?"

Melanie laughed. "A vagina doctor. Once when Bastien and I were talking about a mortal friend's pregnancy, he couldn't think of the term OB/GYN, so he just said vagina doctor." She shrugged. "Immortal Guardians aren't real big on physicians. Most were raised in times when medicine was still in its infancy. Or even *before* its infancy."

Emma shook her head. "Being married to a man who was born two centuries ago must be a trip."

"It is." She grinned. "But it's a very *fun* trip."

The rest of the visit went well. As it turned out, Melanie really *was* there to discuss female issues. As a physician and newly proclaimed friend, she wanted to ensure Emma understood the consequences of getting pregnant.

Learning that any baby she conceived by Cliff would most likely be infected with the virus and—*if* it matured mentally—might forever remain trapped in the body of an infant sobered things quickly. But Emma appreciated Melanie's candor and the matter-of-fact way she offered up information that Emma admitted she *did* need to know and hadn't let Cliff impart the previous night. She'd even come prepared and gave Emma a shot since Emma wasn't currently on birth control. Once Emma had met Cliff and fallen hard, the idea of sleeping with another man had just been too unappealing, so she'd stopped taking it.

Melanie also walked Emma through what she could expect if she continued to see Cliff. The mental decline that would take place. The guilt and more he would suffer once the psychotic breaks began to strike on a regular basis. Though she tried to remain clinical, tears glimmered in her eyes by the time she finished.

Throat thick, Emma drew the woman into a hug. "Thank you for helping him."

Melanie shook her head. "I can only try my best to address the medical side of it. I can't make him happy. Not the way you do."

Hearing the difference she made helped Emma feel better. "Does Cliff know you're here?"

"No. And he doesn't know Bastien and I are aware of his coming here last night." Leaning back, Melanie brushed a tear from her cheek. "But Emma, I also want you to know that Cliff won't blame you if you decide it's all too much. Whether you conclude that now that I've laid everything out for you or at some point in the future. He *won't* blame you."

Emma shook her head. "I love him too much. I want every minute I can have with him, good or bad." She covered Melanie's hand where it rested on the sofa between them. "Wouldn't you want the same with Bastien?"

"Yes," she answered without hesitation. "Just know that Bastien and I are here for you. If you ever need to talk or are concerned about anything, you can call us." Taking out her cell phone, she exchanged numbers with Emma. "And if Cliff ever inadvertently hurts you, call me immediately."

"Cliff would never hurt me," Emma declared and braced herself for a denial rife with warning.

But Melanie surprised her. "I don't think he would either." Tilting her head to one side, she seemed to consider it. "Even during their psychotic breaks, the part of Vince and Joe that cared about us seemed to linger and kept them from injuring Linda or me." A flush crept up her cheeks. "But sometimes immortals — and I assume vampires — can be a little rough in their, ahem, exuberance during sex. You know, preternatural strength and all that. I'm immortal now, so any bruises that form fade just as quickly. But you *aren't* immortal, and I worry Cliff might..."

"Panic if he thinks he hurt me?" Emma glanced down at her arms. She hadn't noticed any bruises earlier and saw none now.

"Yes." Melanie's look turned thoughtful. She narrowed her eyes as though she might be mentally hatching something. "You know, Linda recently started seeing Alleck. Linda is the other doctor who works closely with the vampires at the network. And Alleck is a German immortal who sometimes helps us with our research. Linda is still mortal and *does* sometimes sport bruises after bouts of loveplay. Maybe I could arrange to have a" — she made air quotes with her fingers — "*spontaneous* discussion with her regarding how she got the bruises and how she feels about them while Bastien hangs out in Cliff's apartment and makes sure he overhears it." She nodded. "Yes. I'll do that. *And* I'll have Bastien mention he bruised me a bit before I transformed."

"Did he?"

"I don't know. I don't really remember." She smiled wryly. "A *lot* was happening at the time. I nearly died twice."

"Sheesh."

"Yeah." They chatted a little longer, then Melanie headed out to her car. "You should probably open the windows and let a breeze flow through the house. I don't want Cliff to know I was here."

"Why?"

"Because I want him to feel free to visit you without looking over his shoulder, wondering if we're there, scrutinizing everything he does. I want him to be happy."

Emma nodded. "I do, too."

As she watched Melanie's car creep back down the driveway and reviewed everything the woman had told her, Emma wondered how long that happiness would last.

Chapter Fourteen

W HEN CLIFF AWOKE THE NEXT afternoon, his mind was wonderfully quiet and his body rested after the best night's sleep he'd had in months.

A smile stretched his lips.

Emma.

He couldn't wait to see her again tonight. Couldn't wait to hold her and talk to her. He'd grab his phone right now and call her if all outgoing and incoming calls to his cell weren't monitored.

Oh well. He could wait. He felt great!

Unfortunately, Cliff's mental reprieve proved to be a temporary one. He was hanging out with Melanie and Linda in the lab shortly before the dinner hour when the whispers began. Not those carried to his ears by the multitude of employees who inhabited the building but the whispers in his head.

Damn it. His mood soured. What had he expected? That one night with the woman he loved would banish the voices forever and miraculously heal the brain damage he'd suffered?

If Melanie and the other doctors here at the network found a cure for the virus that wouldn't kill him, they didn't even know if the brain damage *could* be reversed or if the voices and violent impulses would continue to plague him for the rest of his mortal life.

Just give up, they taunted. *Give in. No point fighting it when you know we'll win.*

Never. He would *never* give in. He had something more than his own sanity to fight for now. If he could beat this, he might have a future with Emma.

And what he wouldn't give for that, to have a storybook happily-ever-after with her. Marriage. Kids. A dog and a white picket fence. The works.

Perfect, a voice taunted. *Then you could yank a slat off the fence and impale the dog with it. They're so nice and pointy.*

Closing his eyes, Cliff rejected the words and abhorrent images they inspired and focused on thoughts of Emma.

She doesn't want you. You're just a novelty to her, the voice continued.

A bad boy, another joined in. *You know how much women love bad boys.*

And a taste of the forbidden.

Once she realizes how fucked up in the head you really are, she'll run — not walk — into the arms of another.

Fury tore through Cliff, so violent he nearly shook with it, but he resolutely tamped it down and headed for one of the specially designed treadmills the lab boasted.

Emma loved him. He wouldn't let the madness take that from him.

Determination fueling him, Cliff ran at speeds that would wreck a normal treadmill, as if by doing so he could outrun the insanity that loomed. Melanie and Linda chatted as they studied whatever medical data the vampires' latest scans provided. One desk had two large desktop computers set up side by side with the backs facing the treadmills. Sometimes Melanie and Linda would sit at them, elbows nearly touching, faces carefully blank. Melanie would type so swiftly her fingers would blur. Linda would look at Melanie's computer screen, then type something on her own. Melanie would read it, then type again.

Cliff had swiftly concluded this was what they did when they wanted to discuss something without the vampires listening in. They also used sign language. He could've easily learned the latter so he'd know what they were talking about but opted not to. He knew how much a lack of privacy sucked and didn't want to take that little bit away from them.

And considering how setbacks could incite the damned voices, he thought it best if he *didn't* know what they discussed in case it didn't bode well for his future.

Stuart woke around sunset and joined Cliff on his run. He was a good guy. Though he hadn't been a vampire as long as Cliff, he seemed to be struggling today, too.

Miguel, one of the other vampires housed at the network, wandered in and leaped onto a third treadmill. He was only just beginning to experience the mental deterioration but wasn't as wary of Cliff as some of the others. Flashing Cliff and Stuart a smile, he tried to race them to see who could clock the highest speed. He even cracked some jokes that managed to take the edge off.

Until Dr. Whetsman made a surprise appearance in the lab.

In no time at all, Cliff found himself grinding his teeth.

It would be so easy to kill him, the voices growled. *To wrap your hands around his throat and squeeze. Watch his eyes bulge and fear fill his face while you cut off his breath and tighten your hold until his fucking head falls off.*

Cliff clenched his hands into tighter fists as he ran on the treadmill. *He's just an asshole. Not worth my time. The world is full of assholes.*

And you can kill them all, the voices pointed out, gleefully providing both verbal and visual suggestions that made *The Texas Chainsaw Massacre* look as tame as a children's cartoon.

Fucking Whetsman.

Even the prick's fear-induced flatulence couldn't diminish the anger that continued to grip Cliff every time the man opened his damned mouth until Doc Linda suddenly slammed her pencil down, swung on him, and nearly shouted, "Oh, come on! What the hell did you eat today? That's disgusting!"

Stuart burst into laughter, stumbled, then flew backward off the treadmill and slammed into the huge padded mat Melanie had fastened to the wall behind them for just such occasions. On Cliff's other side, Miguel did the same while the vamps down the hallway burst into guffaws.

Even Melanie couldn't hide her laughter as Whetsman's face flamed and he beat a hasty retreat from the lab, muttering something about unprofessionalism.

Cliff slowed his speed as the anger within him receded. With Whetsman gone, he could once again focus on thoughts of Emma, which reduced the voices to annoying mumbles. His jaw loosened, as did his fists.

A moment later, Bastien strolled in. "What was Whetsman doing in here? I thought that asshole worked the day shift."

Melanie shook her head. "I don't know. It was weird. I thought he'd already left."

Bastien grimaced. "And what the hell is that smell? Did someone die?"

That sent the vampires into another round of laughter.

"*I* would have," Linda muttered, "if he'd stayed any longer."

Melanie's face creased with a combination of amusement and disgust. "It's Whetsman." She nodded at Cliff, Stuart, and Miguel.

Bastien glanced at them, then rolled his eyes. "The man is a menace."

"You'll hear no argument from me," Melanie grumbled.

Curling an arm around her waist, Bastien bent to press a kiss to her lips. "Did he say anything I should kick his ass for?" he asked hopefully.

"No."

"Damn." Releasing her, he turned and headed toward the treadmills.

Cliff slowed to a stop and hopped off. Because the equipment had required serious advancements to allow the vampires to run at top speeds, the belt surface was higher off the floor.

"You ready?" Bastien asked.

"Sure." Cliff followed him out of the lab and down the hallway. The guards stationed in front of the elevator and stairwell door all nodded as they approached.

The ride up was a quiet one.

As always, guilt assailed Cliff. When some of the vampires had begun to grumble about him being the only one allowed to leave the network, Seth had stepped in and shut that down fast.

"When Bastien came to me, he sought permission to take *all* of you along on his hunts," the powerful leader of the Immortal Guardians had said. "I told him he could take *one* of you and *only* on a trial basis, something I have never allowed in the past. This is not fun and games, gentlemen. This is an experimental treatment, if you will, the equivalent of a Hail Mary pass that we hope will reduce the aggression this virus spawns and buy us more time to find a cure. Cliff has been a vampire years longer than the rest of you, so he is the logical choice. And he has a history with Bastien that makes him far less likely to bolt."

He had paused then and met each vampire's gaze, one by one. "Do not forget the purpose of Immortal Guardian hunts. You were wise enough to accept our aid so you would not become monsters. Immortal Guardians hunt and slay the vampires who do not so they won't prey upon innocents. If you think going out and killing vampires who have succumbed to the same madness he's battling himself is easy for Cliff, then you're too foolish to be allowed to join him."

The vampires had voiced no complaints since.

When the elevator deposited Cliff and Bastien on the ground floor, they crossed the building's foyer.

John, the brother who held the highest rank among the guards, nodded and tossed them a greeting.

Bastien and Cliff exchanged a few words with him before they headed outside.

Bastien paused. "Do you want to drive or run?"

"Drive."

They ducked into Melanie's Chevy and soon left the nondescript network building in the rearview. Cliff suspected Bastien felt as guilty as he did over having to leave the other vamps behind because he always avoided discussing the night's hunting grounds until they were far enough away that the vamps couldn't hear them.

True to form, Bastien halted some miles down the road. "How are the voices?"

Cliff grimaced. "They're back." He shook his head. "I really had to fight the urge to attack Whetsman."

Bastien grunted. "Me, too. And all I did was pass him in the hallway. Damn, that man's annoying."

Cliff nodded. He shouldn't have mentioned Whetsman because the voices roared even louder, calling for blood.

"Where do you want to hunt tonight?" Bastien asked.

"How about Duke?"

"Duke it is."

They found what they sought shortly after arriving on campus. Four vampires. Two victims. Even with extraordinarily enhanced strength on their side, the bastards remained as cowardly as they'd been as mortals, only attacking smaller numbers of humans they knew were weaker.

And they delighted in terrorizing and torturing their victims.

Well, two could play at that game. Drawing his weapons, Cliff cut those fuckers up. And while it dampened the voices, the pleasure he took in the act disturbed him.

What would Emma think if she could see him like this? How would she feel as she watched him tear into those vampires with such viciousness? Would she loathe him for it? Would she fear him?

He didn't think he could bear either one.

Bastien studied him carefully while they waited for a cleanup crew to come wash down the pavement and collect the dead vampires' belongings. "You okay to run around on your own, or do you need to hunt again?"

"I'm okay," Cliff told him. Or he *would* be once he saw Emma.

"Okay." He motioned to Cliff's shirt. "It occurred to me that we wouldn't have to sneak back into network headquarters without the other vampires seeing you if you changed your clothes first." Because Cliff hadn't felt comfortable returning to sublevel 5 and greeting Stuart and the rest with the blood of other vampires on his clothing, Bastien always texted Melanie first to determine when they could slip in unnoticed. "So I brought you an extra pair of hunting togs tonight. Do you want to change now before you head out looking for other vampires or after you get back?"

Cliff glanced down. "The blood should alleviate any doubts they have about me, so I'd better keep these on, but I'll take the clean clothes with me."

"Okay."

A network cleanup crew arrived, composed of two men and three women. The men wore jumpsuits that bore a pest control company logo. Each carried a tank in one hand and a sprayer in the other. The women were dressed casually and could pass for students.

"Mr. Newcombe?" the tallest woman greeted them.

"Yes."

"Hi. I'm Tami. Mr. Reordon sent us." She glanced at the two injured, unconscious males, at the shriveling-up bodies of the vamps, then took in the copious blood that painted the pavement and grass. If the gruesome scene disturbed her, she let no hint of it show. "We'll have this cleaned up for you in a jiffy."

"Thank you," Bastien said.

Cliff couldn't help but notice the uneasy sidelong glances the men slid his way and tried to take a page from Bastien's book. When mercenaries had shot Melanie and nearly killed her, Bastien had flown into a rage and left a bloodbath in his wake. One that had required the network to send a cleanup crew *bus*. And Bastien hadn't given two shits about the network employees' responses when he had helped them tidy up the mess by leaping from rooftop to rooftop and hurling mercenary bodies at that bus.

"Do you know if anything was caught on video?" Tami asked.

Bastien shook his head. "Not that I'm aware of. No surveillance cameras were aimed our way while we fought, but the vamps attacked the men before we arrived, so you might want to double-check."

"Yes, sir."

"Do you need any help with the victims?"

"No, sir. We'll take it from here."

The second woman knelt beside the unconscious males and set her large purse on the ground. As Cliff watched, she began to remove first aid supplies from it, check the men's vitals, and tend their wounds with an efficiency that reminded him of Melanie.

Bastien turned away and walked with him back to the car. Once there, he drew a cell phone from an inner pocket of his coat and handed it to Cliff. "If you come upon vampires who are harming mortals, text me and wait until I arrive to confront them."

"Unless they're killing the mortals."

"Unless they're killing the mortals," Bastien agreed, "and they don't outnumber you too badly." Leaning into the back seat, he grabbed the duffel bag and drew it out. "How are the voices?"

"Lower."

"But still there?"

"Yeah."

He glanced at his watch. "We're coming up on the top of the hour. Why don't you meet me in four hours instead of two? You don't have to track down other vampires the whole time. Go for a run or... hell, I don't know. Go see a movie." Delving into another pocket, he withdrew his wallet and handed Cliff a lump of folded bills.

Cliff grinned as he pocketed them. "Gee thanks, dad."

Bastien laughed. "Are movie theaters even open this late?"

"I doubt it." Anything that wasn't either a twenty-four-hour superstore or gas station tended to close before midnight.

He shrugged. "Well, whatever you think might help clear your head." He passed him the duffel. "Just don't do anything I wouldn't do."

Cliff looped the strap over his shoulder. "*Is* there anything you wouldn't do?"

"Hmm. Good point. Have fun then."

"You, too." Grinning, he raced away.

Though Cliff wanted to shoot straight to Emma's house, he needed to fulfill his obligations to Bastien and the Immortal Guardians first.

With that in mind, he headed to NCCU to see if he could *accidentally* run into some other vampires.

He *did* find—in record time—two out hunting and watched them for a bit before approaching them. Neither one harmed the victims they chose beyond drinking from them, something he thought promising. Unfortunately, they weren't interested in making friends or engaging in small talk. The first was good. They didn't seem to be part of whatever new vampire army was amassing. But the second made it impossible for him to try to win them over to the Immortal Guardians' side.

Tonight anyway. Maybe he could find them another night and try again.

Having performed his duties, Cliff sped to Emma's quaint country home.

Excitement and nerves battled inside him. Would she really be happy to see him again? She had said she would, but...

Last night seemed like a dream.

The voices, dampened by his violent clash with the sadistic vampires earlier, tried to resume their constant diatribe.

Cliff ignored them as he skidded to a halt on her neatly mown lawn.

Lights inside brightened the windows, but blinds kept him from peering within.

He glanced down at his blood-soaked clothing, then at the bag Bastien had given him. Dropping to one knee, he set the bag on the ground, unzipped it, and rifled through it. Clean clothes, clean boots, and — *yes!* — scentless hand wipes.

It took Cliff mere seconds to doff his hunting garb and wipe the blood from his exposed skin. He couldn't imagine what Emma would think if she were to look out and see him standing bare-ass naked in her front yard but considered it worth the risk. It suddenly felt incredibly important that he come to her tonight as clean and gore-free as a normal man would.

A full minute later, he wore clean clothes. Once he stuffed the hunting garb and red-smeared hand wipes into the duffel, he zipped it and gripped the handles.

His heart pounded in his chest as he left the grass, strode up the stone path, scaled the wooden steps to her porch, and stopped before her front door. He raised a hand to knock but hesitated. He glanced down at his clean clothes and the duffel. What was he missing?

A thought dawned. Swearing, he set the duffel down and zipped back to one of the fields he'd run through on his way here.

Seconds later, he once more stood before Emma's door, this time with a bouquet of pretty wildflowers clutched in one fist.

Please let it have been real, he thought.

Raising his hand, he knocked, then picked up his duffel bag. If both hands were full, maybe he would be less tempted to touch her as soon as he saw her.

Footsteps padded across the floor inside. Locks clicked. The door swung open.

Then Emma stood before him.

His breath left him in a rush. *She's so beautiful.*

She wore a colorful dress tonight that hugged her breasts and slender waist before it fell loosely to a few inches above her knees. No shoes adorned her feet. Instead, pink-painted toenails gleamed in the porch's light.

Tilting her head back, she smiled up at him. "Hi."

Joy filled him as he tightened his hold on the duffel. She was happy to see him! "Hi."

Stepping out onto the porch, she rose onto her toes, wrapped her arms around his neck, and drew him down for a kiss.

Every voice in his head fell silent as Cliff dropped the bag and wrapped his arms around her, careful not to crush the flowers. Or Emma. She felt so good in his arms that he just wanted to squeeze her closer and never let her go. Instead, he reveled in the touch of her lips against his and poured all the love and affection he felt for her into the kiss.

She hummed her approval, tightening her arms a moment before she slowly withdrew and lowered her heels to the floor. She didn't move away though. The front of her body still pressed into his, inciting fiery desire he could do nothing to cool. "I missed you today," she said softly, a smile toying with the edges of her lips.

"I missed you, too," he admitted with a smile, then offered her the flowers. "These are for you. Some of the blossoms have closed for the night, but they'll open again in the morning if you put them in water."

Her lovely features brightened. "They're beautiful, Cliff. Thank you. That's so thoughtful."

Even *that* made him happy... that she would take pleasure in something as simple as wildflowers he'd picked for her instead of disparaging them. Back in college when he'd still been human, he'd dated a girl who considered anything short of a dozen roses an insult and frequently complained that he didn't buy her nicer things than her friends' boyfriends bought them.

Taking his hand, Emma turned and tugged him after her. "Come inside."

Snagging the duffel bag, he followed her in and closed the door behind them. When he turned back to face the living room, he stilled.

The coffee table in front of the sofa bore a crisp white runner it hadn't before. Two long, thin candles rose from silver stands on it and loomed over a pair of plates and neat place settings with carefully folded napkins beside them.

Since she had no dining table, Emma had set the coffee table for a romantic dinner for two… without the food, though the mouthwatering aroma of something pasta related filled the room.

He set the duffel down.

Emma watched him carefully as she toyed with a daisy-like flower. "I wasn't sure how much time we'd have. Last night we only had a couple of hours and…" Shrugging, she sent him a sheepish smile. "I don't know. I thought it might be rude to just pounce on you as soon as you walked in the door."

"Hell no. Pounce away," he retorted with a grin, drawing a laugh from her. "I nearly pounced on you, too. But *this*…" He motioned to the coffee table. "This is perfect, Emma. I love it."

She beamed.

Cliff glanced at his watch. "We have three and a half hours." He cast her a hopeful look. "Could we maybe have a date night?" He hadn't been on an actual date in years and craved the normalcy of it.

"Yes." Her lovely face lighting with excitement, she rushed into the kitchen. "The lasagna is ready. I was just keeping it warm in the oven. Let me put these beauties in water first."

In the time it took her to find a vase and arrange the flowers in it, Cliff removed the lasagna from the oven, filled both plates, lit the candles, and found a bottle of sparkling grape juice in the fridge.

When she saw him filling a couple of wineglasses with it, she wrinkled her nose in apology. "Sorry. That's all I have. I've kind of been on a health kick lately."

He sent her a reassuring smile. "This is fine. I can't get buzzed from alcohol anyway."

"Oh. Right. I forgot. That kinda sucks."

He chuckled. "Yeah. But on the plus side, it keeps half-crazy vampires from going on drunken rampages."

She laughed. "True."

They settled beside each other on the sofa, close enough that their arms brushed. Then they picked up their wineglasses.

"To us," she said with a soft smile.

"To us," Cliff repeated, stealing a tender kiss before they clinked their glasses together and took a sip.

Emma's stomach rumbled as they spread napkins on their laps and tucked into the tasty pasta.

Cliff grinned and took a bite. "Mmmm. This is delicious."

"Thank you."

His mind cycled back to the sparkling grape juice and her health-kick comment. "You aren't having any health problems, are you?" If so, he'd have to find a way to bring it to Melanie's attention. Maybe he could say he heard Emma mention it in the cafeteria or something.

"No." With what appeared to be great reluctance, she said, "It's just how I'm dealing with the aftereffects of the mercenary attack."

His chewing slowed as he eyed her with concern. He hadn't really thought about the lingering effects the mercenary attack might have on network employees. He studied the arms left mostly bare by her dress. Cliff ran himself ragged on the treadmill to try to silence the voices that battered him. He'd noticed the increased muscle definition in Emma's arms, the slight narrowing of her waist and slimming of her hips. Did she exercise vigorously to combat... what? Nightmares?

She shook her head. "It isn't what you think. I'm fine. I just want to be in better physical condition if something similar goes down in the future so I can be like you and help others out."

Cliff stared at her. Did she have any idea how much those words meant to him? That she saw him as someone who *helped* others rather than someone who was destined to lose his mind and *harm* them?

"I've been meaning to pour more effort into my health anyway," she added, "so it's a win-win."

Swallowing, he nodded and asked her about her day, much of which she'd spent singing off-key to *Sly and the Family Stone* while she scraped old paint off the siding out front.

He laughed when she claimed her warbling had scared off two squirrels and stunned every bird within a mile's radius into appalled silence. She laughed when he told her about Linda's outburst in the lab that sent Stuart and Miguel stumbling and flying off the treadmills. And the two of them continued to laugh and talk as they enjoyed their dinner, just as they would have on an ordinary date.

Cliff loved it. And loved Emma all the more for it.

As soon as both plates were empty, he drew her onto his lap.

Smiling, Emma looped her arms around his neck and toyed with his dreadlocks.

"Thank you for this," he murmured, rubbing noses with her.

She shook her head. "I love you, Cliff. Not just your perfect body and handsome face, but your intelligence and sense of humor and caring nature. I love every minute we spend together, however we choose to spend it."

Chapter Fifteen

A MBER LIGHT FLARED TO LIFE in Cliff's eyes as he brushed her lips with his. Once. Twice. Then deepened the contact.

Desire shot through Emma when his arms tightened around her and his tongue stroked hers. She could feel Cliff's erection trapped beneath her, but that wasn't where she wanted it. Dropping her hands to his shoulders, she rose onto her knees, slung a leg over his, and straddled him.

As soon as she sank onto his lap, Cliff gripped her ass in both hands and tugged her tight against him. *Yes.* His hard cock, still constrained by the fabric of his pants, rubbed her clit. Moaning, she rocked against him as his kisses grew more feverish, his hands more bold.

Cool air wafted across her back as he drew her zipper down. Emma abandoned his lips long enough for him to yank her dress over her head and toss it on the floor. Then she kissed him again, loving his taste, the fervent exploration of his hands.

His thumbs skimmed the lace that covered her breasts. Fire shot through her as he teased the hard tips.

"Cliff," she breathed. "I want you." She fisted his shirt, dragged the hem up out of his pants, and drew it over his head.

He was so damn hot. Broad shoulders. Bulging biceps. A muscled chest that bore dark hair that tempted her. She *loved* hairy chests. Curling her fingers in it, she gave it a tug.

His eyes flashed bright amber. He unfastened her bra with deft fingers and flung it aside. Then, bending her back over his arm, he closed his lips around the stiff, sensitive peak of one breast.

Emma moaned. Arching against him, she gripped his hair. Every touch and brush of his lips set her on fire. She had never in her life wanted a man more.

Slipping a hand between them, Cliff tore her panties off. "I'll replace them," he murmured before delivering a love bite to her breast.

She jerked against him. "I don't care. Just take your pants off. I don't want to come until you're inside me, and I'm already close."

He growled against her breast.

"*Yes*. More, Cliff. Please."

He didn't take the time to pull off his pants, clearly impatient to be inside her. Or maybe she just didn't give him time to. As soon as he unfastened them and freed his erection, Emma curled her fingers around his long hard length and began to stroke him.

He hissed in a breath as she drew her thumb over and around the crown. "Emma," he groaned.

Rising to her knees, she guided him to her slick entrance and sank down, taking him deep inside her, loving the way he stretched her.

His arms tightened around her as he groaned. "You feel so good," he uttered, his voice hoarse with desire.

Then both began to move, urgency driving them, hands stroking, mouths tasting, the passion building and building until she cried out as ecstasy crashed through her. Her body clamped down around him, squeezing his hard length in rhythmic pulses that drew her name from his lips as he came hard.

Her heart battering her ribs, Emma sank against him. Little aftershocks of pleasure continued to ripple through her as she nuzzled his neck and felt his pulse race beneath his warm skin.

Cliff wrapped his arms around her and snuggled her close. He pressed a kiss to her hair before he rested his cheek atop her head.

She smiled. Cliff was a cuddler. She loved that about him. Or perhaps he was just starved for physical contact. He had been at the network for almost three years now and certainly hadn't had any other girlfriends in that time.

Some of the glow from their lovemaking faded.

Three years. Melanie said most vampires would've succumbed to the madness by now.

"How are the voices?" she asked softly, needing to know despite her reluctance to spoil the mood.

"Gone." Leaning back, he cupped her face in his big hands and smoothed his thumbs over her cheeks. His eyes still bore an amber glow as he smiled at her, then touched his lips to hers in a kiss so tender it made her heart melt. "You silence them, Emma."

If only she could silence them permanently so he could be free.

She forced a smile. "Maybe they heard the birds and squirrels talking and are afraid I'm going to sing."

He laughed. "Maybe so."

Once their breathing calmed, they opted to shower together. Hot water sluiced down around them as steam turned the glass door opaque. As the two of them lathered each other up, Emma began to sing a playful tune.

Cliff grinned. "Wow. You weren't kidding. You really *can't* sing. I can't even tell what song that is."

Laughing, she punished him by singing louder until he silenced her with his lips, lifted her into his arms, and took her against the wall.

It was the first time she'd ever had shower sex. And she vowed it wouldn't be the last.

Once dry, they stumbled into the bedroom and tumbled onto the bed where he took her again, swiftly driving her to a third, then fourth, climax. Emma was so exhausted afterward that she had to fight to keep from falling asleep when he rolled them to their sides and spooned up behind her.

"I wish every night could be like this," he murmured, his breath teasing her hair as he tightened his hold.

Reaching back, she curled a hand around the nape of his neck. "Then every night *will* be, Cliff."

"I love you, Emma," he whispered.

"I love you, too."

After Cliff left, fatigue hit Emma like a sledgehammer.

Having worked the day shift for the past year or so, she had—of necessity—had to maintain an early-to-bed, early-to-rise schedule. So her body didn't appreciate the sudden late nights.

Shuffling into the bedroom, she tumbled face-first onto the covers and drew the pillow that carried Cliff's scent to her chest. "Totally worth it," she mumbled as she fell asleep with a smile on her face.

An explosion of sound jerked her awake.

Jackknifing up in bed, heart slamming against her ribs, she glanced around with wide eyes. What the hell? It reminded her of the time golf-ball-sized hail had fallen when she was a little girl. The noise had been deafening and had utterly terrified her.

It did the same now. Especially since there had been no rain in the five-day forecast, let alone hail.

Racing to her window, she speared the blinds with her fingers and yanked them apart so she could peer out at... a tranquil backyard just beginning to lighten with dawn.

What?

She didn't realize until then that the sound was concentrated at the front of the house.

Quiet fell.

She held her breath.

The thunderous racket began anew.

Swearing, she glanced down at the tank top and pajama shorts she'd donned to see Cliff to the door. In record time, she tugged on yoga pants and a hoodie. Grabbing her cell and the 9mm, she headed into the living room.

A shadow passed across one of the front windows.

Sucking in a breath, she ducked back into the hallway and waited.

When no one busted in the window, she crept over to the back door. A peek out the curtained window showed her the same tranquil meadow she'd seen from her bedroom window. Turning the lock, she eased the door open and slipped outside.

Another of those quiet pauses struck. Then the noise resumed.

Try though she might, Emma could not identify what hell was making it... until she headed for the side of the house, eased along it, and peered around the front corner.

Her eyes widened. Her jaw dropped.

No longer attempting stealth, she strode onto her front lawn. The dew-covered grass cooled her bare feet as she stopped and stared.

Tarps covered her lawn and shrubs as a large black form moved up and down and side to side on a ladder so quickly that he blurred. On the left side of the ladder, every millimeter of flaky paint had been removed. On the right, it still looked like crap.

"What the hell are you doing?" she called.

The form solidified and spun to face her with a snarl, eyes glowing bright amber.

Fear sliced through her, driving her to back away a couple of steps and grip the gun tighter.

As soon as the man saw her, his features smoothed out and his eyes stopped glowing. "Oh. Sorry about that," he said with a British accent as he offered her a chagrined smile. "You startled me. I didn't hear your approach over the noise."

"Uh-huh." Was this Bastien? "What the hell are you doing?"

Leaping down from the ladder, he motioned to the house behind him with a scraper tool. "Melanie mentioned you were scraping old paint off the siding when she arrived. So I thought I would"—he shifted his weight, looking for all intents and purposes like a precocious child who'd been caught doing something he shouldn't—"swing by and, uh... help?"

Amusement trickled through her, easing some of the tension in her muscles. Oh yeah. She could definitely see this man using the phrase vagina doctor. "I take it you're Sebastien Newcombe?"

Nodding, he strode toward her. "Apologies. Yes, I'm Bastien." He wiped his dusty, paint-flecked hand on his pants, then offered it to her.

Emma transferred the 9mm she held to her left hand and shook. "I'm Emma."

"Good to meet you, Emma."

She motioned to the house. "I know *what* you're doing. I just don't know *why*. And aren't you supposed to be sleeping right now? The sun's up." Fortunately for him, it would take the sun a couple more hours to climb high enough to top the oak trees that shaded the front of her home.

He shrugged. "I'm immortal. I don't need as much sleep as a human or a vampire. I also came early enough to get the work done while your house was still in the shade. And I'm doing it because..." He shrugged. "I love Cliff like a brother. I've never seen him as happy as he's been the past two nights after spending time with you. So I wanted to thank you."

"By scraping old paint off my siding?"

His lips quirked up in a smile. "Well, I'm not really a flowers-and-chocolates kind of guy."

She grinned. "That's okay. I actually appreciate this a lot more. That shit is tedious."

He laughed. "Especially when done at mortal speeds?"

"Absolutely. But next time knock first and let me know it's you. You scared the bejeebers out of me." Her eyes widened. "Not that there will *be* a next time. You really don't have to do this. Loving Cliff is its own reward. I don't need any others."

His hard features softened. "That almost makes me wish I were of the freely-distributes-hugs sort."

Her responding laugh transmogrified into a yawn, catching her unawares. "Sorry about that."

He swore. "I woke you up, didn't I?"

"Yes."

He grimaced. "I forgot that humans who work the day shift often like to sleep in on weekends."

She waved away his concern. "Don't worry about it."

"You look tired."

"Um. Thank you?"

"Damn it. I'm not supposed to mention things like that, am I?"

She smiled. "No."

"Apparently I'm about as adept at social interaction as Roland Warbrook is."

She nearly laughed at the comparison. Roland was notoriously antisocial. And Bastien *was* often described as having a bit of a fuck-you attitude.

"I didn't mean to be impolite," he said, his deep voice full of contrition. "It just occurred to me that Cliff's late-night visits might adversely affect your health. Don't humans need eight hours of sleep?"

"Ideally yes. But we can get by on less when we have to. I think most adults *do* get by on less. I got *way* less than eight hours when I was in college. So don't worry about me. I'll be okay."

"Not if Cliff keeps you up late seven nights a week."

If Emma were a morning person and had gotten more sleep the previous night, she most likely would've reacted better to the innocuous statement. But crankiness and the fact that her relationship with Cliff was entirely dependent upon other people *letting* them see each other sparked anger and resentment. "Well, don't even *think* about limiting the nights Cliff can see me, Bastien. As long as no one wakes me up at the crack of dawn, I can catch up on my rest on weekends. And if that isn't enough—"

He raised his hands in a gesture of surrender, one still gripping the scraper. "I wouldn't do that, Emma. Cliff loves you. And I can see you love him, too. I was simply worried that not getting enough sleep would eventually wear you down and make you ill. Cliff wouldn't want that. And I wouldn't either. That's all."

"Oh. Sorry about that." She wrinkled her nose. "I'm not really a morning person."

"Nor am I," he said with a smile. "I'd let Cliff have his roaming time and come here *before* we hunt together so you could go to bed earlier, but..." He hesitated a moment, expression sobering. "He needs the hunts to alleviate the aggression that grips him."

Her stomach sank. Swallowing hard, she nodded. "I appreciate your being frank with me about that."

"I will always be so when it comes to Cliff," he vowed, voice softening. "You quiet the voices."

"I do."

"But he needs to hunt to eradicate the violent impulses that constantly build within him. And I think it best that he do that before he comes to see you. If Cliff ever hurt you—"

"He won't."

"But if he *did*, it would kill him."

"He won't hurt me, Bastien. I'm sure of it. And I can sleep late on weekends. If I get too tired during the week, I can always nap after I get home from work." She shrugged. "And even if I couldn't do either of those things, I'd still be okay because I'm a *gifted one*."

His eyebrows flew up. "You are?"

She nodded. "According to the network, I'm the descendent of a healer, so I never get sick. Ever. I've never even caught a cold." She also had a photographic memory that enabled her to remember with crystal clarity everything she'd ever read.

He stared at her, an almost comical look of horror dawning on his handsome features. "You aren't a descendent of Roland Warbrook, are you?"

Emma grinned. "No."

Relaxing, he pretended to wipe sweat from his brow. "Whew. That was a close one." He grinned. "For a moment there I thought I was going to have to start playing nice with the surly bastard."

She laughed.

He jerked a thumb over his shoulder. "I'd better get back to work. I want to finish the whole house before the sun tops the trees."

"You really don't have to do that."

"I know. But I want to." He smiled. "I'll come back on a weekday to sand it and paint it so I won't keep you from sleeping in again. Just leave the paint on your back porch."

Without another word, Bastien turned and strode toward the ladder.

Chapter Sixteen

A YEAR PASSED. ONE WONDROUS year illuminated by nights with Emma that Cliff could hardly believe. Though some might mock him for saying it, to him Emma was the light that kept a sea of darkness at bay. Without her, he would have long since drowned in it.

The voices seemed to grow louder and louder every day. Emma still silenced them. But as soon as he left her, the damn murmurs began anew, swiftly escalating in volume.

The aggression and violent impulses grew stronger, too, threatening to consume him. To rob him of who he was. But Cliff continued to fight it.

Most days he won.

Some days he didn't.

He began to have psychotic breaks. Mild ones compared to those Vince had experienced.

He usually didn't even know he'd had one — that he'd flown into a rage — until he awoke, afflicted with the telltale lethargy and mental bleariness that resulted from being sedated with the only drug capable of knocking out a vampire or immortal.

Fear and dread always consumed him in such instances. His stomach would roil, his skin would break out in a cold sweat, and his hands would tremble as he wondered what he'd done. Whom he'd hurt. Or worse, if he'd killed anyone.

He had not yet slain anyone while in the grips of a psychotic break. But he'd broken bones.

Shame filled him. He didn't even remember doing it. But he had injured Stuart once when his friend had struggled to restrain him long enough for Linda to tranq him. And the reprieves that followed the breaks — the quiet after the storm — seemed to shorten with each one he experienced.

Even now, while Cliff sat on the sofa in his apartment, the voices clamored at him to maim, dismember, and kill. It sickened him.

"This is not who I am," he whispered, as if saying it aloud would ensure some part of him would never forget it and would help him defeat the looming madness. "This is *not* who I am."

He should be sleeping. He had only left Emma's arms a few hours ago. Members of the day shift had just arrived. But the damn voices wouldn't let him rest.

Rising, he crossed to the kitchen, opened one of the cabinets, and drew out a box of graham crackers. The top showed a bit of wear from being opened and closed so often but shouldn't draw undue attention from the network employees who stocked his cupboards. Flipping it up, he dumped out two thick sleeves of long brown crackers and retrieved the cell phone he'd hidden beneath them.

As soon as he turned it on, Emma smiled up at him from the lock screen.

Cliff clutched the device like a lifeline as he returned to the sofa and sank down on the cushions. Bastien had never asked him to return the phone he'd given him to use while he roamed alone. The one the network had provided was constantly monitored. But Cliff didn't think Bastien had told them about this one. So he figured as long as he kept the Wi-Fi and Bluetooth turned off and the cell set to Airplane Mode, Reordon shouldn't be able to detect it or access anything on it unless he somehow learned of the device and got his hands on it.

Fortunately, there were no cameras in the vampires' apartments to clue him in. Bastien had insisted on it and had gotten Seth's okay.

Unlocking the screen, Cliff opened the photos app and scrolled through the pictures.

Most were of Emma. Smiling. Laughing. Teasing. Goofing around. But there were selfies of the two of them as well. And videos. Nothing exciting. Nothing pornographic. Just snippets of everyday, ordinary life that seemed utterly extraordinary to him. The two of them cooking together in her small kitchen. Cliff helping her assemble wooden shelves for her growing home library. Him mowing the lawn for her while she nurtured the pretty flowers in her hanging baskets under the porch's light. Emma sitting on the floor between Cliff's knees while he sat on the sofa and carefully combed the tangles from her beautiful hair, oiled her scalp, and tried to fashion yet another intricate braid she'd found online.

They had discovered during the past year together that tasks that occupied his hands and required him to focus on learning how to do something new helped calm him. So there were quite a few photos of him braiding her hair in increasingly complex patterns, as well as of the two of them putting together five-thousand-piece puzzles while they chatted and listened to music.

He continued to scroll through the pictures until he came upon the one he sought.

Emma had taken it. She had caught him laughing, and he looked young and carefree.

THIS IS WHO YOU ARE, she'd written across the bottom.

He studied it a long moment. *That is who I am.*

He swiped to the next photo.

She'd taken this one as well with one of those extender things that let you take better selfies.

Emma was perched on his lap. Cliff had wrapped his arms around her and ducked his head to press his cheek to hers. Both were grinning over a joke she'd just cracked.

AND THIS IS WHO WE ARE, she'd written.

He swallowed hard, wanting desperately to believe that would always be true. But he was having a hard time today. The voices were almost deafening. And restless energy constantly plagued him.

He wished he could call Emma or Facetime her or something. But he couldn't risk the network picking it up and learning of their relationship. Reordon and Seth were both incredibly protective of *gifted ones*. There was just no way they would be okay with Emma seeing a psychotic vampire whose tenuous grip on sanity weakened every day.

Rising, he returned the phone to the box of graham crackers and tucked it back in the cabinet. He needed to find something to get the voices to shut the hell up. If he slept, he wouldn't hurt anyone.

If he slept long enough, then when he woke he would only have to make it through a couple of hours before he went hunting with Bastien and loosed this aggression.

He fetched his earbuds and plugged them into the cell phone the network had given him. A quick scroll through his playlist and Disturbed began to roar in his ears, blocking out the twenty-four-hour-a-day bustle at network headquarters. Blocking out the voices. But it did little to rid him of the restless energy that soon drove him to pace like a caged tiger.

He needed a good long run on the treadmill.

Or maybe he should ask Linda to sedate him. She and Melanie sometimes gave him and Stuart diluted doses of the drug to take the edge off when they could feel the pressure building. He hated the way it made him feel — like his limbs were twice as heavy and his mind full of fog. But he *did* often sleep better afterward.

Swearing, he shut off the music, tossed the cell and earbuds on the sofa, and left his apartment. Melanie and Bastien had headed home shortly after he and Bastien returned from hunting. But Linda was still around.

He gave the guards at the end of the hallway a nod of greeting, then headed into the lab only to find it empty. He checked her office next.

Empty.

Maybe she was in the restroom.

Opting to pound the treadmill until she returned, he headed back out into the hallway.

The elevator dinged, drawing his attention.

His lips tightened when Dr. Whetsman emerged and headed toward the lab.

Kill him! Kill that motherfucker! the voices bellowed. *Gut him! Feed him his own fucking entrails!*

Cliff clenched his teeth. His hands curled into fists.

No way could he be around that bastard today. The treadmill and Linda would have to wait.

Cliff strode toward his apartment, intent on ignoring the asshole.

Whetsman's nervous gaze fastened on him as they approached each other. A bead of sweat trailed down one temple.

Even that infuriated Cliff.

Then a scent wafted to him. Linda's.

Damn it. Now he'd have to talk to him. "Have you seen Linda?"

Whetsman's eyes widened slightly. His pupils shrank as he swiftly looked away and quickened his pace. "No."

Cliff's steps slowed. "Bullshit. I can smell her on you."

Another bead of sweat rolled down to join the first. "I passed her when I came in just now. She was on her way out, probably heading home. That must be what you're smelling."

Highly doubtful. Just walking past someone didn't imbue you with her scent. You had to come into physical contact with her for that to happen.

Cliff stopped.

Whetsman scurried past him, eyes averted.

When he did, the slight breeze he created carried another scent to Cliff's ultrasensitive nose.

Blood.

Linda's blood.

Over the years, Cliff had infused himself with blood donated by almost every employee that worked for the network. And even if he hadn't, Doc Linda had gotten enough paper cuts for him to recognize the scent as hers.

Alarm struck. Spinning around, he grabbed Whetsman by the arm. "Where is she? What have you done?" he demanded, his voice low and guttural. Too low to carry to the guards down the hallway whose attention, he sensed, sharpened on him.

Whetsman gaped up at him with terror-filled eyes. "I didn't do anything. I don't know where she is. Probably out fucking that German immortal who thinks he's smarter than me."

Liar! the voices cried, slavering for action. *Kill him!*

"Bullshit," Cliff snarled. Crowding the man up against the wall, he scanned the white lab coat.

There. On the cuff of the arm Cliff held. Crimson speckles.

"Cliff?" Todd called from the end of the hallway. "Everything okay down there?"

Cliff ignored him and yanked Whetsman's arm up to sniff the droplets of blood.

Whetsman's heart pounded in his chest as he trembled in Cliff's grasp and watched him touch his tongue to the spots. "What the fuck are you doing? That's disgusting!"

"Cliff?" Todd called again.

Fury rolled through him, exciting the voices and amplifying their calls for violence.

That's Linda's blood! He killed her! He tortured her! He cut her up! Cut him up! Butcher him!

"What did you do?" Cliff growled, tightening his grip on Whetsman's arm.

Bone snapped and crunched beneath the pressure.

Whetsman screamed.

Cliff shook him like a dog with a toy. *"What did you do?"* he bellowed. Spinning, he yanked the scientist across the hallway and slammed him into the wall.

More! Fuck him up! Fuck him up! the voices demanded, filling his mind with gruesome ways he should punish the bastard for killing Linda. For killing his friend.

"Help me!" Whetsman screeched. "Kill him! Kill him!"

Like Whetsman had killed Linda?

Fuck that.

An alarm began to blare. Boots pounded up the hallway.

Cliff threw the man across the hallway again, taking pleasure in the crack that sounded as Whetsman's head struck the wall.

A dart skimmed past Cliff's nose. He ducked a second one, then a third.

The *snicks* of suppressed gunfire filled the air.

Bullets struck his torso. Agony tore through him, merely heightening his fury.

Roaring, he bent over Whetsman where he'd crumbled to the floor, picked him up, and hurled him at the guards who ran toward them, weapons raised.

The gunfire stopped. Swears erupted as bodies tumbled to the floor.

Cliff started toward them, seeing nothing now but the man he wanted to rip to shreds.

More bullets peppered him.

Cliff stumbled backward, howling in pain and fury as Whetsman picked himself up and limped toward the elevator.

That fucker was getting away!

Cliff shot forward at preternatural speeds, bowling through bodies, seeing no faces, only impediments keeping him from reaching Whetsman before—

The asshole ducked into the elevator and the doors slid closed.

"No!" Cliff slammed into them full force. The heavy metal dented with a thunderous rumble but didn't halt the elevator's ascent.

Something jabbed him in the back. Ignoring it, Cliff dove for the door to the stairwell, plowing through more obstacles he barely acknowledged were guards. Men cried out as he batted them aside and leaped up to the first visible landing. Dizziness rose. Lethargy threatened, dragging at his legs like a strong river current as he raced upward, one floor after another, passing shadows that emitted screams so loud they matched the voices that kept yowling in his head, lending him strength and driving him onward.

Cliff stumbled out of the stairwell onto the ground floor.

Halfway across the lobby, Whetsman tripped and fell to the floor. A dozen guards followed and hovered over him while he clutched his arm and shouted, "He's crazed! He's fucking crazed!" When the scientist spotted Cliff through the dark legs surrounding him, he shrieked, rolled onto his belly, and started scrambling away.

The guards spun around.

Too late.

Cliff covered the distance between them in one leap. Grasping the back of Whetsman's coat, he lifted him above his head and slammed him down again.

The scientist screamed.

That's it! Hurt him! the voices clamored. *Make him bleed! Make him scream! Make him beg for mercy!*

More *snicks* sounded while the alarm continued to blare.

Bullets struck Cliff in the back and burst from his chest. Breathing became a struggle. Blood poured from his lips. But all Cliff saw was Linda's blood on Whetsman's coat.

Fuck him up! Make him bleed the way he made her bleed!

Lifting the scientist, he threw him across the lobby. The sound of bones snapping brought Cliff joy as the fucker hit the wall.

Leaping across, Cliff caught him before he hit the floor and hurled him at the granite desk.

More crunches and snaps. Blood spewed from the man's mouth and trailed down his face as he collapsed in a heap.

Sharp pain erupted in Cliff's neck.

His head swam. The voices in his head slowed, slurred, and stuttered to a halt.

"Hold your fire! Hold your fire!" someone—was that Todd?—shouted.

Staggering, Cliff reached up and found something protruding from his flesh at the nape of his neck. He yanked it out. His balance wavered as he stared down at a tranquilizer dart.

His arm fell to his side. The dart clattered to the floor. He lurched backward a step.

A few feet away, Whetsman moaned.

Cliff sank to his knees.

Finish him off, a drunken voice mumbled in his head.

The warm blood saturating Cliff's clothing cooled beneath a ceiling fan that rotated lazily above him.

He shivered.

All strength deserting him, he collapsed onto his side.

Pain careened through his head when it rebounded off the hard floor.

Blood rattled in his lungs as he struggled to breathe.

The entrance of the building... the door that led outside to sunshine and blessed oblivion... was the last thing Cliff saw before darkness enveloped him.

⋙◦◉◦⋘

Emma's knee bobbed up and down as she stared at her computer screen without seeing it.

Something had happened. Something big. Something bad. She just didn't know what.

An hour ago the network's alarm had begun to *wonk, wonk, wonk,* startling the crap out of her. A male had spoken over the intercom, issuing a shelter in place order. Then a loud rumble had echoed up the elevator shaft.

Screams erupted from the stairwell. Seconds later a few bodies ran past her closed door.

Emma thought she caught the *snicks* of suppressed gunfire and broke out in a cold sweat.

Were mercenaries attacking again?

Fearing the worst, she ducked under her desk and exchanged her pumps for the running shoes she always kept on hand now. Then she waited, heart pounding in her chest, hands shaking.

The alarm ceased blaring.

Mr. Reordon's voice came over the intercom. "Attention, all personnel. Thank you for your patience and cooperation. A security breach took place that required our immediate attention. It has now been resolved. The threat has been neutralized. And all is well. You no longer need to shelter in place. Be advised, however, that as a purely precautionary measure, the building will temporarily remain on lockdown. I will notify you as soon as the lockdown is lifted."

What the hell had happened? He'd said nothing in the hour since, so she assumed they were still on lockdown.

Emma tried and failed to concentrate on the task at hand.

When knuckles suddenly rapped on her door, she jumped about a foot. "Come in."

Cynthia poked her head in, her face somber. After glancing over her shoulder, she ducked inside, closed the door, and crossed to seat herself in the chair on the other side of the desk.

The grim look on her friend's face made everything within Emma go still. Her knee stopped bobbing. For a moment she even forgot to breathe. "What is it?" she asked, unable to bear the silence.

"Todd just texted me."

"What happened? Did mercenaries attack? Is Todd okay?"

"It wasn't mercenaries. And he's okay. He wasn't injured. But, honey…" She bit her lip and shook her head.

"What?" Emma prodded, so tense she wanted to scream.

"Todd said Cliff had a psychotic break."

Alarm set Emma's heart to pounding. She gripped the edge of her desk, holding on so tight it was a wonder her blunt fingernails didn't score the wood. "Is he…?"

"He isn't dead," Cynthia told her. "But it was a bad one. He attacked one of the doctors."

Oh no. "Was it Dr. Lipton?"

"No." Her brow furrowed. "I think his name started with a *W*."

Whetsman. Anger rose. That bastard was *always* antagonizing Cliff.

"Apparently Cliff really tore into him. I mean, he beat the shit out of him. And the guards had to shoot Cliff multiple times to get him to let the doctor go. Todd said he might have brain damage."

Tears blurred Emma's vision, then trailed down her cheeks when she blinked. "Cliff?"

"No. Whetsman." Cynthia shook her head, her features full of regret as sympathetic tears welled in her eyes. "Todd said Cliff was crazed, Emma. That he also injured some guards." Every word cut like a knife. "A *lot* of them. They had to sedate him to... to bring him under control again and keep him from killing the doctor. A few of them were so angry that..."

"What?" Emma said, her voice thick. "Tell me all of it."

"They wanted to shove him out into the sun."

Her chest hitched with a sob.

"But they didn't!" Cynthia blurted hastily. "They didn't, Emma. Todd wouldn't let them. Neither would Mr. Reordon."

"Where is he?"

"Cliff?"

Nodding, Emma opened a drawer and fumbled for a tissue to dab her eyes.

Again Cynthia bit her lip. "They chained him up in a holding room and are waiting for Seth to arrive."

To heal him or to execute him?

That question coupled with the image of Cliff chained down, unconscious and bleeding in some cold cell, tore great gasping sobs from Emma's chest. Folding over, she buried her face in her hands.

"Oh honey." Cynthia hurried around the desk, wrapped her arms around Emma, and hugged her close. "I'm so sorry. I know how much you care for him."

But she didn't. Cynthia thought Emma loved Cliff from afar, like a shy teenager with a crush on the high school quarterback. She didn't know the two of them had been meeting in secret. That they spent hours together every night. That Emma had kissed him. Made love with him. Learned every aspect of his personality and constantly craved his company. Cynthia didn't know that Emma had laughed with him. Teased him. Enjoyed long, relaxing bubble baths with him. Lost herself in passionate encounters in the shower. Held him while they talked for hours and kept the voices at bay.

She couldn't lose him. It was too soon. She wasn't ready.

She would *never* be ready.

But she could do nothing to stop Seth from taking him from her. Or Reordon. Or Bastien who — despite his love for Cliff or perhaps because of it — would take Cliff's life in a heartbeat if he thought it would end his friend's suffering.

Emma couldn't even tell Cliff goodbye because she wasn't allowed on sublevel 5.

More sobs rocked her as Cynthia tightened her hold and stroked her hair.

Chapter Seventeen

A BREEZE COOLED CLIFF'S WARM skin as four vampires shriveled up at his feet.

Bending down, he used the shirttail of one to wipe the blood from his blades before he slid them into their respective sheaths.

"Any wounds I should know about?" Bastien asked.

Cliff shook his head. "You?"

"No."

He didn't have to look to know his friend's gaze followed his every move as Cliff collected the fallen vampires' weapons.

Almost a week had passed since he'd fucked up Whetsman so much that the man had suffered traumatic brain damage even Seth couldn't reverse. Cliff had no memory of it. He remembered being with Emma the night before, then… nothing… until he woke up in the infirmary with Bastien, Melanie, and Linda hovering over him while the German immortal Alleck loitered nearby.

Apparently Whetsman had been mind controlled by Gershom into stealing vials of the sedative that could be used to knock out Immortal Guardians. Linda had thought his behavior in the lab odd, noticed some vials were missing, and followed Whetsman out to his SUV to ask him about them. When she confronted him, Whetsman shot her with a 9mm equipped with a suppressor Gershom must have given him and left her to bleed out in his back seat while everyone inside remained unaware.

According to what everyone had been able to piece together, Cliff had been restlessly prowling sublevel 5 when he noticed specks of blood that smelled of Linda on Whetsman and went medieval on his ass. No one had known what had instigated the attack, however, until Seth scrutinized Cliff's thoughts.

Cliff couldn't bring himself to overly regret hurting Whetsman. The bastard had almost killed Linda. But the guards...

The constant acidic burn in his belly worsened.

He'd injured *so* many men in his blind determination to get to Whetsman. Guards on sublevel 5 who had previously been friendly and shot the breeze with him now tensed at his appearance and watched him warily. At Cliff's request, Reordon had shown him footage of it, from the time Cliff had left his apartment until the second he'd collapsed in the lobby, where Todd and John had had to restrain some of the guards topside to keep them from shoving his unconscious form out into the sunlight.

Cliff thought the guards had been more than justified in calling for his death. But surprisingly Reordon had disagreed and had torn into the men when he'd arrived on the scene.

It had come as quite a shock. Reordon was very protective of those who worked for him. Cliff would've thought he'd be calling for his head after seeing the damage Cliff had wrought. But he hadn't. Reordon had even allowed Bastien to resume taking Cliff hunting, though he'd put an end to Cliff's eating lunch on sublevel 1.

"I hate to do it," he'd told Cliff in the privacy of his soundproof boardroom, "but there were some civilians in the stairwell you stormed up—"

"I didn't hurt any, did I?" Cliff had asked with alarm.

"No. You just scared the hell out of them. And I can't chance your having a psychotic break like that on sublevel 1. Dealing with that isn't part of the civilians' job description. The guards, on the other hand, all know their position is dangerous. They know what they've signed up for. They're aware of the risks. And they agreed to take them. That's why I reassigned the guards who wanted to roast you to desk jobs at another location that will bore the pants off them."

"I injured some of their colleagues."

"And they knew that could happen. What they did was the equivalent of someone signing up to work at a mental health facility that cares for patients with psychological disorders that cause violent tendencies, then beating the shit out of the patients if they become violent. It was bullshit."

Cliff hadn't really thought about it like that. Turning to Bastien now, he held up the weapons he'd collected. "What do you want me to do with these? This dagger isn't bad, but the rest are crap."

Bastien produced a bag for the weapons and personal belongings of the vampires. Since the two of them had caught the vampires *before* they could pounce on the unsuspecting women they stalked, there were no mortal victims that would necessitate a cleanup crew tonight.

Once he tucked the weapons in the bag, Cliff bent to collect the wallets and clothing that remained after the vamps finished disintegrating.

He hadn't seen Emma since his break. No access to sublevel 1 meant no lunches with her. And since Bastien had resumed taking him hunting two nights ago, Cliff had remained with him the entire time instead of roaming alone.

As soon as they finished tidying the battle scene, they headed back to Melanie's car.

"You want some time to yourself tonight?" Bastien asked casually as he tossed the bag in the back seat.

"No, thanks."

"You sure? I brought the duffel with a change of clothes."

"No. I'm good."

Bastien slammed the door shut and stood staring at it for a long moment. A long sigh escaped him. "That's bollocks."

"What?"

Lips tightening, Bastien rounded on him. "I said that's bollocks. How long are you going to keep beating yourself up about this, Cliff?"

He stiffened. "I killed Whetsman."

"No, you didn't. *Seth* killed him."

"After I brain damaged him beyond repair."

"He fatally wounded Linda and left her bleeding to death in his car," Bastien said, his voice rising. "I would've done the same damn thing to him. Hell, Melanie probably would have, too." Cliff seriously doubted that. "And if she didn't, Alleck sure as hell would have."

Frustration rose. What did Bastien expect him to do, just brush it off as if he'd accidentally tripped someone? "He only did it because Gershom mind controlled him. And what about the guards?" He glared. "Did you forget about *them*? How many guards did I hurt, Bastien? How many fingers did I break when I yanked their weapons out of their hands with preternatural speed and strength? How many arms did I snap and legs did I shatter trying to get past them to Whetsman? How many concussions did I give them?"

Bastien made a scoffing sound. "How many guards did *I* give concussions and how many arms did *I* break when I forced my way into network headquarters after they refused to let me see Vince when he was suffering? Do you think I lie awake, agonizing over that?"

"This is different."

"No, it isn't."

"Yes it is!" Cliff shouted. "Because *you* know you won't do it again, and *I* know I will! And I'll do it *again* and *again* and *again* until someone puts me down like a rabid dog!"

Silence fell.

Cliff began to pace slowly, forcing back the violent impulses that threatened to rise again, tamping down the voices that urged him to fly into another full-blown rage.

Bastien drew a hand down his face and let out a long weary breath. "Well, fuck."

Exactly.

"Technically speaking," his friend mused, voice calm now, "I *don't* know that I won't do it again because some of those guys at the network still chap my ass."

A laugh caught Cliff by surprise.

"Honestly, the only one who doesn't is Todd."

"Yeah. He's a good guy." And the only one who didn't walk on eggshells around Cliff now.

"So... what?" Bastien asked. "You're going to punish yourself for something you neither asked for nor have any control over by denying yourself the only happiness you've found since transforming?"

Cliff shot him a look. "I didn't say I wanted to stop hunting."

"I'm not talking about the hunting."

His pacing ground to a halt. Cliff turned to face him. Surely he didn't mean…

Bastien shrugged. "I know about Emma."

Of course he did. Cliff slid the car a look, thinking of the duffel bag packed with clean clothes and hand wipes. The cash Bastien had forked over. "How long have you known about her?"

"Since the first night you went to see her." Crossing his arms over his chest, Bastien leaned back against the car. "When you started roaming around on your own, infiltrating vampire groups and pumping them for information, I was afraid you'd pull some superhero martyr bullshit and get yourself killed, so I followed you and stayed downwind, ready to jump in if you needed me."

Yep. That sounded like something Bastien would do. He wasn't the coldhearted bastard so many Immortal Guardians painted him.

"Once I saw you with Emma, I stopped worrying. Because I knew you had something to live for. Something precious. Something so rare it took me two damn centuries to find it for myself."

The love he and Emma shared *was* precious. "Does Reordon know?"

"About you and Emma? No. I'm sure he would've put a stop to it if he did. Like Seth and his Immortal Guardians, Reordon tends to be *very* protective of the females who work for him. Even more so if they're *gifted ones*."

Which only lent credence to Cliff's own assumptions about the network head.

Straightening, Bastien reached beneath his coat and withdrew something from a back pocket. "Here."

Cliff crossed to him and took it. It was a jump drive. "What is it?"

"Footage of what happened. All of it."

"I've already seen it. Reordon showed it to me."

Bastien tapped the drive. "This isn't for you. It's for Emma. She's heard snippets of what happened. *Everyone* at the network has. And I'm sure your absence is scaring her. You should go to her."

Cliff held up the device. "You don't think this will scare her more?"

"No, I don't. Any woman smart enough and strong enough to love you isn't going to run screaming from footage of you beating the shit out of an asshole who tried to murder someone you care about. *You* are the sole reason Linda is alive today. Had you not confronted Whetsman when you did, she would've died in the back of his SUV without anyone the wiser. Zach said she was mere minutes away from death when he healed her." He rubbed his jaw. "Aaaaaaand, full disclosure, Melanie had a talk with Emma quite a while back and laid out everything she could expect if she chose to have a relationship with you."

Cliff supposed some might resent their interference, but he chose to appreciate it. "I did, too."

"I knew you would. Just like I knew you wouldn't continue seeing her unless she fully understood what happened with Whetsman and the others."

Cliff curled his fingers into a fist around the drive. "I love her."

"I know you do. That's why I couldn't stand to watch you keep torturing yourself—torturing *both* of you—by staying away from her. So go. Don't worry about infiltrating other vampire ranks. We're done with that. From now on, as soon as we finish hunting, you can head straight for Emma's place."

If Emma still wanted to see him after this. "Could I get that duffel bag?"

Bastien smiled. "Yeah."

Chapter Eighteen

E MMA SNIPPED A DANGLING PIECE of yarn, then held up her latest creation.

The soft winter hat was sprinkled with every color of the rainbow and sported a cheerful pom-pom on top. "Cute."

Leaning over the sofa arm, she dropped it atop the growing pile of similar hats that would soon fill the cardboard bankers box she'd bought to contain them. A week had passed since Cliff's psychotic break. Tales of it still circulated the building and whispered through the cafeteria Cliff no longer visited.

Cynthia gave Emma daily updates, courtesy of Todd, in the soundproof restroom after ensuring they were alone. If she hadn't, Emma wouldn't have known that Mr. Reordon had banned Cliff from having lunch in sublevel 1 and was once more restricting him to sublevel 5.

Had he also banned him from hunting with Bastien? Or from roaming alone?

Because Cliff hadn't visited her once since his break.

At least half a dozen times she had picked up the phone to call Melanie or Bastien. But she wasn't sure she wanted to hear what they'd say. According to Todd, Cliff was struggling and having a hard time coming to terms with what he did.

Emma couldn't stop thinking about the guards who'd wanted to shove Cliff out into the sunlight while he was sedated. Knowing just how close she had come to losing him terrified her. And she had feared those guards might seek retribution until Cynthia told her Mr. Reordon had been furious over their actions and had either fired or transferred every single guard who'd called for Cliff's death.

Slumped on the sofa in a tank top and pajama bottoms, Emma rubbed tired, gritty eyes.

She hadn't been sleeping. Even though exhaustion shadowed her, she was too tense to nap in the evening as had become her habit. And she'd been staying up late at night, hoping Cliff would show up, ring the new doorbell he'd helped her install a few months ago, and sweep her into his arms as soon as she opened the door.

Sighing, she glanced at the bag full of yarn at her feet.

Like Cliff, she had discovered that occupying her hands helped reduce the restlessness that plagued her, so she'd dug out the loom and gone to work. She'd made dozens of the damn hats so far but didn't stop. Once the box was full, she figured she'd pick out a few to send to her parents, her brother and his wife, and her two nephews, all of whom lived in Michigan. The rest she would donate to a homeless shelter.

Something thumped on the front porch.

Jumping, she twisted around to stare at the door. Her heart began to beat a little faster, not with fear this time but with hope.

The doorbell rang.

Tossing the loom on the table she jumped up, tripped on some of the tangled yarn, and lunged for the door. Though she wanted to open it as soon as she reached it, common sense forced her to pause long enough to look through the peephole.

Relief rushed through her.

Her hands shook as she fumbled with the locks and yanked the door open.

Cliff stared down at her, garbed all in black, his handsome face somber.

Breath hitching, she threw herself against him and hugged him so hard she knocked him back a step.

Swiftly regaining his balance, he wrapped his arms around her and rested his chin on her head while he let her squeeze the stuffing out of him.

"Are you okay?" she murmured.

A moment passed. "Yeah," he said softly. But he wasn't. She could hear it in his voice.

It only made her hold him tighter. "If you want to come in, you're going to have to carry me, because I'm not letting go for at least five minutes."

A rusty chuckle rumbled beneath the ear she'd pressed to his chest. Then he lifted her a few inches so her feet dangled loosely above the wood slats of the porch. Pressing a kiss to her hair, he strode inside and nudged the door closed behind them.

True to her promise, Emma didn't let go of him for at least five minutes.

Cliff didn't object. He merely continued to hold her and seemed willing to do so for as long as she needed it.

At last she loosened her grip.

Cliff gently lowered her feet to the floor and released her.

Tilting her head back, Emma cupped his face in both hands and studied him.

On the surface, he looked good. Hale, hearty, and drop-dead gorgeous.

But his dark brown eyes were haunted.

"Do you want to talk about it?" she asked softly. If he didn't, she wouldn't press him.

A sad smile tilted his lips as he drew a hand over her hair, which remained in the lovely braids he'd fashioned for her shortly before his break. "You're too damn selfless."

She arched a brow. "Because I'd rather hold you and cop a feel than jibber-jabber?"

He laughed, his eyes crinkling with genuine amusement that warmed her heart. "Or maybe you aren't."

Wrapping her arms around his waist in a loose embrace, she leaned into him. "I was worried about you."

Looping his around her waist, he linked his hands at the base of her spine and lowered his forehead to hers. "I know." A weary sigh soughed past his lips. "You're the best thing in my life, Emma. The absolute best. But in a way, that makes dealing with these psychotic breaks even harder." His forehead rocked against hers. "Every time I lose control, I am damn near paralyzed with fear afterward, wondering how you're going to react to it."

She shrugged. "By loving you."

A faint amber glow lit his eyes but failed to conceal the very fear he spoke of. She could read it clearly and knew he was afraid to believe that.

"Tell me what happened," she encouraged him gently.

Releasing her, Cliff backed away a step and drew something small out of one of his pockets. "Here." He pressed it into her palm.

Emma stared down at the unadorned jump drive. "What is it?"

"Surveillance footage."

Her heart sank.

"I want you to see it for yourself."

"Cliff—"

"I *need* you to see it for yourself."

Swallowing hard, she nodded and led him over to the sofa.

Cliff said nothing as she shoved the knitting paraphernalia aside to make room for him. Though he glanced at it curiously, Emma offered no explanation. She was too nervous.

Face grim, he sank down on the cushion beside her and waited patiently for her to open her laptop and insert the drive.

It only bore one file.

Vowing to keep all expression from her face, Emma opened it and let the video play.

The hallway down on what she assumed was sublevel 5 filled the screen. It wasn't all that different from the one on her floor if she discounted the heavy-as-hell doors that secured the vampires' apartments. Cliff emerged from one such apartment. Clearly agitated, he headed up the hallway.

"Where were you going?" she asked, voice muted.

"I was looking for Doc Linda. I was going to ask her to give me a milder dose of the sedative so I could sleep, but I couldn't find her."

A man who was about Emma's height and a little on the portly side exited the elevator and walked toward Cliff. "Is that Dr. Whetsman?"

"Yeah. I'm about to ask him if he's seen Linda. He lied and said he hadn't, but I caught her scent on him and saw blood on his sleeve."

In the video, Cliff grabbed the man's arm and brought it close to his face.

"What are you doing?"

"Confirming it's her blood."

Oh shit. Cliff's eyes flashed bright amber as he attacked the man. Violence erupted in the hallway.

It was hard to watch. Not so much the Whetsman part, because he had hurt Linda. And Linda had been good to Cliff. But the rest…

Cliff was such a sweet, gentle soul, more prone to laughter than to anger. To see him snarl and tear through those guards with such fury and ferocity…

And they shot him soooo many times.

It took every ounce of control to keep her eyes dry and her expression blank.

On the screen, Cliff attacked Whetsman again in the network's lobby, then dropped to his knees and collapsed.

The sofa cushion beneath her sank a little as Cliff moved to halt the video, but Emma stayed his hand. "Let it finish."

Todd, bless him, was shouting at some guards who had made a move toward Cliff's unconscious form. John, the brother in charge of security on the ground floor, joined him and helped Todd hold the others back.

Then Mr. Reordon skidded around the corner with a semiautomatic rifle in his hand and ran up to them with three more guards.

"Do you know what they were arguing about?" she asked. Had anyone told him?

"Yeah. Some of the guards wanted to shove me out into the sunlight because I'd injured so many of them."

"And Mr. Reordon wouldn't let them."

"No."

"Neither would Todd or John or that guy there or that one." At last she met his gaze. "Because they know what *I* know—that you're a good man, Cliff, who's worth saving. And they haven't given up on you." She stroked his tight jaw. "I haven't either. And I never will. I love you."

His Adam's apple bobbed in a swallow. "You can still say that after watching me injure so many?"

"Yes."

"And you can say that knowing I'm going to do it again?"

She shook her head. "You aren't going to do it again."

When he opened his mouth to protest, she touched a finger to his lips.

"You've had other psychotic breaks. Did you hurt anyone while you were in the grips of them?"

"I hurt Stuart once."

"A fellow vampire who healed within minutes and didn't hold it against you." Cliff had told her about that. "Did you harm any humans? Or *gifted ones*? Did you attack any of the guards?"

"No."

"These were extenuating circumstances, honey. You thought Whetsman had killed Linda, your friend. If I thought Whetsman had killed Cynthia, I would've fucked him up, too."

Reaching up, he clasped her hand and pressed her palm to his lips. He closed his eyes as he kissed it, then just held it there. "I don't want that to be who I am," he murmured despondently.

"That *isn't* who you are."

Opening his eyes, he lowered their clasped hands to his thigh. "It's just going to get worse, Emma. You know it is."

Leaning in close, she held his gaze. "If it does, we'll face it together."

He shook his head. "This isn't the life I want for you. Always waiting for the next outburst, the next psychotic break. Watching me lose every bit of myself that you fell in love with."

"That isn't going to happen."

"Emma," he said, his expression tortured, "you *have* to face the reality of my future. I've been with the network for almost four years. They were studying the virus and seeking a cure long before they found me. And they've made no progress since then beyond finding a sedative that can knock me out. The chances of us having a happy ending together are infinitesimally small."

She swallowed hard, everything within her rebelling against his forecast. "I'll take those chances if it means I'll have more time with you." When he would've spoken—another protest no doubt—she again touched his lips. "If it were me, would you walk away?"

He recoiled slightly as though appalled by the mere thought of it. "What?"

"You heard me. If I was the one infected with the vampiric virus and I was the one in the video we just watched, would you walk away?"

He stared at her helplessly. "No."

"Why?"

He exhaled a sigh of defeat. "Because I would want every moment I could have with you."

"Then what would you do instead?"

"Fight like hell to keep you sane."

"Exactly." Moving over, she settled herself sideways on his lap and pulled his arms around her. "You're strong, Cliff." She held out an arm, flexed her biceps in an exaggerated show of muscle, and arched a brow. "I'm strong, too."

His expression lightened. "Yes, you are."

"Together, we can do anything. We can fight this. We can *beat* this. Even though you may think it's futile, we have to give Melanie and the other doctors more time." She pressed a tender kiss to his lips. "I know it's hard, honey, and that things may get worse. But I'll be here to help you through it. All of it." She kissed him again. "I'm not going anywhere."

Those eyes of his brightened further as he dipped his head and claimed her lips in a longer, deeper kiss.

Heat swept through her as his tongue met hers, stroking and teasing.

The fear that had plagued her all week fell victim to the need to feel him against her, to assure herself he was still here, that he was still hers.

Shifting, she straddled his lap.

I thought I'd lost you, she wanted to say but didn't, knowing it would merely spawn more guilt. "Cliff," she said instead, "I need you."

"I need you, too," he uttered, voice gravelly with desire. Clamping his hands on her ass, he rose. A breeze buffeted her as he sped to the bedroom and lowered her to her feet. He blurred. The sound of cloth tearing filled the room as she felt a tug.

When Emma glanced down, she discovered she was naked with her clothes scattered on the floor around her. Looking up, she met his burning gaze. "Hell yes. Now do you."

He was bare in seconds, and together they tumbled to the bed. His touch was rough, carrying a hint of desperation that matched her own. But it only made her want him more as she writhed against him, hands exploring. She moaned and urged him on, just wanting him to fill her. But Cliff made her wait while he stroked and teased her until her breath came in short gasps and she balanced on the precipice. Then he plunged inside, his long hard length stretching her and eliciting moans of pleasure as he drove deep, again and again, his luminous amber eyes catching and holding hers until she threw her head back and cried out in ecstasy.

Cliff growled as he came hard, pouring his heat inside her.

Their harsh breaths filled the silence as he braced himself on his elbows, burrowed his arms beneath her, and hugged her close for many long minutes.

Then he made love to her again, their coming together slower, gentler, and full of affection as they took their time exploring each other anew.

When at last they rolled to their sides, his face was once more relaxed, his expression full of love rather than fear and dread. And his beautiful eyes had lost that haunted look.

Emma cupped his strong jaw. "Always?"

His pressed a kiss to her lips, achingly tender. "Always."

<hr />

Cliff continued to hunt with Bastien. He also resumed seeing Emma every night.

Or *almost* every night. As they both had known, the psychotic break he experienced the day Whetsman shot Linda was not his last. More seized him in the months that followed. Sometimes he recognized how close he was to having one and asked Melanie or Linda to sedate him. Sometimes they struck without warning. Either way, Emma didn't see him on those nights because he ended up tranqed.

But Cliff was surrounded by friends who loved him at the network. Melanie and Bastien. Linda. Aidan, a Celtic immortal who practically lived there now. Stuart. Miguel. The other vampires, who began having psychotic breaks of their own. And they all kept Cliff from hurting any mortals in his vicinity... or himself, which helped him recover faster so only one or two nights would pass without her seeing him.

Though his love for Emma only seemed to deepen — as hers did for him — he smiled less and less when they were together.

"Take heart, Emma," Bastien told her on one of his rare visits. "When Cliff isn't with you, he doesn't smile at all."

She took no comfort in the knowledge. She wanted Cliff to be happy. She missed his smiles and treasured all the more each one she was able to coax forth. Every laugh, too. Those were few and far between now. But she knew he still drew solace from her company and the affection she offered him.

Some days that and his desperate desire for a future with her seemed to be all that held him together. The voices in his head grew louder. So loud that when the two of them sank onto her sofa and watched movies together, his muscles never completely relaxed. When he held her, she could feel the tension thrumming through him. And he'd stare at the screen as though some other movie were playing in his head. A muscle would twitch in his jaw while he clenched and unclenched his teeth. His eyes would begin to glow.

The first time he erupted in anger around her, they were watching a sci-fi flick. She couldn't say whether it was a good one or a bad one. She only half paid attention to it because worry coursed through her. Cliff was tense. More so than usual. Instead of relaxing back against the cushions and tucking her up against his side with an arm around her shoulders, he leaned forward with his elbows on his knees, twisting his dreadlocks. Every once in a while he shook his head a little as though he were silently arguing with someone and disagreed with whatever he or she said. His eyes began to glow, creases forming at their corners as he squinted them ominously.

Lips tightening, he lowered his hands and let them dangle between his knees. His fingers curled into fists. The muscles in his biceps and forearms flexed and jumped. His eyes brightened.

"Shut up!" he bellowed suddenly, so loud they could probably hear him in the next county.

Emma just about jumped out of her skin.

"Shut up! Shut the fuck up! That *isn't* who I am! That is *not* who I am!"

She stared at him, pulse racing, heart aching for him as it slammed against her rib cage.

Cliff glared at the coffee table a long moment, muscles coiled so tight she thought he might spring to his feet and start punching the walls. Then his fists unclenched. His eyes widened as he sucked in a breath. Swiveling to face her, he gave her a look of such agonizing dismay. And she knew it was because he could hear the frantic beating of her heart.

Emma couldn't bear it. He was already fighting asshole voices in his head. She wouldn't let him kick himself for startling her, too.

Sitting up straighter, she gave him a decisive nod. "Damn straight. You tell 'em, honey. Give those voices hell."

Cliff blinked, a look of surprise sweeping over his face, so comical that despite the gravity of the situation, she couldn't keep her lips from twitching.

A big, beautiful grin banished the darkness in his features.

Emma so rarely saw that expression on his beloved face anymore that she drank it in like water in a desert.

Shaking his head, Cliff drew her onto his lap and claimed a kiss. "I love you so much."

She smiled back and tapped his forehead. "You're just saying that because I'm so good in bed, I shut those fuckers up."

He laughed. And the sound of it made her so happy you'd think she'd just won the lotto. "You aren't good in bed. You're *fantastic*." He kissed her again and arched a brow. "Speaking of which..."

Looping her arms around his neck, she rubbed noses with him. "Want to go see just how quiet those voices can get?"

"Hell yes." Rising with her in his arms, he carried her to the bedroom.

Chapter Nineteen

C LIFF BRACED HIS ELBOWS ON his knees, dropped his head into his hands, and closed his eyes. Tension thrummed through him as the voices in his head called for him to commit grisly acts of violence, their cries relentless. It took every ounce of strength he had to refrain from acting upon them.

Roughly a year had passed since he'd attacked Whetsman. And the growls and snarls in his head did their damnedest to deafen him now, the impulses they sparked overpowering.

The only time he ever slept was when he was sedated or when he held Emma in his arms. The sun had not even reached its zenith today, yet Cliff had to fight like hell to remain in control. He wouldn't be able to hunt with Bastien again until sunset. How could he possibly hold out that long?

Loosing a growl, he slid his fingers into his dreadlocks and strained to hear Emma's voice up on sublevel 1. There had been times in the past when just listening to her shoot the breeze with Cynthia, banter with Sadie, or hum under her breath while she worked had helped. The thunderous demands screeching through his head, however, had reached such levels that he could barely even hear the goings-on in sublevel four.

He curled his fingers into fists, the tugs on his hair punishing. Gratifying.

He had waited too long. He was terrifyingly close to losing himself entirely. There were still fractured pieces of him in there, remnants of the Cliff he saw in the photos Emma had snapped, but the twisted monster rising within him seemed to devour more of them every day.

He *never* wanted Emma to see that monster.

He would die first.

The past few months, he had poured himself into helping her remodel the rest of her home. He had retiled her bathroom, painted the cabinets, and installed new faucets. He'd replaced most of the light fixtures throughout the house and — much to her relief upon learning he had no actual experience with such — *hadn't* discovered what electrocution would do to a vampire. He'd sanded and painted her kitchen cabinets. Restained her wood floor.

Emma thought he did it because working with his hands distracted him from the war perpetually raging in his head. And the distractions did help. But he *really* did it because…

Well. He did it for the same reason a man whose doctor had told him he only had a few months to live might. He was getting his affairs in order, taking care of things now that he knew he wouldn't be around to do later. Emma loved that house. Cliff did, too. It felt like home to him now. She *made* it feel like home to him. A home he had fantasized about filling with decades of love and laughter. Boisterous children and barking dogs.

She'd told him how she intended to fix it up, all the changes she'd like to make when both time and her budget allowed. She'd even asked for his input and suggestions, still clinging to the hope that they would have their happily-ever-after together.

And the more she'd included him in her plans, the more Cliff had wanted to make those changes for her himself. *He* wanted to be the one to transform her house into her dream home. He *needed* to be the one to transform her house into her dream home, to leave her that tangible evidence that he was more than what the madness was making of him, to give her something good to take away from their last months together. When she opened a cabinet in her sleek kitchen a year from now, he wanted her to remember him smiling over her singing off-key while they bobbed their heads to music and installed the new hardware. Not him destroying romantic dinners by bellowing at people who didn't really exist but wouldn't stop yammering in his fucking head. And an infusion of funds from Bastien had helped him pursue that goal.

He'd been reluctant to take the money at first.

"Why?" Bastien had asked. "Everyone who hunts vampires is supposed to be on the network's payroll. Just consider me the middleman. Reordon pays *me* to hunt. Then I pay *you* to do the hunting *for* me so I can sit back, relax, and think up new things to try with Melanie the next time I get her naked."

Cliff didn't so much do the hunting as the killing, but Bastien's argument had made enough sense for him to accept the funds. Because it enabled him to accomplish what he needed to.

Cliff knew how hard all this was on Emma. Yet she offered not a single complaint. She didn't grow short-tempered or weary of his sudden angry outbursts, none of which he directed at her. Nor of the creepy way he would mutter to himself, engage in snarled one-person arguments, and pace when agitated. Nor of the way he would sometimes pounce on her as soon as she opened the door, tear her clothes off, and take her rougher than he intended in a desperate bid to shut out the damn voices.

Remorse would always sour his stomach afterward. Some nights he didn't even say hello first. He had even left faint bruises on her where he had gripped her too tightly and had panicked... until he harkened back to a conversation he'd overheard Melanie and Linda having once in which they had laughed about their immortal lovers leaving the same marks on them.

That alleviated some of the fear. Emma, as usual, dispatched the rest.

"You weren't too rough," she'd mutter sleepily. "You gave me three orgasms, honey. You think I'm going to complain about that?"

But he knew she must miss the gentler, playful couplings they'd shared in their early months together.

Cliff tried so hard to balance the bad with some good.

When he was gone, he wanted Emma to only remember that man in the pictures. The one who had saved her life the morning mercenaries had attacked. The one who treasured even the most mundane moments with her.

The man who loved her.

If he didn't end it soon...

He tugged harder on his hair and shook his head.

What if she saw the monster that grew inside him?

If he didn't end it soon, how would that monster manifest itself to her?

He never, *ever* wanted to frighten Emma, let alone harm her. And while he'd never had such impulses around her before...

No. He couldn't bear to think it. Melanie seemed sure Cliff would never harm Emma. Cliff would like to think the same. The violent impulses he constantly battled had certainly never focused on her. But the words his father had spoken to him shortly before Cliff went away to college came back to him again and again:

"Whenever you're contemplating an action that comes with even minimal risk, son, ask yourself this question: Is it a gamble you can afford to lose?"

This was not minimal risk.

And this was *not* a gamble he could afford to lose.

He would *not* let the madness win. And there was only one way he knew of to ensure it wouldn't.

Melanie and Bastien would take it hard. Melanie would blame herself for failing to find a cure in time or a way to reverse the brain damage. Bastien would stoically deliver the death blow if Cliff asked him to, no matter how much it ate him up inside. But that wouldn't stop either of them from offering Emma whatever support she'd need once he was gone. He knew he could count on them for that. Todd and Cynthia would be there for her, too.

Cliff ground his teeth as the voices howled in his head, rejecting his intention to eradicate them.

Emitting a bestial growl, he pulled at his dreads.

Light thuds reached his ears.

A deep voice with a Scottish accent spoke. "It's Aidan. I'm coming in."

Aidan had landed himself in hot water a couple of years ago by breaking into network headquarters, bypassing their security protocols, and altering the memories of multiple guards and employees so he could obtain a list of *gifted ones* he hoped might lead him to a woman who could love him and alleviate the roughly three thousand years of loneliness he'd experienced.

Once he'd gotten back into Seth's good graces (Reordon still held a gargantuan grudge), Aidan had befriended Cliff and asked him to assist him in his quest to find love. Cliff had been shocked speechless, something that had made the ancient immortal burst out laughing. But the peculiar request *had* made sense. Cliff had resided at the network for over three years when Aidan came to him. And he'd spent much of that time listening to the lives of the employees play out like a massive soap opera. Who better to help him sift through the list of *gifted ones* from the network's employee roster and select those who might be amenable to the Celt's approach?

Cliff didn't think he'd be up to the task today, but he was desperate for a distraction.

The lock on the heavy door clunked. Clinging to control by his fingertips, he didn't look up as Aidan entered.

The ancient immortal closed the door, then sat down beside him. Aidan had been born with several astonishing gifts, one of which was telepathy. It shamed Cliff to know that Aidan could hear the vile demands of the voices and see the horrific images that flickered through his mind like loathsome subliminal messages.

Aidan never blamed him though, or disparaged him. Having glimpsed what transpired in Cliff's fractured mind—the things Bastien and Melanie could only guess at—Aidan actually seemed to respect Cliff and hold him in high esteem for being strong enough to reject it.

His big hand clasped Cliff's shoulder. "Do you trust me?" he asked softly.

"Yes," Cliff whispered, trying hard to modulate his tone and resist the urge to shout over the noise only *he* heard.

"Stand up," Aidan ordered.

Lowering his clenched fists, Cliff did so and focused on his friend.

"Don't be afraid," Aidan murmured.

Before Cliff could respond, a feeling of weightlessness engulfed him as darkness replaced his apartment.

In the next breath, blindingly bright light bathed him. Not indoor lights, but…

Oh shit.

Sunlight.

Cliff tensed.

Aidan's fingers tightened on his shoulder, preventing him from bolting for the trees nearby. "Don't."

Panic flooding him, Cliff threw up his hands to shield his face and gritted his teeth against the pain he knew would come. The violent voices in his head shrieked and wailed.

A moment passed.

Agony failed to surface. Flaming pain did not sear his skin. His eyes hurt a little from the brightness, driving him to squint. But other than that...

Nothing.

Slowly lowering his hands, Cliff stared down at his exposed arms.

His smooth brown skin remained healthy. No blisters formed. No pain struck.

The heartbeat that had begun to slow picked up once more as he looked up at Aidan with wide eyes. "How is this possible? Am I hallucinating? Is this...? Am I having another psychotic break?" If he was, he hated to admit it but he hoped it would last a little longer. He'd been a vampire and only ventured out at night for so long that he no longer even dreamed of being in the sun.

"No." Aidan smiled. "I can heal with my hands and am using my gift to heal the damage the sun is doing in real time."

Astonishment rippled through him. "You can do that?" He'd never heard of such a thing.

Aidan nodded. "I wasn't sure I could until I tried it with Ethan. I can't say he was very pleased about being my guinea pig, but he owed me."

A little huff of laughter escaped Cliff. "Well, you *did* transform his wife for him so she'd be superstrong." As the last of his fear drained away, Cliff closed his eyes and tilted his face up to the sky. "It's warm," he murmured with a hint of wonder. "I'd forgotten how warm sunlight can be. That you can feel it on your skin." It even banished the chill contemplating his own demise had spawned.

"With your heightened senses, you feel it a little more now."

A lump rose in Cliff's throat. Even this simple bit of normalcy had been denied him for six long years. When he opened his eyes, he had to blink back moisture. "I never thought I would feel it again. Not unless..."

Not unless he decided to spare Bastien and Melanie by choosing to end things by walking into daylight and letting the sun sear the madness — and his life — away.

Aidan squeezed his shoulder. "Every day you hold out, Cliff, every day you keep fighting, I'll give you this. I'll give you the sun."

Cliff stared at him, stunned speechless, afraid to grasp yet another tenuous thread of hope. "Doesn't it hurt you?"

The Celt shrugged. "It's a mild discomfort at most."

Bullshit. Aidan might be ancient enough to tolerate some sunlight. But Cliff wasn't. As soon as sunlight touched him, he began to sunburn and blister, something that had tipped him off something was seriously wrong after he'd transformed. And the longer Aidan healed him, the more pain the immortal siphoned away from Cliff and into himself.

Yet there he stood, doing just that and promising to repeat the action every day if necessary. "Why would you do that for me?"

"Because you're my friend," he said simply. "My brother. And this is what brothers do for each other."

The two had become good friends since Aidan had transferred to North Carolina.

Cliff now considered Aidan one of his *best* friends. And when Emma's voice surfaced in his mind, asking him if he would do the same if the tables were turned, Cliff nodded. "I *would* do it for you."

After a moment, Aidan arched a brow. "You hear that?"

Cliff cocked his head to one side, listening. "What?"

Aidan grinned. "I think we shocked the voices into silence."

It was true, Cliff realized with amazement. All he heard was birdsong and the rustle of leaves as a breeze passed through the trees.

Cliff laughed, his shoulders loosening with relief. "I think you're right. My mind hasn't been this quiet in a long time." Still smiling, he took in the beautiful scenery. Verdant meadows and forests adorned lovely hills. He drew in a deep breath, reveling in the sweet scents carried to him on the wind. "Where are we?"

"My home in Scotland."

Cliff motioned to the trees around them. "All this land is yours?"

"Yes."

"Wow. You're a lucky man." Happiness suffused him. Standing here with the sunlight bathing his skin and his mind blessedly quiet, he felt more normal and at peace than he had since his early months with Emma.

Squinting his eyes, he sent Aidan a sly glance. "Are you sure you aren't just trying to keep me alive longer so I can help you find a wife?"

Aidan laughed. "You've caught me. That's exactly why."

"Any luck yet?" A hawk floated above them on the breeze, capturing Cliff's attention. How wonderful was it to be able to observe the majestic bird without voices clamoring for him to butcher it, slowly and painfully?

Aidan shrugged. "I met Veronica Becker."

"You did?" That surprised him. "I thought you crossed her off the list because she's still mourning her husband." Based on the conversations he'd overheard, Cliff had concluded that Veronica and her husband had loved each other as deeply as he and Emma did. Veronica had taken her husband's death hard.

"I did. But she got a flat tire."

Cliff gave him a pointed stare. Aidan hadn't wanted to approach the women on network premises, where they would instantly know who and what he was. He preferred to arrange casual, *accidental* meetings which—on more than one occasion—had entailed flattening one of their tires on their drive home from work, then *happening by* to help them.

"It wasn't me," Aidan protested.

"Sure it wasn't," Cliff replied drolly.

Aidan laughed. "It truly wasn't, but she thought it was."

That sparked a grin. "Figured it out, did she?" Not surprising. Veronica was brilliant.

"Yes, and kindly suggested I find another MO."

Cliff laughed. "I told you so. North Carolina is like a small town. Word gets around."

"Well, when I didn't show up to change her flat tire, she got out to do it herself and was attacked by vampires."

His amusement vanished, replaced by concern. "Is she okay?"

Aidan nodded. "She's fine. I escorted her and her son home, then went to see Dana Pembroke."

"The psychic?"

"Yes."

"How'd that go?"

"She had a vision of the two of us making love."

Cliff's eyebrows flew up as he smiled. "That's awesome!"

"Aye. And she agreed to go out to dinner with me tonight."

Hot damn! "Do you think Dana's the one?" he asked, happy for his friend.

Aidan shrugged. "I don't know. But I like her."

"And she's psychic and saw you two naked together. Holy hell, that's a good sign."

Aidan grinned. "I hope so."

The hawk's shadow swept across them as it took off after whatever prey had caught its attention.

Cliff soaked in the beauty that surrounded them. "It's weird, the things you take for granted. The things you wouldn't expect to miss much if they were taken away." He wished Emma could be here to experience this with him. "I've always been a night owl." Despite his strict adherence to the early-to-bed, early-to-rise schedule school and work demanded before his transformation, he had always felt more rested during the summer months when he could stay up and sleep later. "So when I realized I couldn't go out in daylight anymore, I didn't think I'd miss it." He drank in the bright light, enjoying the tangible warmth of it on his skin. "But I do. I really do."

"Not anymore," Aidan vowed.

He really did intend to take Cliff out into the sunlight, every day if necessary, to help him fight the madness. And Cliff, curse his selfish hide, would let him, wanting to put off saying goodbye to Emma for as long as he could.

"Listen," he began, thinking of Emma and his concern for her. "There's something I need you to do."

"Name it," Aidan replied without hesitation.

Cliff was so damned fortunate to have friends like him. He really wished he didn't need to do this. He just couldn't accept what might happen if he didn't. "I wouldn't ask," he said. Aidan had done so much for him already. "I had hoped I wouldn't have to. But Bastien can't teleport and—"

"What would you have me do?"

Cliff drew a folded piece of paper from his jeans pocket and held it out. "I need you to go to this address."

Aidan took the paper with his free hand. Flipping it open, he read the numbers and words scrawled across it.

Emma's address. Cliff needed Aidan to provide her with tools she could use to safeguard herself should the madness ever reach the point where Cliff failed to recognize her when he flew into a rage.

As long as he still *saw* her, he steadfastly believed he wouldn't hurt her. But if he didn't... Or if he was wrong...

Aidan nodded. "Consider it done."

Cliff studied him. "You know what I'm asking?"

"Yes."

"I'd ask Richart, but I don't really know him well. And Seth..."

"You'd rather Seth not know, if he doesn't already."

"Yes." Emma was Cliff's lifeline. His reason to keep fighting. If he lost her, he would lose himself. He would lose *everything*.

"I understand." Aidan tucked the paper into his back pocket. "Shall I go tonight?"

"No. It doesn't have to be tonight. I don't want you to cut your date short. Just... soon."

Though Aidan smiled, it didn't reach his eyes. "I'll take care of it."

"You don't have to bring me out in the sun again," Cliff told him. Preventing him from harming the woman he loved meant far more.

"I didn't *have* to bring you out into the sun today," Aidan responded. "I did it because I wanted to. And I'll do it again tomorrow for the same reason. And every day after that as long as you continue to fight."

Cliff wished he had a way to repay him. Sharing what he knew about the names on Aidan's list of female *gifted ones* seemed woefully inadequate. "You're a good man, Aidan."

"So are you, Cliff," his friend said, his voice earnest. "Nothing that happens in the future will ever negate that."

Sorrow filled him. "You don't know how much I want that to be true."

Chapter Twenty

EMMA JERKED AWAKE. DISORIENTED, SHE glanced around and realized she'd fallen asleep while trying to lose herself in an e-book.

Boots thumped on her front steps, as loud as a bass drumbeat in the night's quiet.

She glanced at the clock. It was too early for Cliff to arrive. The sun had barely set, so he probably hadn't even started hunting with Bastien yet.

Hard knocks rocked her door.

Unease shot through her. Cliff didn't knock. He rang the doorbell they'd installed together.

Careful not to make a sound, she padded over to the door in bare feet and peeked through the peephole.

A black shirt and coat blocked her view until the man inside them bent his knees to reduce his height enough for her to see his face.

Oh shit. Her heart began to slam against her ribs.

Aidan O'Byrne, a nearly three-thousand-year-old Immortal Guardian who had pretty much moved into an apartment down on sublevel 5.

What the hell was he doing here?

A full minute passed while she wondered what to do.

A sigh wafted to her ears. "I can hear your heartbeat through the door, so pretending you aren't home isn't going to work, Emma."

She swore. "What do you want?"

"I need to speak with you. Open the door please."

Hell no. Not until she figured out why he was here. But the late nights with Cliff had left her somewhat sleep-deprived, so her mind was sluggish.

Another masculine sigh. "You know who and what I am, so you know no locks can keep me out. I'm asking you as a courtesy."

Well, crap. Emma turned the locks on the door and opened it only enough for her to stand in the gap and speak to him. No way was she inviting him inside.

She tilted her head back. She'd passed Aidan in the hallway a time or two at network headquarters. He was handsome. And tall. Taller than Cliff, who was six feet, making her feel at even more of a disadvantage.

But he didn't charge in or make any threatening moves. "You know who I am," he stated again.

She gave him an abrupt nod. "You're Aidan. I've seen you around at the network."

"And Cliff has mentioned me."

She debated the wisdom of answering that one and wondered if he was one of the telepathic immortals, capable of reading others' thoughts. "Yes."

"As I said, we need to talk."

Emma hesitated another moment. Cliff had never spoken poorly of Aidan. Quite the opposite. So she ultimately decided to ease back and open the door wide enough for him to enter.

Aidan stepped inside and glanced around while she closed the door.

"So?" She folded her arms just under her breasts and wished she wore a T-shirt instead of a tank top.

"So," he parroted and actually looked as awkward as she felt. "You've been seeing Cliff."

Emma kept her expression neutral. Should she deny it? Feign ignorance? Brazen it out?

Then reason penetrated the fog of fatigue and pointed out that if Aidan knew her address, he probably knew a hell of a lot more.

"How did you know?" she asked finally.

"Cliff is my friend," he told her. "I sleep at the network during the day and have spent a lot of time with him since transferring to North Carolina." He considered her carefully. "You know that immortals and vampires have heightened senses."

She nodded.

"Well, I couldn't help but notice that—on the nights Bastien takes Cliff hunting with him and lets him roam alone for a few hours—Cliff always returns carrying a woman's scent."

Emma lowered her gaze to her bare feet. *Curse their heightened senses.*

"I catch the same scent each time I pass your office at the network. And even if I didn't, I'm telepathic and see you in his thoughts."

As always, resentment that her relationship with Cliff was entirely dependent on the approval of others welled within her. Cliff still worried over Seth or Mr. Reordon discovering their relationship, convinced they would put a stop to it to protect her. So if Aidan was here to warn her away, he could go fuck himself. "If you're here to tell me not to see him anymore, you can—"

"That's not why I'm here," he said. "Because I'm telepathic, I also know that Cliff is always in better shape mentally after spending time with you. He's calmer. More at peace." He shrugged. "I'm his friend. I wouldn't take that away from him."

All defensiveness fled. Emma lowered her arms. "He says I quiet the voices."

"You do." Regret darkened his features. "But Cliff is struggling, Emma."

Her throat worked in a swallow. "He's been struggling for a long time now."

Aidan shook his head. "Yesterday was different."

Fear and dread returned, making her stomach churn. "What happened? He didn't come by last night. Did he have another break?" His rare absences always terrified her but usually only lasted a night.

"No," Aidan told her. "But the voices clamoring in his head were so loud that they woke me from a sound sleep. And when I went to him…" Every second he hesitated, her fear escalated. "He was contemplating ending it."

All strength left her legs. Her knees buckled.

Aidan hastily grasped her upper arms to keep her from sinking to the floor.

Emma gripped his forearms with desperate hands, fingers

twisting the material of his sleeves. Moisture welled in her eyes. "Is he...? Did he ask Bastien to...?" End it for him? Was that why Aidan, not Bastien, had come to her? Because Bastien was too torn up over having ended his friend's life?

"No," Aidan hastened to assure her. "Cliff is alive."

Tears spilled over her lashes as her chest rose and fell with harsh breaths taken to hold back sobs. "I thought you were going to tell me..." Shaking her head, she swallowed hard. "He's okay then?"

Aidan guided her over to the sofa. "Let's sit down, shall we?"

Nodding, she released him and sank down on the soft cushions. Her hands shook as she swiped at the tears cooling her cheeks.

Aidan retrieved a wingback chair from the corner and plunked it down across from her so he could face her. Seating himself in it, he leaned forward and placed his elbows on his knees. "I tried something new yesterday that I hoped would help him. I teleported him to a sunny meadow on my estate in Scotland."

Shock stole her breath, bringing a halt to the sobs. "You *hurt* him?" she demanded furiously. "How could you? He's been helping you—"

Aidan held up a palm. "I didn't hurt him. I'm a powerful healer and kept my hand on his shoulder the entire time, healing the damage the sun wrought so quickly that he didn't feel it."

She frowned. "You can do that?"

"Yes. I tried it first on Ethan, an immortal who is only a century old and can tolerate very little sun exposure, to confirm it would work."

She stared at him. "So Cliff was able to stand in sunlight without it hurting him?"

Aidan smiled. "Yes. And we discovered that sunlight silences the voices as effectively as you do."

Hope welled. "So he's better now?"

"He's better."

Relief left her light-headed. Smiling, she reached out and took one of his hands. "Thank you." That had been incredibly thoughtful. And it was a relief to know they had someone else in their corner who could help them find new ways to help Cliff.

"I was happy to do it," he replied as if he'd done something far simpler, like let Cliff borrow his car.

"Do you think, if it gets bad again," she asked hesitantly, "that maybe you could do it again?" Wasn't healing the wounds of others painful for immortals?

Aidan patted her hand. "I've already told Cliff I'll take him into the sunlight every day he continues to fight." That was a hell of a thing to offer.

She clutched his hand. "Really? You would do that for him?"

"Of course. He's my friend."

"But doesn't it hurt?" she asked. "I thought immortals healed others by absorbing the damage into their own bodies."

Aidan shrugged. "I told Cliff it's a mild discomfort at most."

She smiled wryly, seeing through the lie. "It hurt like hell, didn't it?"

He laughed. "Yes. The longer we stood in the sunlight, the worse the pain grew. But I can tolerate it for Cliff. He's a good man, well worth saving."

"I wouldn't love him if he weren't," she professed with a sad smile. "Did you know he saved my life?"

Aidan shook his head, his face lighting with surprise. "No."

"I work the day shift now but used to work nights at the network. And I was there when mercenaries bombed the original network headquarters just before dawn. I worked on sublevel 1. Part of the ground floor collapsed before I could evacuate. Something hit me on the head and knocked me unconscious. And when I woke up, I was buried beneath the rubble and couldn't move." She shook her head. "I didn't even have a chance to call for help before the concrete and whatever else was piled on top of me began to shift and groan as someone lifted it away. The next thing I knew, Cliff was staring down at me, his eyes glowing bright amber while he told me not to be afraid, that he was there to help me."

"Did you know he was a vampire?" Aidan asked curiously.

"Not with certainty." He'd been covered in dust and debris that made him look different enough from the man in the photo Cynthia had shown her that Emma hadn't been sure it was him until Melanie confirmed it after Cliff handed Emma over to her. "But I had heard that one of the vampires housed on sublevel 5 was a brother. And I figured he wouldn't keep telling me not to be afraid if he were an immortal." She remembered the mercenaries dropping down through jagged holes in the ceiling as Cliff spirited her away. "I wouldn't have made it out of the building alive if Cliff hadn't saved me."

"So *that's* how you two met."

She grinned. "Yes, but he doesn't remember it. I was pretty unrecognizable when he found me." She opted not to mention the torture he'd endured shortly thereafter that had deprived him of the memory.

Aidan drew a piece of paper from his front pocket and handed it to her along with a small box.

"What's this?" she asked as she took them.

"Cliff asked me to speak with you."

She frowned. "Why?"

"He's worried he's going to hurt you."

"He won't," she countered. "I've already told him he won't hurt me. I'm sure of it. But he—"

Aidan held up a hand. "You didn't see him yesterday, Emma. You didn't hear his thoughts. And you've never seen a vampire who has completely succumbed to the madness and lost all knowledge of right and wrong."

She shook her head. "Dr. Lipton told me that—even during psychotic breaks—the other vampires have never attacked her or Dr. Machen."

"Melanie knows about you?"

"Yes. Bastien told her Cliff and I are lovers. And she came to see me, afraid I might not understand the consequences of getting pregnant by him or that I might not understand fully what the virus would do to him."

"Did she try to talk you out of seeing him?"

"No. She loves Cliff and wants him to find whatever happiness he can. She just wanted me to be prepared."

Aidan sighed. "Well, Vince asked Bastien to end his life before the damage progressed too far, so we don't really know if he would've attacked Melanie eventually. Cliff has held out far longer than the others but, despite his valiant efforts, is beginning to lose the battle. His greatest fear now is that he may hurt you."

"He won't," she insisted and wished Cliff wouldn't worry about that. Even when fury rose within him like magma in a volcano and erupted in the form of shouts and bellows, he *never* directed that anger at her.

Aidan pointed to the piece of paper she held. "That's my cell phone number." He pointed to the box. "And that is one of those cell phone wristwatch gadgets with voice activation. If you want to continue seeing Cliff, program my number into it and keep that watch on you at all times. And I mean *all* times. When the two of you are making love. When you take a shower. Never take it off."

She frowned. "Is it waterproof?"

"Yes. And if you have even the slightest fear that Cliff is about to have a break or that he may hurt you, call me immediately. I'm a teleporter, so I can be here in half a second to protect you and help Cliff."

Everything within Emma demanded she reject this. She didn't need protection from Cliff. He wouldn't hurt her. But did she really have a choice? Cliff was the one who'd sent Aidan to talk to her. "He'll stop coming here if I don't agree to this, won't he?"

"Yes. He loves you, Emma. If you love him as much as you appear to, then do this for him and ease his fears. He doesn't need those on top of everything else he's facing."

No, he didn't. If this would give him some relief, she'd do it.

Nodding, she opened the box and fastened the watch to her wrist. Emma hadn't worn a watch in years since she always had her phone with her. And she'd certainly never had a smartwatch. So it took a while and several consultations of the instruction manual for them to figure out how to add Aidan's number and achieve voice recognition. But they finally succeeded.

"Call Aidan," she said.

Aidan's cell phone chirped in his pocket.

Both grinned.

"Now," Aidan said, sobering, "here is something Cliff *doesn't* know about." Reaching into his coat, he withdrew two tranquilizer guns identical to those she'd seen the guards at network headquarters carry.

"Uh-uh," she said. "No way. I am *not* going to shoot Cliff."

"These are tranquilizer guns, already armed with darts that can sedate Cliff should the need arise."

Shaking her head, she held up her wrist. "I don't need those. I have this."

"You need to have a defensive measure that Cliff doesn't know about, Emma," he insisted. "Once the brain damage progresses to a certain point, psychotic breaks can occur without warning. If Cliff flies into a rage and rips the watch off your arm, you'll have to go for one of these. They've been specially designed for vampire hunting by the network's weapons experts, so each can fire up to five darts. A single dart should calm him. Two will knock him out. Three will kill him. Avoid the last if at all possible." He placed the guns beside her on the sofa. "Hide these where they will be handy in an emergency but where Cliff won't accidentally happen upon them."

She eyed them with dread, unable to imagine *aiming* one at Cliff, let alone shooting him.

"If Cliff hurts you, Emma, it will kill him. He will end it himself in a heartbeat, even if the wound is so minor you shrug it off. If you want to hold on to him, you need to ensure he can't hurt you."

She nodded, so inundated with despair she could barely speak. "He said I quiet the voices," she murmured again.

Aidan nodded. "You do. But the voices are getting louder. And soon you will only dampen them a little."

She lived in constant fear of that.

Returning his chair to the corner, Aidan headed for the front door. As he reached for the doorknob, she spoke.

"Aidan?"

He turned.

Her limbs weighted with weariness, Emma forced herself to stand and closed the distance between them. Rising onto her toes, she kissed his cheek, then hugged him hard. "Thank you for giving Cliff the sun again." Though the tranq guns upset her, Aidan was a good man who, like her, was just trying to do whatever he could to save Cliff.

He hugged her back. "Thank you for loving him and bringing him happiness."

If only that were enough to heal him.

Releasing him, Emma backed away.

"Are you going to see him tonight?" he asked.

"Yes. He's supposed to come over after he and Bastien finish hunting."

Aidan smiled. "Then you should shower and wash my scent off you. We don't want to tempt fate."

She laughed. "I'll go do it now."

As soon as he left, Emma locked the door and headed for the shower.

———◦◦◦———

Cliff skidded to a halt in Emma's front yard, dropped the duffel bag, stripped, and cleaned up within seconds. Even on his worst nights, he abided by the ritual. Just the idea of her seeing him coated with the blood of the vampires he'd slain made him cringe.

Then he smiled, thinking of the night she'd peeked through the blinds and caught him.

Her eyes had widened. And when she'd opened the front door and stepped out onto her porch, the look of baffled astonishment on her face had made him grin. "Hi, beautiful," he'd called, buck naked in the moonlight. He had just finished wiping off every speck of blood and hadn't yet put on clean clothes.

Mouth hanging open, she'd shaken her head. "What... is happening? Are the voices telling you to streak now?" she'd asked incredulously.

Cliff had burst out laughing.

"Seriously, did you just run all the way here with no clothes on? Because if you did, you're going to have to tell me what route you took so I can go kick the ass of every woman who saw you naked. That body is *mine*."

Once he'd gotten his mirth under control, he had grudgingly confessed that he always changed clothes before he saw her and why.

She'd told him he didn't have to. He'd insisted he did. It remained vitally important to him that he keep the violence of the hunt separate from his time with her.

So here he stood again, naked on her front lawn.

Cliff swiftly garbed himself in clean clothes, headed up the stone walkway, and rang the doorbell. Emma had tried to give him a key, but he drew comfort from the routine of it... *and* wanted to leave her the choice of whether she felt like seeing him and dealing with his insanity. He would think that sooner or later she was going to need a break.

The door swung open.

Emma smiled up at him and greeted him with a kiss as she always did. "Hi, honey."

As he entered, however, a new scent reached his nose. He drew in a deep breath and held it as she closed the door. Turning to face her, he studied her carefully. "Aidan was here."

Her pretty face crinkled up with consternation. "Yes. And let me just say that sometimes your heightened senses freak me out a little. Do you know how creepy it is that he can *smell* me on you?"

Cliff stared at her. "He told you that?"

"Yes, when I asked how he knew we'd been seeing each other."

"Oh. I figured he'd probably just seen you in my thoughts."

"He said that, too." She scowled. "He better not have seen any hot naked times."

That gave him pause. "If he did, I'm sure he skimmed past them. He's a good guy."

"Yeah. I think so, too." She bit her lip. "Ooh. I hope he wasn't reading my thoughts the first few minutes I spoke with him."

"Why? What were you thinking?"

She titled her chin up in a gesture of defiance. "That if he was here to tell me I shouldn't see you anymore, he could go fuck himself."

Cliff would smile over that later. Right now, however, his attention fell to her wrist and stayed there. Setting the duffel bag down, he gently clasped her hand and her elbow and raised her forearm so he could study the new smartwatch. He'd never owned such a device and wasn't sure how they worked. The watches he wore were standard fare, inexpensive and easily replaced since vampires shattered them periodically.

The watch that now graced Emma's slender wrist, however, was sleek and black with a numberless face that boasted dancing flames.

He met her gaze, uncertain of her response to the gift and his friend's visit.

"You didn't have to do this," she said softly, nodding at the watch. "It isn't necessary."

"Yes, it is."

Moving closer until her body nearly touched his, she stared up at him. Love and certainty gleamed in her brown eyes. "You aren't going to hurt me, Cliff."

How he wished he shared her confidence. "You don't know that."

"Yes, I do," she countered, her voice still soft and full of affection. "You aren't going to hurt me. And you don't frighten me even when you fly into a rage. Does it startle me sometimes?" She smiled. "Yes. Because that deep, sexy voice of yours can get *loud*. But whatever horrible things are going on up there" — she tapped his forehead — "will only ever hurt me if they drive you to harm yourself." Arching a brow, she gave him a stern look. "And if that ever happens, I'm telling you right now that I'm going to paddle your ass and give those voices a stern talking to."

Relieved that she wasn't angry over his sending Aidan to her, Cliff drew her into a tight hug and buried his face in her hair. "Damn, I love you."

"I love you, too." Snuggling into him, she released a contented sigh. "But I'm dead serious about paddling your ass."

Cliff laughed.

"How was your day?"

"A lot like yesterday. Not great in the beginning because I couldn't sleep." He pressed a kiss to the top of her head, taking comfort in the familiar scent of coconut oil. "But Aidan took me into the sunlight again."

She tilted her head back. "It really doesn't hurt?"

"Not at all. I feel like shit though because I know it hurts *him*."

"He wouldn't do it if he didn't want to, Cliff."

"I know."

"And it quiets the voices?"

"Yeah. At least it has both times we tried it. Between that and working out my aggressive impulses while hunting, I feel better than I have in months."

"Excellent. What would you like to do tonight?"

"Dinner and dancing?"

She grinned. "Dinner and dancing it is."

They prepared a meal together, creating what Cliff hoped would be another fond memory for her. With the voices reduced to angry murmurs, he could enjoy teasing and bantering with her, stealing kisses and caresses while he put together salads and she whipped up some fettuccine Alfredo.

They ate at the coffee table, sitting cross-legged on the floor across from each other, knees touching. Cliff smiled and nodded as she told him about her day. He laughed when she relayed Cynthia's description of Todd's latest attempt to spice up their love life with more role-playing.

"Where does he get these ideas?" he asked around a chuckle.

She shook her head. "He knows she likes historical romance novels."

"So he thought a full suit of armor would be sexy?"

She laughed. "Until he fell down and couldn't get back up again because it was so damn heavy."

Once they cleaned the dishes and tucked away the leftovers — activities so wonderfully domestic that he didn't find them tedious as some did — they took her phone and Bose speaker out onto the front porch.

Emma donned some sneakers while Cliff programmed a playlist with both fast and slow songs. Then he led her down the steps, onto her front lawn, and drew her close.

They danced for almost an hour before the cursed voices rose in volume.

Sensing the change in him, she took his face in both hands and drew him down for a kiss. "Take me, Cliff. I want you."

He wanted her, too. Lifting her in his arms, he carried her inside and lowered her to the bed. He wanted to go slow. Wanted to remind her of the tenderness of which he was capable. Wanted to show her the reverence and adoration he felt for her. But the fucking voices kept bellowing in his ears. Fury and frustration rose as he fought to block them out. And desperation once again roughened his touch.

"I'm sorry," he murmured afterward, his body curled around hers. "I wanted to go slow. To be gentle."

Reaching back, she rested a hand on his hip and urged him tighter against her. "Three orgasms, honey," she mumbled as sleep crept up on her. "Three orgasms." She sighed. "You're the only man on the planet who would apologize for that."

Because she deserved so much more than he could give her.

"Love you," she breathed.

"I love you, too."

Sleep claimed her.

Cliff held her as long as he could before the fury and aggression within him approached dangerous highs. Slipping silently from the bed, he dressed, grabbed his duffel, and left.

A sojourn in sunlight and slaying multiple vampires had only given him a few hours' respite from the voices and the violent impulses they inspired.

What would happen when those few hours were reduced to mere minutes?

The question haunted him long after he returned to the network.

Chapter Twenty-One

E MMA STARED, UNSEEING, AT HER computer screen.
    She couldn't seem to concentrate on anything today. She was supposed to be arranging new identities for five Immortal Guardians and facilitating their transfer, along with their Seconds, to new locations here in the States and overseas. But she'd gotten nothing done.

She blinked hard. Her eyes felt as if she had rubbed salt into them. Her shoulders slumped with weariness.

Cliff hadn't come by last night.

It happened from time to time and almost always stemmed from a psychotic break.

But he'd seemed so much better two nights ago. They'd made dinner together. They'd danced. He'd smiled and laughed more than he had in months. And despite his concern that he'd been too rough when they'd made love, his touch *had* carried hints of the tenderness he felt for her. The tenderness the madness rarely let him show now.

Had something happened?

Had Aidan changed his mind about taking Cliff into the sun?

Cliff *had* been struggling more lately and —

Ding. A message popped up on her computer screen.

She frowned at it.

> Good afternoon, Emma. Mr. Reordon would like to see you in his office. Please make your way here without disclosing the contents of this message to anyone you encounter.
>
> Best,
>
> Kate Buchanan
> *Executive Assistant to Mr. Reordon*

What the hell? Was he pissed because she hadn't finished fabricating the new identities and — ?

Her eyes widened.

Oh shit. Had he found out she and Cliff were seeing each other?

Her heartbeat picked up.

The message vanished. Another appeared.

Be advised, Mr. Reordon does not like to be kept waiting.

Best,

Kate

Pushing back her chair, Emma rose.

The message vanished.

Limbs stiff, anxiety coursing through her, she left her office and headed for the elevator.

It opened at her approach. Three guards waited within.

"Ms. Williams?" one said.

"Yes."

Nodding, he moved aside and motioned for her to enter.

One of the physical therapists who worked on this floor approached the open doors of the elevator.

The same guard who spoke to Emma held up a hand to keep him out and addressed the man. "We'll send it back for you."

Crap. She wasn't being fired, was she? Were these guards here to ensure she didn't make a fuss when Mr. Reordon handed her her walking papers?

She looked at the burly, heavily armed men who towered over her despite her average height.

How big a fuss did they expect her to make?

Once the elevator completed the short climb to the ground floor, the guards guided her down the hallway that led to Mr. Reordon's office. Emma had only been there a couple of times. The last had been after the mercenaries attacked. One by one, Mr. Reordon had called every employee who had been working the morning of the mercenary attack into his office to ask how they were doing, if they needed anything. Counseling? Maybe a change of hours?

She glanced at the guards from the corners of her eyes.

Something told her this visit wasn't going to be as pleasant.

A dozen guards manned the entrance to the reception room at the end of the hallway. There had been no guards outside it the last time she'd come.

Inside the reception room, Kate Buchanan sat at a large desk situated in front of a wall of file cabinets. An elegant, formfitting business suit hugged the lines of her hourglass figure, making Emma feel dowdy in her jeans and blazer.

Todd and a dozen more guards bracketed the entrance to Mr. Reordon's office.

Seriously, what the hell *was* all this?

Kate glanced up as Emma and her armed escort entered. When she rose, Kate's unbuttoned jacket gaped just enough for Emma to glimpse what looked like a weapon housed in a shoulder holster. "Thank you, gentlemen." As she rounded the desk, she addressed Emma. "Thank you for coming so quickly, Ms. Williams. Would you follow me, please?"

Emma could detect no rancor in the woman's tone. She could detect no emotion at all. Kate was all business as she led Emma to Mr. Reordon's office, motioned for her to enter, then slipped inside and closed the door behind them.

Emma frowned. The large office was empty.

"It'll be just a moment," Kate murmured.

A door on one side opened. Chris Reordon stepped into the doorway and glanced over his shoulder. "I'll be back in a minute."

A minute? Was that all it would take to fire her? Closing the door behind him, he met Emma's disgruntled gaze and pressed a finger to his lips.

Her frown deepened.

He motioned to a doorway in the wall opposite the one he'd just exited.

Emma jumped when a hand touched her arm.

Kate. Her face was no longer devoid of emotion. Now her lips curled up in a faint smile as she nodded that it would be okay.

Her mind blanking, Emma crossed to the doorway and headed inside... an executive bathroom? Really? She glanced around, taking in the double sinks with high-end fixtures, the beautiful tile, the modern toilet, a shower big enough for four, and what appeared to be a closet full of clothes.

What the hell?

She turned around.

Kate and Mr. Reordon entered and closed the door behind them.

"Thank you for coming, Emma," Mr. Reordon said. "I know this is an unorthodox meeting place, but I needed to speak with you in a room that was soundproof. I asked Kate to join us in hopes that her presence would make you feel more comfortable."

It didn't. "Speak to me about what?"

"Cliff," Kate said.

Emma's gaze bounced back and forth between them like a Ping-Pong ball. "Cliff in Accounting?"

Mr. Reordon's lips twitched. "No. Cliff the vampire. We know you've been seeing him."

How? She knew damn well Cliff hadn't told him. So how else could he have figured it out, unless…? Her eyes widened. "Did you bug my house?" she asked, appalled. But it wasn't out of the realm of possibility considering he LoJacked all employee cars so he could track them *in case of emergency* and was notoriously paranoid.

"No," he answered. "We found the unauthorized cell phone in his apartment."

Anger rose. They had searched Cliff's apartment? That was bullshit! The vampires were supposed to have *complete* privacy in their rooms.

"It isn't what you think," he hastened to add. "One of the employees who delivers Cliff's groceries found it by accident. She noticed a box of graham crackers in his cabinet that had expired and replaced it with a new one. When she dumped the crackers out so she could recycle the box, she found a cell phone hidden beneath them."

Kate nodded. "She brought the phone to me because she didn't know what to do about it. As soon as I turned it on, I recognized you. Your picture is on the lock screen."

"And I had one of my tech guys hack the passcode," Mr. Reordon admitted.

Emma again opened her mouth to protest.

"I had to do it, Emma," he said. "I don't *like* having to do that shit, but I needed to make sure he wasn't leaking information about vampires, immortals, and *gifted ones* to outside sources or contacting his family."

"His family thinks he's dead," she reminded him.

"Which is why I needed to know if he's been contacting them."

"He hasn't."

"I know," he said calmly. "I know that now. It's all good. We put the phone and the graham crackers back before Cliff noticed they were missing."

Oddly, Mr. Reordon didn't seem upset with her. Rather, he and Kate both seemed to want to put her at ease. "How long have you known?"

"Almost a year."

She stared at him in surprise. He'd known about them for a year and hadn't done anything? Hadn't intervened? Hadn't tried to stop them from seeing each other?

She shifted her weight from one foot to the other as she studied them. "Why exactly am I here? Why tell me this now?"

Again, Kate touched her arm. "It's Cliff," she said gently, regret entering her pretty features.

Trepidation gripped Emma. "What about him?" Reordon looked grim as hell. "Has something happened?" His absence last night now worried her even more. Had he—?

"There was an incident," Reordon said, his voice so gentle it actually increased her alarm.

The last time there had been "an incident" that produced such grave expressions, the guards had wanted to shove Cliff out into the sunlight. "Did you kill him?" she blurted, terror rising.

"No!" they practically shouted, expressions horrified.

"No," Reordon repeated, softer this time. "But it left him agitated. And Aidan couldn't take him out into the sunlight today. Bastien and Melanie were called away to a meeting, so Bastien had to postpone tonight's hunt, and..."

"He's struggling," Kate said.

Reordon nodded. "Linda is with Alleck in Puerto Rico, consulting a virologist there. And none of the other physicians feel comfortable getting close enough to Cliff to sedate him."

"Why the hell not? He isn't a monster. He's a good man."

"I know that," Reordon said and motioned to Kate. "We know that. But Cliff injured a lot of guards the day he went after Whetsman and scared some of the other employees."

"He also saved a lot of lives the morning the mercenaries attacked," Emma pointed out. "He saved *my* life."

"We're aware of that and—" Reordon drew his hand through the air in a slicing motion, as if he wanted to cut off that line of conversation. "Look, I can't make everyone who works for me see what I do in Cliff. And we don't have time to talk about shit I can't change. Cliff is struggling, Emma. I'm worried that if we don't do something soon, he's going to have another break. I don't know how to dose him with the sedative, and I don't want to shoot him with a tranq gun. I also would prefer not to call Seth if possible or draw his attention by delaying or interrupting the meeting so Melanie can return and sedate him, because…" He glanced at Kate. "Well, all things considered… I'm a little worried Seth's sudden appearance might just agitate him more."

"Where is he?" she asked. "I can calm him. Let me see him."

"That's what I was hoping you'd say. He's in my boardroom. It's soundproofed like this bathroom. I didn't want the other vampires to hear us talking and find out you two are seeing each other, because they'd all start bitching about not having girlfriends of their own."

Kate nodded. "And we didn't want to open the boardroom door and just shove you inside without any warning."

"Consider me warned."

Reordon reached for the doorknob.

"Wait," she said.

He paused.

"Will you be going in there with me?"

He glanced at Kate, then back at Emma. "Do you want me to?"

She hesitated. When Cliff would erupt in rage at her home, she'd usually try to say something that would make him laugh and defuse the moment. But sometimes the only way to reach him and dampen the voices was to distract him with sex. Which she did *not* want to tell them. "No."

Reordon nodded. "Okay. I've shut off all sound going into the boardroom and can't hear anything that takes place inside it." He glanced at his watch. "I'm running late and need to head to the meeting. But Kate will remain in my office until I return. If you need anything, you'll have to open the door to tell her. Are you okay with that?"

"Yes. That's fine." If she failed to reach Cliff, she'd just call Aidan and damn the consequences.

"Do you want a tranq gun?"

"No. I won't need it. Cliff would never hurt me."

"Understood." Opening the door, he led them back into his office.

He and Kate stopped at his desk.

Emma kept going, anxious to get to Cliff and try to calm him. Without even pausing, she opened the door, entered, and found herself in a large, very swanky boardroom. She closed the door, sealing herself inside.

The instant, complete lack of sound was a bit disconcerting as she took in the long, gleaming wood table and the twenty-five or thirty upscale chairs pulled up to it. At the far end of the room, looking oddly out of place, a sofa long enough for even Seth to stretch out on butted up against the wall.

Cliff sat on it, his head in his hands, his fingers tugging on his dreadlocks as his knee bounced up and down.

"Cliff," she said softly.

His head jerked up. The amber glow in his eyes flashed brighter as he rose. "Emma?"

Nodding, she slowly approached him.

Cliff stared at her as though he were seeing a ghost. His Adam's apple bobbed in a swallow. "Are you here?" he asked, voice hoarse. "Or am I hallucinating?"

The backs of her eyes began to burn with tears she refused to let fall. "I'm here, honey." As soon as she reached him, she rested a hand on his chest so he could feel that she was real.

He instantly covered it with one of his own, clasping it tightly but careful not to hurt her. His gaze shifted to the door.

"Mr. Reordon knows about us."

Fury twisted his handsome features. "Did he threaten you?" he demanded in a very un-Cliff-like voice that sent a chill down her spine.

"No, honey," she assured him, keeping her voice soft and calm. "He's known for a long time and is fine with us seeing each other. He just noticed you were struggling tonight and thought I could help."

He searched her face a long moment.

"Come here." Stepping close, she slid an arm around his waist. "I didn't see you last night and need you to hold me so I know you're okay."

A long breath soughed out of him as he released her hand and wrapped both arms around her in a tight hug.

Emma held him close as he rested his cheek on her hair. Long minutes passed. "Did something happen?" she asked tentatively.

He nodded. "I tried to kill Seth yesterday."

Shock seized her. "What?"

"I tried to kill Seth. Or someone I *thought* was Seth. Or both."

"Seth—the leader of the Immortal Guardians—Seth?" she asked, trying and failing to keep the alarm out of her voice. No wonder Mr. Reordon had thought Seth's appearance would increase Cliff's anxiety.

"Yes." Sighing, he loosened his hold enough to place a little space between them. He looked so damned weary and pained it broke her heart.

Instead of bombarding him with the many questions that desperately want to pour forth, she sought a response he wouldn't expect. She'd learned early on that catching him off guard, particularly with something he might find amusing, could sometimes diminish the voices.

Arching a brow, she cast him an admiring look that caressed his muscled body from his head to his boots and back up again. "Damn," she said, infusing her voice with awe. "That was ballsy."

A startled chuckle escaped him, chasing away some of the darkness.

"How'd he respond?"

A wry smile lingered on his lips as Cliff took her hands. "The bad Seth? He cut me and hurled me into a tree. I broke several bones."

She scowled. "What a total asshole!" she blurted, outraged on his behalf.

That drew a full-fledged laugh out of him, pleasing her despite her concern for him. "Yeah. He's an asshole all right."

Squeezing his hands, she sat on the comfy sofa and tugged him down next to her. "Tell me everything."

A little bit of the tension in his rigid form eased as he wrapped an arm around her and tucked her up against his side.

It was a fantastical tale. An ancient immortal by the name of Gershom who apparently was determined to launch freaking Armageddon had posed as Seth—so well he could pass for his twin—and attacked Aidan. What the hell?

"Did you attack the asshole before or after you found out he wasn't Seth?"

"Before. Then I attacked the real Seth when the fake one fled."

"Well, you're just all kinds of ballsy, aren't you?"

He shook his head as he toyed with her hand, one knee bobbing up and down again. "I didn't really see him. Either one of them. I just knew someone was trying to hurt Aidan and… lost it."

"How did the real Seth react?"

He looked down, his chin nearly touching his chest. "With kindness I didn't deserve," he murmured.

Biting her lip, Emma cupped his stubbled jaw in her free hand. "You know that's bullshit, right?"

Turning his head, he buried his lips in her palm and said nothing.

"Cliff?"

Still nothing. Just his lips in her palm and his knee bobbing up and down.

"Look at me, honey," she ordered gently.

For a moment, she thought he wouldn't. Then he regarded her with a now familiar, haunted look in his luminescent eyes. The one that told her he feared he was the monster he'd been trying so hard not to become.

"Do you remember me telling you that sometimes you wear blinders? That you're so focused on the bad that the good eludes you?"

He nodded reluctantly.

"Well, that's what you're doing right now. You're wearing those damn blinders again. You're so focused on the fact that you attacked Seth that you don't seem to realize you played an integral role in helping Aidan, Ethan, and Heather keep this Gershom asshole busy until Seth and Zach could arrive. You did exactly what you intended, honey. You kept the bad guy from killing

Aidan. You leaped in and had his back before anyone else did." She shook her head. "Don't you think Seth appreciates that?"

Rising, he strode away from her. "Aidan, Ethan, and Heather could've handled Gershom without me. I was a hindrance."

Emma stood. "Again, I call bullshit on that, honey. Because Ethan and Heather didn't jump in to defend Aidan until they were absolutely sure the asshole he fought wasn't Seth. If you hadn't helped in their stead, who knows what might have happened? For all you know, he might've gutted Aidan."

Upon reaching the far end of the room, he swiveled and started back. A low growl rumbled in his throat as he shook his head the way he did when he was arguing with himself… or with the voices. When he was a few feet away, he spun and headed back to the far end of the conference room again, reminding her of a caged panther. His hands curled into fists as he muttered to himself. The veins in his arms stood out as the muscles beneath them flexed. "I need to hunt," he rasped.

"I know. But Bastien and Aidan are both at a meeting. So it might be a little while."

He swore. "Ask Melanie to sedate me."

"She went to the meeting with Bastien."

He shook his head, his fists clenching and unclenching at his sides. "Right. She and Bastien left together. Have Linda do it."

"Mr. Reordon said Linda's in Puerto Rico."

Again he swore. "Then shoot me with a damn tranq gun," he ordered, voice rising with frustration.

Hell no. And she didn't want anyone else to shoot him either. The voices in his head wouldn't perceive that as anything less than an attack. How would *that* calm him? "I'd much rather you work off some steam with me." When he strode back toward her, she smiled, motioned to the sofa, and waggled her eyebrows. "This *is* big enough for two, you know."

He paced away again. "No."

Stubborn man. He knew it would help. It always did. But he was so afraid of hurting her… "Cliff—"

He rounded on her furiously. "I said no! I don't want you to feel like you have to fuck me every time I start to lose it!"

He might as well have slapped her. Emma straightened, lips

tightening. It was the first time he had ever directed his anger at her. "Well maybe this isn't just about you," she bit out. "Maybe Mr. Reordon scared the shit out of me when he called me into his fancy office bathroom, told me he knew about us, then somberly informed me that there had been *an incident*. Maybe I thought he was going to tell me you'd had another psychotic break and that this time the guards had killed you." Tears welled in her eyes despite her efforts to keep them at bay. "And maybe I wasn't just offering to *fuck you* into a better frame of mind. Maybe I needed you to hold me because for a minute I thought I'd lost you and—"

He crossed the room so quickly he blurred. His arms banded around her as he crushed her to him. "I'm sorry," he whispered. "I'm sorry, Emma. I'm sorry."

She squeezed him tight, sorry too for her outburst. None of this was his fault. He would never have lashed out if the damned voices weren't bellowing who-knows-what at him. But she was too choked up to speak.

She didn't want to lose him.

She just didn't want to lose him.

And if he tried to shut her out now, if he tried to distance himself from her out of some misguided belief that he was somehow *sparing* her...

Framing her face with his hands, he pressed fervent kisses to her forehead, her cheeks, and her lips. "I'm sorry," he whispered again. "I'm so sorry, sweetheart. I didn't mean it. I just..."

"I know," she choked out. "And I'm sorry, too." She fisted his shirt as she met his bright amber eyes. "It really did scare me. I didn't see you last night. And that usually only happens when you have a break. Then Mr. Reordon and Kate looked so damn grim when they faced me..."

"It's okay." He kissed her. "I'm okay." Sliding his arms around her, he kissed her again, deepening the contact as his hands began to explore her back with heated caresses. "You said I saved the day, remember?" he murmured in a way that suggested he was trying to convince *himself* it was true. "You said I did good." He trailed his lips down her neck in a series of fervent kisses, then drew her up onto her toes and pressed her hips to his, letting her feel how hard he was.

She moaned, clutching fistfuls of his hair as desperation turned to desire.

"I held off the bad guy," he murmured, tugging her blazer off and letting it drop to the floor. "I'm okay." His fingers went to work, deftly unfastening the buttons on her shirt.

"You're okay," she agreed breathlessly as flames danced through her. She needed him so much. As much as he needed her.

She couldn't lose him.

How could she ever survive losing him?

Their clothing hit the floor. Then they came together on the sofa, remorse and a longing for reassurance driving them. Their time together suddenly seemed alarmingly short, on the brink of ending. And the fear and despair that spawned made their lovemaking all the more intense as they found ecstasy together.

Afterward, they reluctantly tugged their clothes back on — unsure how long they'd have before Kate and Mr. Reordon poked their heads in — then lay back down on the sofa.

Cliff spooned up behind her, his biceps pillowing her head.

Some of the tension left his form, the muscles in the arms corded around her relaxing as he snuggled closer. And Emma let her own anxiety drift away.

Quiet fell.

Their heartbeats slowed.

Their breathing deepened as exhaustion settled upon them.

Cliff pressed his lips to her neck. "I don't think we're going to get our happy ending," he whispered.

A tear spilled down her cheek. And it took Emma a moment to find her voice. "Just give us as much time as you can, Cliff."

Nodding, he breathed a heavy sigh against her nape and let sleep claim him.

Chapter Twenty-Two
6 Months Later

A S CLIFF SLOWLY WOKE, THE first thing he noticed was that the voices weren't as loud.

They still growled and snarled, feeding him sadistic suggestions and fueling vile urges. But even the aggression that vampire hunting and nights with Emma could no longer eradicate seemed to have decreased.

What had happened? What was different?

He turned his head, almost expecting to see Emma's lovely face beside his on the pillow. His condition had deteriorated to such an extent that now the only time he slept without being sedated was when she was in his arms or vice versa.

Alas, she wasn't there.

Of course she wasn't. He was in his apartment at network headquarters. Emma never ventured down to sublevel 5. She didn't have the security clearance required. And even if Reordon gave it to her, Cliff wouldn't want her to come down here.

He wasn't the only vampire having psychotic breaks. And since they lacked a personal connection to her, he didn't trust the others not to harm her.

In rare instances, if all else failed to calm Cliff, Reordon would summon him and Emma to his office and allow them to sequester themselves in his boardroom for a time.

When Cliff had first come to the network, he would never have imagined Reordon would become such a strong ally. But he'd turned out to be a real stand-up guy. He had even provided Cliff with video footage of his worst post-Whetsman psychotic breaks so he could show Emma.

Cliff never wanted her to underestimate the danger he posed. And too, he'd wanted to ensure she wasn't laboring under any illusions that his condition wasn't worsening.

Yet she still she loved him. She still fought for him, bolstering his strength whenever his determination to continue fighting wavered.

Sitting up, Cliff swung his feet over the side of the bed and rose.

Yeah, he thought as he headed into the bathroom to perform his usual wake-up ablutions, *something is definitely off.* His movements felt sluggish, as if he'd been drugged. And the voices in his head were definitely more muffled.

Had one of the guards tranqed him? Sometimes they hit him with a double dose that lingered after he woke. Or maybe he had asked Melanie to sedate him? It took quite a lot of the sedative to put him to sleep now.

He frowned as he tried to puzzle through it. Hadn't he seen Seth last night?

Memory slowly forced its way through the fog as he grabbed his electric razor.

Yes. He *had* seen Seth.

A smile slowly stretched his lips as he removed his beard stubble.

Cliff had gone hunting with Aidan and Bastien and...

His eyes widened

They had found two of the missing immortals! A man and a woman. He couldn't remember their names... or many details other than the two had been prowling UNC Chapel Hill's campus with a fairly large group of vampires.

Gershom had captured and transformed a dozen *gifted ones*. And until last night, the Immortal Guardians had only managed to locate and retrieve one.

Now they'd found two more.

Hadn't a battle taken place?

Hmm. There *must* have been a battle. Because he remembered Seth praising him afterward for keeping the vampires busy and killing them all so Aidan and Bastien could disarm and hold the immortals until Seth arrived.

Joy rushed through him, accompanied by relief.

Finally. He *finally* had good news he could share with Emma when he saw her later. *I helped Bastien and Aidan rescue two of the missing immortals!*

It had been so long since anything good had happened. He couldn't wait to see her and watch her face light up when he told her.

He glanced at his watch. Unfortunately, he'd have to. The sun hadn't set yet.

He shrugged. Maybe he could find the new immortals and help them settle in here at network headquarters. Tessa, the only other missing immortal they'd been able to find, had warmed up to him pretty quickly considering she'd met him on one of his...

Well... he couldn't say one of his bad days. They were *all* bad says now. So maybe one of his *worse* days?

Cliff listened to the goings-on outside his door while he dressed in a T-shirt, cargo pants, and boots—all black. The other vampires often teased him about what they called his IG-wannabe attire. They didn't know that he wore black because he never knew when his mental state might deteriorate so much during the day that Aidan would have to teleport him to the other side of the globe where it was still night and take him hunting because Cliff couldn't hold out until the sun set.

As soon as he finished tying his shoes, he left his apartment.

Todd and Jin, another guard, walked toward him in the hallway, heading back to their post from he didn't know where.

Jin nodded, his expression aloof but not hostile.

"Hey, man." Todd proffered his fist. "How's it going?"

Cliff fist-bumped him. "It's going. How's Cynthia?"

He grinned. "Out of my league."

Cliff smiled. "But she loves you anyway?"

"Hell yes, she does."

They had greeted each other thusly for what seemed like forever, and Cliff took comfort in the routine of it. "Hey, do you know the names of the two new immortals? I can't remember them."

"Jordan and Liora."

Cliff silently repeated the names, committing them to memory.

"Do you know where they are? I thought I'd say hi and show them around sublevel 5 if no one else already has."

Todd jerked a thumb over his shoulder. "They're down in 10. We just came from there. Liora wanted to talk to Melanie, something about blood work. I saw her chatting with Tessa earlier and think she's starting to grasp the reality of it all. But Melanie and Bastien haven't arrived yet. Aidan either. They had a long night last night."

He would imagine so with two new immortals to initiate to the truth.

Todd shrugged. "Sunset isn't that far away though. Until then, Jared is here if you need anything."

"Okay. Thanks."

Cliff strode toward apartment 10.

Before he reached it, the heavy door swung inward and a man and woman stepped out. The man—whom he took to be Jordan—was tall and broad-shouldered with dark, closely cropped hair. Liora was shorter with long auburn hair. They appeared to be carrying on a rather heated discussion and didn't notice him at first. Though their lips moved, they spoke so low that even with his preternatural hearing he couldn't hear them over the damned voices in his head.

Cliff continued forward, the thuds of his boots drawing their attention.

The moment they saw him, they froze.

He smiled. "Hi. I'm Cliff. We met last night."

Liora's eyes widened and color fled her face as she took a hasty step backward.

Jordan's eyes widened, too. Then his brows drew down in a scowl as he thrust an arm out in front of the woman as if to shield her and pointed at Cliff. "You stay the hell back!"

Caught off guard by the malice reflected in the man's expression, Cliff halted. "What?"

"You heard me," he snapped. "Stay the hell away from her."

"Jordan," Liora protested softly. But unease darkened the eyes that didn't stray from Cliff… as though she feared he might attack if she looked away for even a second. "Take it easy. While you were sedated, I chatted with the other vampires. And it isn't what you think."

Nodding, Cliff held up his hands in an attempt to appear harmless. "Yeah. I think there's been some kind of misunderstanding."

If anything, Jordan's expression darkened further as his eyes acquired an amber glow. "I'm not misunderstanding shit. You tried to kill Liora last night. And you would've succeeded if that British immortal hadn't intervened."

Ice filled Cliff's veins. His breath stopped. "What?"

"You tried to kill her!" Jordan repeated furiously. "You *would've* killed her if —"

Jared appeared at Jordan's side, startling him into silence. "Shut up," he ordered, face grim.

Jordan scowled up at him. Recovering quickly, he opened his mouth.

Jared waved a hand.

Jordan flew off his feet and through the doorway into apartment 10. A crash sounded just before the door clunked shut.

Cliff's heart began to pound.

Jared's expression softened as he looked down at Liora. "Are you all right?"

She nodded.

But she wasn't. Her hands trembled visibly, and she looked poised for flight.

Jared turned to Cliff. "Ignore Jordan. He's having difficulty accepting the truth. He doesn't want to believe it, so he's lashing out at everyone."

Jordan's voice carried through the door. "That's bullshit and you know it! Keep him the fuck away from her!"

Eyes flashing golden, Jared stared at the door. Another crash resounded inside, followed by a curse.

"What's he talking about, Jared?" Cliff asked, his voice hoarse with dread as he stared at the ancient immortal. "Did I hurt her? Did I…" He swallowed, then forced himself to continue. "Did I try to kill her? Was he telling the truth?"

Seth had *praised* him. Cliff had thought he'd *helped* Bastien and Aidan. He thought he'd *helped* Liora. But when he forced himself to look at her again, the truth lay in her posture as she edged closer to Jared and in the eyes that held Cliff's with both fear and sorrow.

No. Not sorrow.

Pity.

Suddenly an image flashed through his mind of Liora stumbling backward as she stared up at him with eyes full of panic, her long hair disheveled. A deep gash on one side of her face bled profusely. More wounds wept on her arms. And Bastien gripped Cliff's wrists, shouting for him to stop as he fought to keep Cliff from delivering a death blow.

Horror filled him, coupled with self-loathing as he staggered back a step. Then two more. He shook his head, not wanting to believe it.

"Cliff," Jared said gently, "it isn't as bad as you think."

"The fuck it isn't!" he shouted. "I tried to kill her!"

Stuart and Miguel appeared in the doorway to the infirmary, skin gleaming with a sheen of perspiration from their runs on the treadmills.

"Cliff?" Stuart asked, his face full of concern.

Cliff shook his head, continuing backward, placing more distance between himself and the woman.

Jared's expression firmed. "Jordan is only telling you half the tale, Cliff. He's conveniently leaving out the fact that he, Liora, and almost a dozen other vampires were doing their damnedest to kill you."

Jared's presence seemed to ease the woman's fear enough for her to speak. "It's true," she said. "We thought you were an Immortal Guardian."

But Cliff, shaken to his core, barely heard her. He had nearly slain an immortal female. If Bastien had been slower to respond, Cliff *would* have!

You cut that bitch up, a voice taunted gleefully.

He had laid open her cheek. He'd cut her arms. He'd *wanted* to kill her.

Why had he thought he'd helped her?

Because Seth lied to you, the voice hissed.

The truth of that simple statement twisted his insides. Seth had lied to him. Seth had even altered his memories. It *had* to have been Seth. Cliff just couldn't see Aidan doing such a thing.

But Aidan had been there. Hadn't he? And he hadn't stopped Seth. Bastien hadn't either.

Jared took a step toward him. "Let me help you. Let me calm you."

Fury consumed him like a flash fire. The voices surged with triumph. "You stay the fuck away from me!" Cliff snarled, not even recognizing his own voice.

Seth lied to you. You trusted him, and he betrayed you. So did Bastien. And Aidan. They all betrayed you. This one will, too.

Kill *them. Kill them* all!

His pulse pounded in his ears as he curled his hands into fists.

He should. He should kill them all. He'd trusted them not to let him hurt anyone. He'd trusted them, and they'd *lied* to him!

Yes! Kill them! Butcher them! Fuck them up!

Jared took another step toward him.

Roaring, Cliff shot back to his apartment in a blur and slammed the heavy door.

Once inside, he stood still, breathing hard, every muscle tense. His whole body shook with rage as bloody image after bloody image flitted through his mind.

How many times had they lied to him?

Bastien. Aidan. Melanie. Linda. Seth.

How many atrocities had they covered up?

Were some of the nightmares he had and some of the images that flitted through his mind of brutally tearing vampires apart... memories? Had he done that?

Did he do that?

He had thought them merely depraved delusions spawned by the madness, like the verbal taunts that maintained a constant litany in his head. But what if they weren't? What if, instead of delivering a quick death, he inflicted unnecessary agony on the vampires he killed? Vampires who might even be more lucid than him?

How many had he savaged?

Stumbling over to the kitchen, he grabbed one of the barstools and hurled it across the room with such force that it splintered against the wall. A large chunk of drywall fell off, revealing the heavy concrete beneath. He hurled a second barstool. Then a third. Tore the sofa apart. Smashed the large-screen television with the coffee table. Swept everything from the bar.

Pain and despair devoured him inside, ramping up the rage.

How could they do this to him? *How could they do this?*

He yanked a door off one of the kitchen cabinets and let it fly.

It embedded itself in the bathroom door.

How many victims had they made him forget?

He yanked another off and threw it, the contents of the cabinets tumbling out and littering the countertops and floor.

How many lies had they told him?

He yanked another off and pitched it at a lamp.

He'd waited too long.

He overturned the heavy refrigerator.

Because he'd trusted them to tell him the truth and they'd lied, he had waited too long!

Liora's bloody face again flashed through his mind as he tore off the oven door with a screech of metal.

What if that had been Emma?

He paused, breathing hard, the oven door clutched in his hands.

What if that had been Emma and Bastien hadn't been around to stop him?

His grip tightened, compressing the metal and forming grooves beneath his fingertips.

What if he'd had a psychotic break and yanked the watch off Emma's wrist before she could call Aidan?

He dropped the oven door.

What if Emma has been lying, too? a demon inside him snarled.

Cliff shook his head. No. She wouldn't do that. She wouldn't lie to him.

Everyone else might. But not Emma. *Never* Emma.

He glanced at the kitchen cabinets, their contents exposed now that he'd obliterated the doors. Stepping over the rubble, he thrust his hands into one and rummaged around.

Panic rose when he didn't find what he sought.

Frantically, he searched through the pile of crap that had fallen on the countertop, then dropped to his knees and combed through the splintered wood, plastic peanut butter jars, broken glass, boxes of cookies, burst bags of chips. He tunneled through cold tubs of ice cream and frozen foods that had spilled from the overturned fridge, and —

There!

Cliff scrambled across the mess and grabbed the box of graham crackers. Hands shaking, he dumped it upside down. Two sleeves of brown crackers fell atop the mess, followed by a cell phone.

Cliff fumbled to catch it before it could hit the floor, then stood up.

As soon as he touched it, the lock screen lit up and Emma gazed up at him.

His hands shook so badly it took him four tries to type in the passcode.

While the voices howled for him to put the phone down and go fuck someone up, he swiped through the photos.

Emma smiling. Emma laughing. Emma teaching him how to knit winter hats.

They must have made a hundred of those damned things.

Emma speckled with paint and grinning as she brandished a wet paintbrush while they painted her kitchen cabinets.

Emma leaning toward him with a smile full of love.

Moisture welled in his eyes as he wondered how the hell he could tell her what he'd done, that Bastien had had to physically restrain him to keep him from killing a female immortal.

How could he tell her she'd been wrong in her fervent belief that he could win this battle?

How could he admit he'd waited too long?

He swiped to the next photo and the next, his heart splitting.

He'd just wanted to give Melanie and the others more time to find a way to heal him.

He'd wanted to have that happily-ever-after with Emma. To have the house and the picket fence and the children and the dog.

He'd been so focused on the dream… so reluctant to give it up… that he'd missed the moment when the monster growing inside him had snuck up and devoured the last lingering bit of him that she'd fallen in love with.

He swiped again.

A photo of himself grinned up at him.

THIS IS WHO YOU ARE, Emma had written across the bottom.

But it wasn't, he acknowledged with utter despair.

Not anymore.

Agony engulfing him, Cliff tightened his hold on the phone until a spiderweb of cracks streaked across the screen, distorting his image. Then he slung it across the room.

It shattered when it struck the wall, tiny pieces scattering like buckshot.

Unfortunately, it couldn't erase the image of himself from his mind.

"That isn't who I am," he murmured hoarsely.

He looked at the chaos that surrounded him, the destruction he had wrought, and saw again Liora's bloody face.

"*This* is who I am."

The voices roared in triumph.

Beneath them, a heartbeat sounded.

Cliff spun around.

Jared stood behind him. Reaching out, he touched his fingertips to Cliff's forehead. "Sleep."

Darkness fell.

Chapter Twenty-Three

E MMA STARED, UNSEEING, AT THE television.
Something had happened.

One knee bobbed up and down much like Cliff's did when he was agitated.

She didn't know *what* had happened, just that it was bad.

Cliff hadn't come by last night, which meant he'd had a psychotic break.

It always meant that now. And those breaks had been coming closer and closer together.

But this one was different. She didn't know the details. She could only guess based on the little bit Todd had allowed Cynthia to wheedle out of him.

Bastien and Aidan had taken Cliff hunting last night, and whatever had happened had taken place outside the safety of network headquarters.

Cliff had never had a psychotic break outside network headquarters before.

She bit her lip.

Had he hurt someone? Someone who *wasn't* a vampire? Had he…

Had he attacked a human?

Todd either didn't know or wouldn't say. But he'd admitted that Cliff had been unconscious when Bastien and Aidan brought him back to the network, his hands coated in blood.

He'd said Melanie had wept. And Bastien's and Aidan's eyes had been suspiciously moist.

Emma had been unable to concentrate for the rest of the day, tears of concern hovering just beneath the surface, so she'd left work early. She would've lingered in case Mr. Reordon allowed her to see Cliff. But Todd said Cliff had been sleeping heavily all day.

Cliff only did that when they sedated him. So at least he...

She closed her eyes.

At least he was still with them. He hadn't asked them to kill him, to let him go.

Nevertheless, the fear and dread and sense of impending doom that had nearly suffocated her all day refused to relent.

Opening her eyes, she glanced at the front windows.

Darkness lay beyond them.

Normally she would have already showered, changed, and succumbed to a nap while she waited for Cliff to work out some of his aggression on a hunt and then come to her.

She glanced down. All she'd managed thus far tonight was to shower and change into a comfy T-shirt and yoga pants, too anxious to sleep despite the fatigue that rarely abandoned her.

She needed to see Cliff. Needed to know he was okay. Needed to feel his arms around her and hear him say he wasn't ready to give up the fight despite whatever had happened.

A tall, dark figure abruptly appeared several feet away.

Yelping, she sprang to her feet.

Oh shit.

Seth, leader of the Immortal Guardians, towered over her. Standing roughly six feet eight inches tall with broad shoulders, a muscled form, and hair down to his hips, he'd been a frequent visitor at the network the past few years.

He held up his hands. "Forgive me for startling you," he said, face grim. "You're needed at the network."

Fear filled her as she hurried toward him, not even pausing to slip on a pair of shoes.

As soon as she was within reach, he clasped her shoulder.

Darkness surrounded her, accompanied by a feeling of weightlessness.

Then light resumed, and she found herself standing in...

Well, she wasn't sure. A shattered big-screen television and what was left of a sofa indicated it was someone's residence. But the place had been completely trashed. Overturned furniture—splintered and barely recognizable as such—cluttered the place, forming disjointed mounds and ragged ridges. Fragments of glass caught the overhead light and glittered like diamonds amid the remains of a coffee table with a missing metal leg.

A crash split the air.

Emma jumped.

"Let me out!" someone bellowed, his voice deep and rough as though he'd been shouting for hours.

Gasping, she whirled around. Something sharp pricked her foot. A piece of glass perhaps. But Emma paid it no heed. Instead, she stared at the man who was doing his damnedest to beat his way out of the room with the missing metal leg from the coffee table.

Sweat glistened on the smooth brown skin of muscled arms left bare by his T-shirt. White powder—Sheetrock perhaps?—clung to the perspiration and speckled his dreadlocks.

Unaware of their presence, he continued to hammer away at the wall. "Let me out!" *Crash.* "Let me out!" *Crash.*

His violent strikes had succeeded in removing a large chunk of drywall beside the door. What looked like concrete lay beneath. But it, too, began to crack and crumble beneath his powerful blows. "Let me out!" he roared.

Tears filled her eyes. "Cliff?" she called softly. She'd never seen him like this before and wondered if she'd even be able to reach him.

Her pulse pounded in her ears as silence fell.

Cliff wheeled around so quickly he nearly toppled over. His brilliant amber eyes glowed with madness as he regarded them, brows lowered, face full of fury as his breath emerged in jagged gasps.

Emma's heart broke. No recognition lit Cliff's eyes as he glared at Seth.

Even when he shifted his gaze to meet hers, she wasn't sure he really *saw* her.

"Calm him," Seth said suddenly. "We need his help." His hand still on Emma's shoulder, Seth reached out with the other and grabbed Cliff.

Dizzying darkness swirled around her once more. Then they stood in Mr. Reordon's swanky boardroom. But this time they weren't alone.

At the opposite end, Mr. Reordon hovered over a laptop while he spoke rapidly into a cell phone. The immortal Zach was there, too, along with an older man in military fatigues.

Emma had seen Zach around network headquarters a few times in recent months. The gray-haired soldier seemed oddly familiar, like someone she'd seen on the news or something. Wasn't he a general?

Yes! General Lane.

Seth released them and moved toward the others.

A thunk drew her gaze to the floor. Cliff had dropped the coffee table leg.

When she looked up, his gaze was fastened on her face. He said nothing, breath still coming in harsh gasps. He just stared at her as though he wasn't sure she was really there.

Reaching out, she slipped her hand into his and twined their fingers together, willing him to know her, to find his way back to her.

He held on tight, the battle he waged palpable.

Her throat thickened.

"I have Scott Henderson on the line," Mr. Reordon announced. "He'll have special-ops teams en route in two minutes. My own team is assembling in the hangar."

"Excellent," Seth said.

General Lane cast Cliff a wary look before addressing Seth. "My team is on standby if you need them."

"Thank you." Seth returned and stood nearly nose-to-nose with Cliff, demanding his attention. "Bastien, Melanie, and the others are being held in a military facility defended by mercenaries."

Emma tensed. *Oh shit.*

"We're about to descend upon it en force. General Lane believes the alarm will trigger fail-safes or booby traps installed in the base to prevent anyone who succeeds in infiltrating it from leaving alive. I need you to help us pinpoint those fail-safes before we trigger them so we won't lose anyone."

Her stomach sank.

A muscle twitched in Cliff's tight jaw before he issued a nod. "I won't let you down."

Absolute terror filled her. As soon as Seth turned away, she tugged Cliff over to a corner. Releasing his hand, she cupped his face in both hands and met his glowing gaze, relieved to find it less wild and more lucid. "Honey," she whispered urgently, "I don't know what's happening, but—"

"Gershom took them," he said, his voice retaining a hint of the roughness that had rendered it unrecognizable earlier. "He captured them all. Bastien, Melanie, Aidan, and every other immortal stationed in North Carolina. He even took Seth's daughter and granddaughter."

Shock stole her breath. "What? How?"

"I don't know. I can't..." His face tight with frustration, he reached up and fisted a hand in his hair. "I can't think straight today."

Releasing him, she gently took both his hands in hers to keep him from pulling his dreadlocks.

"I think I had a break earlier," he said. "I blacked out. And when I woke up, I was locked in my apartment and everything was trashed." He shook his head. "There were so many voices. Not just the ones in my head telling me to kill everyone..."

Her blood chilled.

"But others. It was the medical staff in the infirmary. When Gershom captured the immortals, he also injured all of their Seconds. So badly they suffered brain damage. I heard Seth tell Linda that Bastien and the others had been taken. I wanted to help. I wanted to help find them. But no one would let me out. They wouldn't listen. They wouldn't let me out. And..." He gripped her hands so tightly it almost hurt. "I-I-I think I lost it. Then you and Seth were there."

Grim-faced Immortal Guardians decked out in black and armed for war began to fill the boardroom, but Emma kept her gaze on Cliff. "Honey, I know you want to help, but—"

"I *have* to help them," he told her earnestly.

"No. You don't." It sounded like he'd already had two psychotic breaks today, another terrifying first. If he went into battle in his current state of mind—

"Yes, I do," he insisted.

And something in his voice made her fall quiet.

His Adam's apple rose and fell with a hard swallow. Moisture filled his amber eyes. "I fucked up," he choked out.

She stared up at him. "What?"

Again he swallowed. "Last night I nearly killed one of the missing female immortals Seth has been searching for."

For a moment she couldn't breathe. It was what he had always feared, that he would harm an innocent. "Cliff—"

"I thought she was a vampire. A male vampire like the others she was hunting with," he said, his tone one of desperation and despair. "She had her hair tucked up under a hat and..."

He shook his head. "Seth tried to make me forget it. He tried to make me think I'd helped. But I'm so fucked up in the head now that it... didn't take or... I don't know. I still remember some of it."

Emma sensed the sidelong glances the Immortal Guardians slid their way but ignored them.

"I cut her, Emma." A tear spilled down his cheek. "Her face. Her arms. I cut her. And I would've killed her if Bastien hadn't stopped me."

"Cliff," she forced out, blinking back tears. What could she say to him? "Honey, you thought she was a vampire."

"If I'd been lucid, I would've known she wasn't." He shook his head once more, his beautiful face full of anguish. "I can't be like this anymore, Emma. I can't hurt innocents. The whole reason I came here was so I *wouldn't* hurt innocents."

Panic screamed through her. This couldn't be it. She couldn't lose him. Not yet. She wasn't ready. She would *never* be ready.

As if mocking her, she heard Seth ask, "Are we ready?"

"Yeah," Mr. Reordon responded.

Cliff released her hands and started to turn away.

Her heart shattering, Emma caught his arm, threw her own around him, and drew him close for a last desperate kiss. "I love you."

His expression softened a little as he gently disengaged her grip and cupped her face. "I love you, too." He smoothed his thumbs across her cheeks in a last caress. "Thank you. For everything."

Biting her lip to hold back a sob, she watched him move away to stand with the Immortal Guardians.

"Everyone grab a shoulder," Seth instructed, his skin now bearing a peculiar glow. "We strike fast and we strike hard."

A unanimous battle cry filled the room.

Cliff's eyes met hers through the crowd.

Then everyone vanished.

Silence fell.

Tears blurred her vision, then spilled over her lashes.

Emma sank to her knees on the floor.

Cliff was gone.

And she knew in her heart she would never see him again.

———◦◦◦———

One second Cliff was holding Emma's tear-filled gaze. The next he stood shoulder to shoulder with a hell of a lot of Immortal Guardians in an airplane hangar. Beyond their grouping, dozens of human soldiers sporting black fatigues, helmets, bulletproof vests, and a shitload of weaponry faced them. Tanks and other large military vehicles filled the space behind them.

Was this it?

When he let go of the shoulder in front of him, the immortal—one he'd never seen before—murmured over his shoulder, "Not yet."

Cliff had just enough time to grab the guy's shoulder again before Seth said, "Here we go."

Darkness and that dizzying sensation teleportation generated struck. Then fresh air filled Cliff's nose as a breeze ruffled his hair. Massive trees rose up around them. A large base stretched in front of them. And every immortal, human, and military vehicle had made the jump.

Cliff hadn't even known teleportation on that scale was possible.

Seconds later, Seth teleported them again. Or rather he teleported David, the other Immortal Guardians, and Cliff to a wide hallway inside the building.

Half a dozen guards manning a checkpoint at the end of the hallway gaped at them.

The immortals surged forward, taking out the guards before they could sound an alarm.

Cliff followed close on their heels, unsure of his role. He'd been so focused on Emma that he'd missed whatever instructions Seth had given the others. And the last thing he wanted to do was to hinder their efforts to find Bastien, Melanie, and the rest.

Gunfire erupted outside.

Inside, the Immortal Guardians plowed through another checkpoint. More guards fell beneath the onslaught. The metallic scent of blood filled the air.

The voices in Cliff's head bellowed for action. But he fought them, determined not to fuck this up, determined to right the egregious wrong he'd committed the previous night.

His last act would *not* be that of a monster.

An alarm blared suddenly. Several grunts reached Cliff's ears. The bodies in front of him halted abruptly.

Zach cursed. "The fail-safes have been triggered."

"So we bypass them," Jared said.

But no one seemed to move.

Wait. Fail-safes?

Cliff shouldered his way through the immortals until he stood beside Seth. A couple of immortals yanked blades out of their chests. More blades, which looked like five- or six-inch daggers without hilts—littered the floor.

This was why Seth had wanted him join them. To thwart the fail-safes.

Cliff studied the floor tiles carefully, then the walls of the hallway. Who would've thought all those years of playing video games that required you to run gauntlets riddled with booby traps might someday come in handy? "I don't see anything in the floor that looks pressure sensitive, so there must be motion-activated sensors in the walls that trip them."

He darted forward at preternatural speed. Pain pierced him when two blades impaled him. Grunting, he stopped and yanked them out. Yep. They were definitely motion activated. But... "These weren't designed to stop humans. They were designed to stop *us*, or at least to slow us down."

"How do you know?" Seth asked.

"Watch." Hoping like hell he was right, Cliff walked up the hallway at ordinary human speed.

Triumph filled him when no more blades struck him.

"Shit," Zach murmured behind him. "They *are* for us."

"Gershom must have had them modified," Seth agreed.

In the next instant, Seth's voice filled Cliff's head, pushing the gruesome ones aside as he addressed the group telepathically. *We're going to teleport ahead. Follow as quickly as you can at mortal speed, but leave every hallway guarded and search every room. We're going after Gershom.*

They nodded.

Gripping David's shoulder, Seth teleported to Cliff's side. He caught and held Cliff's gaze. *Guide them.*

Cliff nodded. *I'll get them through safely,* he vowed, hoping Seth could hear him over the clamor in his head. *You won't lose a single immortal tonight.*

Seth looked at something behind Cliff, then teleported away with David.

The other Immortal Guardians strode toward Cliff at a normal pace.

Cliff's nerves jangled. He didn't doubt that every single one of them knew he was a vampire. They might have even overheard him confessing to Emma that he'd nearly killed Liora. And they were supposed to follow *him*?

The big guy in the lead was one of the immortals who had been impaled with a fail-safe dagger. He caught and held his gaze. "You're Cliff, the vampire."

"Yes." The voices in his head surged, balking at being the object of so many piercing stares.

"I'm Mattheus. It's an honor to meet you."

The greeting stunned him. "It's an honor to meet you, too." He looked at the others. "All of you. But time is short. Seth has tasked me with getting you through the fail-safes, so if you'll follow me at a distance—"

Boots clomped beneath the *wonk wonk wonk* of the alarm.

Cliff whirled around just as three soldiers swung around a corner up ahead.

Swearing, the soldiers opened fire.

Cliff shot toward them. Blades flew from the walls, slicing his flesh, two embedding themselves in his side. Bullets peppered him.

Growling, he dove at the soldiers and slew them all.

Pain inundated him.

Gritting his teeth, he turned toward the immortals and motioned them forward. "Move forward at mortal speed." He drew the blades out and dropped them to the floor.

Mattheus was the first to reach him. "Let me go through the next one."

"No. I can guide you through safely." Three doors opened onto the hallway. Cliff nodded to them. "We should check those so we'll know if the rooms have fail-safes, too." It only took seconds, and none did.

"Okay. Follow me." Cliff headed up the hallway.

Behind him, Mattheus ordered two immortals to remain behind and take out any guards they encountered.

At the next intersection, Cliff called a halt. This was taking too long. He needed to find the damn sensors so they could pick up the pace.

Guards at the far end opened fire but only managed to hit Cliff twice before an immortal teleported behind them and snapped their necks.

Cliff darted forward with enhanced speed. Pain struck. He jerked to a halt. Something whizzed past his front, missing him by a hair's breadth.

He looked down. What looked like a tranquilizer dart—much larger than the compact ones the network had developed—stuck out of his shoulder.

He plucked it out.

Mattheus and the others caught up to him.

"What is it?" Mattheus asked.

A slight lethargy drew Cliff's notice. He shook his head. "I think it's the tranquilizer."

"You think?"

He nodded. "The virus fuels me with so much energy and aggression now that one dose hardly affects me." He pointed at the hallway at the far end of this one. "Don't go down that without me doing it first."

He returned to the primary corridor while Mattheus again assigned men to search the rooms.

"I can see the sensors now," Cliff announced with relief. They were ingenious, blending seamlessly with the rest of the wall. But now that he knew about where they should be situated and what to look for, he could spy them. "Watch carefully." After backing up a few steps, he raced forward at preternatural speed, angling toward one side, and—just before he reached the first sensor— jumped up. His right foot hit the wall a foot above the sensor as his body canted sideways. His left foot hit the wall yards away above another. His right hit the wall again and pushed off. Then he landed on the floor at the next intersection, having triggered not one fail-safe.

Yes!

Bullets plowed into him.

Snarling, Cliff swung around to face the soldiers firing at him from the end of the long corridor.

"Rafe," Mattheus called.

The teleporting immortal appeared behind the humans and took them out.

A river of black flowed up the wall behind Cliff, following his exact path.

Cliff didn't wait for them. He entered the adjacent hallway. Saw the same sensors. Showed them the path to take. Did the same with the next hallway. When he reached the next, a quick scan revealed no motion sensors. He checked the floor. Nothing. Had they thought the immortals wouldn't get this far?

He shot toward the opposite end.

Pain lacerated his arms.

Skidding to a halt, he took in the new gashes and the blades that had carved them.

Damn it. What had he missed?

He saw no sensors in the walls. Nothing on the floor.

He looked up. *There.* "The sensors are in the ceiling on this one." Sticking close to the wall, he darted forward again and made it safely to the end. "Hug the walls and you'll get through." A burning began at the site of the wounds, as if the blades had been coated with cayenne pepper. But the ground began to tremble beneath his feet, a rumble accompanying it, reminding him they needed to hurry.

Wiping it from his mind, he lunged forward.

And so it went. Cliff took the lead in every hallway, racking up wounds while he found routes of safe passage for the others. They could have navigated the hallways at mortal speed, but time was tight. The roar of gunfire filled the air constantly. And they couldn't afford to give any mercenaries a chance to flee.

The base was big and boasted many corridors, almost every one of which sported fail-safe measures of one kind or another. Every blade that cut or impaled Cliff, every bullet that pierced him, seemed to clear his head more. The pain that buffeted him intensified by the second. But he kept pushing forward, kept clearing paths, showing the immortals how to remain unscathed, hoping every life he saved would redeem him for those he'd taken. And those he had *almost* taken.

Mattheus tried to stop him, tried to take the lead to spare him. "We can take more damage than you, damn it."

But Cliff shook his head and continued onward. "It has to be me."

"Seth wouldn't want you to—"

"It has to be me," Cliff repeated resolutely. Because this had to end. Tonight.

He had lost his battle with the madness. But he would win the war. He'd let these fail-safes bleed the monster right out of him and deny it dominion. Instead of killing innocents and having to be put down like a rabid dog, he would sacrifice himself for others. It was the closest thing to a heroic death he could hope for.

So he ran the gauntlet. Again. And again. And again.

And as he did, he stopped seeing the guards who shot him.

Instead he saw Emma's beautiful face.

He stopped hearing the monster inside him howl its fury over being thwarted.

And instead heard Emma's off-key singing. The musical sound of her laughter. Her gasps of ecstasy. And the affection that laced her voice as she told him she loved him.

He stopped feeling the cuts, the gashes, and the blades sinking deep into his flesh.

And felt her lips brush his instead.

Too late, he noticed something off about the floor in front of him. The tile beneath his foot sank a millimeter. The wall beside him exploded. Fire scorched him. Agony assailed him as the blast swept him off his feet. So much pain battered him that he couldn't make a sound as he flew through the air, then hit the floor, skidded across it, and slammed into something hard.

A crack sounded. More pain ricocheted through his head.

All strength left him as he lay there, stunned into immobility.

Blood rattled in his lungs as he struggled to draw breath.

Blurring, dark forms swarmed forward and crouched around him.

His heart strove to beat as a face appeared before him.

Not that of the Immortal Guardian bending over him. But Emma's.

Instead of large fingers searching for a pulse in his neck, he felt Emma's delicate fingers caress his face.

His lips turning up in a faint smile, Cliff surrendered to oblivion.

Chapter Twenty-Four

E MMA DIDN'T KNOW HOW LONG she sat there, crumpled on the boardroom floor, sobbing her heart out, before murmuring voices carried to her from Mr. Reordon's office through the open door.

Footsteps approached, alerting her that someone had entered.

"Oh shit," Cynthia whispered.

Emma forced herself to look up as her friend hurried toward her.

Dropping to her knees, Cynthia wrapped her arms around Emma and drew her into a tight hug.

Emma sagged against her, crying so hard she couldn't speak.

"It's okay," Cynthia whispered, rocking her and patting her back. "It's okay. You don't have to say anything. You just cry it out, honey. I'm here for you."

Kate appeared a moment later with a box of tissues and two bottles of water.

"Thank you," Cynthia murmured.

Nodding, Kate set them down within reach and left.

"Here." Yanking a few tissues from the box, Cynthia pressed them against the back of the hands Emma wept into.

Emma accepted them gratefully and wiped her running nose.

Keeping one arm around her, Cynthia grabbed a bottle of water, twisted the lid off behind Emma's back, then offered it to her. "Take a sip."

Leaning away a little, shoulders slumped, Emma did as bidden. Her choppy breathing didn't make it easy. But her eyes, cheeks, and nose were hot from weeping, and the cold liquid felt good sliding down.

Cynthia opened the other bottle and wet a wad of tissues with it. Like a mother tending a child, she patted Emma's heated skin and puffy eyes. "What can I do?" she asked gently.

More tears spilled over Emma's lashes as she shook her head. "N-Nothing." Her breath hitched. "He's gone."

Her friend's eyes widened with dismay. "What?"

"Cliff's g-gone."

"Oh no. Oh honey." She pulled Emma into another hug.

Emma blew her nose and wiped her eyes but couldn't seem to stem the tide of tears as she gave Cynthia an abbreviated account of what had happened.

"But Cliff's tough," Cynthia said. "You know that. I'm sure he'll kick ass, take names, then come back and give you all the—"

"No. He won't," Emma told her. "I saw it in his eyes. He isn't coming back. This is how he wants to go. He's going to die tonight."

Saying it out loud just sparked another round of sobs.

Cynthia stayed with her, holding her, rocking her, and making soothing sounds.

What felt like hours passed before a throat cleared.

"Cyn?" a masculine voice said tentatively.

They looked over.

Todd stood in the doorway, his expression somber and uncertain. "Kate asked me to come. She thought you might want me to drive you and Emma home."

Cynthia glanced at Emma. "Do you want to go home?" She dabbed her face with more cool tissues. "Or you could come to our place. Why don't you do that? Why don't you stay with us tonight? I promise Todd won't snore."

Todd nodded as if he were silently vowing not to snore.

"Home," Emma said softly. "I want to go home."

"You got it, honey. Whatever you want." Cynthia rose, drawing Emma up with her. "Sweetie, would you get the tissues and the water, please?"

"Sure." Todd hurried forward and grabbed the bottled water and box of tissues. "You want me to pick these up?" He motioned to the tear-soaked, snotty tissues that littered the floor around them. "I saw a wastebasket in Reordon's office. It'll just take a minute."

Kate's voice carried to them from the next room. "Don't worry about that. I'll take care of it."

"Okay." He hovered behind them as they left the boardroom.

Kate stood beside Mr. Reordon's desk. "Here." She handed Cynthia her purse, then turned to Emma. "These are for you." She held out a pair of scuffed running shoes. "I think we wear about the same size."

"Thank you." Emma sat on the sofa she and Cliff had occupied several times and slipped her bare feet into the sneakers, which fit comfortably enough. As soon as she stood, Cynthia wrapped an arm around her once more and Todd resumed his hovering.

"Don't worry about work, Emma," Kate said as they left the office. "You take as much time as you need. We've got your back." Even *she* didn't believe Cliff was coming back.

"Thank you." Emma straightened her shoulders before they hit the lobby but still drew stares as Todd and Cynthia escorted her out of the building because she couldn't calm her damn breathing.

Or maybe it was just the shattered look on her face or the grim expressions on the others'.

When they reached a dark SUV, Cynthia climbed in the back seat with Emma and gave Todd directions. Once they reached Emma's home, Cynthia dug out her keys and used the spare Emma had given her to unlock the door.

The TV was still on.

So much had happened since Seth had popped in and told her they needed her at the network that Emma couldn't believe so little time had passed.

"Wow," Cynthia said, looking around. "This place looks fantastic."

Emma hadn't realized until then just how long it had been since she'd had Cynthia over for a girls' night. "Cliff helped me fix it up."

Cynthia and Todd both swung around to stare at her.

Ignoring them, Emma shuffled into her bedroom and dug out a pair of pajama pants and a loose tank top, adding panties and a bra in deference to Todd's presence. "I'm going to take a shower," she mumbled.

"Okay." Cynthia whispered something to Todd, then joined Emma in the bathroom.

Emma found a faint smile. "You planning to join me?"

Cynthia laughed. "No. I just don't want you to be alone."

Emma didn't either. "Thank you."

"Anything you need, I'm here. Todd is, too. I hope you don't mind, but I told him to order a couple of pizzas. He was wringing his hands and looking adorably anxious because he wants to help but has no idea what he should be doing right now."

"He's a good guy."

Cynthia smiled. "Yeah, he is."

Aside from cooling her puffy face, the shower did little to make Emma feel better. Her eyes continued to water like a leaky spigot. Every limb seemed heavier. She just felt utterly and completely exhausted. Too much to partake of the fragrant pizza Todd had ordered. "I think I'm just going to go to bed."

"Okay." Cynthia followed her into the bedroom. "You want me to sit with you?"

"Yes, please." Emma curled up under the covers with her knees practically touching her chest, faced the wall, and closed her eyes.

Cynthia sat behind her on the bed and leaned back against the headboard, reaching over to rub Emma's shoulder.

"Would you turn the TV on?" Emma asked after a minute. "It's too quiet."

"Sure. Anything in particular you feel like listening to?"

"I don't care. I just need something to drown out my thoughts."

"All righty. You got it."

Soon tense music and explosions filled the bedroom as Cynthia chose what sounded like an action flick.

Emma closed her eyes, trying to visualize whatever took place on the screen.

But all she saw was Cliff's face and the love and finality that had filled his glowing amber eyes as he'd cupped her face and said, "Thank you. For everything."

⋘◈◈◈⋙

Cliff blinked. Dark arboreal giants towered over him, their limbs forming a complex canopy. Stars winked down at him between the branches. Cool ground cushioned his back.

Flexing his fingers, he curled them around crisp brown leaves, pine needles, and soil.

Slowly he sat up and looked around.

Where was he?

Several moments' thought failed to enlighten him.

The stars in the sky and darkness beyond the forest indicated it was nighttime. But nighttime where? He and Bastien usually hunted on college campuses.

Again he glanced around.

This was not a college campus.

And Bastien was nowhere in sight.

He rose, every limb oddly heavy.

His ears felt funny. Like someone had stuffed cotton in them or something.

Had he been tranqed?

He sniffed.

Trees. Soil. Decaying leaves. And smoke.

He glanced to the right. The smoke didn't smell like the kind produced by burning wood in a fireplace or cooking over a charcoal grill. It reminded him instead of the smoke that had suffused the air the morning mercenaries had attacked network headquarters.

He faced that direction.

Was network headquarters through there? Had mercenaries attacked it again?

He waited for alarm to fill him at the prospect, but it didn't. He felt oddly… detached.

Voices floated to him on the breeze, managing to penetrate the cotton in his ears. Using them as his guide, Cliff stumbled forward.

After a minute or two, the trees and foliage began to thin. Then he stepped out into a large clearing.

About fifty yards away, a group of men and woman garbed all in black clustered together on a cement slab.

He looked around. Why would a cement slab lie in the middle of a clearing with no other structures in sight?

Two figures raced toward him.

Bastien and Melanie. Both drew him into a hug.

"What happened?" he asked dully. "Did I have another break?" It would explain why the voices in his head had gone eerily silent and why he felt so out of it. "I don't remember what happened. Where are we? How did I get here?"

Melanie shook her head. "You helped Seth save us."

"I did?"

Bastien nodded.

Cliff could call forth no memory of that.

Melanie's eyes bore a faint glow as she blinked back tears and rubbed his arm. "Are you okay?"

He glanced down. Moonlight provided enough illumination for him to see the numerous holes, tears, and burn marks that marred his clothing. Though blood streaked his arms, nothing hurt. How long had he been unconscious? "Yeah." It must have been quite a while if his wounds had healed. "My ears feel funny." And everything else just felt… off. Sluggish. His mind foggy or something.

Had they given him too much sedative?

Bastien and Melanie exchanged a concerned look.

Gently clasping Cliff's chin, Melanie turned his head from one side to the other, then ran her hands along his limbs. Her brow furrowed. "I see blood, but I don't see any wounds."

Across the way, Seth frowned. "His wounds are all healed?"

Melanie nodded. "There isn't a scratch on him."

Then he *had* been wounded.

He hadn't chased someone into the forest and drained him, had he?

If so, he hoped like hell it was one of the bad guys… whoever the bad guys were. He still had no idea what had happened.

The sound of a vehicle approaching distracted him.

A Humvee sped into view, kicking up dust on the dirt road. Tires locking, it drifted to a halt inches from the concrete slab upon which Seth and the rest of the Immortal Guardians stood.

Chris Reordon stumbled out, eyes wide, hair mussed. He took a few steps toward the others, stopped, turned in a circle, then met Seth's gaze. "Okay. I don't know how the fuck I'm going to cover this up."

Everyone but Cliff burst into laughter.

Chris strode over to Seth and wrapped him in a bear hug. "Glad to see you made it."

Seth clapped him on the back. "Glad to see you did, too. Did the other Immortal Guardians and network soldiers all make it out safely?"

"Yeah. They're guarding the prisoners we took a couple of miles away. I didn't know what to expect after that big-ass explosion, so I told them to keep their distance and watch the flock while I came to see what had happened."

Cliff stared. Prisoners? Explosion? He didn't remember *any* of that.

"There was an explosion?" a tall woman hovering close to Seth asked.

"Well, yeah," Chris said as if he couldn't believe she'd asked. "I don't know how you could've missed it. Honestly, I expected all of you to be toast when I came back. It was *that* fucking big. And loud. And bright as hell. It stopped just short of creating a mushroom cloud."

What?

Again Cliff glanced around. Maybe that explained it. His difficulty remembering. His ears feeling weird. The confusion riding him. Maybe he had been caught in the blast.

He glanced down.

And maybe he wasn't the only one. Maybe he found one of the bad guys—he *really* hoped it was a bad guy—in the forest and drained him, then passed out on his way back to…

He looked around.

Wherever the hell they were.

"Don't worry about the cleanup," Seth told Reordon. "Have Henderson get his crew back to network headquarters here in Texas and…"

Cliff missed whatever the Immortal Guardians leader said after that.

They were in Texas? Why? He drew a complete blank when he tried again to remember, something that always filled him with anxiety after having a psychotic break.

Chris nodded. "I'm on it."

Seth caught his arm as Chris turned away. "Would you take Cliff with you and have Dr. Machen examine him once you're home?"

"Sure." Chris gestured to Cliff as he strode toward his vehicle. "Hop in."

The odd lethargy lingering, Cliff followed him and stepped up into the Humvee.

"You okay?" Chris asked as he wheeled the vehicle around.

"Yeah," Cliff said slowly. "I think so."

"Okay. Let's get you back to network headquarters."

"Emma?"

Emma frowned, cursing the tentative female voice that drew her back to consciousness. That way lay pain and despair and grief so deep she feared she might drown in it. She didn't want to go there.

"Emma?" A hand touched her shoulder and gave it a light shake. "I'm sorry to wake you, but Kate from Mr. Reordon's office is calling."

She could hear it now, the dinky incoming-call alert her phone issued. "Let it go to voice mail," she mumbled. If she didn't answer it, she wouldn't have to hear Kate confirm Cliff's death and could pretend there was still some tiny smidgeon of hope that he might have survived whatever the hell had happened at the military base he'd helped the Immortal Guardians blitz.

"Are you sure?" Cynthia asked.

"Yeah."

"What if she calls again?"

"Ignore it." Emma would return her call tomorrow.

"Okay." Cynthia patted her shoulder. "Can I get you anything before you go back to sleep?"

"No, thank you."

"Okay."

Fortunately, oblivion claimed Emma before more tears could fall.

"Emma?" Cynthia said, jostling her shoulder again.

She jerked awake. Damn it! "What?" she growled, squeezing her lids closed. Why wouldn't they just let her sleep? If she slept, she didn't have to think about—

"I'm sorry to wake you again, but Kate has called three times in the past hour and now she's at your front door."

Emma's eyes flew open. "What?"

"She's here. At the door. I'm surprised you didn't hear the doorbell ring."

She hadn't heard the doorbell ring because she had been blissfully ensconced in sleep.

Why would Kate come here?

Emma would ask how the woman knew where she lived, but working so closely with Mr. Reordon, Kate probably knew everything he did. And Chris Reordon knew freaking everything. He'd even known Emma and Cliff were seeing each other.

Pain sliced through her at the thought of Cliff.

Throwing back the covers, she rolled out of bed and stomped up the hallway to the living room.

Todd stood across the room, one arm on the open door, the other on the doorjamb, barring Kate entrance.

As Emma approached, he lowered his arm and stepped aside.

Kate stood on the porch, bathed in the warm light that spilled out of the pretty fixture Cliff had installed. Her face lit with relief when she saw Emma. "He's alive," she blurted.

Emma stopped short and sucked in a breath. "What?"

"Cliff's alive," Kate repeated. "I'm sorry to bother you at home. But you weren't answering your phone and I thought you should know that he made it, that Cliff survived the battle."

All breath whooshed out of Emma's lungs as she staggered a step.

Todd hastily reached out and grabbed her elbow to brace her.

Shock rendered her speechless. Cliff was alive? How could that be? He'd looked so determined to end it, his face so full of despair when he'd said, *I can't be like this anymore, Emma.* She had been sure when he left that she would never see him again.

"Where...?" It was all she could manage to force out.

"He's at network headquarters. Mr. Reordon and a couple of Immortal Guardians brought him back about an hour ago."

Emma's heart began to pound in her chest.

Cynthia stepped up to her side and wrapped an arm around her shoulders. "Is he okay?"

Kate nodded. "We believe so, yes. He's quiet and seems a little dazed the way he often does after a break—"

"He had a break?" Emma asked. That would be three in one day!

"No. Mattheus—one of the immortals—said Cliff did exactly what Seth asked him to do. He led them through the base and got them all past the fail-safes unscathed." She bit her lip. "He *was* injured quite badly while doing it. But his wounds had already healed by the time the dust cleared. Mattheus got him out of the base before the explosion."

There was an explosion?

"But he lost track of him in the chaos that followed. The general belief is that Cliff stumbled into the forest, came across one of the fleeing mercenaries, and drained him." She shrugged. "Since those mercenaries were helping Gershom and trying to kill the Immortal Guardians and network special-ops soldiers, everyone's fine with that."

More tears filled Emma's eyes. "So he's really okay?"

Kate smiled. "He's really okay. Although I should mention that he has no memory of the battle."

Emma frowned. Why would he have no memory of the battle if he hadn't had a psychotic break? "Can I see him?"

Kate shook her head, her smile slipping into an expression of regret. "I'm afraid not. There's just too much going on at network headquarters right now. It's locked down in case Gershom had a plan B waiting in the wings. I wouldn't have been allowed out myself if I didn't have the highest clearance. And I doubt even *I* could get you back in with me. We're still working on making sure everyone is accounted for and…" She waved a hand as if to cut herself off. "Well, I won't go into all that. Cliff is sleeping deeply right now anyway. Mattheus said Cliff was hit with darts he was pretty sure were loaded with the tranquilizer. So he'll probably sleep for quite a while. Dr. Machen is keeping an eye on him." She glanced at her watch. "I actually need to head back there. Mr. Reordon is probably wondering where the hell I am. I just wanted you to know that Cliff is still with us."

Emma drew the woman into a quick hug before she could leave. "Thank you."

Kate smiled. "If it were me, I would've wanted to know." Turning away, she headed down the steps. "Oh, and don't worry about coming in to work tomorrow," she said over her shoulder as she crossed to a shiny gray Tesla parked behind Todd's SUV. "You've really been through the wringer tonight. So just get some rest. If you don't see Cliff tomorrow night, don't panic. If he received a heavier than usual dose of the tranquilizer, it may take him longer to sleep it off and recover. Higher doses tend to leave him pretty out of it after he wakes up. So no news is good news."

"Thank you," Emma called again.

Once Kate ducked into the car and drove away, Todd closed the door.

Silence fell.

Emma looked at Cynthia as more damn tears slipped over her lashes. "He's okay."

Cynthia drew her into a hug. "I'm so glad."

Todd wrapped them both in a bear hug and sighed. "Me, too."

Emma emitted a watery chuckle.

It felt like the weight of the world had just been lifted from her shoulders. Or some of it anyway. She had no idea what state of mind Cliff would be in when he awoke. Would he feel better once he heard that he'd helped Seth and saved lives? Would that alleviate some of the remorse he felt over harming the immortal woman?

That had to count for something, didn't it?

Would it be enough to compel him to keep fighting? Or would he still…?

Mentally, she shook her head. She couldn't think about that. Not yet.

Tonight she just needed to revel in the knowledge that she hadn't lost him and bask in the little spark of hope that ignited.

Her stomach growled.

"Was that you or was that me?" Cynthia asked against Emma's hair.

"I think it was me," Todd said, his big arms still banded around both of them.

Cynthia snorted. "How can you possibly be hungry? You ate a whole pizza by yourself."

"I can't help it. I eat when I'm stressed."

Emma smiled. "Actually, it was me." Usually she'd be sitting down to dinner with Cliff right about now.

Cynthia squirmed but couldn't break free. "Sweetie," she protested.

"Oh. Right." Abandoning his hold, Todd straightened.

Cynthia did, too, and studied Emma's face. "Even though Todd pigged out while you were sleeping—"

"I can't help it," he huffed.

" — there's still some pizza left. If I warm it up, do you think you could eat some?"

Emma nodded. "I think so."

"Excellent."

Within minutes, the three of them were slouched on the sofa, eating what was left of the pizza. Emma doubted she'd eat more than a slice. She was too wiped out from everything. But Cynthia and Todd went to town.

Cynthia shook her head as she scrolled through the photos on Emma's phone. "I can't believe you had this beautiful, heartwarming, heartbreaking romance going on all this time and didn't tell me."

Emma shrugged. "We didn't tell anyone."

"Not even Bastien?" Todd asked around a mouthful of pizza. "I thought Cliff told Bastien everything."

"Not even Bastien," Emma confirmed. Bastien had discovered it on his own. "We were afraid if anyone found out, they'd rescind Cliff's hunting privileges... or at least stop allowing him to roam around on his own afterward."

A hint of hurt entered Cynthia's expression. "I wouldn't have told anyone."

"I know you wouldn't have told anyone *intentionally*," Emma agreed. "But you do sometimes forget the vampires down on sublevel 5 can hear everything we say. And I couldn't risk you letting anything slip while we were chatting in my office."

Todd nodded. "You *are* pretty bad about that."

Cynthia frowned at him. "How do *you* know? You don't have preternatural hearing."

"I know. But the vampires do. And they tend to razz me about some of the things they hear you tell Emma about us."

"They do?" Cynthia's eyes widened with dismay. "Why didn't you tell me?"

He shrugged. "Honestly? Because those guys could use a few laughs." He winked. "And it's easy to shake it off when I get to come home to you."

She grinned. "You are so freaking awesome."

"I know," he retorted with a grin. "I keep telling the vampires that, but they don't believe me."

Cynthia's look turned sly. "Now I feel like I should mess with them. Maybe the next time we're in Emma's office, I'll tell her you did something in bed—something so unbelievably mind-blowing... and arousing... like multiple orgasms arousing—that no other man could possibly satisfy me again."

He stared at her, eyes wide, then grinned big. "Yes! Do it. They'll go crazy wondering what the hell I did."

Cynthia laughed.

Emma smiled as they continued to banter and tease each other, occasionally trying to draw her into the conversation and cheer her up. But all the while, she silently counted the minutes, the hours, and wondered how long she would have to wait to see Cliff again.

Chapter Twenty-Five

S OMETHING WAS WRONG.
    Cliff sat on his sofa, one knee bobbing up and down.

Something was *very* wrong.

He glanced around his apartment. On the surface, it appeared the same as it had last week. Last month. Last year. But it wasn't. Everything looked a little too perfect. Too new. And the faint scent of fresh paint lingered in the air.

When he'd asked Melanie about it, she'd broken the news that he'd had not one but two psychotic breaks, back to back. Jared had refuted that, claiming he'd only had *one* break and that the second time he had merely flown into a rage. But that was just mincing words.

Cliff apparently trashed his apartment so badly that Reordon had to replace every piece of furniture in it *and* one of the doors. Cliff was pretty sure Reordon replaced the refrigerator and the doors on his kitchen cabinets, too. But Reordon hadn't complained. He had even upgraded the TV and gaming systems, all while Cliff slept like the dead.

Rising, he crossed to the kitchen and opened one of the cabinets. A graham cracker box stared back at him. He took it down, opened the top, and looked inside. Two sleeves of crackers huddled within, just as they should. When he dumped them out, a cell phone slid after them. Cliff caught it with a spark of hope. But like everything else in his apartment, it looked too shiny and new. When he turned it on, Emma's face didn't appear on the lock screen. A generic beach scene did. And every app he opened was newly installed and bore none of the information or progress that should have been stored in them. There were no e-books, movies, or TV shows. No music. And the only photo on the device was the one he'd seen on Emma's employee ID badge.

He must have broken the other phone. Knowing Reordon, he'd probably had his tech team try to retrieve the photos and other information off the old one. If *anyone* could do it, they could.

Cliff stared at the new phone in his hands. He must have decimated the old one for them to have failed.

After stuffing the crackers back in the box, he tucked the phone in his pocket and began to pace.

Even that was different. His feet felt weighted, as if his shoes bore concrete soles. His limbs felt heavy. His mind was... quiet. *Too* quiet. The only voices that filled it were those that carried to him from the other occupants of sublevel 5.

Was this the calm before the storm?

"Knock, knock," Melanie called.

Cliff glanced toward his open doorway. Melanie and Bastien had thought he'd feel more comfortable resting in his apartment than he would in the infirmary, so they'd let him sleep in here and just kept the door open so they wouldn't have to keep typing in the code every time they wanted to check on him.

Melanie entered. "How are you feeling?"

"Okay." He shrugged. "Tired. Out of it."

Nodding, she approached him. "That's probably your body still working the last of the sedative out of your system."

Sounded logical. But doubt assailed him.

"What about your ears? Are they bothering you? Back at the base you said it felt like they were full of cotton."

He touched one ear. "Yeah. They still feel funny. Everything sounds muffled or something."

Her look turned clinical. Drawing an otoscope from the pocket of her physician's coat, she motioned for him to lean down. "Let me give them another look."

Cliff ducked down so she could peer into his ears.

"I don't see anything," she murmured. "Is anything else bothering you?"

"Not really."

She pressed a palm to his forehead, then touched her fingers to his neck. "No nausea? Swelling of the throat? Fever? You feel a little warm to me."

The questions struck him as odd. "I'm okay." Once vampires transformed, they didn't get sick. Ever.

Tucking her hands in the pockets of her coat, she studied him. "What about the voices?"

"They're quiet today."

Her eyebrows flew up. "Well, that's good. Mattheus said you were badly wounded in an explosion." She frowned. "One of those damn fail-safes. Maybe it scared the voices away for a bit."

"Maybe."

Silence settled upon them, becoming awkward as she shifted her weight and just stared up at him, her brow furrowed. Hesitance crept into her expression.

"What?" he asked when she seemed disinclined to speak.

She sighed. "Something has come up."

He frowned. "What is it?"

"Mattheus said after he tripped the first fail-safe and was hit with a couple of blades, he felt a little sluggish. It didn't last long. But he suspected the blades had been coated with something."

"Like what? The sedative?"

"That would explain why you slept for nearly two days. But he wasn't sure. So he pocketed some of the daggers and darts, and the researchers up on sublevel four have been examining them."

"What did they find?"

"The darts contained the tranquilizer. The dosage varied, so we aren't sure exactly how much you were hit with."

"Not enough to be lethal."

"No, thank goodness. A few of the blades were coated with it, too. But the thing that concerns me isn't the sedative. They also found a poisonous substance on some of the blades. That *shouldn't* have affected you. The virus is tough as nails when it comes to neutralizing chemicals. But since your ears are still bothering you, I'd like to do some blood work just in case."

"Okay." Cliff followed her to the infirmary.

Stuart and the other vampires were up and running on the treadmills. Across the room, Tessa, Jordan, Liora, and the other newly inducted Immortal Guardians sat at a long table covered with file folders and papers, no doubt reviewing the results of the many medical tests Melanie had performed... and finally acknowledging the lies Gershom had told them.

Cliff tensed when everyone looked up at his entrance. Guilt suffused him again when he looked at Liora, but he found no condemnation in her gaze. Jordan eyed him with a blank expression that rankled, but at least he wasn't shouting at Cliff to stay the hell away.

"Hey, Cliff," Miguel called from a treadmill. "I heard you saved the day the night of the big showdown."

"Yeah," another vamp said. "Mattheus said you were a real badass, getting the Immortal Guardians through all the fail-safes injury-free."

"That's so cool," Stuart added, his eyes glowing as he struggled to block out the voices in his head. "I wish I could've been there."

Cliff forced a smile. "It'd be cooler if I could remember it." All he knew was what they told him, and he wasn't sure he could trust that now. Not after they tried to make him forget he'd hurt Liora. But Mattheus wasn't invested in Cliff the way Melanie and the others were. He had no emotional attachment to him at all, so he had no reason to lie about it.

"Hi, Cliff," Tessa called, offering him a smile and a wave.

"Hi, Tessa. How's it going?"

Her smile acquired a wry twist as she shrugged. "It's going."

He chuckled because he knew it was expected of him and followed Melanie over to the exam area.

It only took her a couple of minutes to draw the blood she needed for her tests.

"Do you need an infusion?" she asked as she labeled the vials. "Your blood volume looked good when they brought you in, so I didn't give you any."

"No."

"Okay. Bastien will be here as soon as the sun sets if you're ready to resume your hunts."

"Sure. I'm going to go rest until he gets here."

"Okay."

Cliff waved to the guys and left the infirmary.

At the end of the hallway, Todd nodded to him.

Cliff nodded back, pretended to check the time on his watch, then ducked into his apartment. There he halted. Glancing down at the arm he wore the watch on, the same arm from which Melanie had drawn blood, he straightened it and stared.

Blood beaded at the bend of his elbow. He touched it, wiped it away to reveal a puncture wound that slowly forced out another crimson bead.

His heart began to pummel his ribs. That wound should have healed as soon as Melanie withdrew the needle. That's why she hadn't pressed a cotton ball to it and topped it off with a Band-Aid the way nurses used to when he was human.

He looked at his open door.

Reaching over, he slowly closed it, feeling the full weight of it in a way he hadn't before.

The moment it latched, silence engulfed him.

Oh shit.

He couldn't hear anything save his own heartbeat thudding in his ears. He might as well have been standing inside his soundproof bathroom. He couldn't hear *anything* that took place outside his door. All the customary sounds that usually bombarded him — the chatter of the guards, the movements and conversations that took place in the labs and infirmary, the vampires razzing each other or working out or playing video games — had vanished the moment he closed the door. And even though his mind was refreshingly clear, he couldn't hear anything that transpired on the floors above him.

Cliff looked at the doorway to his bedroom. Clenching his hands into fists, he jumped toward it... and didn't even make it halfway there.

Anxiety rising, he sprinted forward... and reached it in about the same time Todd would.

Shit! He wasn't feeling tired and sluggish because his body was fighting off the lingering effects of the sedative. He felt tired and sluggish because he was used to the strength, speed, and energy being a vampire constantly infused him with.

And he was no longer a vampire.

Cliff hadn't slept for two days because he was sedated. He had slept for two days because whatever poison those blades had been coated with had been systematically killing off the virus that infected him. And if the poison had killed off the virus...

Panic filled him.

He had no functioning immune system and would die soon.

Emma.

He had to see Emma. As quickly as possible. He wanted to spend whatever time he had left with her. Wanted to remind her who he had been before the damned voices began bellowing in his ears and ramping up his aggression. Wanted his last moments with her *not* to be full of despair but full of the laughter, teasing, and tenderness he hadn't been able to give her for so long.

He *needed* to see her. He had no idea how long someone could live without an immune system but thought he'd once heard Melanie say it could be as little as a day.

Striding into the bathroom, he stripped and took a shower. Had he not been so desperate to get to Emma as quickly as possible, he would've laughed at how long it took him. Usually he zipped through his showers with preternatural speed.

As soon as he dried off, he donned the usual T-shirt, cargo pants, and boots—all black.

Grabbing the new cell phone, he slipped it into a pocket just as the door to his apartment clunked and opened.

Bastien stood in the doorway. "Hey. How're you feeling?"

Cliff strode toward him. "Good. Are you ready to go?"

Bastien's eyebrows flew up. "Sure."

They headed for the elevator.

"Hey, man," Todd said. "Good to see you up and around."

"Thanks."

Bastien said nothing as they sequestered themselves in the elevator and rode it up to the ground floor. But Cliff could feel his steady gaze.

"You want to run or drive?" Bastien asked once they were outside.

"Drive." He couldn't run to Emma's without the enhanced speed he'd lost.

"Okay."

Cliff fidgeted in the seat as they drove away from network

headquarters, waiting impatiently to reach the point at which the vampires could no longer hear them.

As per his usual habit, Bastien pulled over a few miles away.

"Could I skip hunting tonight and just go straight to Emma's?" Cliff blurted.

Bastien studied him a moment. "How are the voices?"

"Quiet."

"And the aggression?"

"Not a problem."

After a moment, he nodded slowly. "Okay."

"Would you give me a ride?"

Bastien stared at him. "You want me to drive you all the way there?"

Cliff usually ran it. "Yeah."

Another pause. "Okay. You want me to pick you up, too?"

"Yeah."

"What time?"

"Just before dawn."

Bastien's face lost all expression as he turned his gaze forward. "Sure. I'll be there."

They rode the rest of the way in silence.

When they were a couple of miles from Emma's home, Cliff said, "Pull over for a minute, would you?"

Bastien swung off the road and brought the car to a halt.

"This will just take a sec." Cliff thrust his door open and got out. Tall grasses swished against his calves as he strode into a field. Fortunately, a full moon hung above him, providing enough light for him to see without the enhanced vision he'd lost.

Halting several yards away, he drew the new cell phone out of his pocket and dialed Emma's number.

"Hello?" she answered.

"It's me."

She sucked in a breath. "Cliff! Honey, are you okay?"

"I'm okay," he told her, and it wasn't *totally* a lie. His head hadn't been this clear in years.

"Kate said you were injured…"

"I was. But my injuries have healed. I'm on my way over there now. Is that all right?"

"Yes! Of course it is! I can't wait to see you."

He strolled a few steps farther into the meadow. "Listen, the voices are quieter tonight. So I was wondering…"

"Yes?"

"Remember the night Aidan gave you the watch?"

"Yes," she said, a hint of caution entering her voice.

He surveyed the pretty meadow. "Could we do that again? Could we have a date night? A nice romantic dinner and maybe some dancing after?"

She sniffed a little. And when she spoke again, it sounded as though she was fighting tears. "I'd love to have a date night, honey."

"Great. I'll see you in a few."

"Okay. I love you."

"I love you, too." Pocketing the phone, he bent and began to gather a bouquet of wildflowers for her. Once he was satisfied with the size of it and the variety of colors it afforded, he returned to the car and sank into the passenger seat.

Bastien didn't move when Cliff closed his door. He just kept staring through the front windshield.

A muscle flexed in his jaw.

"Bastien?"

"Are you sure this is what you want to do?" he asked, voice grim.

Go to Emma's without hunting first? "Yes."

Without another word, he turned the key and completed the drive to Emma's house. He kept the engine running once he pulled into her driveway.

Cliff exited the car and closed the door. "Thanks. I'll see you before dawn."

Nodding, Bastien backed out and drove away.

Cliff strode up the walk, his heart light. For tonight at least, he would achieve his greatest dream: he would come to Emma as a mortal man bereft of insanity.

The door opened before he reached it.

Emma stepped out onto the porch, wearing the colorful dress from their second night together and no shoes, just sparkling toenails he always thought adorable. "I heard a car."

"Bastien dropped me off." Shaking his head, he smiled as he walked toward her. "Damn, you're beautiful."

Skipping down the steps, she jogged forward and threw herself into his arms.

Laughing, he caught her and swung her around as she hugged him tight. "This is exactly the greeting I was hoping for." He pressed his lips to the soft skin of her neck where it met the gentle curve of her shoulder, loving her scent and the feel of her in his arms. Peace suffused him as he sighed in contentment. "I missed you."

A chuckle escaped her, but it sounded forced. "It's only been two days."

Lowering her feet to the stone pathway, he drew back just enough to look down at her. "I always miss you when we're apart."

A tear spilled over her lashes as she stared up at him. "You're really okay?"

Cupping her face in his free hand, he smoothed his thumb over her cheek and wiped away the moisture. "I haven't felt this good in years."

A tentative smile touched her lips. Then she rose onto her toes and touched her lips to his. "I thought I'd lost you," she whispered.

"I know," he said softly. "But I'm still here. And for once the voices are quiet. So..." He stepped back and proffered the flowers, happy to see he hadn't inadvertently crushed them while swinging her around. "These are for you."

Her face lit with a smile as she took them. "Thank you. They're beautiful."

He stole another kiss. "So are you." Looping an arm around her shoulders, he guided her up the path. "Let's go start our date night."

Chapter Twenty-Six

E MMA WRAPPED HER ARM AROUND Cliff's waist and leaned into his side as they climbed the steps, crossed the porch, and headed inside, so happy to have him here with her. She hadn't known what to expect. If he would be struggling the way he had been the last time they'd been together in Mr. Reordon's boardroom. If she would even see him at all. But he looked good.

Reluctantly relinquishing her hold on him, she moved away and watched him close and lock the door.

No. He looked *great*.

Really great.

His manner had been tense, his body taut with carefully restrained aggression, for so long that she'd forgotten how freaking hot he used to look when he strolled toward her. Spellbound, she watched him approach, every movement deliciously fluid, his muscles loose and rippling beneath his clothing.

How long had it been since she'd seen him this way?

It made her heart pound as swiftly as if it were their first date.

His stomach growled.

She grinned.

His lips turned up in a wry smile as he rested a hand on his muscled abs. "Sorry. I think it's been a couple of days since I ate."

Emma lost her smile. "They wouldn't let you eat?"

He shrugged. "I *couldn't* eat. I fell asleep shortly after I got back to network headquarters and didn't wake up until a couple of hours ago."

"Kate said you were tranqed."

His eyebrows rose. "Kate from Mr. Reordon's office?"

"Yes." Crossing to the kitchen, she breathed a sigh of relief when he stayed with her. She felt clingy as hell and didn't want to let him out of her sight. "She thought I'd want to know you made it back safely."

"That was kind of her."

"I thought so, too." She studied him. "*Were* you tranqed?"

He shrugged. "That's what they tell me."

Worry nibbled at her. "You don't remember?"

"No. I don't remember any of it."

Did that mean he didn't remember basically telling her goodbye or the determination she'd read in his eyes to end his existence?

Did that mean he intended to keep fighting?

Taking a vase down from a kitchen cabinet, she filled it with water and arranged the flowers in it. "Todd said everyone has been singing your praises. He said you impressed the hell out of them by safely guiding the immortals through all the booby traps and fail-safes."

He nodded. And she loved seeing happiness light up his deep brown eyes again. "That's what they're saying. I worried at first that Bastien and Melanie might be bullshitting me to make me feel better, but…" He shrugged. "Mattheus—one of the immortals who went with us that night—said it was true. He said I got them all through injury-free."

Not without great cost to himself, but Emma could see how much it meant to him that he'd done something truly heroic. "That's wonderful, honey." She couldn't resist giving him another hug.

His hands settled on her hips as he dipped his head and pressed his lips to hers in a slow, sensual kiss.

Emma moved closer, leaning her body into his as she parted her lips. His tongue gave hers a teasing stroke, inciting a hum of approval.

His hands tightened, urging her even closer.

His stomach growled.

Both laughed.

Emma patted his chest. "Let's get some food in you."

The hours that followed reminded her of the early days of their relationship. Side by side, they worked together to whip up a quick meal of salad, pasta, and the baguettes Cynthia had brought when she'd visited earlier. While they did, they laughed and talked, exchanging quick kisses and affectionate caresses. By some unspoken mutual agreement, neither mentioned the battle, his condition, or his future. They simply enjoyed each other's presence.

Emma set the coffee table with a white runner and candles. Then they sat cross-legged on the floor across from each other, knees brushing.

Emma told him Cynthia's plan to spark the vampires' curiosity about Todd's prowess in bed. He laughed and shared some of the things the vampires teased Todd about.

She couldn't remember the last time she'd smiled so much. And Cliff seemed wonderfully happy and carefree. Charming and funny. Every time a tiny voice inside wished he could always be thus, she pushed it back into the deepest recesses of her mind. Tonight she would forget everything else and enjoy this eye of the hurricane, this calm between storms. Tonight they were just an ordinary couple, completely enraptured with each other.

Once they finished dinner and cleared the dishes, they headed outside. Cliff arranged her speaker on the front porch and cycled through her phone's playlists. Then Nat King Cole began to sing "Unforgettable."

"Perfect," she said. This whole night was unforgettable.

Smiling, Cliff took her hand. "Most Immortal Guardians like older music. And I've spent a lot of time around Bastien and Aidan, so I've really grown to appreciate it."

She smiled. Her grandparents had sparked her own love of oldies.

Cliff led her down the steps and onto the grassy dance floor. There he issued her a gallant bow, then drew her into his arms.

Emma hadn't danced with many men in the past. The boys in high school had just linked their hands at the base of her spine and swayed a little. College guys had done the same.

Not Cliff though. Cliff entranced her. He made her feel special. Loved. It reminded her of the way her parents danced. Her mom and dad had been married for going on forty years. And no matter how busy or chaotic life got, they *always* danced together on their anniversary.

Cliff took Emma's right hand in his left and pulled her close. His right arm slid around to her back, his warm hand delivering a soft caress. Emma slid her left hand up his arm to his shoulder, happy to discover his muscles still loose and limber instead of tightened into knots. And when only inches separated them, they began to move. To the side. Backward. To the side. Forward. Angling in such a way that they traveled in slow circles. Every once in a while he would step back and raise their clasped hands, encouraging her to walk a slow twirl beneath them before returning to his embrace.

And his gaze always held hers, making her feel as if she was the most beautiful and most loved woman in the world.

Tonight he even sang, his deep voice joining Nat King Cole's in professing her unforgettable as they danced beneath the moonlight. It was magical.

He was magical.

"I'm so in love with you," she murmured.

Smiling, he swiveled slightly and lowered her in a gentle dip. "You're the love of my life, Emma."

She had never been happier than in that moment.

Once the song ended, Nat King Cole began to croon "Darling, Je Vous Aime Beaucoup." Then "Pretend." "For Sentimental Reasons."

And when at last they abandoned the dance floor and went inside, Cliff made love to her with aching tenderness, then with a playfulness that sparked laughs and chuckles as well as gasps of ecstasy, then once more with a tenderness that stole her heart all over again.

Afterward, instead of spooning, they lay facing each other, their limbs entwined, and talked softly, laughing and teasing. Instead of tightening with tension, his muscles remained relaxed. Instead of darkening with frustration and anger as he struggled to combat the voices in his head, Cliff's beautiful face lit with frequent smiles.

He was captivating. He was loving. He was everything she'd ever wanted.

Emma wished the night would never end.

Alas, dawn waited for no man. So they dressed quietly and

headed for the door. Leaning into him, Emma touched her lips to his. "I wish you didn't have to leave."

Cliff kissed her again, pouring so much emotion into the contact that it brought tears to her eyes. "I love you."

"I love you, too."

He pressed his forehead to hers, a gentle smile touching his lips. "You're the best thing that's ever happened to me, Emma. Don't ever forget that."

A sense of foreboding infiltrated her.

He stepped back.

"Cliff?" she asked, afraid all of a sudden. Reaching out, she took his hand.

Still smiling, he brought it to his lips and kissed the back of it. "I have to go. The sun will rise soon."

But when he turned away, she didn't let go. She couldn't. Her heartbeat picked up. "Cliff," she repeated.

"Bastien's waiting," he reminded her as he carefully tried to extricate his hand.

Emma shook her head. Something was wrong. She could feel it.

Her mind raced, reviewing their evening together.

Everything he'd said. Everything they'd done. Every minute of it.

It had been perfect.

It had been *too* perfect.

When Cliff managed to free himself, she ducked around him, planted herself in his path, and refused to let him leave.

He closed his eyes. "Emma," he protested softly.

And there it was, a flicker of finality in his expression that terrified her.

Raising her hands, she cupped his face. "Cliff, look at me."

He opened his eyes.

Hers filled with tears, those born of both anguish and denial. "You're telling me goodbye," she choked out. "That's what this has all been about. The flowers and the dinner and the dancing." The aching tenderness with which he'd made love to her. "You're going to die today, and you're telling me goodbye."

His silence betrayed his guilt.

Releasing him, she shook her head and backed away. "Why?"

He seemed so well tonight. Like his old self. She knew it wouldn't last. His lucid moments never did. But... if he could still have nights like this, didn't that mean there was still hope?

She couldn't give up. *He* couldn't give up.

Sadness darkened his beloved features. "I wanted one more night with you," he acknowledged. "I *needed* one more night with you and —"

"But you're better," she blurted. "You were smiling and laughing. You didn't mutter to yourself or pace or shout at the voices once. And Todd said you did great the night of the battle, that you were a true hero."

He shook his head. "That doesn't make up for the fact that I almost killed an immortal female."

Damn it. He *did* remember that. "But you *didn't* kill her. And you *saved lives* the night of the battle. Doesn't that count for anything?"

A weary sighed escaped him. "Sweetheart, you knew this was the way our time together would end. You've always known it. Please don't make this harder than it already is."

She stared at him. "Harder?" Anger rose, as did her voice. "You don't want me to make it *harder*? I thought you died two nights ago! I thought you died and that I'd never see you again. Then you show up here, looking so damned handsome and healthy and are happy and charming and loving and we have the best night of my life and you give me this perfect memory, then tell me not to make it harder —" Her breath hitched as the truth dawned.

More tears welled in her eyes and spilled over her lashes. Pain inundated her. "You wanted to give me the perfect memory," she whispered.

His throat worked in a swallow. "Yes."

"Cliff," she murmured, both a thank-you and a plea.

This hadn't just been about what he needed. It had been about what he'd known she needed, too. He hadn't wanted her last memory of him to be what it would've been if he hadn't come tonight: him standing before her, eyes glowing, face full of anguish and self-loathing and — yes — suffering as he told her *I can't be like this anymore.*

He'd wanted her last memory of him to be a good one, a loving one she could hold close and cherish in his absence.

Biting back a sob, she spun around, yanked the door open, and left the house.

"Emma," Cliff called after her.

Ignoring him, she hurried down the steps and stomped across the grass toward the car parked beside hers in the driveway.

The driver's door opened and Bastien stepped out.

"Did you know?" she demanded. "Did you know he was coming here to tell me goodbye?"

His jaw clenched. "I suspected it."

"Well, you need to talk him out of it. Whatever he has planned, you need to talk him out of it, Bastien."

"I can't," he said, face grim.

"That's bullshit."

"I *can't*," he repeated. "It's his choice, Emma."

"A choice he made before he went into battle to rescue *you*." She jabbed him in the chest. "*You* and Melanie and Aidan and everyone else who was captured. He went there to save your asses, and he did. He led all of your immortal brethren safely through those fucking booby traps, suffering injury after injury so *they* wouldn't and could rescue you." Again she poked him. "He *saved* you. Now *you* need to save him."

Cliff spoke softly behind her. "He can't save me, Emma."

"Bullshit." She shifted so she could see them both. "He can and he will."

"No, he can't." The certainty in Cliff's words pierced her like a knife.

She stood there in the silence that fell, her heart breaking, absolutely devastated. "So… what? You're going to wait for the sun to rise and let it burn you to death?" Was that why he'd stayed longer than usual?

"No."

She looked at Bastien. "You're going to decapitate him?"

"If he asks me to, I will."

She stared at Bastien helplessly. "How can you do that? He's your friend."

His throat worked in a swallow. "That's *why* I can do it."

"He isn't going to decapitate me," Cliff said. "He won't have to."

So Cliff intended to take his own life?

She didn't know why that seemed worse, but it did. Emma took a step toward him. "Cliff, honey, you don't have to do this. Look how much better you are tonight. If you just give it a little more time—"

"I don't have more time."

"I know you're worried this lucidity won't last, that things will get bad again, but—"

"I don't have more time, Emma," he repeated. "Even if I *wanted* more time…" He shook his head. "I'm all out of it. It's over."

He almost sounded as if he *did* want more time, that he wasn't ready to give up the fight, that the choice wasn't his.

"I don't understand."

Closing the distance between them, he took her hands. "Something happened at the base."

She stared up at him. Something *other* than him nearly dying? "What do you mean?"

"When I triggered the fail-safes…" He squeezed her hands, then shook his head. "Some of the blades that cut me and stabbed me were coated with chemicals. Melanie thinks most of it was the tranquilizer. But they found poison on some."

"Poison doesn't affect vampires and immortals," she said.

"This one does."

From the corner of her eye, she saw Bastien take a step toward them. "What?"

"Emma," Cliff said, holding her gaze. "The poison cured me."

Chapter Twenty-Seven

I T TOOK A MOMENT FOR Emma's beleaguered mind to catch up with what Cliff was trying to tell her.

She sucked in a breath. "You mean... you think the poison destroyed the virus?" she asked in a whisper. The fear that had consumed her the night Cliff had gone into battle returned full force. If what he said was true, then they *were* out of time. Everyone knew the vampiric virus came with a fucked-up catch-22: kill the virus and you leave the vampire or immortal who'd been infected with it with no functioning immune system.

"Yes," Cliff answered solemnly.

Bastien took another step toward them. "Are you sure?"

"Pretty sure, yeah."

"What did Melanie say?"

"I didn't tell her," Cliff admitted. "I wanted to spend whatever time I had left with Emma. And I knew if I told Melanie, she'd want me to stay at network headquarters so she could run tests and —"

"So she could *stop* it," his friend said, looking as alarmed as Emma felt.

"She can't stop it, Bastien."

"You don't know that," Bastien nearly shouted.

"Yes, I do!" Cliff shook his head, then motioned to his face. "Look at me. Saying goodbye to Emma is wrenching my fucking heart out. Do you see my eyes glowing?"

Bastien scoffed. "That could be the sedative's influence."

"And the fact that I no longer have superspeed or strength? No preternaturally enhanced senses? No fucking fangs?"

His fangs were gone, too?

Despair filled Emma. Cliff *hadn't* chosen to die tonight.

He had been dying ever since he'd returned to network headquarters.

He had simply wanted to spend his last moments with her as soon as he'd realized it.

And she'd yelled at him for it.

"Cliff," she said, full of remorse.

Bastien pointed at her. "No. He isn't dying." Then he scowled at Cliff. "You don't know that the poison killed the virus. What if it merely suppressed it? Or counteracted the most notable symptoms?"

Cliff gave him a sad smile. "You're grasping at straws."

"No. Those are valid fucking questions."

Cliff held out his arm. "Do you smell the virus on me?"

Frowning, Bastien gripped Cliff's wrist and brought it to his nose. He drew in a deep breath. Held it. Let it out. "No. But I'm not an elder. I can't always smell the virus on vampires and immortals."

"You can't smell the virus because it's gone."

"You don't know that," Bastien insisted.

Emma bit her lip as the two stared at each other, apparently at a stalemate. "Maybe we should call Aidan."

Seconds later, a tall, dark figure abruptly appeared right in front of her.

Shrieking, Emma stumbled backward.

"What happened?" Aidan demanded. "Your watch called me. Are you hurt? Is Cliff okay?"

Shit. She'd forgotten they'd programmed her watch to call him if she ever spoke the words *Call Aidan*. "I'm okay," she told him. "But Cliff needs you."

Aidan turned to examine the scene.

Cliff stood placidly while Bastien gripped his wrist.

"What's going on?" the ancient Celt asked.

Bastien thrust Cliff's wrist toward Aidan. "Smell this."

Aidan's eyebrows flew up. "What?"

If Emma wasn't so damn distraught, she would've laughed.

Even as upset as he was, Cliff cracked a smile.

Bastien's face, however, remained dark and angry. "Smell him. Tell me if you smell the virus."

His expression saying he questioned Bastien's sanity, Aidan accepted Cliff's wrist and sniffed it. His brows drew down. Then he sniffed again, drawing in a deeper breath. "What the hell?" he muttered. Palming a dagger, he sliced open Cliff's palm.

Cliff hissed in pain.

Emma cried out and started forward, but Cliff thrust out his other arm and stopped her.

Latching onto his hand, she gripped it in both of hers.

Aidan brought Cliff's bleeding palm to his nose and drew in another deep breath. His eyes widened. He looked at Bastien, then Cliff, his face full of... confusion? Fear? "I can't smell it. I can't smell the virus."

Cliff tugged his hand free. "Because it's gone. The poison destroyed it."

"What poison?" Aidan demanded.

"The poison that coated some of the blades that cut me at the military base."

Aidan shook his head. "Poison doesn't affect us."

"This one does," Cliff snapped. He held up his hand. "The wound is still bleeding and is showing no signs of healing. My eyes no longer glow. My fangs are gone. And I no longer have enhanced senses, speed, or strength."

Dread filled Aidan's features. "If the poison killed the virus..."

"Then I'm dying."

"Seth," Aidan said.

Emma jumped when the Immortal Guardians leader appeared beside them. His hair was shorter than the last time she'd seen him, stopping above his shoulders.

Seth took in the tableau—the devastation on her, Bastien, and Aidan's faces—then turned to Cliff, his face solemn.

"It isn't what you think," Cliff said. "They didn't call you here to kill me. The poison already did that."

Seth frowned. "What poison?"

Cliff sighed as though he'd grown tired of recounting it. "Some of the blades loosed by the fail-safes were coated with poison. I don't know what kind it was, but it killed the virus in me."

Aidan nodded. "I can't smell it on him. I can't even scent it in his blood."

Seth met Emma's gaze. "Release him."

She did so immediately, hoping Seth could help him. If Bastien was right and even a tiny shred of the virus remained...

Seth rested a hand on Cliff's shoulder. A look of concentration overtook the powerful immortal's features.

Emma's pulse thudded in her ears as she awaited his verdict.

Seth's frown deepened. Moving to stand beside Cliff, he released his shoulder, then rested one hand on the center of Cliff's chest and touched the fingers of the other hand to Cliff's forehead.

Birdsong twittered from a nearby tree, reminding Emma that sunrise approached.

"You're right," Seth murmured. "There's no sign of the virus. At all. It's been completely eradicated."

———◦◉◦———

Cliff felt no surprise at Seth's proclamation. He hadn't needed the powerful Immortal Guardian leader to confirm it. But the others had.

Bastien and Aidan looked utterly devastated.

And Emma...

He swallowed hard.

Biting her lip, she regarded him with glistening eyes full of anguish.

How he wished he could've spared her this. Cliff knew if he asked her what she would change if she could go back in time and do it all over again, she'd say nothing. Not one damned thing. But awareness of the grief she'd suffer after he was gone tore him up inside.

Heat arose at the points Seth touched him. When Cliff lowered his gaze, he discovered Seth's hand on his chest had acquired a golden luminescence.

"It wasn't the poison," Seth murmured.

Emma blinked. When tears spilled down her cheeks, she absently wiped them away. "What?"

The golden glow faded, as did the warmth. Then Seth stepped back. "It wasn't the poison."

Cliff frowned, confused. "If it wasn't the poison, then what was it?" It sure as hell hadn't been the tranquilizer.

Seth glanced at Emma, then at Aidan and Bastien as if he wasn't sure he should disclose it.

Emma sidled closer to Cliff and slipped her small hand into his. "Please. If Cliff is going to die, we should at least know why."

Seth rubbed his palms together, almost as if doing so would magically conjure the answer he sought. When that failed, he sighed and placed his hands on his hips. "That's just it. Cliff isn't going to die."

Shock rippled through him. "What?" How was that possible? "Why?" Network researchers unanimously agreed that the virus destroyed vampires' and immortals' immune systems.

Seth shrugged. "Because it would appear my father healed you."

Bastien's and Aidan's mouths fell open.

Cliff was pretty sure his did, too, as the most absurd thought flashed through his mind. "You have a father?"

Emma looked up at him. "I'm so glad you asked that, because I was thinking the same thing."

Seth laughed. "Yes, I have a father. One whose powers make mine seem paltry by comparison." He smiled at Cliff. "And apparently your willingness to sacrifice yourself to spare me and members of my Immortal Guardian family pain, injury, and even death made an impression on him. Because he not only eradicated the virus, he reversed the brain damage you suffered and fully restored your immune system."

Cliff tightened his hold on Emma's hand as his heart began to pound. "You're sure?"

Seth's smile widened. "I'm sure. You are now a wholly healthy human, Cliff." His brow furrowed. "Although you've lost the greater regenerative properties the virus gave you, so you *will* age now."

Awe and wonder swept over Cliff as he turned to Emma. "I'm going to age now." Joy made his chest swell and his heart expand. "We can grow old together."

Smiling through her tears, Emma nodded. "We can grow old together."

Elation filling him, Cliff swept her into his arms and buried his face in her neck. When that wasn't enough, he swung her around. He was free of the virus! After years of struggling and suffering, of fighting and desperately clinging to hope, he was human again!

And they could have their happily-ever-after.

Emma laughed and cried at the same time while Cliff wept against her shoulder.

They could have their happily-ever-after!

Lowering her feet to the ground, he raised his head and stared down at her, reveling in the love and joy that lit her beautiful features, knowing she saw the same in his. "This is who we are," he murmured, thinking of the photo she had taken of them so long ago in which they'd been so happy.

A tear slipped over her lashes and trailed down her cheek. "This is who we are, honey. Now and always."

Smiling, he dipped his head and kissed her trembling lips, pouring all of the emotion that overwhelmed him into it. He couldn't believe his long battle was over. Couldn't believe that he was once more that man in the picture. Couldn't believe this was real.

He lifted his head. His smiled faltered as fear and dread slithered through him. "Wait." Releasing Emma, Cliff stepped back and regarded them all with dawning alarm. "This *is* real, isn't it? It's not a delusion or a hallucination or" — he looked at Seth — "false memories you planted?"

Seth winced. "No, I only did that the one time, Cliff, and realize now the error of it. This is real."

Cliff looked at Aidan.

"It's real," the Celt told him, his voice gruff with emotion.

Bastien nodded as he closed the distance between them. "Real enough that I need to get my ass inside soon because — unlike you — I still roast in the sun, you lucky bastard."

Cliff laughed with relief as Bastien yanked him into a hearty hug.

Then Aidan hugged him.

Cliff shook his head as he stared up at Seth. "I don't know how to thank you. Or your father. You've given me…" Taking Emma's hand, he twined his fingers through hers. "Everything."

Seth clapped him on the shoulder. "You deserve it, Cliff. You've had a long, difficult journey that robs all others like you of their honor. But you clung to yours with admirable tenacity and deserve every ounce of happiness you find now."

Skillet's "Monster" filled the air as the sky began to lighten.

Seth fumbled in his pocket for his phone. "Yes?" He was quiet a moment as he listened. His gaze slid to Bastien. "I know why you're calling, and everything is all right. Bastien and I will be along shortly to explain." He listened another moment. "We'll be there momentarily." He pocketed his phone.

Cliff smiled. "It's weird not being able to hear both sides of the conversation now."

"That was Melanie," Seth told him. "I believe she's discovered the absence of the virus in your blood work. She said she needed to see me immediately and sounded panicked. Bastien and I will let her know what happened."

Unease trickled through him. "How are we going to explain this to Stuart and the other vampires?" And how would the other vampires react to the knowledge that Cliff had been healed but their struggle would continue?

Guilt suffused him.

"I don't know," Seth said. "We'll speak to Melanie in Chris's boardroom so the vamps won't hear us. We need to bring Chris into the loop anyway." His countenance turned contemplative for a moment. "Maybe he can help us figure out a way to reunite you with your family as well."

Cliff stared at him, eyes wide as he tried not to get his hopes up. "Do you think that's possible—that I could see my dad?" His mom had died of cancer when he was a boy, and his dad had never remarried. So it had just been the two of them, with his grandparents visiting as often as they could to try to fill the void.

Bastien snorted. "Are you kidding? Reordon is like Seth. With him, *anything* is possible."

Seth nodded. "But we'll need time to come up with something."

"That's fine," Cliff assured him.

Seth looked at Bastien. "Are you ready to go?"

"Yes. Melanie doesn't know I'm at Emma's and will worry if I don't get my ass back before sunrise." He looked at Emma. "I'll return for the car tomorrow."

"No need," Aidan said. "I'll drive it to the network for you. Maybe we can put our heads together once I get there and come up with a plausible explanation for the vamps."

Bastien nodded. "Sounds good. The keys are in the ignition."

Seth glanced at Cliff. "I assume you'd like to stay?"

"Yes."

Seth smiled. "We'll leave you two to celebrate then."

In the next instant, he and Bastien vanished. Tossing them a wave, Aidan ducked into the Chevy, started the engine, and drove away, leaving Cliff and Emma alone.

Still holding her hand, Cliff looked down at her and smiled. "Hi there."

"Hi yourself." Emma swiveled to face him. Offering him a mischievous smile, she slid an arm around his waist and leaned into him. "Has anyone ever told you you're the hottest human on the planet?"

He laughed. "No. But I believe *you* have that honor."

"Flatterer."

He shook his head. "I still can't quite believe it," he admitted softly.

"I know. I think it hasn't fully hit me yet."

He glanced around. The gray sky began to acquire a golden glow. "Would it be okay if we stayed out here for a little while?"

She gave his fingers a squeeze. "I'd like that."

Turning, they strolled toward the front porch, where they sank onto the steps, sitting side by side with their hips pressed together. Cliff kissed the back of her hand, then rested it on his knee.

The soft sounds of nature helped calm his chaotic thoughts as he absently stroked her fingers. Now that the trauma of thinking he would die today had passed, his mind quieted, needing a reprieve.

Birdsong floated on the cool breeze. Scuttling sounds arose as two squirrels chased each other around and around an oak tree at the edge of the yard.

Peace fell upon them as he and Emma leaned into each other and let it all gradually sink in.

A third squirrel joined the other two and drove the chase to another tree.

A crow *caw, caw, cawed* in the distance.

Cliff sighed, his lips curling up at the edges as happiness suffused him. "How would you feel about adding a picket fence?" he asked softly.

Emma surveyed the yard, her expression thoughtful. "I'd like it. If we had a dog, a fence would keep him from chasing after whatever wildlife happens by and getting into trouble."

He squeezed her hand. "And keep the children from wandering too far?" His heart swelled as she looked up at him, her face filling with wonder at the realization that they could have children now.

She smiled. "That sounds perfect, honey."

Dipping his head, he pressed a kiss to her lips. "I love you, Emma."

"I love you, too."

Releasing her hand, Cliff wrapped an arm around her and held her close as the two of them watched the sun rise.

Thank you for reading *Cliff's Descent*. It's a story I've wanted to tell for quite some time now. For the many Immortal Guardians fans who have asked me to *please* find a way to save Cliff, I hope you're as satisfied with his happily-ever-after as Cliff is.

If this was your first time reading an Immortal Guardians book, I hope you enjoyed Emma and Cliff's story and liked meeting some of the crew. Just a note: Cliff's tale is more somber than others in the series because of his unique circumstances. You'll find more humor sprinkled throughout the rest. Though their personalities and backgrounds vary, my Immortal Guardians are deeply loyal to each other and—despite the sometimes dark and violent lives they lead—love to laugh and tease each other. The men also *all* adore strong women. So if you appreciate heroines who kick ass, you'll find a lot of them in my series.

Thank you again for reading *Cliff's Descent*. If you enjoyed it, please consider rating or reviewing it at an online retailer of your choice. I appreciate your support so much and am always thrilled when I see that one of my books made a reader happy. Ratings and reviews are also an excellent way to recommend an author's books, create word of mouth, and help other readers find new favorites.

Dianne Duvall
www.DianneDuvall.com
Dianne's Newsletter - http://eepurl.com/hf/T2Qn

About the Author

Dianne Duvall is the *New York Times* and *USA Today* Bestselling Author of the acclaimed **Immortal Guardians** paranormal romance series, the **Aldebarian Alliance** sci-fi romance series, and **The Gifted Ones** medieval and time-travel romance series. She is known for writing stories full of action that will keep you flipping pages well past your bedtime, strong heroes who adore strong heroines, lovable secondary characters, swoon-worthy romance, and humor that readers frequently complain makes them laugh out loud at inappropriate moments. Reviewers have called Dianne's books "fast-paced and humorous" (*Publishers Weekly*), "utterly addictive" (*RT Book Reviews*), "extraordinary" (*Long and Short Reviews*), and "wonderfully imaginative" (*The Romance Reviews*).

The Lasaran (Aldebarian Alliance Book 1) was a #1 Audible Mover & Shaker. *The Segonian* (Aldebarian Alliance Book 2) was a Barnes&Noble Top Indie Favorite. Audible chose *Awaken the Darkness* (Immortal Guardians Book 8) as one of the Top 5 Best Paranormal Romances of 2018. Her audiobooks have been awarded multiple AudioFile Earphone Awards for Excellence. One was nominated for a prestigious Audie Award. And her books have twice been nominated for RT Reviewers' Choice Awards.

When she isn't writing, Dianne is active in the independent film industry and has even appeared on-screen, crawling out of a moonlit grave and wielding a machete like some of the psychotic vampires she creates in her books.

For the latest news on upcoming releases, contests, and more, please visit www.DianneDuvall.com. You can also connect with Dianne online:

Website — DianneDuvall.com

Newsletter — http://eepurl.com/hfT2Qn

Books Group — facebook.com/groups/128617511148830/

Blog — dianneduvall.blogspot.com

BookBub — bookbub.com/authors/dianne-duvall

Facebook — facebook.com/DianneDuvallAuthor

Instagram — instagram.com/dianne.duvall

Twitter — twitter.com/DianneDuvall

Dianne's Street Team — facebook.com/groups/137705883031474

Amazon Author Page — amazon.com/Dianne-Duvall/e/B0046IHUO6

YouTube — youtube.com/channel/UCVcJ9xnm_i2ZKV7jM8dqAgA?feature=mhee

Pinterest — pinterest.com/dianneduvall

Goodreads — goodreads.com/Dianne_Duvall

Made in the USA
Monee, IL
09 September 2021

77656174R10173